RESCUED

RENE GERACI

First Edition 2025
Published by Geraci Publishing

For permissions or inquiries, contact: ReneGeraciAuthor@gmail.com

Editing and Proofreading Services completed by
Melanie Campbell, Romantic Realms

Cover Design and Formatting completed by
Rene Geraci

TABLE OF CONTENTS

For the ones who open their hearts to the broken, quirky, and forgotten.

For those who rescue, foster and fight,
who love fiercely, and rage quietly
against every act of cruelty.
And for anyone who ever found love
in the wag of a tail,
or the eyes of a stranger
who became family.

TRIGGER WARNINGS

Reader discretion is strongly advised. This dark romance contains mature themes and content that may be distressing to some readers, including graphic language, graphic sexual acts, on-page sexual assault, murder, physical violence, references to deaths of animals, and references to animal abuse. Please proceed only if you feel comfortable with intense and potentially triggering subject matter. Your mental health matters. If you are struggling, or are in need of support, please don't hesitate to reach out to a mental health professional or call or text 988 for the *988 Suicide and Crisis Lifeline.* You are not alone.

Chapter 1
Olive

On the Rocks and Off the Rails

The bar is loud tonight. People crowd in like sardines, elbow-to-elbow. Every table is taken, every stool claimed by a guy in a Boise State Broncos jersey who thinks shouting louder will help us win. The floor shakes every time the Broncos score, and grown men roar at the TV in celebration. It's all beer, nachos, and testosterone—and I'm right at the center, slinging drinks behind the bar like it's an Olympic sport.

"Two Coors, a pickleback, and water." I give the guy his drinks and take his money.

"Next."

"Four Bud Lights and four shots of Hornitos. And water for yourself. You need to stay hydrated to make it all night with me."

I smile sweetly and lean in just enough to make him hopeful. "It looks like you'll spend your night with the dude you're sitting with. He's watching Twilight on his phone and clearly waiting for you, not the game."

The bar bursts into laughter, including the guy, who throws his hands up in surrender.

Brian snorts as he drops a fresh tray of clean glasses next to me. "Brutal! How you still get tips with that attitude is beyond me."

I nudge him with my elbow. "Game days bring out the best in me."

"Pretty sure that guy you roasted is still gonna tip you twenty bucks. It's a true talent."

"He better. That's top-shelf sass."

Brian's been working here longer than I have. We get along great and hustle with the best of them. We've got a rhythm. He cleans, clears, washes, and closes tabs while I charm and get people to drink more, and we split all the tips. Sophia, my best friend, is working the floor tonight.

A guy at the end of the bar waves at me. He's wearing a vintage Broncos hoodie and grinning like he's trying to impress someone. "You guys got any drink specials for Boise State fans?"

I wipe my hands on a towel. "Sure do. If you can name three Broncos who went pro in ten seconds, I'll give you half off."

He blinks. "Uh..."

"Clock's ticking."

"Um... Ezra Cleveland... Rypien... and..."

"Go on..."

"Uh... my cousin, Travis?"

The people in earshot laugh. "Nice try. Full price, as I slide him a beer."

He raises his glass. "Fair enough."

Brian leans toward me, "You running trivia now?"

"Just keeping the bar lively. Don't tell him, but I don't think I could even name a single player. He could have made up the names." I give him a wild smirk.

The Broncos score, and the entire room erupts like we've won the Super Bowl. Someone spills their beer in the celebration, and I grab a towel without missing a beat.

"These games are the worst, but if they drink enough, maybe I'll forgive the universe for making me work them."

He laughs and slides me a shot of tequila. "To suffering."

"To tips," I correct, tapping his glass before tossing it back.

And just like that, the next wave of screams hit when the other team scores, and everyone fumes. More orders, screams, and people.

This bar feels like home, like family. I'm in my element, and even though this isn't exactly where I thought I would end up, I love it here.

The Broncos lose, but barely. As soon as the game ends, the bar empties to only a few regulars and strays. Sophia and I bus all the dirty tables and make the place somewhat normal again.

We mostly see the regulars and college kids, so when someone comes in wearing a suit, we notice. A burly, mafia boss-looking man goes to the corner, removes his jacket, and takes a seat. He's young, maybe twenty-six or twenty-seven. I go over to his table, flashing him a big smile.

"Hey there."

Nothing but crickets... Is this guy ignoring me? I keep a smile on my face.

"Can I get you something to drink? A menu?" I ask the scowling dark-haired guy.

"Coors."

"Coors it is." He has a tattoo on his neck, covered by his shirt, but I can see the tips of wings coming out from under his collar. Maybe a bird or an angel?

I fetch his beer and set it in front of him. "Here you go, it's five dollars, or I can start you a tab."

He slaps a five-dollar bill on the table.

I pick it up and walk away. “What a jerk,” I mutter to myself as I go back to the bar.

“Hey, Olive?”

“What’s up, Todd?” I reply.

“Why isn’t there a pregnant Barbie?”

I internally roll my eyes at the lame joke heading my way. “Why?”

“Because Ken came in another box.”

I give him a sweet, fake smile and giggle at the dumb joke. Some of his jokes are good, but most days they’re not. Most days, they’re grossly inappropriate, or worse, just not funny.

“Good one,” I say.

Sophia comes back from asking our boss if we can cut someone. It’s dead in here now that the game is over.

“What did Jan say?”

“She said we can both go as long as Brian’s good with it.”

We both turn and stare at Brian, and he feels it because he immediately looks over and asks what we want. We both give our best smiles and puppy dog eyes and ask if we can leave. He rolls his eyes.

“Go clean off the rest of the dirty tables, clean the bathrooms, and get out of here.” We both smile and go to get it done.

“Ugh, the bathroom is a mess,” I say out loud.

I hate cleaning them after games. Every stall needs toilet paper; the sinks are gross, so I clean them out. I sweep and stock the paper towels. Next, I head to clean the men’s room. This would suck if we hadn’t made bank in tips today.

I knock twice to make sure it’s empty. I don’t hear anyone, so I open the door. Only to walk right into the rude guy who’s been hanging out in the bar’s corner since the game ended. He said a whole three words all night—Coors, Coors, and Coors.

He glares at me as he walks by. What an ass. I finish cleaning the disgusting men’s room and clock out.

"Hey, Olive, wanna shoot some pool before we go home?" Sophia calls as she clocks out.

"Definitely. I'll grab the first round. Beer for you?"

"Yeah, I'll take that sour beer we got in."

I return to the table with her beer, my favorite–Stoli Blueberry Vodka and lemonade, and two shots of tequila. Because after the night we've had, I'll take them both if she doesn't want one.

"Thanks, Liv. What are you doing tomorrow? You're off, right?" she asks.

"Yes, I'm off. Probably just going to the gym and running some errands."

"I don't have to work until 4:00 p.m. Do you want to meet for coffee in the morning?"

"Of course I do! Acai bowls and coffee at The Naked Bean?"

"Duh!" she says with a flip of her long brown hair. I give her a warm smile, appreciating my friend for a moment.

Sophia and I met when I was still in college for nursing. She'll finish school soon; I dropped out. We get along great. Her heart is big and full of kindness. She's the most thoughtful friend I have ever had. She doesn't judge. Ever. And that's so rare.

As I reach over the table to take my shot, I look up to see Mr. Grumpy focused on me. I get this dark feeling in the pit of my stomach. I aim for the seven ball and miss, like always.

I lean over to Sophia and whisper into her ear, "Have you ever seen that guy in here before?"

She eyes him over her shoulder and smirks a bit. I roll my eyes, elbowing her in the side, "Stop making it obvious."

She giggles, "No. I've never seen him here. Why do you ask? Because he kind of has a tall, dark, and handsome thing going? Do I need to play matchmaker?"

"No, he's kind of an ass. I guess he's hot, if you like them rude and scary."

"I mean, he's kind of more my type than yours, Olive." She's had a hard life. Her parents were pretty terrible. You wouldn't know that by looking at her. She's full glam, cute outfits, designer purses, the works, and she loves dark and broody men.

I laugh because that's accurate. I like the pretty Golden Retriever type.

A few shots later, Todd and Christi, two of our bar regulars, come over to the table.

Christi asks, "Can we join you ladies?"

I'm on my third drink and am convinced I can still play pool. "Sure!" A few minutes pass, and Brian brings us another round of shots.

"Great, guess I'm walking home tonight." Which is fine because my apartment is less than a mile away. I take a shot of tequila and lime.

After the liquid burns my insides, I challenge everyone to a game of doubles, despite having the hand-eye coordination of a drunken toddler. "Me and Sophia versus you two."

Todd racks the balls and tells me to break.

"Alright, losers," I announce, chalking my cue stick with way too much enthusiasm as I slide my hand up and down the stick suggestively. "Prepare to witness greatness."

We all laugh at my antics. It's kind of my thing. I don't mind giving as much as I take. All in good fun.

"Last time you said that, you scratched on the break," Sophia reminds me.

"Yeah, well, this time, I have... strategy." I pause, pretending to measure the angle with my cue like a pro.

"Strategy is not whatever this is," said Christi, gesturing with her finger, whirling it at me. I take my shot. The cue ball jumps off the table, ricocheting off a barstool and landing on the floor, rolling to none other than Mr. Grumpy. Silence falls over the group. The man stares at his beer, the ball sitting next to his foot, and then at me, looking so annoyed.

"Oh, fuck," I mumble to myself.

"Sorry, could you hand me the ball?" I ask, trying to keep a straight face while walking in his direction to take it back. I'm not sure if I want to laugh, cry, or hide.

Todd facepalms after seeing my horrendous break. Sophia and Christi are already howling with laughter. Mr. Grumpy picks up the ball and sets it in my hand. He stares at me and says, "Watch yourself."

I walk away, feeling like I might shit myself.

I mouth, "What the fuck?" as I join the group again.

The game continues, mostly consisting of my shots going anywhere but where they're supposed to. When I finally sink a ball, I celebrate like I've won a gold medal. "Did you see that?! I fucking made it!"

"That was the other team's ball," Sophia deadpans.

"But it went in, and I put it there," I say, smiling at them with utter joy.

Todd groans. "You're ridiculous, but thanks for helping us, not that we need it with your skills."

"My amazing skills, you mean. You're welcome. Happy to help those in need," I correct him with some sass.

Todd pipes up after he takes his shot. "Have you heard this one?"

We all groan, knowing another bad joke is in the works.

"A woman I slept with told me I had the biggest penis she'd ever seen." We all glance at each other and then back at Todd. "Turns out she was blind. She was just pulling my leg."

I am mid-drink and spit it out, spraying it all over our bar table, and snort from laughter. The slightly drunk version of myself finds his jokes much funnier. As I'm attempting to clean up my mess, I notice Mr. Grumpy is leaving; his eyes follow me as he walks out, making my hands clammy and my heart race. Finally, he's gone, and I feel a little lighter. He was a dark cloud in here and was giving me the creeps.

Chapter 2
Olive
The Short Walk Home

By the end of the night, I had pocketed five balls—one belonging to the other team, another the cue ball—knocked back three more drinks, and was ready to call it a night.

As we all stumble out laughing, sometime around closing, I turn to Todd and Christi with absolute confidence and ask, "Same time next week?"

Todd sighs. "You're lucky you're fun to be around. We will definitely see you soon."

"Damn right, I am."

Sophia and I linger in the parking lot for a moment while she waits for her Uber. "Are you sure you don't want to stay over at my place?" I ask her.

She flashes me a wicked grin and a wink, "Nah. Robbert and I have plans...some horizontal bonding time."

I laugh. "Don't do anything I wouldn't do." We both chuckle, knowing that's not much. I'm a free spirit, confident in my own skin, and sexually adventurous. Once her Uber arrives, I walk home, passing by The Naked Bean, already dreaming about our acai bowls in the morning.

Food. When I get home, I need food.

As I make my way to my apartment, I can't help but feel a little nervous despite nothing seeming out of sorts. I can't shake the feeling that something is off.

The small town we live in is one of the safest places in the country. I've made this walk home hundreds of times; I've never really felt this uneasy. I try to get the thought out of my head and think about something else. It's cold outside, but not too cold given the time of year. October in Boise is pretty comfortable, but an involuntary shiver ripples along the length of my spine like cold water. I pick up my pace, trusting my gut, and try to get home as fast as I can.

I live in a cute apartment building outside of downtown. My parents own the building, so my rent is next to nothing. Mostly younger couples and college students live here. As soon as I'm inside, I immediately lock the door, feeling safe now that I'm home.

I change into my pajamas–a pair of soft black shorts and an old t-shirt that says, "Do I run? Yes, I run my mouth a lot." A gift from Sophia. I go into the kitchen and open the fridge. Nothing. I've got nothing but a bit of sour milk, a jar of pickle juice, and a pack of ham with no bread to put it on. Tired and hungry, I decide to order some late-night delivery from Roberto's Tacos. It's open twenty-four hours, and it's not too far away. I open the delivery app and order four chicken tacos and a drink. I submit the order, and the screen says it'll be here in twenty minutes.

I turn on the TV and flip through a few channels before I get a little tingle between my legs. Why do I have to be hungry and horny? Deciding I have enough time, I jump up and head to my nightstand and pull out my trusty purple vibrator. Lying in bed, thighs spread, I run the little vibrating tip on my clit, instantly feeling the sensations I need. About five minutes later, on the edge of release, I hear a knock at the door.

"Fucking great," there it goes, another lost orgasm, never coming to fruition. I debate whether to keep going and try again, or go get my food—food wins. This can wait. I can always finish later. I toss the vibe on the bed and pull back on my shorts. I look at the time on my phone. "Thank God! I'm starving," thankful the food was so fast.

I swing open the door to find a hulking man in a black ski mask. Panicking, I try to shut it, shouting, "What the fuck, get out!" But he has his foot in the door and pushes me backward with little effort. I'm no toothpick of a girl, and I'm strong, but he's at least eight to ten inches taller and overpowers me. The masked figure lunges toward me, the glint of something sharp catching the light.

I try to scream, but a fist connects with my ribs, knocking the air from my lungs. He follows me inside and grabs me. I stumble back, trying to get away from him, and crash onto the coffee table. I go still, lungs tight with suspense and fear. His hands are firm, unrelenting, and grip my wrists, pinning me down as I thrash beneath him. My breaths come in short, panicked gasps, trying to muster up a cry for help, but between fear and pain, my screams catch in my throat.

He stuffs a cloth in my mouth and holds his callused hand over it. It tastes like dirt and carries the scent of mildew, like an old rag left in a closet for years. A low, rasping chuckle fills the space between us as the man leans in, his breath hot against my skin. He smells of stale beer and too much expensive cologne, something with saffron and cedarwood.

"You remember me?" he murmurs, his voice dripping with something dark and cruel.

He lands a blow to my cheek, pain exploding across my face; the world tilts into chaos. He puts a piece of duct tape over my mouth, keeping me silent as I struggle to reorient myself.

Fuck, what was happening? He presses down on me, heavy and solid. Between his weight and the gag in my mouth, it's difficult to keep breathing. After a couple more hits to my sides and face, he drags me by my hands. I squirm and kick, attempting to get away. In response, he uses his other hand, grabs a handful of my tangled hair, and walks me to my bedroom. The sharp stinging pain in my scalp paralyzing my energy and will to fight back.

He throws me down onto the bed. I land on my side, immediately trying to crawl up the bed, latching onto the blanket and sheets. I need to escape and try to put as much space between us as I can. I start pulling at the tape around my mouth, but I don't get it off. He stands at the side of the bed, pulling my hands up and duct-taping them to the bronze bar of my headboard. My mouth is open in a scream, but no audible sound escapes. I'm crying, shaking, trembling, kicking, making every effort to get away. I'm desperate to gain some control.

He's at the foot of my bed now. Asking me if I remember him. With my eyes full of tears and his face hidden, there's no way to tell.

"I know women like you, women who think they can do whatever they want. Women who are sluts, and a good time for anyone who takes it." I scream again, but the only noises I make are muffled sounds that don't reach beyond the bedroom walls. The man grabs his knife, straddles me, and holds the blade to my neck. "Do what I say, and I'll let you live."

And then, without warning, I see his fist coming at me again. My face throbs, and my whole body trembles with terror and agony. He pulls at my shirt and begins to cut it off up the front.

Laughing, he says, "Guess you can't run your mouth now."

Air catches in my throat. I don't blink. Don't breathe. Just stare. Every muscle locks tight, not wanting to get cut. The knife is cold against my skin as he cuts the collar off, exposing my chest to him. He leans up onto his knees and pulls my shorts and panties down. Realizing what's about to happen, I thrash, and kick, and try to get him off me. I'm frantically looking to see if I can find something to use as a weapon, but I'm bound and powerless, incapable of defending myself. Given the amount of pain I'm in and the energy I've already spent, I'm running out of steam to fight. I manage to kick him once in the gut.

"Fucking bitch."

He moves to put his body on top of my legs, completely holding me in place. I'm barely breathing, choking on my saliva, tiring of fighting, and I look down to see him unzipping his pants. My eyes widen as he pulls his dick out, and I am aware of what he's going to do to me. How could this be happening to me? Who the hell is this? I close my eyes, wishing it away. Hoping for some escape to come.

"Oh, don't act like you don't want this, you slut. You have a vibrator right here, and now you can have the real thing instead. An even better one. I could tell you wanted me. Don't you remember teasing me?"

He's crazy. I don't recognize his voice or know what he's talking about. It's been years since I had a boyfriend, and the last guy I connected with was from Tinder last New Year's. Who is this guy? He climbs over me and puts the knife to my throat again.

"Spread your legs for me. Now!" As tears roll down my face, silenced, I feel trapped and helpless, still struggling to breathe. I don't know what else I can do. I can't bring myself to spread my thighs, but as he grabs my legs to open them, I find it difficult to resist very much. Every limb feels drained, and I'm barely hanging on.

The cold knife is on my throat. I feel a prick on my neck; a cut. I scream again, no sound escaping the gag. His dick pushes into me, and I shut my eyes. Feeling him move in and out of me, hard, grunting above me, taking what he wants.

I look at my tied hands and try to focus on that. I do everything I can to leave my body and focus on my hands. My hands that were cleaning tables and bathrooms a few hours ago, my hands that played pool with friends, and almost hit that guy with the cue ball. I study the bar of my metal headboard. It gives off a vintage-meets-modern vibe. I do anything I can to leave what's actually happening, to focus on something else.

He continues thrusting in and out of me. His hands are on my face, then running down my body, over my breasts. Violating every part of me. Squeezing them painfully. He grunts in my ear.

"You like this dick, don't you, you little slut? I'm going to use every single hole of yours. I'll fuck your pretty ass next." When he lowers his head to talk into my ear, I see it. The same fucking wings sticking out of the guy's shirt from earlier. It's the same tattoo. It's the guy from the bar. My eyes widen in realization, and my brain tries to process what the fuck is happening.

He leans up, grabs my body, and flips me over. The movement is unnatural, and I get a shooting pain in my hand. The tape won't let me turn properly, and I think something broke or popped out of place. Recognizing his identity and intentions, I panic and jerk, kicking again, desperate for anything to save me. Hearing him spit, I feel wetness in my crack. I freak out; this cannot be happening. I'm shaking and begging for him to stop when he hits me over the head with something hard, and everything goes black.

CHAPTER 3
OLIVE

THE BODY REMEMBERS

I'm barely able to open my eyes; I think one is still shut. My whole body aches with pain. I see a bit of light coming through the window. As I come to, I hear knocking on the door. I'm still taped to the bed. I can't move. Struck with instant terror, not wanting the masked man to be here or to come back for more. Closing my eyes painfully tight, I lay in disarray, wishing it all away.

I hear Sophia. She has a key to my apartment. I internally thank God, happy she's here, but also go white, not wanting her to find me like this.

"You didn't eat your tacos last night, Olive? How could you? That's a party foul. Are you still sleeping? Hello? We had plans like thirty minutes ago!"

Sophia comes into my room. She walks in and stops, gasping at what she's found. On my side, still taped and naked, I'm fully exposed to her. Feelings of shame run through me, to be found like this, broken and weak. It's a whole new level of pain. Within seconds, she runs over to my side.

Rescued

"Are you ok? What the hell happened here?"

I look up at her, and she sees that I still have my mouth taped shut. Her eyes go wide, unblinking, as if she's trying to unsee what's in front of her.

She leans over and says, "I'm going to take the tape off. Hold still."

"One, two," she rips the duct tape off my mouth. I attempt to spit out the cloth. She helps me by pulling on it. I gasp for air. Relief floods me with that first deep inhale, like I finally came up for air.

"Calm down, you're ok, I'm going to get your hands free. Stay here while I get some scissors to cut the tape."

I shake my head. "No, no, please don't leave me," I beg. She puts her hand on my back. I immediately flinch at the contact, causing Sophia to pull back and startle.

She puts her hand back down to reassure me and says, "It's ok, I'll be right back, I'm just going into the other room."

I heave and panic. My chest tightens like a vice, each breath shallow and sharp, as if the air itself is too thick to swallow. I look down to see I am covered in bruises, some still forming, and blood on my chest and sheets. I don't even know where the blood is from. My heart thunders and my hands tremble as a wave of fear and memories crashes over me.

"Ok, I'm back," Sophia says.

She sits next to me, not touching me but close.

She says in a gentle tone, "I'm going to cut the tape; I'll need to hold your skin back. Just hold still."

The second her hand touches me, I jerk, but my hand can't move. The pulling on my arm sends throbbing pain into my wrist.

She waits for me to calm down and says, "It's ok, you're going to be ok," and cuts the tape. I feel the familiar cold metal cross my skin, and I shudder, lowering my head in utter disbelief. As she pulls the tape off my wrist, I scream out from the pain shooting through my arm and hand.

Sophia talks to me after she removes all the tape, but I can't hear her. I'm too focused on the overwhelming pain and the chaotic emotions running rampant through my mind. My ass is sore. My ribs hurt when I breathe. Looking at my wrist, I see that it's completely swollen, probably broken. I'm not even sure what else is hurting because I go numb. I'm covered in blood, bruises, and who knows what else.

"Hello? Hello! Olive!" Sophia is waving her hand in my face. I snap up. "I'm going to get you dressed, and I'll call the police."

I look at her. I can't move or speak. I can't even register what she's saying. But I give her the smallest of nods, agreeing to whatever it is she's trying to tell me.

As she's helping me dress, I look up at her face and see tears streaming down her cheeks. "What's wrong?"

She looks at me, confused.

I glare back, not sure why she's crying.

"I found you beaten and raped. You're my best friend. Of course I'm crying."

Raped. Even though I knew, it hadn't fully registered, but he raped me. Raped, in my apartment, by that guy.

"The guy from the bar," I say.

"What?"

"It was that guy from the bar last night. I saw his tattoo."

Her face goes from sad to angry in a flash, her jaw clenching, eyes full of fury. "What? Are you sure?"

"Yes, I'm sure," I say in a clipped tone.

"Oh my God, Olive. I should have come home with you. I shouldn't have let you walk home alone. Why didn't I just stay? I'm so sorry, Olive. I should have made sure you got home safe." I shake my head, "It's not your fault. He came after I got home."

Sophia helps me stand and puts my pants on. She wraps a blanket around me, and we walk to the couch.

She picks up her phone and walks into the kitchen. "Yes, hello. My name is Sophia McGrath. Last night, an attacker sexually assaulted my friend, Olive Smythe. I found her in her apartment, 1856 South Leadville Avenue, this morning."

I stop listening after that.

A few minutes later, she hangs up the phone and joins me on the couch.

"Ok, babe, the police and EMTs are going to come. After they finish investigating, I'll take you to the hospital."

I wrap my blanket tighter and lean into her arms. She holds me while I cry. Tears stream down my face so hard that my head throbs again. I don't know how long we sit here, but a loud knock sounds on the front door. Sophia stands to answer it. I pull the blanket around me to shield myself. I don't need more humiliation from strangers seeing me like this.

Two cops are at the door, one male and one female, and an EMT. Sophia greets them and lets them in.

The EMT comes over first. "Hi, my name is Steven. Can you tell me your name?"

"Olive Smythe," I mumble. I curl into myself, my body tensing. I can't even look at him.

"Good. Do you know where you are, Olive?"

"My apartment."

"Good. Are you having any trouble breathing?"

"No, I'm fine."

"Do you mind if I check your vitals and pupils?"

"Sure," I say with hesitation.

He reaches for my arm, and as soon as he makes contact, I pull my arm in retreat, my eyes wide with panic.

"I won't hurt you; I promise. Can we try this again?"

Sophia is sitting on my other side now. "It's ok, Olive. I'm right here. Focus on me."

Steve reaches for me again, putting his fingers on my wrist to check my pulse. My breath catches. Sophia watches me, reassuring me. I let him do what he needs to do, but it feels like another violation.

"You seem stable enough to answer questions. After that, you need to go to the hospital. You can ride in the ambulance, or your friend can take you. When you get there, you will be able to talk to a female doctor who has been trained to manage assault cases. How does that sound?" I nod, thankful that for the moment, this is over.

Sophia says, "I'll take her in. Thank you."

The female cop walks toward me. "Hello, Olive, my name is Sergeant Persimmons. Do you mind if I sit and ask you some questions?"

I give her a slight nod to avoid speaking for as long as possible. I want to crawl into a hole and never speak about this.

"Great, Olive. Can you tell me about what happened last night?"

The words don't come at first. They stick in my throat like jagged glass. I force them out, my voice barely a whisper.

"I thought, when he knocked, it was the taco delivery I ordered. I opened the door, and he stood there. He had a black ski mask on. He had a knife and hit me in my side until he could put the cloth in my mouth."

Sophia cut in. "I took the tape and gag out of her mouth when I got here. She was taped to the bed. I left everything in the bedroom."

The male cop points, asking where, and Sophia nods that it's the room over to the right. He goes in. I assume to collect evidence.

Sergeant Persimmons continues, "You're doing great. Can you tell me what happened next?"

I finish the statement, avoiding eye contact with both Sophia and the police officer. Telling them all the gory details, recounting as much of the night as I can remember.

"At one point, he leaned over me, and that's when I recognized the tattoo on his neck from earlier. He was in the bar, where I work, after the Broncos game. He was rude and creepy."

The officer asked, "Can you describe him and the tattoo?"

"He was around six feet, maybe. Dark hair, long on top. He's twenty-six or twenty-seven, I would guess.

"I couldn't see the whole tattoo, but I noticed it in the bar. There were wings on the side of his neck. Maybe a bird or an angel? I could see a few inches of them. He paid cash; we hadn't seen him in the bar before."

Time passes in a blur of more questions, paperwork, and waiting for them to finish their investigation of my apartment.

"Good, thank you, Olive. We'll contact you if we have any updates or more questions."

Finally, they leave. My body feels like lead, too heavy to carry, as if gravity is working against me. I stare blankly with dead eyes because I have nothing left to give. I'm exhausted; I'm in pain, and desperate for this day to be over.

"I'm so proud of you, Olive. You are so strong. You will get through this. I'll be with you every step of the way, ok? Will you let me take you to the hospital?"

I nod, not even having the energy to fight her.

The sun is bright, and I'm not prepared to see the world right now.

I look at her with utter gratefulness; we're both still teary-eyed. I don't know how I would've gotten free if she hadn't found me, or survived any of what I just went through without her.

He left me there to die. Maybe he thought I was dead. Right now, I wish I were...

Chapter 4
Olive

BEDSIDE MANNER

As soon as we pull up to the hospital, my stomach drops, and I realize I don't want to do this. Sophia looks at me with warm eyes.

"Are you ready?" she asks, her tone soft.

"No!" I snap. "I don't think I can do this. I can't walk in there and talk about it again."

Sophia looks at me, and with care and concern, she places her hand over mine. I want to pull away, but she looks at me closer. She holds my attention and says, "I'm here with you, I won't leave your side, but you have to go in there and let them help you." As I cry, she wraps her arm around me. She lets me break down, the tenth time in just a few hours.

I don't know how long we sit here, but I finally look at her and tell her, "Ok."

The emergency room smells like antiseptic and bad coffee. The fluorescent lights are too bright, making me feel like I'm under a spotlight. People stare at me; it feels like they are burning their judgments into my flesh, like they know. I, once again, wish this wasn't my life. I want to crawl under a rock and never come out.

A nurse calls my name, gentle but firm, and I flinch at the thought of going back and having someone poke and prod.

"It's ok," Sophia whispers. She settles her arm around my waist and helps me to my feet.

I want to tell her I can't do this. That I want to go home, burrow into my bed, and pretend last night never happened. But home doesn't feel safe anymore. I have nowhere to go.

I follow the nurse down a sterile hallway, void of anything significant. She leads me into a small room with an exam table, a chair, and a countertop holding a computer.

"The doctor will be in shortly."

Sophia and I sit in silence, no words left to exchange. The weight of it all and the quiet press in around me, but no words come–nothing that fits, nothing that could change anything.

The doctor walks in, her blue eyes warm and soothing. She offers a warm smile, "Hi, I'm Dr. Clark. I assume you are Olive?" She says as she gestures to me sitting on the exam table.

"Yes, I'm Olive."

"Do you consent to your friend staying in the room with you today?"

"Yes, I want her to stay."

She looks at me the way people look at injured animals–like I might bolt. I know she's trying to be gentle, but I'm so embarrassed.

"We're going to take care of you," she says, her voice soft but steady. "Take your time, you can stop anytime throughout this entire process. Everything I do will be completely consensual and at your own pace. Do you want to tell me what happened? "

I don't, but I open my mouth and tell her anyway. His hands. The blows. The knife. The unbearable weight of him. The way my screams couldn't pierce through the gag. The way no one came.

I had to relive this all over again. It's some kind of cruel joke that women have to tell people about their traumatic experiences, and let strangers violate them all over again.

Dr. Clark didn't flinch. She only nods, taking notes. When I finish, she explains what will happen next. The rape kit. The exam. The photos of my bruises and injuries. The swabs.

She hands me a gown and a blanket.

"Can you please put this on? I'll step outside and give you a moment."

As she walks out, Sophie says, "I'll stay, but I'm going to turn around and give you some privacy. This can't be easy, and I don't want to make it any harder."

My hands shake, and I can barely remove my shirt. I catch sight of myself in the mirror. "Fuck," I mutter to myself.

My lip is swollen, my cheek is black and blue, and there's a large softball-sized bruise under my left breast. I look at the bruise, realizing that's where my ribs hurt. I have another on my side, a slight bruise on my breast, and dried blood running down my neck from where he nicked my skin with the knife. That must have been where the blood on the bed came from.

I turn away. Changing into the paper-thin gown leaves me more exposed than I'm ready for. I ignore most of the exam, only hearing the clanking of instruments before the doctor shoves cold metal into my body. Sophia holds my hand the whole time.

The exam was cold, sterile, and clinical. The doctor and nurse moved gently, explaining each step before they did it, but it didn't stop the feeling that my body wasn't mine anymore.

"Ok, Olive. You have some small lacerations and tearing. Nothing that won't heal on its own, but you will feel some additional discomfort for the next few days. I've taken all the samples I need. I'll have you pee in a cup after this, and we can run all the basic STI and pregnancy tests. The pregnancy test won't be accurate this early, but they are part of the protocol, so I will also give you a Plan B if you'd like."

I tighten my eyes shut and nod. I hadn't even thought about that; I can't think about what those tests might show. How did I end up here? I want to disappear, to hide from everything, from everyone, and pretend none of this ever happened. But it has, and the proof is in those tests.

After the exam, I curl into myself, my body tensing involuntarily. I can't even look at the doctor as she leaves.

Sophia, still holding my hand, says, "You did so good, Olive. Seeing how resilient you are makes me so proud. I'm in awe of how strong you've been. I'm so sorry you had to go through all this. You're almost done, though."

I had to have X-rays of my ribs and wrist. Luckily, the doctor said the rib fractures were minor, and my wrist was sprained, not broken. I went home with a splint on my hand, some pain meds, Plan B, and several brochures about finding a therapist or support group. Great, I'm a fucking statistic.

Sophia was waiting with me when they finally let me go. She stands, opening her arms, and I collapse into them. She helps me walk back to the car.

"I got you," she whispers into my hair. "You're not alone."

I want to believe that. I really do. But as we walk out of the hospital into the morning sun, I know one thing for certain: I will never be the same.

Sophia called out of work and came home with me. As I walk into the apartment, nothing feels familiar. The entire apartment is tainted. My coffee table is the first reminder. The air carries a faint stench of stale paper and metal. Even the light filtering through the curtains feels wrong. Too many shadows are here now. It is no longer my home; it's a shell of who I was, who I used to be.

I used to be loyal, loud, funny, and endlessly curious. I thrived on connections with people, new experiences, and finding joy in the little things. Now, I am a creature of fear–skittish, withdrawn, flinching at every sound and touch, shrinking from light, from movement, from people. Even my shadow feels like a threat.

"Let's get you in the shower," Sophia says, walking towards the bathroom, and I follow her.

She turns on the shower, puts a clean towel on the counter, and tells me she'll be right outside the door if I need her. I nod and close the door.

I stand in front of the mirror, my fingers brushing the icy surface of the glass as if it can help me understand what I'm seeing. The reflection isn't mine, not really. The eyes staring back are empty, glazed over from all the crying. My body is out of tears. My face is battered, swollen, and pale, but the damage goes deeper than that. The person looking back at me isn't the person I was before. The wild, confident girl who used to smile at her reflection. This woman in the mirror is a stranger, marred by darkness. I doubt I will ever see the old me again.

The steaming water burns and stings my skin, but I don't care. I want new skin. I want this skin to burn off me. I let the water run down my head and back. I turn and let it pound into my face, despite the pain and aching feeling it causes. Anything to take away the pain from last night. I cry into the sensation, letting the shower blend in with my reappearing tears. I don't know how long I've been standing there crying, but I hear a knock at the door and jump, remembering the piercing knock from last night.

"Are you ok? You've been in there for almost an hour; I just wanted to check on you. "

"I'm ok," I respond, realizing the water is barely lukewarm now. "I'll be out in a minute."

For the next week, Sophia moves into my apartment, refusing to let me be alone. She calls out of work for us both, for our shifts this week. Her boyfriend, Robbert, brings over fresh blankets, groceries, and movies. She is an unwavering presence that I am so thankful for.

At night, I attempt to sleep on the couch with the TV humming in the background, some mindless show playing to fill the silence and darkness. The light and company keep the nightmares away. During the day, Sophia makes sure I eat, even if it's only a few bites of toast, and sits beside me when the weight of everything feels too heavy to carry alone.

Sophia doesn't push or force conversation. There isn't a lot to say. She already knows what happened, and she can't do anything to take away the pain. She's there with me. And in the moments when the world is unbearable, when I think I might drown in the memory of that night, it's Sophia's hand in mine that reminds me I'm not alone.

She had an abusive father and neglectful mother; both were alcoholics. She told me stories about covering her bruises before school. I wish those things had never happened, but I felt some relief in the solidarity. Someone who could relate to pain and suffering and come out on the other side alive and relatively happy. But after a few days, I realize Sophia can't stay here forever; she needs to go home and live her life. I'll soon have to live in this apartment alone, and that thought truly terrifies me.

Ten days was long enough, the time had come. I told Sophia she needed to go home, that her boyfriend wanted to spend some time with her, and that she had done more than enough for me. She admitted an actual bed was calling her name. Of course, I told her to go. Her staying here couldn't last forever. At some point, I had to put on my big girl pants and be here alone.

For the first time since that night, I'm by myself. The nightmares are so intense most of the time that I stay awake. I sit in my room, my old bed, made with the flowery, blue and white comforter Sophia ordered. The bronze headboard remains. It's hard to look at now. I had stared up at it during the worst moment of my life, and now it feels like it's staring back. I can't sleep, I can't eat, I can't leave, but I also don't want to stay.

I pick up the book on the nightstand that I had read halfway through, and stare at it. I love, well, loved, romance books, and was enjoying this one, but the thought of reading about two people getting it on makes me want to puke. So, I shove it back in the drawer. Is everything I love ruined? Am I just a shell of a person with nothing to hold on to?

I opt for TV. I've been sleeping on the couch all week with Sophia, so maybe I'll sleep out here forever.

Sophia convinces me to come to work with her a few days later, promising she will take me home as soon as she's off work and stay the night. It will be good for me to get out. She's working a slow lunch shift, only a few hours. It sounds terrible, but not as terrible as sitting in this apartment alone for another day.

It's been thirteen days since that night. All the bruises have faded from my face, and the big ones on my body are improving. I took the brace off my hand, too. I haven't told anyone about what happened. Sophia told our boss, Jan, that I had an emergency and needed some time, but nothing else. When I walked into the bar, I saw Todd and Nash, another regular, and went to sit near them. I knew them and figured they were safe.

"Heya, Olive, I haven't seen you in a while. Where ya been?" Todd says.

Sophia glares at him and says, "She's been busy. Don't ask dumb questions."

I smirk at her, and he leaves it at that, given the death stare Sophia gives him.

A moment later, Todd pipes up again and, to no one in particular, says, "There's something about the clitoris. I can't quite put my finger on it." The empty bar is silent.

"I'm shocked you can't find the clitoris, Todd," Sophia deadpans.

My face reddens. I can't help but look away. I can't listen to this crap right now. My saving grace of a boss comes in, breaking the unbearable awkward silence. "Olive, would you come chat for a moment?"

I almost leap out of my chair to get away from whatever hell is going on at the bar. "Sure."

We enter Jan's messy office. She is an excellent bar owner and friend, but damn, her office is a wreck. Stacks of paper are everywhere, there's an overflowing trash bin, and if you ever get a glimpse of her email inbox, you'll see she has over 150,000 unread messages. On the plus side, you can't find a better boss in this industry.

"I know you had an incident and missed work last week, but I want to discuss that with you. Do you plan to come back next week? Or will it be longer?"

I am hesitant to answer. She doesn't know I was attacked, and I don't want to share, but I have to tell her something.

"Olive?"

"Yeah," I mumble, trying to think of what to say. "Someone broke into my apartment, and I don't feel ready to come back to work. It might be a while yet. I understand if you need to hire someone else."

She looks a bit stunned. "No, dear, that's not what I was getting at, but I'm sorry to hear about the break-in. Are you ok? Is that why those police officers asked if I had surveillance recordings? Unfortunately, I don't have any fancy tech stuff."

"Yes, I'm ok," I mutter. "It was someone I recognized from the bar; maybe they were hoping to identify him." I leave it at that, hoping she realizes I'm not interested in talking about it.

"Can you move out of your apartment?"

"No, my parents own the property and let me live there for pretty much nothing. I don't have the money to find another place. I just want to feel safe in my home again; To feel like it's my home again."

Jan looks at me and nods. "Is there anything I can do?"

I answer simply, "No, I'll figure it out. I need a little time to sort myself out."

She reaches out to grab my hand and gives it a squeeze. I go rigid, trying not to jerk my hand back. Attempting to calm myself and tell myself it's just Jan. I look up at her and see a worried expression in her eyes. I stand to leave, feeling like I want to go jump into bed, or off a bridge.

"Wait. If you want to feel safer in your apartment and have some companionship, have you considered a dog? I volunteer at a local rescue, Only Dogs. There are a couple of dogs that are in our care that are pretty protective dogs."

I look at her and think for a moment. "Do you mean a guard dog? Like they're trained or something?"

"Well, no. I mean if that's what you're comfortable with, then I'm sure there is a way to find a trained dog. It would probably involve more costs to you, but definitely doable. The rescue has a handful of dogs that are skittish about meeting new people, some more than others. Once they know you, they're great, loving companions. However, if someone were to break in, they would surely go into guard mode. Given that, there are some differences in adopting a dog like that. They need to be contained when people come over."

"How would I adopt one of them?" I ask, feeling nervous, but a little excited for the first time in almost two weeks.

"Fill out an application. I process most of them, but it's necessary to have one on file. Once approved, I can set up a meet and greet. Depending on which dog you choose, it may take a few meetings before you can bring them home."

I have butterflies in my stomach at the thought of having someone else at home. Someone to protect me, not to fix me, but to fill the emptiness gnawing at me. Maybe a dog is what I need. For a moment, the thought feels like a lifeline, like it anchors me to the ground.

"Can you text me all the info and what dogs I should look at?"

"Of course, Olive, I'd be happy to. And please, take all the time you need. You will always have a job here when you are ready to come back. I'll figure it out in the meantime."

With that, I walk out and back to the bar to sit with Sophia while she works.

Chapter 5
Olive

Paws and Consider

Sitting through the lunch shift and trying to 'people' for a couple of hours was brutal. Once off her shift, Sophia finally takes me home. As we relax on the couch and I settle my nerves, I tell her, "I talked to Jan today."

Sophia looks at me, concerned. "About work? Are you going back already?"

"No, I don't think I'm ready for that, especially with how hard it was to be friendly with Todd and Nash today. I would be the worst. But Jan mentioned she volunteers with a local dog rescue. She said I might feel safer with a guard dog. What do you think?"

Sophia furrows her brow and tilts her head. "A guard dog? You think that's a good idea? Can you handle a pet? Have you ever had a pet before?"

"No, my mom is afraid of animals, so we never had pets. Although I had a goldfish that I won from a fair once, it only lived a couple of days, though. But thanks for the vote of confidence."

"You know, my concern is only out of love. I don't want to see you get overwhelmed while trying to deal with everything. Dogs are an enormous commitment; they need care and walks outside several times a day. You can't give them back if it doesn't work out."

"I get that, and I appreciate the concern, but this is the first time since my assault that I'm a little excited. I hate this apartment, but I'm stuck here. I think I would feel safer. Plus, I love dogs. It will be good to take care of something else. I've always wanted one. I figured I could check into it, maybe learn more about it before deciding for sure."

Sophia looks at me with narrowed eyes for a second, and then her smile lights up, "Well, let's do it, lady! What's the first step?"

Giving me the reassurance I need, I reach for my phone and open the text Jan sent after our conversation.

Jan: Hey, Olive. Here is the info you will need.

Only Dogs Rescue, here is a link to their website. Onlydogsrescue.com. Fill out an application; list me as a reference if you'd like! A few dogs that I think would make excellent guard dogs are Tallulah, Laika, and Kong. Look over their bios and let me know if you have questions.

I click the link and glance at Sophia to see a huge smile on her face. It makes me smile, too.

The website looks nice. It has a picture of three guys, Jan, and another woman on the front page, with four dogs all sitting in front.

"I didn't realize Jan was so involved in dog rescue; she's on the cover photo and everything. I wonder what she does," Sophia says, looking over my shoulder.

"She told me she processes most of the applications, but I bet she does more than that."

"Look! Dog bios–click there!" Sophia points to the button.

I do, and I see a ton of dogs, all with happy faces. They're all so cute. The title reads, "Are You My Furever?"

We both exhale a sing-song, "Aw." I find the dog named Laika, and click on her picture. She's a cute shepherd-looking dog with a big smile on her face and her tongue hanging to the side. She's all black instead of having the usual shepherd markings.

Laika-Female, 3 years old, German Shepherd Mix

Laika is a special girl who needs a special home. She has a fear of people and that can come across as feisty with new people. But she loves her people once she knows you. Someone left her behind in an empty house for weeks, alone to fend for herself. She was starving when we found her. She had some skin issues, which we have remedied, and now is as healthy as can be. She is high-energy and playful. She would benefit from an active owner. She is generally good with other animals, but would do best with male dogs. She is ready to find her special people.

I look at Sophia, and we both beam in pure delight.

"Oh my God, she is so cute!" I say, covering my heart with my hand.

Sophia says, "She is adorable, but shepherds are a whole other ballgame. They shed a ton and are pretty active. She might not be content to stay on the couch all day."

"Yeah. I say, a bit disappointed. Well, let's look at the next one."

I like this idea more and more. The thought of having something else to focus on, to forget my own problems for a few minutes every day, sounds like heaven.

"Find the next one Jan said to look at," Sophia says.

I scroll through and find Tallulah next. She's a big-headed brown dog with the absolute biggest Pittie smile that I have ever seen. Her cute little ears stand to attention, but flop forward at the tips. She has a white patch on her chest with little brown spots, and the picture shows her lying in a small pool enjoying the sun. We both giggle and read on.

Tallulah-Female, 9 years old, Pitbull Mix

Tallulah is a petite but feisty little thing. She will need a very special home. Tallulah is not fond of anything new. She doesn't particularly care for new people, other animals, or new environments. She must trust the person she is with. Tallulah also suffers from separation anxiety and would do well with someone who is home the majority of the time. She makes new friends only on her terms and after multiple meetings. We don't know a lot about her past. We found her dumped out in the hills with what appeared to be cigarette burns. She had several puncture wounds and was completely emaciated. Because of this, she has some issues with food. She will need to be kenneled when food is around. This tiny lover needs someone who can keep her safe, show her what it means to be loved, and give her the life she's always deserved.

My eyes well with tears for this poor, broken girl, left to die after being tortured. My heart immediately goes out to her.

"What do you think, Soph?"

"You know a dog like that will need someone who understands dog body language and behaviors. Someone experienced. You will also need to keep her safe. Maybe since you have never had a dog before, you should consider whether that is a good fit for you right now. I'm with you on this whole dog thing. I think you should take some time to think about what you can handle. Whether you can take on her care. Let's look at the last one."

I scroll to the next dog, Kong. He is a bluish-gray colored pitbull with short-cropped ears and a white patch on his chest. His picture differs from the others. He doesn't have a big smile, and his eyes are sad, but piercing gold. He's adorable, but those eyes show a broken spirit.

Kong-Male, 5 years old, Blue Nose Pitbull

Kong gets along with some smaller animals, but will need a special home. Kong has severe stranger danger and will need his adopter to earn his trust before they can bring him home. We took Kong into care after finding him chained in a backyard, where he'd been his whole life. He was abandoned by his owner with several others, and we were asked to assist and bring him into our care. He was underweight, with a large mass on his hip.

Once he received medical care, a large obstruction was found in his abdomen. Had he not been saved when he was, he wouldn't have made it. Four feet of rope was found in his intestinal tract. He's lucky to be alive today. Kong is a pretty easygoing dog, aside from meeting new people. He doesn't require a lot of exercise; he's more of a Netflix and nap kind of dog.

I look into his sad eyes, I feel his pain, and know that Kong will be my new companion. I don't care what Sophia thinks. I'll give him all the love in the world, and he'll keep me safe in return.

"He's the one," I say. My words tumble out in a breathless, high-pitched rush; my hands flutter with excitement. I can't contain the flush of my cheeks and the huge grin on my face.

Sophia claps her hands and cheers. "I think he sounds perfect; I can't wait to meet him. Now, go fill out the application. This is the first time I've seen you look happy, alive, whatever, since I found you. I'm really glad to see it."

Rescued

Chapter 6
Loch

The Weight of Goodbye

"Hey, Loch! There's a girl who works for me who applied for Kong, and I think she's a great match," Jan says while joining me in the office.

I can't help but glare at her. Kong? My Kong? He's been my longest foster. He's been with me for almost two years, and honestly, I didn't think his issues would ever allow for adoption.

"Do you know this girl? Does she have experience with dogs like Kong?"

"Well, no. Her apartment was broken into recently, and since she lives alone as a single woman, she wants a guard dog. I actually suggested him to her. She may not have a lot of experience, but she's worked for me for almost four years. She's a wonderful, responsible person who needs a companion. Since Kong will need a few meetings, maybe you can spend some time with her, educate her on some dog basics, and set her up for success." She winks at me and smiles.

Internally rolling my eyes, I say, "Ok, well, set up a meeting for us, and I'll see if she can handle him. I'm free tomorrow afternoon if she's available."

"Thanks, I appreciate you taking time for this. Do you want to meet her first, before you bring Kong in?"

"That would be great," I say.

About an hour later, Jan texts me.

Jan: Olive Smythe will come to the rescue at 2:00 p.m. tomorrow to meet with you.

Loch: Got it.

Later that day, when I get home, I head straight for the sunroom; I use it for my foster dogs. Not having personal dogs allows me to give more back to the animals that need my help.

I see Kong lying in his kennel like a good boy. My chest feels tight, in a mix of sadness and relief to think he might have a real home.

The two other fosters I have start spinning around in their kennels and barking at me, knowing it's time to go outside and time to eat.

I let the first dog out, a black and white spotted pitbull named Moo. She's wild but sweet. She runs around the enormous yard I have for them. Moo loves trying to catch squirrels and lying in the sun. She trots inside after a while, and I give her dinner in her kennel.

Next, I let out Thor. He's an all black pitbull, quite larger than an average pit, so I'm guessing he's mixed with a large breed. He's a wonderful dog. He loves people and kids, wouldn't hurt a fly, unless that fly is a cat. Thor comes in and I give him dinner in his kennel, too.

Now, it's Kong's turn. He darts outside, catching the rays, does his business, and comes and sits by the door. I can tell he doesn't care to be outside for long; I think he spent so much time outside that he would rather curl up on my couch. I let him in. He goes to his kennel and eats his dinner. He's a simple dog with simple needs.

Thinking about him leaving makes my heart hurt. I had to earn his trust on day one. I had to get him to trust me and get him off that chain. I remember walking through the disgusting house that smelled like urine and rotten food. His owner was gone, believed to have left town and abandoned the dogs, but I knew the truth.

Kong was aggressive toward the cops that were on scene, so they called me to come try to get him off the chain; otherwise, they would catchpole and euthanize him. I walked into the backyard. He stood on a piece of cardboard, and he immediately started growling and pulling on his heavy chain, secured with a padlock. The chain was so heavy that I could see wounds on the top of his neck from the weight of it embedded into his skin. Which meant I would also have to get close enough to cut the lock off.

Kong had a rickety-as-fuck dog house, looking like it was a hundred years old. He had no water or food bowl, and someone had wrapped his chain around a tree. The chains pulling around it had worn the bark off the tree. It had taken years to do that, and I had watched many dogs come and go on these chains. He'd lived out there on that chain his whole life. It took a couple of hours, but I was able to calm him down, throwing pieces of hotdog at him until he would let me get close enough. I sat on the muddy ground and let him come to me, at his own pace. We developed a bond eventually, and now it's as strong as can be.

I keep telling myself he'll be better off, but every time I picture his empty bed, my throat goes tight and my eyes sting. If he finds a home, this is a win, but God, why does it feel so much like losing?

As I watch him lie on his fluffy bed, I hope this new home works out for him. I hate that my fosters spend so much time in kennels, but it's better than the hellholes most of them come from.

Rescued

I'm sitting at the front desk of Only Dogs, waiting for my meeting with Olive. We have a facility about forty minutes outside of Boise's downtown area. It's a simple operation where people can meet dogs ready for adoption, and houses about thirty dogs until they're placed in a foster home or adopted.

I have my laptop out reading emails, when I hear the door open. The most beautiful woman I've ever seen walks through my door. I look up at her, noticing her messy bun, and a few pieces of long blond hair framing her face. She's stunning, curvy in all the right places, casual, wearing leggings and a gray t-shirt that clings to her chest. Her beautiful eyes hold mine, and a sweet, awkward smile crosses her lips.

"Hello." I see her mouth move, but I'm transfixed by her pouty lips. "I'm here to meet Kong."

"W–what?" I stutter, not able to focus on what she said.

"Are you Loch? I'm here to meet Kong," she says, again.

"Oh, yes." I stand up to greet her.

"Hi, I'm Loch. I run Only Dogs, and I'm Kong's foster. You must be Olive." I reach out to shake her hand.

"Hi," she shifts her gaze to the floor, and takes a step back, not taking my hand in return. "Sorry, I..."

"It's ok. No need to explain, let's sit down and chat a bit. I didn't bring Kong today because I wanted to go over some basics and make sure you're up for the challenge."

I hold my hand out, asking her to have a seat on the large bench in the front window. She sits down at one end, and I keep my distance, sensing she isn't comfortable with me. Trying to stay calm and friendly, keeping this very light, I ask her, "What made you decide to adopt a dog, especially a dog like Kong?"

She doesn't answer for a moment and looks at her feet. "I want a protective dog to help me feel safe in my apartment."

It's barely audible, and I can tell she doesn't want to talk about it. So I ask, "Have you had a pet before?"

Quiet, but without hesitation, she says, "No, but my aunt has a dog, and I've spent time with many friends' pets over the years. I love animals. I've never considered a dog before because I work nights and didn't want to leave a dog home alone too much."

She focuses on my eyes for the first time, only for a moment. But, in that moment, her blue-gray eyes look back at me. I've never seen eyes that color. The gray color is a striking blend of cool tones, giving them a mysterious, unreadable quality. I'm at a loss for words, but I know I need to keep talking to this woman. I want to know more about her.

"I assume you have read Kong's bio?"

"Yes, something about him spoke to me. His eyes looked so sad."

My lips curve in a subtle smile, and I say, "I get it. I see it in your eyes, too." Then I freeze, realizing I said that out loud, to her. Crap.

She looks up again with a furrowed brow, looking at me like I just told her she's broken.

"I mean, you seem like you could use a companion," I try to recover quickly.

She searches my eyes for a moment and says, "Yeah, I guess so."

If I could slap myself right now, I would. Why is this woman making me so nervous? I'm here to talk about a dog, not why she's sad. Get it together, man.

"So, do you have a lot of visitors at your house? Some things you will need to keep in mind, since Kong isn't great with new people. The reason he will make a great guard dog is the same reason you will need to put him in a kennel or separate room when you have guests over—repair men, maintenance people, friends, family. Unless someone comes often enough that they will take the time to get to know Kong, then he can make new friends over time. I can teach you how to introduce him once he's settled in. How does that sound?"

She looks like she's thinking about that, and then says, "Well, I only have a few regular visitors, but I'm comfortable with that. Will it upset Kong to know people are over and he's locked away? I'd hate to upset him."

I smile at her thoughtfulness. "He will love meeting your friends eventually, but he will be fine kenneled up. Even though he has these quirks, he is a very chill, low-key dog. A dog bed and two meals a day, and he's good. He won't be the type of dog you can take to busy parks, walks around town, or busy places. He can't handle that, and it puts him at risk of biting someone, which will cause him to lose his life. There is an element of responsibility that comes with owning a dog like Kong. You are also responsible for keeping him safe."

So I ask again, "Do you feel comfortable with this?"

Just then, someone else walks through the front door. An older woman with a small white dog in her arms.

"Excuse me, I need to check this out. Hang here and I'll be right back," I tell Olive.

"Sure, no problem." She smiles, gesturing for me to address the new visitor.

"Thanks." I walk the five feet over to the woman. "How can I help you, ma'am?"

"I need some help with my dog," she sobs hysterically. "I left my abusive husband, and my kids and I are trying to use local resources to get back on our feet, but none of them will allow me to bring my dog." I nod and hold her shoulder, offering support.

"Take a deep breath, it's going to be ok." I glance over at Olive, realizing she is watching all this unfold, but I also need to help this woman. "Who do you have here?" I ask as I pet the little white poodle.

"This is Princess; we love her, and I know this is a rescue, but I was hoping you could take her for me until I get back on my feet.

We would really like to get her back. She's my kids' first dog, and it's going to be hard for us to leave her short-term... " She trails off, sniffling.

I walk her to the front desk so our conversation is more private. I get her number and where she hopes to stay. I tell her I will keep her dog for her. We don't take in dogs that will go back to the owners, but I can tell this woman is desperate, and her small dog won't be a burden. We chat for a few more minutes; I take Princess to the back, and the woman leaves.

When I return, Olive's eyes are softer now, more at ease. "That was kind of you to help her out. You won't adopt her dog out, will you?"

"Of course not. On occasion, people don't come back for their pets, but we'll do our best to hold on to the dog as long as the owners continue to respond and let us know what's going on. Ok, back to you and Kong. Do you feel comfortable with what I said about keeping him safe?"

"Yes, I still want to meet him."

"Great, so it's going to take some time for you to fully meet him. The first few meetings he will be on edge, barking, and snapping. Can you handle that?"

Olive looks at me, her eyes wide, "Will he bite me?"

"I have a process, and if you'll trust me, I'll make sure you're both safe, and in time, you'll bond. I know dog body language, and if you follow my directions, you'll be fine. It's easier to introduce him to you in his own home, where he already feels comfortable. I can have Jan join us at my house if it would make you feel more comfortable coming over?" I see her stiffen. Her back is straight, and she stares at me like she's still trying to figure out what I said.

But when I am about to repeat myself, she squeaks up, "Yes, I can go to your house. Jan doesn't need to come."

I'm surprised by her answer, but maybe she wants to do this on her own. She brings her hand to her mouth and nibbles on a fingernail, drawing far too much of my attention to her mouth.

She says, “It’s ok, I can do it alone.”

I give her a warm smile, reassuring her she has nothing to worry about. I can’t look away from her mouth as her lips turn up at the corners. I feel like a perv, drooling over this gorgeous woman who is clearly struggling.

We set a date next week for her to meet Kong. This should be interesting.

Chapter 7
Olive

Fetching More Than a Dog

I slump onto the couch, exhausted from venturing outside the confines of my apartment and interacting with another human. My limbs are heavy, like I'm moving through wet cement.

God, I'm so worthless. I can't even talk to a man like a normal fucking person. But was he a normal person? To be fair, he might have been the best-looking man I have ever seen in real life.

A few weeks ago, he would have been exactly my type. A total golden retriever, with a mysterious side, so put together and confident. Meanwhile, it took serious effort for me to shower and put on leggings today. I pick up my phone and text Sophia.

Olive: I met Kong's foster today, and I'm going to meet Kong next week.

Sophia: YAY!

Sophia: Wait, you didn't meet the dog today?

Olive: No, his foster dad wanted to make sure I knew what I was getting into.

Sophia: What was he like? How did the meeting go?

Olive: Well, it's the first time in weeks I've even looked at a man without shaking, so that's something. He was nice. It was easier for me to stay calm because he didn't push me or try to pry. I think he could tell I didn't want to talk. I almost felt comfortable around him.

Sophia: Aww, that's a big step! Cute?

Olive: I mean, if you like a masculine, godlike appearance, then yes.

Sophia: Details. Now!

Olive: Ugh, I can't even think about men right now. This is not helping.

Sophia: I didn't say you had to ask the guy out. Just tell me what he was like! I need to know.

Olive: Lol! He was about six feet, light brown hair, longer on top. He was like an extra-large version of that hot guy from The Office, but built like an ox. He had a muscular dad bod. So hot.

Sophia: STOP! And he fosters dogs?!

Sophia: Is he gay? He seems too good to be true.

Olive: Lol! OMG! Sophia, stop it! But no, I didn't get those vibes. He actually owns and runs the rescue. It's kind of cute. His picture is on the website. The one we were on the other night.

Sophia: Hold.

Ninety seconds later.

Sophia: OMG! He's hot!

Olive: I couldn't even shake his fucking hand, Sophia, and I agreed to go to his house... alone.

Sophia: What do you mean you couldn't shake his hand? Like, did you leave him hanging or what?

Olive: He reached for me and tried to shake my hand, and I kind of froze. I took a step back and stared at the floor like a freaking loony person.

Sophia: Lol! You didn't. Well, baby steps. You let me touch your hand and hug you. Maybe getting out of the house and talking to other humans will help you slowly adjust. Do you feel comfortable going to his house?

I can come. Or you could ask for a different meeting location. Don't do something you're not comfortable with.

Olive: It's weird. I feel super anxious around him. After everything that's happened, being around people is hard. And he's gorgeous, which also makes me nervous. But somehow he also makes me feel relaxed and normal. I think you're right about leaving the house.

Olive: Do you think it's ok for me to go to his house?

Sophia: As long as you feel safe. You deserve to be happy. You deserve to get your dog and be around other people.

Olive: Thanks, Soph, I can't truly explain it, but I feel ok.

Sophia: Girl, I am so proud of you. As long as you're sure, then so am I.

Olive: Yeah, maybe. How's the bar?

Sophia: Same shit, different day. Brian said to tell you hello, though. And Todd actually told us a funny joke yesterday.

Olive: Wow, let's hear it.

Sophia: Ok... My girlfriend dumped me, so I stole her wheelchair.

Sophia: Guess who came crawling back?

Olive: Wow.

Sophia: Maybe you had to be there.

Olive: Guess so...

Sophia: So, how are you really doing?

Olive: You mean, do I still want to jump off a bridge while simultaneously never leaving my house? Yes, I do. But I took a shower today without you making me, and I went to that meeting. So, I guess that's a step forward.

Sophia: I'm always here to nudge you into the shower. I love you so much, Olive. Just one day at a time. I think once you bring Kong home, you'll start to really feel at home again.

Sophia: Have you contacted any of those therapists that the doctor gave you?

Olive: No

Sophia: Maybe you should?

Olive: I'll think about it.

Sophia: Well, I'll call you in the morning, ok? I'll bring you some breakfast and coffee.

Olive: Sounds good.

A week later...

I sit in my car at 10:00 a.m. on Sunday morning, thinking about walking to Loch's front door. I can't do it. I'm nervous to see him and to meet Kong. It seems like I've been waiting for weeks for this moment, and now, I can't get out of the fucking car.

It's freezing today, our first big snowstorm of the year. I sit in the driver's seat, watching the snowflakes drift down, each one delicate and fleeting, melting the second they touch the glass. I feel like one of them–fragile, dissolving under the weight of something so much stronger than I can bear. But as I watch, the flakes fall faster, layering over each other, sticking, refusing to disappear. Alone, they are nothing; together, they become something solid.

Maybe I'm like that, too. Maybe I won't be as frail, as long as I'm not alone. If Kong were with me, I wouldn't be so alone. Fear is what keeps me frozen, but even in winter, the world doesn't stop. The snow keeps falling, and I can keep moving forward through the fear and pain until I'm strong again.

Now, I only need to work up the courage to get out of the car. Olive, you can do this. Get out of the damn car. I swing the door open, climb out of the car, and feel the snowflakes on my face the moment I step outside. I close the door and stare at the house. Walk, Olive. Put one foot in front of the other.

Taking a deep breath, I step up onto the wide porch that wraps around the front of the house and knock on the wooden door. The house sits comfortably on a quiet suburban street. Its white siding and dark blue shutters give it a classic, welcoming feel. There's even a wooden porch swing. All that's missing is the white picket fence.

I knock on the door, nervous to enter a stranger's house, but excited to finally meet Kong. My heart pounds and my legs wobble. It feels like hours before the door opens. His smile is the first thing I see, a huge grin giving Loch the smallest dimples, so faint I didn't even notice them the first time we met. Probably, because I was staring at the floor half the time.

His large frame takes up most of the doorway, and he moves inside. "Come in, it's freezing out there. Can I take your jacket?" I look at him. He's not trying to reach for me; he's just looking at me with his striking golden brown eyes. They have a deep luminous quality and color shift in different lighting, from a solid brown to having golden flecks scattered throughout their irises. I take a shaky breath and remove my puffy coat and scarf.

It's warmer inside, not only the temperature, but it's homey. It smells like coffee and cinnamon, warm and comforting. Above his oversized brown leather sectional, there is a series of black and white photos of adorable dogs. The original hardwood floors are worn but stunning. The living room leads back into a kitchen, and there's a hallway past the mounted TV on the right. I'm assuming the hallway leads to bedrooms and such. It's somewhere between a bachelor pad and grandma's house. It makes me smile at his eclectic style. Not exactly where I pictured a guy like him living.

He leads me into the kitchen and pulls a chair from the four-seater wooden table. "Would you like something to drink? Water? Tea? Coffee? I just made a pot?"

"Uh, sure. Coffee sounds great."

"Cream? Sugar?"

"Neither, black is fine."

"A woman after my own heart. I pictured you as a pumpkin spice latte type of woman."

I give a loud, audible snort. And I'm so shocked and embarrassed that my cheeks flush bright pink. Did I snort within one minute of being here? Olive, get your shit together here.

"Glad that made you laugh. Don't worry, I wouldn't have judged you even if you did like pumpkin spice lattes." I smile and look up at him, surprised at how relaxed I am. His presence makes me nervous because he's drop-dead gorgeous, but also somehow calms me. He turns and hands me my cup, and I catch his eyes. We're still, and it becomes awkward. We realize we're staring a moment too long and both look away.

"Ok," he says, attempting to make it less awkward. God, why am I so weird?

"I'm going to get Kong, but you need to follow my rules. Can you follow rules, Olive?"

Another slight flush of my cheeks. Is he serious? What is he going to do? Call me a good girl, like a kid, if I do?

"Yes, I can follow rules," with a slight lift of one side of my lip.

His eyes narrow, and he sips his coffee. "When I bring him in, I want you to look at me, or the table. Do not look at him; no eye contact. Do not reach out to touch him, do not make any sudden movements, and don't speak until I say it's ok. However, I am going to give you a safe word of sorts; you can use it at any time."

I snap my head to his and say, "What exactly am I dealing with here that I need a safe word?"

"I don't want you to have to talk or explain, but if you feel scared, overwhelmed, or just need a break, I want you to communicate that to me. So if you say 'peanut butter,' I will take him to the back room, and we can talk about it after. Ok?"

A little skeptical, and now, even more nervous than I was before I knocked on the damn door, I mutter, "Ok."

"It will be fine, Olive. Just ignore him," he says, reassuring me.

Chapter 8
Loch

On the Edge of a Snarl

I let Kong out of his kennel. He's a big boy, muscular and strong. I put a thick, red collar on him. It partially covers the bald patch on the back of his neck from the heavy chain he was left on before I found him. I attach his leash and walk him through the door into the kitchen, where Olive is waiting. He's a mopey dog most days, so I think he expects to walk in and lie on his bed.

Once the door is open and he sees Olive, he immediately lunges, his head darting upward to try and bite. He's snarling, pulling, and trying to claw with his feet to get to her. Then, he starts barking his head off at her when he realizes he can't reach her. I lead him to his bed across the room. He doesn't take his eyes off her, but lies down when I give the command. I toss him a treat.

Olive remains calm in the chair. She isn't moving or watching us like I asked. I see her head dip down; her hair is up in a messy bun again today.

I talk to her so that Kong knows that she is safe.

"Reach for your cup of coffee, slow and steady." He lunges again, but I'm prepared for his reaction and get him to lie back down.

"It's ok, boy. You're ok. Lay down, calm down."

I ask her, "Can you do it again?" She does, and he gives a low grumble, then barks a couple of times, but stays in place. I give him another treat.

"Good boy. It's ok, buddy. You're ok."

"When you have a friend or family member who wants to meet Kong, you will need to follow this same process. It keeps everyone safe and allows him to make good decisions, to calm down on his own, and at his own pace. He'll know you're protecting him, too. Take another sip."

I see her drink. No grumbles from Kong. I give him another treat and tell him he's a good boy. We repeat this process for another five minutes. I have a small stool beside his bed, so I sit down and give him another treat.

"Olive, I'm going to ask you some simple questions, so he can get used to us talking. You can keep drinking your coffee and answering my questions, but don't turn around or move. Ok?"

She barely nods and whispers, "Yes." Kong grumbles again at her voice.

"Take a deep breath. We're doing fine."

Her back straightens, and her head lifts. I'm struggling to take my eyes off her. She's at a slight angle from me, and I can see her large chest heaving above the tabletop. What the hell? Stop getting distracted. This girl is scared, and you're leering at her chest. I take a deep breath to refocus.

"What's your favorite color?"

"Red," she says in a hushed tone.

"Good." I'm not sure if the compliment was for her or for Kong, but I toss him a treat.

"Where are you from?"

"San Diego."

"Ahh, a Cali girl. Ok. You're doing great. How are you feeling?" I ask her as I toss another treat to Kong. He's still alert, but is calming down faster than usual.

"Pretty nervous. I guess it's good he has a scary bark. That's what I signed up for, isn't it? He wouldn't make a very good protector if he barked like a little Chihuahua."

We both chuckle. "True. I'm going to walk Kong back out for a minute. You alright?"

"Yes."

I let him outside for a minute, giving him and Olive a break, a few minutes to decompress.

When I come back in, Olive glances up at me. Her eyes are watery, and she wipes a tear from her cheek.

Oh, fuck! "What's wrong?" I sit at the table with her.

"Nothing, I'm fine. That was a little more intense than I expected." She glances up at me. I see her beautiful, sad eyes. Something more than a break-in has happened to this girl. I can see it all over her face.

"Do you want any more coffee?"

"Sure." So I top off her cup.

We both start to speak at the same time. She says, "I'm sorry." I ask her, "Do you want to talk about it?" but we cut each other off, interrupting each other. We both smile.

She's sorry she's crying? I reassure her. "It's totally ok. I am not judging you at all. If you want to talk, I'm happy to listen." I could listen to her talk all day. I almost asked her twenty more questions earlier, just to keep her talking.

She looks down, almost shameful, and says, "I'm fine, it's fine. I'm ok." Yeah, like that was believable. She is not fine, but I can't make her open up or talk to me.

"Would you like to come back another day? Do you need time to think about whether Kong is the right dog for you? We have lots of dogs that are actually friendly, but also have scary barks."

This makes her chuckle, and she wipes another tear from her cheek. I hate seeing her cry, but it makes the gray in her eyes look the color of the deepest water. Like looking down into a crystal clear, frozen lake. It's stunning.

"No, I'm fine; let's continue. Please. I really want him to like me."

"Are you sure?"

"Definitely, I'm ok."

I nod, "This time I want you to turn your chair to his bed. I'm going to leave this bowl of hotdog pieces here for you to toss to him when I say so. You can still drink your coffee, but make slow movements at first, stay calm, and do not look him in the eyes. Dogs can interpret staring as a threat. Look at me. Keep your eyes on me, even if I'm looking at him. Sound good?"

"Yes, I'm ready," she says, her eyes crinkling at the corners, and a side smile peeks out. I watch her lips and imagine what they'd feel like to kiss. Fuck, I can't seem to focus around this girl.

I get Kong from outside and bring him into the room again. He's barking again, but not lunging or trying to get to Olive. He's calmed down a lot. I reach down, give him a scratch and a treat, and ask him to lie down again. I sit back on the stool and say, "Olive, we are going to do the same thing as before. Drink your coffee and look at me." She gives a small nod. Olive reaches for her coffee mug, pulling the cup closer to her mouth. Kong leaps up and barks at her. He snaps at her and bares his teeth. She startles and spills some coffee on her shirt. But she stays calm and sets her cup back down.

"Oh, shit. Let me go put him back."

"No, it's fine," Kong barks again and lunges for her. She startles, jumping a bit and putting her hand on her chest, but Kong stops. He looks at her for a moment and lies back down.

What just happened? She jumped, and he went to lie down. I've never seen him react that way before. What did he see?

"Do you need a break?"

"No, let's keep going. It was a few drops of coffee, no big deal."

Her face flushes, and her voice cracks a little like she's trying not to cry. Her sad eyes are glaring at me to move on, darkening and silently begging.

I look down at Kong; there's no reaction from him. He's as calm as can be. I'm puzzled, in all honesty, with each of them. I toss him a couple of treats, tell him he's a good boy, and to stay.

"Let's try this again," I say.

She takes her sip of coffee, looking right at me. We're not talking much, or at least not about anything of substance, but our eyes are having their own conversation. A sense of intimacy, understanding, and desire rolls through me, a feeling of want and need for this woman. I see the spots on her chest where the coffee spilled. Every time I look at it, my dick twitches. After she sets her cup back down and Kong has no reaction, I toss him another treat.

"Now, grab a treat from the bowl, and slowly toss it to him."

Shakily, she says, "Ok." She grabs a treat and looks at him for the first time. I watch a moment between the two of them. Like she's asking him to trust her. Their sad eyes meet. When she tosses the treat, it lands on the floor between them. This time, he lunges for the treat, not for her, but scaring her nonetheless, and because she jumps back, he goes after her. I barely hold him back. Goddammit, fucking hell.

"Kong. No. Off! Kong, lie down!" I command, my voice harsh.

I definitely fucked that up. He's lunging and snarling again. I see her eyes welling up with tears once more. Shit.

"It's ok, Olive. This is who Kong is. He's slow to trust, but once you win him over, I know he will love you with all his heart. He's special." She's looking at me like she's failed, but it wasn't her that failed, it was me. I walk him back out of the room and put him in his kennel.

Olive is already putting her coat back on when I return. My body goes rigid. She's leaving? I can't let her drive home like this.

"Olive, please stay for a few minutes so we can talk about this. I don't want you crying while you're driving home. Please, stay and calm down. You did great today. It'll get easier every time you visit him."

She has her scarf in her hand, ready to bolt. I look at her, trying to stay calm and not push her or scare her. She looks up at me, and I point back to the kitchen table. "Please, let's talk for a few minutes."

She takes her coat off and sits back down. She's staying, just to talk to me. I mean, that's probably not true in the slightest, but I feel like I just won the lottery.

I push her coffee cup towards her. She's looking at me, almost in question of what comes next. I need to say something. I did ask her to stay. But before I can, she does. "Can I ask you something, Loch?"

Half in shock, I answer, "Pretty much anything." I give her a cheeky smile, letting her know she's safe.

"What made you get into dog rescue?"

"Well, that's a complicated question." I pause. "I guess it's because I've always loved dogs and felt the need to help them out of critical situations."

"I had this dog growing up; he was a long-haired wiener dog. My parents got him for my seventh birthday. I named him Rufus. I had loving parents, but they worked long hours. My mom is a doctor, and my dad was the head of a big bank. I stayed with my grandma a lot of the time, and we were close. But watching Wheel of Fortune was about as exciting as it got in the house. So Rufus, well, he was my best friend. He slept in bed with me. I played ball with him and walked him. I took care of him, mostly. My dad really loved him, too, but he didn't have the time to dedicate to him. Rufus was a rescue. My dad picked him out at the shelter. Rufus had terrible storm anxiety. We tried everything, but every time it would thunder and lightning, he would hide in a closet, shaking, crying. The only thing that helped was if I sat in the closet with him.

"About three years later, my family moved across town. Dad got a raise, and we moved to a nicer area. They told me there were better schools, more opportunities. But we had this nasty neighbor, who had dozens of dogs in and out of his house. They were always outside, barking at all hours of the day and night. We could see some of them fighting, and with visible wounds. So my parents called animal control to complain about the noise and ask for a welfare check. The next day, we saw two police cars in front of the house. I watched out the window to see if they would take the man to jail. I was about ten years old by this point; his house smelled like urine every time you passed by. The dogs were always barking, but there were also people yelling and screaming at each other on a regular basis. I knew he was a dangerous man. Unfortunately, nothing happened with animal control. He didn't go to jail; the dogs were left to fend for themselves, and we didn't hear another word about it.

"A week later, Rufus got sick. Dad was home, and Rufus started throwing up, seizing, and became completely lethargic. His body was shaking; he was stiff, like a board. So we took him to the hospital."

I look down at the table and close my eyes, remembering that hospital room. "That smell of bleach and wet dog. I remember the older lady coming out to talk to us and bringing us into a smaller room. Rufus wouldn't make it."

"My dog, my best friend, lay on the metal table right in front of me, barely moving. The vet knelt in front of me; her face was soft, but her eyes were sad. Too sad. That's how I knew. 'Please,' I whispered, my voice breaking. 'Please save him.'

"But no one could stop it. No one could fix it. He had been poisoned, and there was nothing they could do for him. And as the vet's voice gently asked if I was ready to say goodbye, I realized something that made my stomach turn even more.

"Someone did this. I suspected the neighbor, but nothing could change it now. Someone wanted my best friend gone. And no matter how much it hurt, no matter how many tears burned down my face, I knew one thing–I would never forget this moment. Never."

I open my eyes and see Olive's face, beet red and stained with tears.

"Loch, I'm sorry," she mumbled through her tears. "I can't imagine the pain you felt. Did they catch the guy?"

"No, animal abusers in this country never get caught. And even if they are, and have done unspeakable things to helpless, innocent animals, they get a measly slap on the wrist. There is no justice for the animals. I've seen too many animals suffer at the hands of evil people, and I had to do something about it."

A jolt of electricity shocks me where Olive's hand now rests on mine. She's ghost-white, looking down at her hand on mine. It's almost painful for her to pull her hand away. She had a vulnerable, raw moment, and I wanted more. She quickly stands up, putting on her coat and scarf. I follow her into the living room with my hands in my jeans' pockets, not sure what to say. She's embarrassed, but I wish she weren't. I want to convince her to stay, but I know I can't.

"Friday at 5:00 p.m.?" she says.

A little stunned she wasn't scared off, I nod and open the door for her to leave. "Yeah, see you again Friday. You did well with him for the first visit."

She looks back at me, her throat bobbing, her eyes welling, and she opens her mouth to speak, but no words come out. She only nods and walks away.

I'm drawn to her and feel protective of her, but how can I get her to let me in? What happened to her? She's so beautiful, and I can see she is hurting. I want to make it better, see her smile again.

After she leaves, I go to my office and get on my laptop. I've developed decent hacking skills while monitoring certain people over the years. I'm able to access the actual records, not just public ones. I search police records to find out more about her break-in. Scanning files, I find what I'm looking for and read the police report.

On October 14, Olive Smythe was brutally attacked in her home. Victim was restrained to her bed and found by her friend, Sophia McGrath, the next morning, brutally raped and beaten. Injuries were sustained to the victim's right eye, lip, neck, left breast, right rib cage, back, wrist, inner thighs. The victim sustained open wounds on face and neck and bruising, on arms, legs, torso, neck and face. Victim was restrained by her hands to the bed with duct tape...

I can't read anymore. I'm going to find this piece of fucking shit and kill him. Someone raped and attacked Olive. All her apprehension towards touch makes so much sense now. Who the fuck did this? After scanning more of the file, I see they are still processing evidence. "Fuck, I need to follow this closely and make sure this piece of shit is punished, and if not, I'll take care of him." I take a deep breath. Knowing my sweet Olive suffered like that has my blood boiling.

Chapter 9
Olive

Teetering on the Verge of Nope

Two days later...

I walk into the police station. The tension in my shoulders makes my whole body ache, and the pit in my stomach deepens as I make my way to the front desk. The unsavory smell of stale coffee and musky body odor hits me, and I try to keep from crinkling my nose. Between my nerves and the smell, I might vomit.

"Hi, my name is Olive. I'm here for a lineup. To identify someone," I mutter, much quieter than I intend.

The guy at the desk says, "I'll let them know you're here. They'll come out to get you when they're ready. Have a seat."

I turn around and head to the waiting room. It's full of old blue plastic chairs and a few other people. I find an empty seat and try to calm my breathing. I'm hot and sweaty even though it's cool in the room. I grip the strap of my shoulder bag like it's holding me up.

I know I should have told Sophia that I was doing this today. God, why did I think I should do this alone? I can't stand the thought of seeing him again, of looking him in his evil eyes. Time drags on as my feet tap against the floor with nervous energy. I alternate my fixation between the clock and the door, wondering if I can bolt.

Finally, Sergeant Persimmons and another woman in a sharp blazer walk in.

"Hello, Olive, I'm Sergeant Persimmons. We met at your apartment; I'm the lead detective on your case. This is District Attorney Melissa Gonzalez. Can you come back to talk with us?"

"Mmhmm," I mumble.

They show me into a small room with dark blue walls, a single desk, some chairs, and a window. It's confining and feels like I'm willingly walking into a coffin.

The D.A. says, "Thank you for coming down today, Olive. I know this is hard, but it's valuable information that can help get you some form of justice."

Sergeant Persimmons speaks up, "We're going to bring in six men. The person who assaulted you might be in the lineup. They might not. If you don't feel confident in who it is, just say you don't know. We don't want your best guess. We want the truth. They cannot see us; they can't hear us. We will push this button to ask them to do something, such as talk or turn. Does that all make sense? Do you have any questions?"

They're treating me with kid gloves, like I'm a fragile little flower. But maybe they know better. Maybe I do need kid gloves. Fuck. What am I doing here? I'm not ready to see him again.

"Yes, I understand."

"I'm going to bring them in. You can speak whenever you want. If you say nothing, I will ask you questions, ok?"

"Yeah." My voice cracks; the emotion already threatens to boil over. Don't fucking cry, Olive. You can do this.

I watch six men enter the room in a line. They all turn to face me, looking similar. All are around six feet, dark hair. They all have either a white, gray, or blue T-shirt on and jeans. I look at each one.

Number one is too young, looks like he is still in college, about to join a fraternity. Number two is close, but his face is different. It's softer. Three, I look at him closely. He has gray hair on the sides of his head. And he has a dad bod. The guy I'm looking for was in shape, he was built. Just like...

"Fuck."

Sergeant Persimmons asks, "Do you see someone you recognize, Olive?"

"Four. It's him, number four. He will have wings, a tattoo, on the right side of his neck coming out from under his shirt."

He wore a blue T-shirt, jeans, and white sneakers. Even though I know he can't see me, I feel his eyes lock on mine. Sending me right back to that night.

Sergeant Persimmons presses the button. "Everyone, please turn to the left."

I watch as the group turns. It's there, on number four. He has wings sticking out of his shirt. Since he has a T-shirt on, I can see a bit more of it, and it's a dragon with wings, the wings sticking up onto his neck.

"It's him," I say. My body trembles, and my breath becomes heavy and panicked. I can't keep the tears down anymore. I break wide open. Unable to keep the memories buried inside. His eyes are dark and mean. He looks pissed, with a scowl on his face and furrowed brows.

Sergeant Persimmons says, "It's ok, Olive, you did good. We don't need anything else from you. Let's go back out front and get some air? Yeah?"

I nod through tears and attempt to catch my breath as she walks me out.

"Why don't you have a seat back up front? I'll bring you some water, and you can wait until you calm down to drive home, or, if you'd like, I can call someone for you?"

I shake my head, sitting down. I watch her walk away to get water for me. When she returns, I take the water and drink. Hoping it will wash away the last ten minutes of my life. I never wanted to see his face again, to think about that tattoo, or what he took from me.

"Olive, you did great. Take some deep breaths and try to calm down. It's all over. I or D.A. Gonzalez will contact you as soon as we have any further updates or information."

I nod. I can hear her continue to talk, but it sounds like she's underwater. My brain is done and unable to take on anything else.

I wait for another few minutes, but as soon as she leaves my side, I bolt. I just want to get out of here and crawl back in bed. Get as far away from him as possible.

I sit on my couch with a cup of coffee, trying to find the motivation to shower and get ready. I dread going back to Loch's house. I'm still so embarrassed. I should forget this.

I'm still reeling from the police station a couple of days ago. It was such a disaster. After I made it home, I stayed in bed for two days, only getting up to pee. I feel like I'm on the edge of a mental breakdown. If someone could see me, they would throw me into a mental institution.

Why should I be adding the stress of owning a dog to my life right now? Am I capable of caring for another living being when I can hardly eat or sleep myself? And, especially one that wants to eat me?

I should talk this through again.

Olive: Hey, am I crazy for wanting to adopt Kong?

Sophia: I don't think so, but what's going on? Are you nervous about the next meeting?

Olive: Yes, I'm about 5 seconds from just bailing and going back to bed, but then I'll feel even more pathetic. I have something to tell you. Don't be mad.

Sophia: Lol, no promises. What did you do?

Olive: I went to the police station on Friday for the lineup. I'm sorry I didn't tell you. I should have asked you to come. I was a fucking disaster. How many times can one person be a complete and utter shitshow in public?

Sophia: Olive, OMG. Why did you go alone?! You know I would've gone with you.

Olive: I know, I thought I needed to do it alone. But the second I got there, I regretted it.

Sophia: Well, I'm a little mad, but I understand the desire to have some independence.

Olive: Well, I also got a call earlier today saying they made an arrest. A guy named Jacob Wright. He's apparently the senator's son.

Sophia: What?! For real? How do you feel?

Olive: I don't know. I mean I'm glad they caught the guy and he's off the streets. But him being a senator's son is crazy. Do you think he will get off because of that? Do you think they won't believe me? You hear about all these girls that are not trusted in regard to sexual assault.

Sophia: Fucking assholes. Either way, it's not your fault, and we are going to fight like hell to make sure that doesn't happen.

Sophia: Why are you nervous about Kong?

Sophia: Or is it the man candy, Loch? Lol!

Ugh, why does she have to make it about him? I mean, yes. Things were super weird the other day, and Loch was nothing but nice, but this is about Kong and whether I should bring him home. Right? I hate when she's always fucking right.

Olive: Does it matter?

Sophia: You bet your sweet ass it does. You signed up to adopt Kong because you wanted to feel safe in your home. So, you have to spend a few awkward days with Loch to do that. Either set those feelings to the side and go get your dog, or admit right now that you want to see Loch, too, and that's why you're scared.

Olive: I don't want to see Loch. I'm a mess.

Or do I? I mean, he terrifies the crap out of me, but when I'm near him, I feel calm. I feel safe. So why do I act like such a complete basket case?

Sophia: Ok. Then buck up and go get your dog. You can do this. Take your life back.

Sophia: And hey, if you feel like flirting with him, do it! Winky face.

Olive: Oh yeah, I'll snort and cry all over him again. He'll love it. I'll call you after.

Sophia: Love you!

I sit by the window, staring at the empty street outside. The world seems so full of uncertainty. Every single time I think of stepping beyond my front door, I'm overwhelmed by an invisible weight pressing against my chest. What if I can't handle it? What if everything changes? My mind races back to the idea of bringing a dog into my life–would it help me feel less alone? Or would it be another responsibility I'm not ready for? I'll have to walk him multiple times a day. I'm not sure I'm ready for that kind of commitment. I bite my lip trying to make the answers come.

Then, there's Loch. His smile lingers in my mind. I can see his dimples, warm and kind. And though I'm terrified of what it means to think of him like that, I can't ignore how I feel when I'm near him.

It's nice to feel my heart beat a little calmer when he's around, to not have this gray cloud of fear hanging over my head. But I'm not ready for that type of connection, am I?

Chapter 10

Loch

Push Dont Shove (Ok, Maybe a Little Shove)

I wasn't sure if she would show up today. My mind has been racing all week with what happened to her. I want to talk to her about it, but I know she's not ready, nor could I explain how I know. When I hear the quiet knock at my door, my heart skips a beat. I feel like I've been holding my breath for hours. I open the door, revealing Olive in the same puffy coat as before. It's still cold, but not snowy. I don't know if it's the cold hitting me or seeing her face again, but a chill crawls up my spine.

"Come in. Can I get you a coffee?" I ask.

She nods and removes her jacket, revealing a V-neck sweater. I can't help but immediately look at her cleavage. When I finally manage to pull my eyes away, we make eye contact. She glowers at me. She knows. Damn, I need to stop looking at her like that. She's not here for you to fucking stare at. Embarrassed, I turn away to avoid her glare, trying to pretend I wasn't staring at her chest.

We sit where we were before, at the table with coffees in hand.

"I'm glad you're here," I say without thinking.

"You are?"

"I mean, I'm glad you still want to adopt Kong." I take a slow sip of coffee, eyeing her, hoping she bought that. My hands are sweaty, my whole body is on fire, and it's short-circuiting my brain, keeping me from forming coherent thoughts.

"Oh, yeah, me too." She stares down at her coffee, her fingers tracing the rim of the cup. She's slumped, but also tense. "It's a big step. I want to apologize for being so emotional last week. It was just a lot."

"You have nothing to apologize for. Your reaction was normal, and Kong can be overwhelming for anyone. You're right; it's a significant step, and I want to ensure you feel prepared. Sometimes, we grow the most by pushing through things that scare us."

"Lately, I avoid things that scare me." Her eyes find mine, apprehension lingering.

"Anything can be a little scary at first. But if you start small and work toward the bigger things, you can overcome any obstacle. That's what I'm doing with Kong. Despite his scary demeanor, his reactions to strangers stem from fear. You can't wait for your fear to subside. Trust me, you'll be waiting forever."

"Do you think I'm ready for Kong? I mean, I struggle to leave my apartment most days, but don't feel safe there either. What if he comes to live with me, and it doesn't make a difference? Then, I'll have all the responsibility of taking care of him, too?"

"You're ready. You might not be perfect, but the thing with a dog is... it's about showing up. Doing your best one day at a time. Kong will be fine with that. All they need is compassion and love, and a meal every day." I watch her closely and try to look into her eyes, but they've been turned down since she sat at the table.

"What if I screw up?" I see a flicker of vulnerability as she finally looks up into my eyes.

"We all screw up, that's life. But you don't have to do this alone. Kong has been my foster for a long while, and I would love to get updates about him and I can help you with him anytime. If you go out of town and need a sitter, or if he needs to go to the vet, I'd be happy to help if you'll let me. You don't have to feel like you are alone with his care." I give her a small smile to reassure her. "You think I'm perfect? I've made more mistakes than I can count."

She interrupts, "No, I didn't mean it like that. What if I end up regretting this?"

I look at her questioning, but she avoids my gaze and looks down at her coffee again. "Look, I'm not asking you to have all the answers, but I am asking if you are ready to take the first step?" I lean in a bit and try to catch her eyes. When she looks at me, I give her a soft smile. "Besides, I'm pretty sure a dog will teach you more about yourself than you think."

"But you already know so much; I don't know what I'm doing. You've already got your hands full fostering these guys and the rescue."

"Yeah, I guess I do, but I've learned more from these dogs than I care to admit." I lean back again, continuing to smile. "The thing is, Olive, you can't run from things that challenge you."

She raises an eyebrow, looking at me like she's not in the mood for a lecture, or she's not sure where I am going with this. I can almost feel her backing away even though she hasn't moved.

"Take the first step; you don't have to take him home until you're sure either way." I pause for a moment until her eyes meet mine in question. "You're stronger than you think. Trust me, Olive."

"What if I do something wrong and Kong hurts me?" she asks.

"I grin for a second. That's the thing. Once Kong lets you in, he's yours. He will trust you. What you experienced in your last visit will only improve. We just have to get him over the hump, and he'll let you into his circle. It's taken time, but he's met all the volunteers and staff from the rescue. He's even good with one of my neighbors who lets the dogs out when I have long days. He'll be the same with you."

She relaxes and lets out a breath. "Well, if I screw this up, I'll blame you." She flashes a playful smile and her eyes soften. She actually smiles; it's magnetic, and I need more of it.

"Fair enough. Just remember, you're not alone in this." I said it to show her my sincerity, hoping that over time she'll open up and learn to trust me.

Chapter 11
Olive

JUMP NOW, SPIRAL LATER

"Ok, so are you ready to see Kong again?" Loch asks.

"Yes," I say, my voice trembling. The truth is, I'm not sure, but I'm trying to push through.

"Try not to be nervous. I know that's hard, but he can sense it, and it can make him more jumpy."

Great, this dog is going to know I'm terrified. I've never had a dog, so I'd probably be anxious anyway, and Cujo over here can smell my fear. Take a deep breath and get your shit together. It's going to be fine.

"Let's start from where we did last time," he says. "Sit facing me and the bed like before. I'll bring him in. No sudden movements or staring at him. Stay calm and keep talking to me. Ok?"

"I can do that," I say with confidence I don't have.

He leaves the room to get Kong. I struggle to breathe, air coming in quick bursts, trying to suppress the feeling of wanting to run out the door. I force myself to take another deep breath. Another. And another. I can do this. It's just a dog, and Loch has been nothing but patient with me.

I sit on the edge of the chair, white-knuckling the seat, and trying my best to ignore Kong. I focus on the kitchen, the cute, old-lady style that decorates Loch's home. He returns with Kong, and he barks at me and growls a little, but is much calmer. He's not lunging or baring his teeth, and Loch easily guides him to the bed.

Trying to avoid eye contact, I notice all the dog pictures on the fridge.

"What are all those?" There have to be hundreds or more pictures on the front and side of the refrigerator. Most are small, wallet-sized pics, some are a little larger, and a couple of big ones.

"Those are all the dogs I've rescued. I took each one in because of neglect, hardship, or health issues. I've found homes for almost all of them."

How had I not noticed them before now?

"Wow, there are so many." Little dogs, black dogs, white dogs, brown dogs, fluffy dogs. He's saved them all. There have to be close to 200 dogs on there.

"How do you not keep them all?"

"Well, some have lived in a foster home, or our facility, for years before finding their forever homes. We do a lot of community outreach and have many people that turn to us when they're ready for a new pet. Most of the dogs we take in are not as difficult as Kong. Many of them need to be the only pets in a home, which can be challenging to find, but they're great with people. Some are friendly and well-trained. Only Dogs specializes in harder-to-adopt dogs. We also have some of the best volunteers and fosters."

I turn to look at him, almost forgetting Kong was even here. He's lying on his bed, his head raised, watching me with intense focus, but his body is rolled to the side in a relaxed position.

Loch says, "Try giving him a few of the treats, like last time. Toss them his way. Don't move too fast and try not to react when he goes for the treat."

I toss one as close to Kong as I can without reaching toward him and making him feel cornered.

He watches it fall, then stands to sniff the air, and then the treat. He looks at me, ears slightly perked, and leans down to eat the treat. He keeps his beautiful golden, honey-colored eyes on me the whole time. They have a slight cross-eyed look to them, making him look a little dopey. It's too adorable.

I toss another one, a little closer this time. He snatches up the treat.

"You're making progress," Loch murmurs, his voice low, like he's talking more to himself than to me. "It's all about trust. Dogs, people... it takes time."

I swallow, the words landing like they're meant for me too. I glance at him, but Loch's expression is unreadable, his focus is on Kong. My stomach rolls into knots, trying to read between the lines. He wants me to trust him.

Kong comes forward, caution in his steps. My breath hitches, and for a moment, I forget to breathe. I look at Loch, and his eyes are on me, steady and waiting to see what either of us is going to do.

I feel like he's testing me. Testing us. And what if I fail again?

For a moment, I wonder if he's earning my trust in the same way I'm earning Kong's.

"You're doing fine," Loch says, like he knows what I'm thinking. "Keep being patient with him. With yourself."

I nod, but I don't look at him. Instead, I focus on Kong, who's now sitting a little closer. His tail wags with a slight movement, and his head tilts to the side, like those cute puppies do in videos. He's looking at me with less wariness and more curiosity, but still strained and stiff.

"Yeah," I say, my voice almost a whisper. "I think I'm starting to understand."

Loch says, "I'm going to let him approach you; stay still, and let him sniff you."

I stiffen and stutter, "A-Are you sure?"

"Yes, I still have his leash. Do what I say and don't move."

"Ok," I say, as I move into statue mode. Like that kids' game, where you have to freeze so no one can tag you.

"He laughs just a little. Don't tense up; he calmed down because you calmed down. Look at the fridge and all the pictures if you need to."

"Ok," I say again. I take a deep breath and look at Loch, and then at the fridge. He leads Kong to my feet and allows him to sniff me. He lingers on my shoes. Maybe he's trying to imagine all the places I've been. I continue to look at the fridge and stay still, trying my very best to stay calm and let him get to know me.

"Now, I'm going to let Kong go outside for a couple of minutes and give you both a break. When he comes in next time, you are going to give him a treat with your hand." And with that, he leaves the room.

Oh, God. He's going to bite my hand off. What am I doing?! I see Kong running outside through the window. Watching him sniff around and roll in the grass. Then Loch walks back in and sits down.

"Loch, I'm not sure I can do this." My heart races.

He sits down next to me, and with a confused look, asks, "Hey, what's happened? You did great today."

A long moment passes. I'm trying my hardest to suppress tears, waiting to speak until I have control of my emotions. The fear, heavy breath, sweaty hands, and the bottomless feeling of fear weigh me down like a truck is on top of me.

"It's ok, you can tell me. I won't judge you. You can trust me," he says.

I look at him. His kind eyes, he's so handsome. It's almost hard to look at him sometimes, but I also can't stop staring. He tenderly puts his hand on mine, like I had done for him the last time I was here. He repeats, "You can trust me."

His hand is like a warm blanket. Somehow, soothing me. How? Most touches these days are like someone is stabbing me, even a lot of the times Sophia has touched me. I tolerate it because I know and trust her, but in some moments, it feels like human contact is strangling me to death. But with Loch, there's an energy; it still burns, but instead of fire, it's electricity. Kind of unsettling, but at the same time, not.

"I... I think I'm a little afraid. After he lunged last time, I don't want to, you know, ruin it again."

Loch smiles and says, "I won't let anything happen to you. It's my job to protect you and Kong. That means it's my responsibility to read his body language and know when he's ok, and when he is not. When you take him home, this will become your responsibility. But I would never let either of you fail. Will you trust me?"

I look at him, wide-eyed. The feeling I felt earlier when he was talking about trust returns. I have an ache in my throat and chest. A warm and nervous energy courses through me like lava. Can I actually allow myself to trust him?

After a pause, I say, "Yes, I trust you." He's never given me a reason not to. He's been kind, patient, and understanding at every turn.

"Grab a treat, put your hand out flat, and when Kong comes in, let him come to you. Don't look him in the eye, but you can watch him. Let him know you're safe, with your heart." He puts his hand to his chest, and a small treat in my hand. The corners of his mouth lift, and he gives me a nod.

"Nah, let's give him a bigger treat for approaching you," he goes to the fridge and pulls out a package of hotdogs. He places half a hotdog in my hand. It feels a little silly holding a hotdog, but I keep breathing and stay steady, even though my hands try to shake. Then, without warning, Loch gives me a wink and a devilish smile as he turns to leave. Pretty much the hottest thing I've seen him do. Now, I'm sweating with nerves for other reasons. I blush as he walks out to get Kong.

Oh my God, I'm such a mess. I can barely talk to the guy. My skin tingled when he touched me, and my whole body flushed when he winked at me. It was an innocent wink and a smile. Olive, get it together; focus on Kong, who's about to turn you into Captain Hook.

I close my eyes, taking deep breaths, like before. I open them when I hear the door handle jiggle with the boys' return. I glance at the fridge. All those rescued pups live happy lives. It gives me a happy feeling, like someday I'll find peace after my trauma, too.

Then there's a wet nose in my hand. I glance down to see Kong has taken the treat from my hand. I don't think anything could take the smile off my face at this moment. I look up at Loch, looking for his approval, and I get the feeling that I just got an A plus on a test.

Loch lifts his chin and puffs his chest. He's proud of me. "Great job, Olive," as he walks Kong to the dog bed. "I want you to give him more treats, but sometimes fast movements can startle him. Until he realizes you're grabbing more treats, we'll keep walking back and forth, allowing him to choose to approach you each time."

"That sounds good," I say. I grab the other half of the hotdog and put it in my flat hand; Kong walks over to me and takes the treat. It feels huge, like I've tamed a beast. Like I've won, or at least won him over. I regain a bit of confidence. He's walking and moving at ease now. We do this for a while, each time making me feel safer and safer.

I toss another treat to his bed, and Kong takes it more confidently this time, licking his lips, glancing at me with those gigantic eyes. The ones that used to look like warning signs but are now more open.

I put more treats in my palm, smaller pieces now, so he doesn't get sick. He approaches each time with less and less hesitation.

Loch finally says, his voice soft but clear, "Try asking him to sit."

My breath catches in my throat, and I swallow. "Me?" I glance at him, unsure. "What if he doesn't do it?"

"Just try," he says. "You've earned enough trust. Now ask for something in return."

My mouth goes dry, but I nod. I turn back to Kong, who's looking at me, tail giving the tiniest wag, anticipating another treat. He's not fully relaxed, but he's watching me now, waiting.

My heart is hammering.

"Kong," I whisper, then clear my throat. My voice, still shaky, I say, "Sit." He blinks. I repeat it, steadier this time, more commanding. I reach for that ounce of confidence I found a few minutes ago. "Sit."

And just like that, he does, like it's nothing. His butt hits the floor with a soft thump, and he looks up at me with that quiet and calm focus dogs have when they're giving you everything they can.

My eyes sting. I don't know why. I laugh a little, caught somewhere between crying and total disbelief. "Holy shit."

Loch smiles a little. "There it is."

I reach for more treats and offer another, my hand trembling enough for me to notice. Kong takes it like it's no big deal, as if I didn't climb some monstrous mountain to get here.

"You ok?" Loch asks, low and gentle.

I nod, wiping the corner of my eye before it betrays me. "Yeah. I... I didn't think I could do that."

"But you did," he says. "You're not the same person who walked in here. You faced your fear, and I'm so impressed by you."

I look at Kong again—sitting like it's the most normal thing in the world—and something breaks open in me, soft and warm and real. For the first time in a long time, I don't feel like prey. I don't feel broken. I'm strong and worthy of something.

Kong settles beside me. He lets out a deep, rumbling sigh and lies down right next to me. I swear it feels like an apology and forgiveness wrapped into one.

"He's amazing," I murmur, not looking up. "I mean... intense, but amazing."

"He thinks the same about you," Loch says, and there's something in his voice that makes me glance up.

He's not smiling this time. Not really. He's watching me with that same unreadable look he's worn since I walked in, like he's trying to decide whether he should say something or not.

"What?" I ask, my voice soft.

He shifts his weight against the gate, eyes flicking to Kong and then back to me. "Most people don't make it this far with him. Not this fast."

I shrug, looking back down at Kong. "He may see something familiar in me."

Loch is quiet for a moment. Then says, "That wouldn't surprise me. I see the sadness."

I glance up at him again, and this time I'm not so quick to look away. "You keep saying things like that, and I can't tell if you're still talking about the dog or me."

A small, crooked smile tugs at the edge of his mouth. "I don't know either," he says. "I feel something between us, and I know you feel it too."

That one hits a little too close, and a nervous laugh escapes a little too quickly, and I give him a soft smile, not sure where he is going with this. Loch says nothing. He doesn't have to. His eyes say it all.

I shift, the room feeling smaller, warmer. My hands are clammy, my breathing is short. His attention is like a grip, pulling me near, and impossible to ignore.

"I haven't felt safe in a long time," I breathe, the words surprising me. But something about this, something about him, and Kong–hell, even his grandma-style house–it feels good and genuine. My body is more relaxed around him, like I can breathe a little easier.

I look at him, and there's something about the way he looks back at me that makes my stomach twist. There's a draw that's sucking me in, but once I have a moment to find reality, I want to turn back and run out the door.

"What about you?" I ask. "Do you make people earn your trust, too?"

He huffs, almost a laugh but not quite. "I make it nearly impossible. I trust very few people."

"Why?"

His eyes darken; his jaw tightens, and I notice something darker behind his eyes. "Because most people don't deserve it."

We sit with that for a moment. The air is heavier; we've both exchanged something we can't take back.

"But some do," he says in the quietest whisper.

I nod, furrowing my brows, and give him a questioning look. I wonder if I'm one of them, but I can't read him.

Kong shifts and starts snoring. I giggle. He's comforting me already, or maybe I'm comforting him. Either way, none of us moves for a long moment.

Loch's eyes don't leave mine, and I should look away, but I don't. I hold his gaze. I'm sick and tired of flinching, avoiding, and running from everything and everyone. I need to do the same as Kong and find baby steps to overcome my issues. Find small ways to face my fears, and maybe Kong will help me do that. Or is it Loch that's helping me so much?

He crouches next to Kong and looks up at me, his eyes never wavering. "He picked up on it, you know."

"On what?"

"You," he says, voice low. "We both knew that the fear was still there, that you were trying to suppress it. Hiding it."

I swallow hard and pick up my coffee cup to give me something else to focus on, feeling called out.

"He doesn't judge you," Loch continues. "Neither do I. But you should know—he still chose to come closer, despite knowing you were afraid."

My chest rises with a sharp breath. "You think that means something?"

"It means everything."

He's too close now. He's trying to open something that isn't his to open. Pushing me, forcing me to look in the mirror.

"I don't know what you're trying to do right now," I whisper.

Loch tilts his head. "I'm not trying to do anything."

"Bullshit," I hiss.

His lips twitch. Not in a smile. Something more dangerous. "Maybe I'm trying to understand you, the real you."

"Why?"

"Because I've seen many people pretend to be fine," he says. "You're not pretending. You're... surviving. There's a difference, and I like the rawness in you."

Heat crawls up my neck, my pulse loud in my ears. "You don't even know me."

"I don't," he says simply. "But I want to."

The silence that falls between us is loud, heavy, and charged.

Kong shifts again, but Loch's gaze stays on me, and it feels like he sees every part I've been trying to keep buried. Does he know what I went through, or know why I am the way I am? Does he see me?

"You should be careful with the whole brooding-and-insightful thing," I murmur, forcing a shaky smile, trying to act like what he says isn't real. Trying to shove it all back down, deep. "It's a little personal, don't you think?"

Loch's voice drops even lower. "You think I'm brooding?"

I look at him, and this time, I can't look away. "I believe you're hiding as much as I am, maybe even more."

The corner of his mouth lifts a fraction, but his eyes stay serious. Intense. "Then, maybe you're the first person who's looked close enough to see it."

My breath catches in my throat. I want to say something clever or disarming. I want to pull away before I fall any deeper into this moment. Kong shifts again; he tilts his head up, ticks it to the side, and looks at me, and I can't help but feel like I'm falling for both of them.

Heat coils low in my stomach as Loch looks at me. What does he want? His eyes bore into mine like he expects me to say something. It's not just attraction; it's a longing ache, like the urge to touch fire to see if it burns. But I'm not ready to burn. I'm too afraid.

After an awkward silence, he returns Kong to his kennel and we part ways with plans to meet again in a few days. My heart is pounding. The urge to stay and let him in fights to overpower my defenses. But I'm not ready. I will continue to build the wall back up, brick by brick, despite him breaking them down every chance he gets.

I can't risk falling, even though it seems like I'm losing my balance at the edge of a cliff.

Chapter 12

Loch

Sit, Stay, Swoon

Three days later...

I've been dying to see her again. During our last meeting, I felt it. I found a kernel of the real Olive. She hides away, fearful of what happened to her, but I could almost reach her until she shut down on me.

She's different. There's something deep down and raw in her that hasn't hardened yet. Something broken that didn't shatter all the way, and I want it.

I want to protect that, and keep it, and that scares the hell out of me. I'll pick up all the little broken pieces, and put them back together one at a time, if it means I can keep her. She's so beautiful, her blond hair and big hips, and those eyes. Fuck, I'm so captivated by her. Her rarely seen smile is infectious. Very few people surprise me, but watching her interact with Kong shows me she is a lot braver than the average person. She hasn't given up on him, and that says so much about her.

I'm knocked out of my thoughts by the soft knock at the door.

"Evening!" I say, almost giving away how excited I am to see her.

She gives me a curious glance. She thinks I'm acting weird, and I am.

"Hello."

I shift my weight, crossing my arms to keep myself still. But she looks up, and fuck–those eyes. They stop me cold. The mix of blue-gray hues, the color of the calm before a storm. She is so intriguing.

"Uh, come in," I say, trying to get my thoughts back in order. I make way for her to come in. I take her big puffy coat and hang it up.

"I was thinking today you might be more comfortable in the living room. It would be good if you could sit on the floor at Kong's level. I've put down a folded blanket to give you some cushion to sit on. Sound good?

"Oh, sure. I'm fine on the floor."

"Would you like something to drink? I'm assuming you don't want any coffee this late. I have water or beer? Sorry, I should have more options, but I'm a simple man."

She laughs, "Not a big entertainer?"

I laugh. "Not at all. You're probably the only person to come here besides the other volunteers from the rescue and a plumber I hired last year."

A wide smile stretches across her face. "What an honor. Umm, sure, I'll take a water, I guess."

I go to the kitchen to grab our drinks. I hang my head in the fridge for a minute to cool down. She's making me sweat. I don't know how to act around her. This should be about Kong, but I want her to be here for me, too.

After I try to reset once again, I walk back in and hand her a glass of water and a bowl of treats.

"I'm going to bring Kong in. I'll put the dog bed a few feet away from you so he can have a spot, but it will be easier for you to give him treats. And we'll try to have you pet him today!"

She narrows her eyes at me, but a second later she relaxes and says, "Ok."

She changed her mind right in front of me. She was about to run again, and then her shoulders fell, her face calmed, and confidence radiated through her. She is the most interesting person I've ever met. I love that her body tells me everything I need to know. It makes it so easy to read her.

"Same as last time, stay still and put a treat in your open palm."

I grin at her, seeing her fear almost gone. The person in my house is vastly different from the woman I met at the rescue a couple of weeks ago. Was it something I said? Did something happen? I ponder the significant change while I walk out to get Kong. I go through the sunroom door and lean down to open his kennel.

"Hey, buddy. Ready to be nice today? I need you to trust me. Olive is going to love you, but I need you to give her a chance." I reach down to pet his head and scratch behind his ears. Then, I leash him up, and we walk back inside, ready to do this. I take a deep breath, not sure if I am more nervous for him or for myself.

He walks to Olive, smells her, and takes the piece of hotdog in her hand. Out of nowhere, he sits down, waiting for more treats. I tell her to inch her hand to the bowl and grab another treat for him. Kong's ears go back, and he goes a little stiff, like he's cautious about what she's doing. No hackles and no grumbles. He sits waiting patiently. Olive hands him another treat. I've never seen him like this before. I walk him over to the bed and ask him to lie down. He does and rests his head on his feet, looking at Olive.

"I, umm... Wow! I can't believe he's so calm. Are you ready to try again?"

"Is he getting used to me?"

"Yes, but usually he doesn't warm up to people this fast. Getting him to approach someone is the hardest part. It's kind of amazing." After a brief thought, I say, "I'm going to ask him to lie down near you, and you can keep giving him treats every couple of minutes."

I walk him over to her. He takes a treat out of her hand and, again, sits and waits for more.

After a couple more treats, I tell her, "Why don't you ask him to lie down? Just say 'down,' point at the ground, and when he does, give him a treat."

She stares at me; the slight frown on her face gives away her hesitation. "It's ok, you can do it."

She takes a deep breath and nods, turns her eyes away from me, and looks at Kong. She confidently says, "Down." Kong obeys and lies down.

I'm in utter shock. I can't believe what I'm seeing. It makes me feel a lot of feelings about Olive that I can't explain. How did Kong accept her so fast? Why is she so much more confident with him now compared to the other times she came to see him? My mind is spinning with questions about the woman sitting on my living room floor.

She continues to give him treats and tell him he's a good boy. She starts talking to him like a baby. It makes me laugh out loud, hearing her coo at this huge eighty-pound pitbull. He's absolutely regal, with super-soft blue fur, and even though I hate cropped ears, he looks tough. But as soon as the laugh leaves my mouth, both Olive and Kong turn their heads at me and glare, as if I've interrupted their moment. I put my hands up, smiling from ear to ear in utter disbelief at how they've bonded today.

"Since it's clear he's feeling comfortable, let's see how he does when you pet him. Give him a treat with your hand closed loosely around it. Let him dig his face in, get it out of your fist, and once he does, give him a little scratch under the chin."

"I can do that," she says with certainty.

Olive does exactly as I say. Her shoulders hang comfortably. Her face is lit up with joy, her eyes are sparkling, and she's wearing a smile that reaches them.

She scratches under his chin, and he nuzzles his head into her hand.

Again, I'm in disbelief. "W–Wow," I stutter.

She gives him another treat and then looks up at me, seeking my approval. I give her a warm smile and a nod.

"You're doing amazing." Then, the unimaginable happens. Kong lays his head on her lap, right on her thigh. She freezes for a second, but he nuzzles his face into her lap and she begins petting him—touching his head, scratching behind his ears. At that moment, I see it. He's hers.

"I've never seen him trust someone so fast. When he did this routine with Jan and Mark from the rescue, it took half a dozen meetings for them to be able to pet him like this. He only ever decided to trust me and, well, now you, Olive."

I should say something neutral. Keep it professional. I should talk about Kong, or the next steps in the adoption. Something with boundaries. But instead, my voice comes out low, filled with emotion at watching them interact.

"You're good with him."

She tilts her head. "You say that like you're surprised."

"A little." I shrug. "I'm not as surprised as I am impressed."

Her mouth twitches like she doesn't know whether to smile or brace for impact. "Does it take a lot to impress you?"

"Yes, to be honest with you, it does."

A beat passes. Then another. I hate this part—the wanting, the need, the ache.

She asks me with a knot in her throat, "So, can I take him home?"

The smile she has on her face makes my chest tight. I look at her with an unsure expression.

"Soon, let's meet a couple more times. I need to have you get him out of his kennel and leash him. Once we get over those hurdles, he can go home with you."

The thought of her not coming to see me, no more meetings, and, well, Kong leaving, breaks me a little. But I can't push her. I like her, but I don't think she's interested in me. One wrong move and I'll become another shadow in her story, another reason to flinch. But I also can't bear the thought of not seeing her anymore.

I choose my words carefully. "I know I'm difficult to read, Olive. I don't say things unless I mean them. But I need you to know..." I pause. She watches me. "I don't want anything from you that you're not ready to give, but you're not alone. I'm here to support you and Kong."

I have to try. I can't live with the regret of not even trying. I want her in every way. She's gorgeous, sweet, and has something that I find irresistible. Whatever I see in her, it's the same thing that Kong sees.

Her expression softens, so I take my chance.

"But if there's ever a moment," I continue, steady and slow, "where you want to let someone in—even a little, even as a friend—I'd like to be that person." Fuck, why did I say that? I'm not trying to end up in the friend zone. God, I'm an idiot. Please don't be just my friend.

She doesn't answer right away. And looks at me with a quizzical look, like she's trying to read me or find something. An answer, maybe. Like she wasn't expecting me to say that. And she probably wasn't. I do my best to remain confident, but the more she looks at me, the more she breaks me open.

Kong shifts beside her. He stretches, yawns, and lays his massive head in her lap again, as if it belongs there.

She runs her hand through his fur, thoughtful. Her voice is barely above a whisper. "I don't know if I can right now."

"I know," I say. "I'm not asking you to. I'm saying, when you're ready, I'll be here. I want you to know that I want to get to know you, and I'm interested in spending more time with you."

She looks at me like she doesn't trust what I'm saying, but wants to, and that's enough for tonight. So, I give her a small nod and lean back, giving her physical and emotional space. I let the silence settle, and let her have space to breathe without the pressure of my presence.

But even as I pull away, I already know.

Rene Geraci

I'm in this.

Chapter 13
Olive

Check Yes or No

As I park my car and look at the front of my building, all the happiness and confidence I felt after having Kong accept me are gone. All the things that Loch said to me before I left are scrambling my brain. I manage to pick myself up and walk inside, but I can't help but look around like a maniac. Coming home is worse than actually being at home. God, I'm such a mess. Thinking that soon, Kong will be here in my apartment to greet me and welcome me home, gives me such a calming feeling.

I keep thinking about the way Kong looked at me—like he knew. It was as if he could see all the echoes of my hurts and bruises, no longer visible, but still there. He could see the trauma I've experienced looking back at him. And it seems like Loch was doing the same.

And Loch... God, Loch.

I mean, it was just supposed to be the dog, to have as a companion. Not this man who brings me a sense of calm as well as makes my whole body pulse. I don't think I'm ready to feel these emotions.

He quiets the noise in my head. And it's not that he does anything in particular. It's that he's safe. I can be myself—my broken, disheveled self—around him. He doesn't ask me to explain anything. He doesn't push. But he gives me the space I need, like he's handing me a key and letting me choose whether to use it. Being near him gives me the good kind of chills, and I'm not sure what to think of that.

His voice is so low and seductive it makes it hard to talk to him. Hearing his voice makes my throat close. Leaving me struggling for air. And the loaded silence between us claws to get out.

When I'm with them, I'm comforted by an overwhelming sense of peace. I can breathe easier. I don't know if it's Kong or Loch giving me that feeling, but I want to find a way to keep it.

But I can't even let someone touch me. What in the hell would I even have to offer? Better yet, what would he want with me? Would he still feel the same if he knew what happened to me? I'm sure he would tire of waiting for me to work through all my shit. Is there even a remote possibility of me being able to do that?

But what if I can't do it? What if he can't handle my trauma? What if I get too close and ruin it because I am a bruised, quiet, broken version of who I used to be? What if I don't know how to let someone in without losing myself even more?

I don't even know who I am right now. I don't recognize myself; I don't even think I like this person I've become. I'm weak, lonely, sad, and useless.

And yet, he pretty much said, when you're ready, I'll be here.

There was no pressure or sign of games. He was letting me know of his presence and desire to be more present. I want to trust that. I want to feel alive again.

So, now I'm sitting here like an idiot, arguing with myself over a guy and a dog, and whether I have the courage to let myself want something good again. Whether I deserve it.

Maybe I need a second brain. A louder one. One with wine and sarcasm and zero tolerance for my negative spiral.

I need Sophia.

Olive: I saw Kong again today. I petted him and he lay on my lap!

Sophia: OMG! Is he just the cutest puppy ever?!

Olive: He's a sweet angel puppy with a resting murder face. But I'm obsessed. Like actually. I think I'm in love.

Sophia: With the dog or the man who rescued the dog?

Olive: Yes.

Sophia: Ohhh, shit. Tell me everything about this smoldering man.

Olive: He's... quiet. Deep. Mysterious. But he's so nice and thoughtful that I can't figure him out. There's definitely something about him I can't put my finger on.

Olive: He's so sweet. But he knows what I'm thinking all the time. And he's a fucking closed book.

Sophia: So, like, emotionally constipated Batman vibes, or what?

Olive: 100% would trust him in an alley and also, maybe cry on his shoulder. He's kind. It's like, somehow, he knows what I've been through, like, he can see through me.

Sophia: Sexy and sweet. And rescues animals? What kind of man-meat jackpot did you win?!

Olive: No, but seriously... he said something to me today. About being there when I'm ready. It didn't feel like a line. It didn't feel like pressure. It's like he was just letting me know. But the whole time I was there, I felt... safe.

Sophia: Babe. You never say that about anything, especially men. I mean, not too long ago, you were not even comfortable in the presence of the regulars at the bar, barely me, let alone a strange man.

Olive: I know. That's what's freaking me out.

Sophia: Ok. So listen. I love you, you know I do. I will throw hands at anyone who messes with you. But also, don't close the door just because it's scary to open again. Life will go on, but it's up to you to decide when. So, when you feel ready, take a baby step. What happened to you doesn't have to define you or your life.

Olive: Ugh. Why are you so good at this?

Sophia: Because I've watched you walk through hell, and you deserve someone, and to be happy. Even if he is brooding and owns thirty pitbulls.

Olive: His fridge door is full of pictures of dogs he's saved. Girl, like hundreds. I had to restrain myself from launching at him like a feral cat. And fuck, the look he gave me when Kong listened to my "lay down" command. I needed new panties after that. Loch said that he had never warmed up to anyone but him that fast. He put his head right in my lap. It was so adorable.

Sophia: Adopt him. Date his human. Fall in love. Let me be your maid of honor.

Olive: Slow your damn roll! I was still awkward as fuck.

Sophia: Fine. But girl, you will kick yourself if you don't at least try to get to know this guy. Go in with low expectations and be honest with him about where you are. Even if it's a half-truth.

Olive: I'll think about it. Thanks, girl.

Three days later...

I sit on my couch eating a bagel when my phone lights up with a message from Sergeant Persimmons.

Sergeant Persimmons: Hello, Olive. Please give me a call when you get a chance. We need to discuss your case. Have a good day. Thank you.

What else could they need from me? My stomach twists as I click to call her. Let's get this over with. It rings twice.

"Sergeant Persimmons."

"Uh, yeah, this is Olive Smythe. I was—"

"Oh, yes. Hi, Olive. Thank you for calling. Some things have developed with your case. We apprehended the man you identified.

He went through an arraignment, and unfortunately, he made bail. He's been released. His lawyers are pushing to get all charges dropped; and his father, Senator Wright, is attempting to pull some strings as well. The D.A. and I are doing everything possible to make sure he pays for his crimes. As of now, he is out on bail. If this ends up in court, the D.A. will absolutely need you to testify to have enough evidence against him for a prison sentence. Your identification is strong evidence, but without a testimony, it likely will not be enough. If you choose not to testify, the judge may dismiss the case."

There's a long pause.

"Ms. Smythe? Are you there?"

"Yeah, sorry. I just..."

"Think about it; nothing will happen for some time. I wanted you to be aware that Mr. Wright is out on bail and to consider testifying when the time comes. Do you have any questions?"

"Uh, no, I don't think so."

"Ok, have a good day, and we'll be in touch with any important updates."

"Sure, thanks."

And she hangs up.

What. The. Fuck. Out on bail? Privileged piece of shit, out on bail, because the rich and powerful have no consequences. That's what she said. Like it was nothing, just another update in some broken, bureaucratic process. He's out. Meaning he's walking around. Breathing free air—smiling, laughing, hanging out with friends. He could already be watching or hurting someone else.

A noise catches in my throat, something between a sob and a choke. My whole body goes rigid. The phone slips from my hand and hits the floor, but I don't move to get it. I can't move at all. It's like the world has tilted under my feet and locked them in place.

My breath turns shallow. Cold. And then it hits, like a freight train crashing through my chest. A dull roar in my ears tunes everything else out. My hands and feet are completely numb. The floor has dropped out from under me, leaving me nauseated, weightless, and sick.

Everything comes back. The weight of him on top of me. The smell of his sweat, cologne, and beer breath. His voice in my ear. The sound of my own muffled screaming. The way my body had given up, gone quiet when my fight finally ran out. The sickening warmth of blood on my neck from the icy blade on my throat.

I fold in on myself, arms wrapping tight around my waist, but it doesn't help. The pain is back. Real and sharp. The pain pounds inside me, making my ribs hurt, as though they've been fractured again. Phantom bruises bloom under my skin, invisible but so damn present.

He's out–free.

And I'm still here, trapped. Silent and so small. Still carrying the night he gave me like a weight I can't get rid of. The worst part, I knew this would happen. Deep in my gut, I knew my rapist would walk.

And he's a senator's son. He has money, power, and connections. The kind of man who's never heard the word 'no.' The kind of man who's going to walk into court with a suit and a smirk, and walk right back out like nothing ever happened, because he's rich and powerful. Rules don't apply to him.

They never designed justice for women like me. Not when the monster wears a last name with clout and can buy his way out of prison.

My fists clench, nails digging into my palms, but it still isn't enough to get me out of my trance. My thoughts are slipping, spiraling, screaming without sound.

He'll get a slap on the wrist, and maybe six months in some cushy white-collar facility where they serve steak and have Wi-Fi. I can see it already, him coming out even more smug than before.

I can't imagine facing a courtroom of strangers, dragging my story, all the painful memories and details, out under cold fluorescent lights. I can't imagine having to say those words out loud in front of him. Reliving what he did to me.

So I don't move.

I lie down on the couch and curl in tight. I ignore my phone when it buzzes, and the world when it tries to reach me. I don't eat. I don't speak. I just... stop.

Because it isn't the attack itself that's broken me. It's waking up to find the world hasn't changed. And I'm the one stuck in the wreckage he left behind.

Chapter 14
Loch
Waiting, Wanting, and Worrying

Olive is thirty minutes late. She was supposed to come and see Kong today, and she's not answering her phone. What if something happened to her? I'll wait a little longer and keep trying to reach her. Did I scare her last time?

She would have called or texted to say that she changed her mind. I don't think she would bail on me or Kong without talking to me. I shouldn't have said that I wanted to get to know her. Fuck, I never meant to make her feel cornered or vulnerable. I wanted her to know where I stood, and that she could do what she wanted; I wouldn't push her.

I spend the next thirty minutes pacing back and forth. I'm trying not to panic and hope this is only a miscommunication about when she was supposed to come back.

After another half hour, I text Jan to see if she can reach her. Jan gets back to me right away. She can't get through to her either, and she doesn't think Olive wouldn't show without a good reason. She says she would've called or texted if she changed her mind, confirming what I already suspected.

Fuck. I'm going to make sure she is ok. I can't assume everything is fine. I need to know. I need to see her.

I get the address from her application and head over there. That's probably a little unethical, but then again, I've done worse. I pull up to her apartment building. It's downtown, but it's nice. Doesn't seem like a neighborhood where an attack like hers would happen. I walk up her stairs and knock on the door, still trying not to panic, and figure out what I'm going to say to her.

CHAPTER 15
OLIVE

FLOODGATES OPEN

In a state of numbness, I hear a loud knock on the door, startling me back into reality. What the fuck? It's him. I need a weapon. Do I call the cops? What the fuck?! I run to the kitchen to grab a knife, open my phone, and begin to dial.

And then I hear "OLIVE... are you in there? It's Loch." He shouts through the door.

I think my heart fell out of my ass. Loch? What is he doing here?

"OLIVE, open up; I just want to make sure you're ok." His knocking is getting louder.

Holy shit. How long was I lying there? Crap, I was supposed to go see Kong today. I completely forgot after finding out about the arrest and bail.

"HEY, OLIVE!" The knocking is harder now. Please, let me know you are ok."

I set the knife and phone down. Thank God I didn't call the cops.

"COMING," I shout, trying to calm him.

Rescued

I look through the peephole to see Loch's face staring at my door. I'm still in sweatpants from this morning, and I probably look like a total slob. I haven't moved from the couch in hours. But who cares? I don't have the energy to worry about it.

I press my forehead to the door. My limbs are heavy, my thoughts foggy, like I've been underwater all day. When my phone buzzed earlier, I didn't even have the strength to check it.

But he came. Not just texted, not just called. He came to check on me. I don't even know how he knows where I live.

I hesitate. It would be easier not to answer, or to tell him to go. That I'm fine. Let him think I'm busy, or sick, or that I forgot.

But something in his voice cuts through the fog. He sounds worried, and he noticed I didn't show up and that something must be wrong. That shouldn't matter. But it makes my heart ache, and my pulse spike.

I open the door slowly. He's there—solid and searching my eyes—watching me, trying to read me.

"Wh–What—are you doing here?" I stutter out.

"You missed your visit. Didn't call. Didn't answer. I... wanted to make sure you were ok."

God, he means that. There's no judgment on his face; there's concern. He has such deep, gentle eyes. His warm whiskey-colored eyes are like quicksand, sucking me in, pulling me under. The more I fight it, the more I sink.

I can't believe he showed up for me.

"I'm not." Shit, that slipped out before I could catch it. Because it's true. And maybe I'm tired of pretending. No, he said it himself. I'm not pretending; I'm surviving.

I step aside and let him in. He walks in and gives me a gentle, but concerned, look. "Do you want to talk about it?" He doesn't press or fill the silence. He waits.

I stare at him for a long moment. The room is quiet, the air is still and heavy. That kind of dangerous stillness that usually makes me shrink into myself.

But not with him; something in me wants to let him in, to let him see who I am, and if he runs, then I'll pick up the pieces like before.

My throat tightens remembering that night. My body trembles, my hands and voice shake, as phantom pain screams from somewhere deep within me. If I don't say it now, I might drown in it forever.

So, I let it out, "I found out... he's out on bail. The guy who... hurt me. He didn't just break in. He followed me home and attacked me."

Loch doesn't move. But something sharp flickers across his face. Quiet and steady, "Jesus. Olive..."

His jaw clenches, and his eyes narrow. I watch as his fists tighten, his knuckles white, but he stays calm and remains silent. He keeps it all together, like he knows how to for me.

I hunch in shame and fear of what he might say or think about me. "He's... walking free. Like nothing happened. Meanwhile, I'm still emotionally bleeding and hurting from what he did, yet he's out there, free. And I'm trapped in my own apartment and a captive of my body."

"Trust me, he won't," he pauses, "he will not get away with it. I promise you that." Loch's voice is gruff, almost angry.

"I didn't want to tell anyone. I don't want pity or judgment. I feel dirty and broken." I can't look at him; I don't want to see the expression on his face as he looks at the damaged person in front of him.

"I won't do either of those things, and I don't see anyone damaged here. I promise. You can trust me. I'm... here for you. You can tell me as much or as little as you're ready for. If you need someone to sit here in the dark with you, I can do that, too. And so will Kong, soon enough."

That hits my chest like a bolt of lightning, shock waves thrum through me. How can he be like this, so... so perfect?

I blink fast, fighting off tears, but one escapes anyway. I wipe it away, embarrassed. Hoping he doesn't notice.

He pulls something from his jacket and hands it to me. I reach for it, our fingers touching, and another jolt of energy hits me. His touch is hot, and his fingers are rough. He's handed me a little Kong keychain. It's a small silver disc with an engraving of Kong's sweet face and his name. My chest tightens and aches with a familiar pain, but this time it's a good pain. I get a sudden feeling of regret that I missed my meeting today. That I didn't show up for Kong. I already failed him.

"He missed you today. But I told him you'd be back. Don't worry, he believed me."

I clutch the keychain like it's fragile, the cold metal smooth on my fingers, slight indentations around the engravings. Kong's sweet face looks back at me, grounding me, resetting me.

Barely above a whisper, I tell him, "Thank you. The key chain is sweet, it feels like he's already here with me. Thank you for coming. I needed this. I'm sorry I missed our meeting today."

I look up into Loch's face. He came here; he gave me such a thoughtful gift, and he's looking at me like I'm the stars and moon. Even though I probably look and smell like old garbage.

"You don't owe me anything. I'll leave if you want me to, but I'd like to stay. All you need to do is tell me what you want."

So, I ask him to stay. His presence makes me feel protected, providing a momentary escape from the memories of my past. Every time I look into those deep-brown eyes and see his gentle smile and strong features, I can forget, for just a minute. And that single minute is pure bliss.

"Can I get you anything to drink?" I ask him with a silly grin.

He's always offering things to me. It's nice to be able to give him something. Even if it's only something to drink.

"Let me. How about water for both of us?" He didn't even ask if he could. He went straight to the kitchen, like he'd been here before. Like he belonged here.

I watch him move, casual and quiet, opening the cabinet where I keep the glasses. How the hell did he even know that? He's so domestic. I squeeze my thighs, trying not to swoon over a man in my kitchen.

The muscles in his back flex under that too-fitted gray T-shirt, the fabric stretching slightly when he reaches up. Holy fuck. And the jeans—Jesus. Who allowed him to wear jeans that tight? That ass should be a crime, or come with a warning label, at least.

I blink, look away, then look back again like some horny teenager.

His body is—God, it's not just hot. It's... He's... breathtaking, so comfortable in his skin, too. Being sexy is natural to him. He knows how to take up space without demanding it. I'd bet he knows exactly how to touch a woman.

I shouldn't be thinking about that. Not today. Not with my emotions feeling like swirling shards of glass cutting me with every breath. But something flutters low in my belly—something warm and familiar. A tingle coursing through me. That slow, curling kind that creeps in without permission and settles between your legs. I haven't felt it in... I don't even know how long. And now it's there, waking something up I thought I'd buried for good.

It's not because he's hot. It's because he's here. He moves through my apartment like he wants to take care of me instead of taking from me.

And suddenly, I'm not watching his body—I'm wondering what it might feel like pressed up against mine. Jesus, Olive, get it together. But I can't look away.

When he turns around to come back to me, he catches me gawking. My cheeks blush pink. I press my lips together, and my heartbeat increases. He smiles at me, knowing and enjoying my embarrassment.

Chapter 16

Loch

Hot Lips, Cold Feet

She asked me to stay, and I'm so glad. I want to leave the ball in her court, so I don't fuck this up. I'm thankful that she opened up to me finally, but she'll take ten steps back if I don't handle this right.

After a bit of awkward silence and small talk, Olive asks me if I want to watch a movie. A movie with her? "Absolutely." I'm almost giddy to get to spend more time with her.

She chooses some chick flick from the nineties. I don't care what we watch. I'm happy she wants me to stay.

I sit beside her on the couch. Not close, not touching, but not too far, either. The couch is plenty big for the both of us, but it's U-shaped, the kind that forces your proximity, whether you want it or not. And I want it too much. I want her to sit on my lap.

She pulls a blanket from the back of the couch and over herself, her knees tucked up, body curled small. Her hair is still a little wild, up in a messy bun, her eyes are tired, but God, she is beautiful like this. Raw and real and still here, and with me. I love that she is so casual. I can't help but look over at her every chance I get. Her breasts, full, heavy, and round, strain against her clothing. She has a beautifully thick, hourglass figure, a huge, round ass I would fucking love to see bent over this couch. She is so sexy.

I keep my eyes on the screen as much as I can. Trying to breathe evenly. Trying not to notice the way her knee keeps brushing against mine, just barely. It's tormenting me. I notice every single move and adjustment she makes, reading into it to see if she is giving me signals. My whole body hums with anticipation. My pulse kicks up; my hands are sweaty. I can't stop thinking about what I want and how I can give her what she needs.

Then, she shifts, repositioning herself, and her thigh presses into mine. Fuck, it's going to make me fucking hard. I stay still. Don't move a muscle, holding my breath again, waiting for her next move.

If I shift away, she might think I don't want it. If I lean in, I may not stop. Her elbow bumps mine a moment later, and we both make awkward little laughs, like people do when they pretend they're not aware of every inch of their skin touching.

She clears her throat, "Sorry."

I shake my head, "You're good." But I'm not. I want to crawl on top of her and touch her body, watch her come undone while I fuck her into this couch. I am losing my goddamn mind.

She smells like citrus and almonds. A smell that makes you want to press your face into her and inhale to take her in.

I don't even realize I'm holding my breath until she moves again. And then, she slips her hand into mine like it's nothing. I look down, slow, unsure if I'm imagining it. Her fingers are laced with mine. Her hand, small, warm, and steady.

My chest tightens, my breath catches, and I can't stop myself from giving her a small squeeze in appreciation. But the rush of adrenaline I get from holding her hand makes me want more. I want to feel more of her.

She doesn't look at me. She keeps watching the screen like she hasn't set me on fire with the simplest touch. My hand is burning. A heat wave shoots through my entire body. I have to focus and control my breathing. If I weren't afraid of scaring her, I would kiss her.

And I... I don't know what to do with that. She's a fragile person in a weak state, and I have to protect her, even though I'm protecting her from myself. Under all the tension, I sense it. This quiet, hurt girl is cracking open for me.

The credits roll, and neither of us moves. The music is background noise to the storm of thoughts I've been trying to hold back since I walked through her door.

Her hand is still in mine. She shifts, her leg brushing mine again, her body moving a little closer. She's testing the space between us. I think she wants to close it, but isn't sure how.

God, I want to reach for her so badly. But I'm afraid I'll ruin it. I don't want to cross a line that she isn't ready for.

I sit here, pacing my breaths, waiting for her to let me know what's next. She turns toward me; her face soft and bright in the dim light of the TV's glow. There is something in her eyes, uncertainty or bravery. I can't tell. She's usually easy to read, but not tonight.

"I haven't felt... safe," she mutters, her voice barely above a whisper. "Not really. Not since it happened."

"You don't have to explain."

"No, I—" she takes a deep breath. "I want to."

I don't move. I let her talk.

"You make me feel safe, Loch. And I haven't even let myself think about why, or what I could even want or offer. But I... I'm more at peace here, around you tonight, than I have been in forever."

She looks down, her fingers tightening around mine, bracing herself.

"I want to kiss you," she says, "but I'm terrified."

Christ. Her honesty is warm and genuine. The vulnerability of it is making my chest tighten. The weight of what it means for her to say that out loud. To trust me with it.

I turn toward her, careful not to increase our contact, and ask, "Do you trust me?"

She hesitates for half a heartbeat, then nods. "Yeah. I do."

My hand moves before I can stop it—lifting gently, fingers brushing the side of her jaw. Her skin is warm, soft. Her body goes rigid for a moment, and I pause, but then she leans into my touch, wanting more. A flutter rushes through my chest and down my spine. My heart races, but I force my body to pull away to watch her reaction.

"I'm not here to take from you," I say. "We don't have to do anything you're not ready for."

"I know," she whispers.

I lean in, slow enough for her to get used to my increasing closeness. Far enough away to back off if she changes her mind. She doesn't, and I kiss her.

Soft. Slow. The kind of kiss that envelops your whole body.

Her lips tremble under mine, and she exhales into me. Her hand still clutches mine, holding on, not desperate, but needing the anchor. And I give it to her.

Everything else fades—the noise in my head, the doubt. It's just the two of us at this moment. Every one of my nerves fires, feeling her soft, plump lips on mine.

She pulls away; I rest my forehead against hers.

"Christ, Olive. You don't have to be afraid of me," I say. "Never. I will never cross any line you don't want crossed. I'm so proud of you for letting me in, letting me kiss you."

Her breath hitches, and she nods again. And in that quiet space, between heartbeats, I know... I'm falling, and I want her to be mine.

Before I know it, she backs away with an unsure look on her face.

"Loch, I'm sorry, I can't. I think you should go. Thank you for staying."

She doesn't have to say any more. It's time for me to go. I don't know what's changed. Is she upset? Did she not feel what I did? Did she not feel the shock waves flowing through our bodies like I did?

"Sure, no problem. I'll go. I should probably get home to take care of the dogs, anyway," I say, trying to act cool about this while wanting nothing more than to hold her. And kiss her again, and fucking stay here with her.

"Yeah. Umm, I'll text you tomorrow so we can plan another meeting for Kong and me? If that's ok?"

"Of course, get some sleep and we'll chat tomorrow."

Chapter 17
Olive

Damage Control

As soon as the door shuts behind Loch, I run to my phone.

Olive: I need to talk to you! Now. 911!!

Sophia: What happened?

Olive: I don't know???

Olive: Loch came over. Like, to my apartment.

Olive: I didn't go to the Kong meet-up because they released my attacker on bail, and he's the rich senator's son who will probably be free unless I testify. So I kind of had a meltdown all day.

Olive: And he just... showed up to check on me. Like some sexy, gorgeous superhero.

Olive: And then... we watched a movie... and I grabbed his hand. And then I sort of told him I wanted to kiss him. He fucking kissed me!!!!

Sophia: OMG. Are you breathing? Is your soul still in your body?

Sophia: And what the fuck is up with bail?! I'm so sorry, hun.

Sophia: SHUT. UP. You held hands and kissed?!?! YES!! Spill the details! Was it good?

Olive: Barely breathing, he was so gentle. Like he asked me if I trusted him... and when I said yes, he kissed me like... like he'd been waiting forever to do it, like it was a fucking movie. But also, I was terrified he might break me and pulled back.

Sophia: Oh my God! Was it good??? Like "curl your toes" good or "eh, he tried" good?

Olive: Soph. It was the kind of kiss that made me forget all the awful shit that happened today for like ten seconds. I felt safe and wanted. But I freaked out right after and told him to leave.

Sophia: Babe. Ok, first of all, I'm crying for you. Second, you DESERVE to feel that. Third, do not self-destruct about this. You are allowed to want him and be HAPPY! Just go slowly, but GO, babe!

Olive: Yeah. I know, but I'm scared. My body and brain are still holding onto everything, like muscle memory. And I don't want to mess this up, or ruin or hurt him.

Sophia: You're not going to ruin anyone. You're healing, and sometimes healing looks like trusting someone again. Even if it's terrifying. Has Loch given you any reason to think you shouldn't trust him?

Has he? I mean, if anyone has ever had a bigger green flag than running a freaking dog rescue, I'm not aware of it. He hasn't pressured me. Even before and after I held his hand, he didn't try to push any physical contact. I told him I trust him, and I do. But my body and brain are literally fighting against each other.

Olive: No, I... I don't know. I'm not ready. I don't know how to get over what happened.

Sophia: One step at a time. A handhold and a kiss was a great step. I'm proud of you. Even if you kicked him out. Which I think is hilarious, btw. Sorry.

Sophia: Ok, back to dumbass rich boy. I'm gonna scream. Like a full primal scream into the void. I hate this system. I hate him. But you're not alone in this. I am HERE! And it seems like Loch wants to be there for you, too. And Kong soon. Loch sounds like the kind of guy who'd burn down a city for you if you let him.

Olive: He would, and the scariest part is... that doesn't bother me. I'd let him.

Sophia: GOOD. Then, let him in. In your own time, when you are ready.

Olive: Also, please come over tomorrow so I can spiral in person.

Sophia: Say less. I'm bringing sweets and gossip, you supply the wine! We're unpacking all of it and making an Olive-gets-laid plan.

Olive: I'll agree to the wine. We'll see about the rest. Love you.

Sophia: Love you more.

I should text Loch and apologize for kicking him out.

Olive: Hey. Thank you for coming to check on me. I'm sorry if I was a mess. Could I come see Kong sometime this weekend? (Back back back)

Hey! Thank you for staying a while last night. It was nice. (Back, back, back)

Hey, are you available this weekend for me to come (Back, back, back)

Ugh, how many times am I going to rewrite this damn text?

Olive: Hey, thank you for checking on me. It was nice. Could I come see Kong this weekend?

Ok, Olive, fucking send it. Send.

Why do I feel like a kid in high school with a crush?

I try to go to bed, but my mind races with everything that has happened in the last twenty-four hours. And sleeping usually leads to nightmares, so I don't get much of it.

The next day, Sophia is already hollering at me as I open the door. Her arms are crossed, and her expression is somewhere between concerned mom and feral gossip gremlin. I hold up the bottle of wine, and she has a box of cheesecake.

"Permission to enter and witness you emotionally unravel?" She snatches the wine like I've offended her by hesitating. "Let's go, bitch."

I laugh despite myself, letting her in. I kick the door shut behind me, lock it, and trail her into the kitchen. I grab two wine glasses.

"You brought the good cheesecake," I say, peeking into the bakery bag. "I can't tell if we are celebrating or spiraling."

"Little bit of column A, little bit of column B," she laughs.

"I kissed the hot dog man, and now I don't know how to exist."

She chokes on a laugh as I pour the wine. "Please tell me that's what we can call him? Hotdog man?"

"Sophia! He's a hot-dog-man, not a hotdog man. I still have some standards."

I pass her a glass, and we flop down on my couch together, curling in, something we've done a thousand times before. This time, though, the mixture of emotion–stress from the asshole's release and nerves from a schoolgirl crush –has my insides buzzing.

Sophia blinks. "Wait. So. You grabbed his hand? You were open about your feelings? And he kissed you? Babe. Are you in a rom-com, or am I dreaming? How are you feeling today?"

I laugh, but it catches in my throat. "It wasn't just a kiss. It was... slow. He was so gentle, afraid to hurt or scare me. I've never been kissed like that. Kissing him threatened to break me open. But, it made me feel more... whole, too."

"Yeah, that sounds horrifyingly healthy," she says. "No wonder you're spiraling."

"I am." I lean my head back against the couch cushion. "I haven't felt like me in a long time. And it's terrifying. I can't even think of a time I was this connected to someone before my attack."

She says nothing for a moment and nudges the cheesecake toward me until I take a bite. My phone buzzes, and I look at the screen and then at Sophia.

"It's Loch. I texted him last night to apologize and make new plans to see Kong."

Sophia leans over me and asks, "Oh! What did he say?"

The text says, "It's fine, no worries. I enjoyed spending more time with you. I hope you're feeling better today. Sunday works for me. Would the afternoon work? Around 1?"

"What should I say back?"

"Tell him you would feel even better with some dick."

"Soph! Oh my God, stop it! Seriously. Help me."

"Is there something else you want to tell him?"

Why does Sophia have to know me so well? What do I want to tell him?

"I like him, and when I'm around him, a wave of calm washes over me. But also, thirty seconds after the calm, I panic. I can't say that to him, though."

"You're allowed to feel all that," she says. "You can want him and still be scared. You can take it slow. You don't have to know what comes next."

"I don't want to screw this up. I don't want to realize I'm too broken, and he leaves when I'm no longer fun or whatever."

"I mean, a handhold and a kiss are barely scratching the surface of fun, yet he still seems to want to see you again."

I roll my eyes at her. "Yeah, thanks. I'm so messed up and fucking damaged goods that a single kiss sends me into a panic."

"Stop, Olive. You're healing, remember? You are so strong, and so resilient."

She says it like it's the most obvious thing in the world. I sit in that for a second, chewing slowly, tasting more than sugar in my mouth. I taste the quiet that has settled in since Loch left. The space he left behind, the unease that returned when he was gone.

"Ok," I type out. "I enjoyed spending time with you as well. I'm trying. I'll see you Sunday at 1." And I hit send before I have time to overthink it and get feedback from Sophia.

"We need to work on your game, girl." Sophia glares at me.

I glance over at her, smiling at my friend. "I can't stop thinking about the bail situation. About him existing out there, like he didn't ruin my life." I swallow hard. "I think that's part of why I felt like I needed Loch last night. He was the only thing that took my mind off it."

Sophia reaches over and wraps her arms around me without a word. She doesn't squeeze too tight, holding me.

"I'm so goddamn glad you have someone who makes you feel more like yourself," she murmurs into my hair. "Do you think it's Kong or actually Loch that's helping?"

"Yeah," I whisper. "I honestly don't know. When Kong lay on my lap, I knew life would be ok. But Loch made me want to participate in that life again. But Soph, I just don't think I'm ready. I want to, but I'm not there yet."

After a few minutes, she pulls back, wiping at her eyes.

"Ok," she says. "Now, let's rewind. Start from the top and walk me through every single hot detail. And don't you dare skip the moment your thighs clenched."

I let out a real, deep belly laugh. "You're the worst."

She grins. "I know. Now spill."

Chapter 18

Loch

SHOW ME WHO'S IN CHARGE

Why am I sweating so much? This is the second shirt I've put on, and I should fucking change again before she gets here.

I've paced around my place like some lovesick teenager waiting for a prom date. Checking the mirror as if anything I do is going to fix the fact that I'm a grown man fully spiraling, because a woman is coming over. But it's not any woman.

It's her. My hand is still tingling from her touch, the way her tiny fingers hesitated before wrapping around mine like she wasn't sure if she was ready to reach for me. The way I have envisioned her hand gripping my cock ever since. When she told me she wanted to kiss me, I swear something shifted inside me. Something big. I want her, and I want to be good for her.

And now, I'm stuck here, hoping like hell that tonight isn't different. I put on my third fresh T-shirt and hope she doesn't walk through my door and pretend the kiss meant nothing. That it was only for comfort or a one-time act of bravery. That she doesn't already regret it.

If she does... If she looks at me like it was a mistake, I'll come undone. It will tear me apart thread by thread. The sharp pain in my chest already aches with worry. Not because I'm entitled to her, I'm not. She owes me nothing, especially not after everything she's been through. I want her anyway, because this is real. There's a tether pulling tight between us, not just sparks, and it's been there since the first time I saw her. I'm not some guy giving her a dog, but someone she can count on. Since the first time Kong leaned into her hand, knowing she was safe, I've wanted her to lean into me with the same trust.

I haven't wanted anyone like this in years. Hell, maybe ever. Not only her body—her curves, hips and thighs, and her lips and that soft little tongue of hers—but all of her. Her fire. Her quiet grief, the feeling of getting her to smile or laugh. When I hear her laugh, my chest aches to have more of her.

But I'm terrified I'll fuck it up. That I'll come on too strong; that I'll never be able to be honest with her about who I really am. That she'll see the part of me that isn't gentle, that doesn't simply rescue dogs, but breaks the people who hurt them. The part I've kept buried deep under the floorboards of my life.

Then, I remember how she looked at me when I kissed her, confident I wouldn't harm her. She knew I would protect her.

And for a moment, I let myself believe it.

I want her to know I'm not running. I'm not afraid of the dark parts. Whatever baggage she's carrying, she doesn't have to do it alone anymore; I'll help her carry it. Because I want to deserve her.

Her knock is soft. Hesitant. It cuts through me like a blade, causing a biting heat across my chest.

I open the door and there she is, hood up, head bowed, in her puffy jacket. She's still, bracing for something.

She lifts her eyes to mine for the briefest second before looking away. That one look is enough. She remembers. So do I. The second those eyes look at me, the sense of need consumes me.

"You came," I say, my voice low.

"Yeah," her tone is neutral, but there's something behind it. A crack she's trying hard to bury.

She steps inside before I can say anything else, no pleasantries. She hangs her coat up, not giving me the chance to do it for her. I trail behind her through the living room, then the kitchen. Her shoulders are drawn tight; she's on a mission to stay guarded.

She doesn't seem mad or upset, but determined to prove something. I follow her into the sunroom. Kong's already up, ears pricked. He barks once, sharp and deep. She startles and stands statue-still, but I let her do her thing, watching in utter fascination.

"Go ahead, give him a treat, and let him out," I gesture, giving her a slight challenge to see if she will ask for my help or not.

She reaches into her pocket, already prepared. Impressive. She tosses the treat through the bars. Kong sniffs it, eats it, then settles—not friendly, but not challenging either.

She crouches in front of the kennel, unlocking the latch with the confidence of someone who's done this a hundred times. Pretending he hasn't snarled at every stranger who's gotten near.

I lean against the doorway, arms crossed, watching her in awe. My voice drops an octave. "Leash him."

She hesitates for the first time. Her eyes fix on mine. There's something in them—want and fear tangled together in those crystal-clear, frozen-lake-colored eyes. I push off the doorframe and step closer. Not touching her, yet enough for her to feel the heat radiating between us.

"Go on," I say, voice smooth but firm. "Clip it on. Show him who's in charge." Her breath halts, and her eyes go wide with confrontation. She knows I'm not just talking about the dog. The ball is in her court.

I hold out the leash, and she reaches for it. Our fingers brush, and neither of us pulls away. Electricity, slow and searing. Her eyes are on my mouth now.

"Unless you'd rather I do it," I goad.

That gets her.

"I can handle him," she snaps, her fingers tightening on the leash. I smirk, but it doesn't reach my eyes. "I know you can."

She turns back to Kong and clips the leash to his collar with steady hands, but her face is flushed. Her breathing has changed. I stand behind her. The tension ripples off her skin as she turns to face me, Kong's leash in hand. She's standing close, feet braced apart, almost challenging. She's close enough to remind me of how her lips tasted when I kissed her.

"What now?" she asks, giving me a deep stare that I can't quite read.

Kong doesn't move. Doesn't growl. He watches her, waiting, respectful, and curious. I don't think I could be more impressed with her.

"Ready?" I ask. "Let's take him for a walk."

She nods, not looking at me. "Yeah."

We step out into the crisp, sunny day. Side by side, with Kong walking a few steps in front of us. Kong's massive frame is tense but manageable. His head is low, nose to the air. She keeps a firm grip on the leash, and I keep one eye on him, the other on her. I'm shocked at how easily she handles him, and that he lets her. He trusts her, almost as much as he does me.

She walks, looking straight ahead, trying to pretend nothing happened between us. Ignoring our kiss, and the fact that it was electric as fuck. She doesn't talk; she holds the leash and walks at a comfortable pace.

I live in an older neighborhood, and the sidewalks are narrow. Her shoulder brushes against mine, making me tense with anticipation.

The way she glances at me when she thinks I'm not looking tells me she wants more. Her shoulders lean in, fingers twitching as if resisting the urge to reach out. Maybe she's afraid of what it'll mean if she says it out loud. Or, maybe she's scared of me after all.

We get halfway down the block. I'm a little lost in my own thoughts, thinking that walking Kong is going to be easy. When a door slams a few feet in front of us. A kid sprints out of a driveway, laughing and yelling something to someone behind him. He's a blur of motion.

Kong snaps. He lunges with a savage bark, and Olive's not ready. The leash jerks in her hand, and she stumbles forward. Hard.

I move fast, one arm around her waist, yanking her back against me as my other hand shoots out and grabs the leash below the clasp.

"Hey now, it's ok, boy!" My voice is sharp but calm, commanding. Kong slows, pulling hard, but calming down. All the hackles on his back are up. He releases another bark and a few low grumbles, but he doesn't lunge again.

I hold him here. One hand wrapped tight around the leash and collar. One arm still locked around Olive's waist, her back pressed tight to my chest. She's not breathing, not moving, and neither am I.

"You ok?" I ask, keeping my tone gentle.

She nods, but she's still not moving. Her body's warm against mine, her hair brushing my jaw. I get a breath of that familiar smell of hers, citrus and almonds. And all I can think about is how easy it would be to turn her toward me. I want to kiss her again.

But I don't. Instead, I steady my voice and say, "You can't let him pull you like that."

She stiffens and moves away from me. I keep talking, gently releasing her from my grip so I don't cross into the creepy-guy-who-touched-her-a-little-too-long territory.

"When you take him out in public, you need to stay aware. Always."

"I didn't see the kid," she mutters.

"Exactly." I shift so we are facing each other, placing us inches apart. "You don't wait to react, Olive. You anticipate. You watch every angle, every door, every sound."

She releases a shaky breath.

"You need to be in control," I continue, quiet and deliberate. "He's powerful. If you're not two steps ahead, he'll take over. And once that happens, it's hard to get it back. If he gets loose, he could hurt someone and lose his life. You are responsible for keeping him safe, but in return, he will keep you safe, too."

Her body is still. I can feel the heat of her skin. Her chest grazes mine. Shame appears on her face, and failure in her eyes.

Wanting to reassure her and return the confidence she had two minutes ago, I whisper, "But if you stay calm..." I guide her hand back to the leash, slowly wrapping her fingers around it with mine. "If you stay grounded... he'll listen. He'll follow your lead."

She lifts her head, enough for our faces to be too close. Her lips part. She wants to say something, but nothing comes out.

I let go of the leash, my hand brushing against hers.

"Let's try again," I say, my voice rough with more than adrenaline.

But I don't move right away. Her lips part, eyes wide, pupils blown enough to make my heart lurch. Her chest rises and falls in shallow, uneven breaths, her breasts pushing against me with every inhale, and retreating every time she exhales. She's right here in front of me, and every instinct I have is screaming at me to take what I want. Grab her and pull her into me.

But I wait; I want her to decide what she wants. She leans forward a fraction, and our eyes lock.

Our mouths meet, and everything else disappears. It's slow at first, a brush of lips that turns into heat and need in a second. She presses into me, her hand finding my shirt, gripping the fabric, looking for a lifeline, not wanting to let go. Making me wonder if she's been wanting this as much as I have.

And then she's gone.

She pulls back like I burned her, eyes flashing with guilt and something that cuts deeper—fear. Not of me, I don't think... of us.

"I'm sorry," I say, breathless, stepping back.

"No," she interrupts, shaking her head, already moving a step away. "It's ok. I just–I can't..."

Those two words hollow out my chest. I nod, but the sting is real. I feel stupid for reading her wrong. For thinking she wanted the same damn thing I've been trying not to want since the second I met her.

The next block is painfully quiet.

Kong walks as though he's forgotten about the earlier incident. No pulling, no barking. He heels beside her as if they've been doing this for years.

I watch them, and there's a tight knot in my throat. Will I see her again?

At the last corner, I tell her, "You're good with him. And he's good with you."

She glances at me, wary. "Yeah?"

"Yeah." I pause. "You're ready, and he is, too."

She stops walking, and so do I.

Her eyes search mine, soft and confused. She doesn't know how to react to the fact that she can finally adopt him. I'm still giving her a piece of myself, even though she just tore into me without realizing how it hurt.

"I can bring him by tomorrow," I say quieter, then add, "and a few things for your place. His kennel, food, and a couple of things that might help him settle easier."

She swallows hard. I see her throat move up and down. Her lips are trembling.

"That would be... great." Her voice is not much more than a whisper, and her eyes are on Kong. "Thank you." She smiles at me. I can tell she hopes having Kong will make it all better. I wish it were me, but I can be happy for her and Kong anyway. I nod, and she doesn't meet my eyes again.

When we get back into the house, she bends down to unclip Kong's leash, gives him a small scratch behind the ear, and returns him to his kennel. He looks at her with respect and trust. She's his now. There's no question. I've never been more jealous of a dog in my life.

She stands up, not looking at me.

"Bye," she says, already turning.

"Yeah," I say. "Bye."

And then she's gone. Pushing me away again. Just like the last time.

Only this time... I think I have ruined whatever was building between us. It might be time for me to let Kong and her go. Let them have the future they both deserve. The thought of not seeing Olive anymore makes my chest ache and my pulse spike, but I have to accept it anyway.

Chapter 19
Olive

Kiss and Confess

The door clicks shut behind me, and I let the breath I've been holding since I left his house escape. I lean back against its solid surface, eyes closed, chest clenching. Why did I pull away?

Because it scared the hell out of me, or because it didn't?

It felt good. Too good. And that's the problem. I don't know how to be normal anymore. I don't know who I am, so how can I possibly know what I want?

The second his mouth touched mine, I forgot how to breathe, forgot everything that's happened over the past few weeks. I've been hiding inside my apartment and myself. It's easier to deal with my past on my own. I don't need anyone else to save me.

But for a second, I wanted to disappear into him. I needed to feel him. I wanted him.

I pace the room, hoping that the answers will find me. I glance at the clock. It's not even that late, but the awkward walk around the block with Loch was as if I'd lived a whole week. I plop on the couch and bury my face in my hands. There are so many feelings I need to sort through, and I don't know where to begin. My skin tingles where his hand caught my waist, and where his voice settled behind my ear like a secret. His scent, amber and vanilla, the perfect, calming, and romantic aroma, has settled in my memory. I can't get him out of my head. He's consuming me.

I shouldn't have left him the way I did. He probably thinks I either hate him or that I'm a total idiot. I want to set things right with him, but I don't know what I could say.

I need to stop thinking about it. Kong, focus on Kong.

Sophia! That's something. Something rational. If he's going to live here, she needs to meet him. Right?

I grab my phone, thumbs already moving.

Olive: Hey. I've been thinking... Would you help me introduce Kong to Sophia at some point? I want her to feel safe around him.

I stare at it, waiting. Not entirely what I wanted to say. But better than: I miss you already, and I acted like a moron today, and I don't know what to do with that.

Another beat. Then–

Loch: That's smart. Let's get him settled first. A week or two will help. Let him learn your space. Let him feel at home with you first. After that, I'll come by and teach you.

Of course. Measured. Calm. Like always. Why is that so endearing?

I should stop there, but my brain won't let me. When we were walking outside, and Kong lunged at the kid, I didn't handle it very well. I was kind of an asshole to Loch, even though he saved my ass. I keep replaying the moment our lips met, and how I felt his breath hitch. How the feeling of my hand on his warm, hard chest made my thighs clench and my clit throb.

I type again before I can overthink it.

Olive: About earlier... You didn't do anything wrong.

Olive: I get overwhelmed when emotions are intense. I'm still sorting things out.

I chew my lip. I don't regret kissing him. I'm not upset that he tried again, but I don't know how to act. I don't know how to be ready to feel all the feelings. When I close my eyes for too long, I get flashbacks of being attacked. His weight, the pain from the next morning. The brace that held my wrist. It is a constant reminder that I'm damaged and afraid.

Loch: You didn't do anything wrong either; I'm not trying to push you into anything you don't want or are not comfortable with.

Loch: We're both figuring it out. But I'm not going anywhere.

God. Is he tossing me a lifeline or baiting a trap? My heart flutters at his understanding.

Loch: Let me know if you need anything. For you, or for him. Even though Kong is yours soon, I'll always be around to help with him.

He doesn't say anything more. But the space between the words makes my heart ache. He's holding himself behind a wall, hoping I'll open the door and let him inside.

I should say something. Offer something back. I don't know what, though.

Olive: Thanks. I will.

I cannot commit to anything else. I'll work up to it.

It's weird to put on makeup again. Even weirder to be going out of the house, voluntarily.

But when Sophia texted earlier, "Come keep me company and have a drink at the bar tonight, I'm off early and can take you home. You need to get out of the house and socialize!"

I didn't overthink it; I didn't think about it much at all. I texted, "Yes," even though my anxiety wants to pull me under the covers, and there's a deep pain in my stomach from nerves. I look in the mirror, trying to see the old me. The fun me, who enjoyed going out and being around people. The me that didn't take any shit and was confident, witty, and always ready for the next adventure. I've only left the house to make necessary runs to the grocery store and for meetings with Kong. All I do is sit in my apartment and watch TV, and sleep. I have become a zombie, living in sweats and T-shirts for weeks.

But tonight, I'm in my black fitted jeans and pink tank. I used to work out and have what I call a softball player's body, thick but athletic. I stare at the reflection looking back at me, admiring the body I love, my thick thighs and waist, and large breasts that I can flaunt. Or, at least I used to flaunt, but I keep the girls covered tonight with a gray flannel over my tank top. I don't want to draw any unwanted attention.

With a sigh, I tell the woman I faintly recognize, "You can do this." Trying my hardest to believe it's a minor victory.

The bar is loud when I walk in. Familiar music thumps through the speakers, and the smells of whiskey and fryer oil wrap around me like an old friend. At first, it's comforting, but as soon as it hits me, I tense, forcing every single step in front of the other. I'm hot and sweaty, looking around, desperate to find Sophia.

"Look what the cat dragged in!" Todd's booming voice cuts through the room.

I manage a smile and a wave before he leans over the chair next to him, grinning.

"You've been dodging us?" he teases. "I got a new one for you—what's the difference between a G-spot and a golf ball?"

I already know I'm going to regret asking. "What?"

"A guy'll actually *look* for a golf ball."

I groan, but the laugh comes out anyway. It feels good. A little rusty, but genuine.

"We've missed you, kid," he says.

"Missed you, too, Todd." I appreciate his affection. I miss parts of my old life and people like Todd, however crazy he might be. He's good people.

Sophia appears across from him, behind the bar. She's smirking, "You're lucky I love you and your horrible jokes."

Todd grins and goes back to chatting with others at the bar.

I take the stool across from her. "Your usual, Stoli Blueberry and lemonade?"

"Thanks," giving her a warm, grateful smile. My hands curl around the cold drink she puts in front of me.

"You look better," she says, eyeing me like she's trying to read past my face. "But something's on your mind. Are you nervous about Kong coming home?"

I shrug. "I don't know. It's... a lot. Coming out tonight. Everything with Loch. With Kong. With me."

"Ok, one problem at a time," she says, tilting her head. "What's actually holding you back with Loch?"

I open my mouth. Nothing comes out.

She waits.

Finally, I breathe the words, "I can't bring myself to think about a relationship. I'm afraid of not being ok if I allow him in. When I think about him touching me, I panic. Who wants to be with someone like that?"

Sophia leans in, her voice soft but firm. "You've already survived so much worse than that. You didn't crawl your way out of that hellhole to live a lonely, half-assed life now. You told me that when you're with him, you can get the past out of your head for a minute. Maybe he's the answer, not the problem."

I glance down at my glass, blinking hard. Her words hit deep, making my pulse rise, and I get hot again. I take three big gulps, downing half the glass.

"You want him," she says. "I know you do."

"I do," I admit. "But I don't know how to let myself want that again and not fall apart."

Sophia's eyes soften. "Then tell him that."

"Tell him what?"

"Next time you see him, when he drops off Kong, ask him to stay and talk to you. Tell him you don't know what you need, but you like him and you feel better when he's around. Then both of you can talk about where to go from there."

I shake my head. "It's not that simple." How can I explain something to him that I don't even understand?

"It's not supposed to be simple," she says. "But it can be honest. If he's worth your time, then allow yourself to see what he's about."

She leans closer. "Tell him you need to push boundaries, but you're not sure how, and that it scares you. That you want to explore what's on the other side of all that fear. And that you don't know how to do it alone. Let him decide what he wants to do with that. If he's willing to go slow, then you're willing to try."

My throat tightens. My eyes sting; I feel them getting heavy with tears. I take another sip, feeling the slight burn from the heavily poured drink.

"Start there," she says. "The rest will come."

I nod. I may not be ready for everything, but I'm done letting fear win over my desire to live my life. I'm ready to stop running from the one person who feels like an escape from my reality. The one who makes me forget the pain.

Changing the subject, Sophia asks, "So, are you excited to finally have Kong come home?"

"I can't wait. I bought him the biggest dog bed I could find. I got like four boxes of toys from Amazon. I'm glad he is a protective dog, but I'm ready for a companion, someone to keep me company. Even though I see you and talk to you and my parents, it's been lonely."

"Girl, I get it. I wish I could come and hang out more, too. I'm so happy for you. When do I get to meet him?"

"Loch said to give him a couple of weeks to settle, to feel at home. And then he'll come help me introduce him to you."

"Damn, I have to wait weeks? Does that mean I can't come over for that long?"

"No, you're still welcome anytime. He'll stay in his kennel or my bedroom while you're over."

"Ok, well, tell me when he's ready and I'll be there, ready to get my hand bitten off." She laughs, like it's not partially true.

Chapter 20

Loch

IN THEN OUT

I heave a breath, standing in front of her door, and knock.

I know she's expecting me, but my chest tightens thinking she's going to open the door and tell me she's changed her mind. About Kong.

The door opens. Her hair is up, as usual. She's in a soft oversized black hoodie, shorts, and her feet are bare. She's smiling at me, thank God, until she looks down and realizes I don't have Kong with me. She glares at me, confused, her heart breaking in the four seconds I've been here.

"Hey," I say with a melancholy smile.

"Hey," she answers, confused. There's a radiating warmth behind her tone. Something I haven't felt the last few times I've seen her.

"You mind coming outside with me to get him?" I ask, jerking my chin toward the car. "It's better if he sees you before the front door. Cleaner reintroduction."

She nods, and her huge smile returns.

"I didn't sleep at all last night. I have been so excited for today!" she says, grabbing her keys off the counter and slipping on her shoes.

I hand her two liver treats as we walk.

"Hold them in your palm when we get close," I tell her. "Let him come to you and give him a second. Like usual."

When we reach the car, I pop the door open.

Kong's head lifts immediately, ears alert, but the second he sees her, he settles. One slow, steady wag of the tail. Then another.

And when she steps forward and holds her hand out? No hesitation.

He jumps down, sniffs her palm, and gently takes the treat. Her fingers brush against his nose, and he's hers. She grabs his leash as it drags out of the car behind him and gives him a scratch behind the ears.

I look at her in time to catch her unfiltered, joyous smile.

As she's petting him, she starts her baby talk, "Hello buddy, who's my big, sweet guy? Are you ready to see your new home? I have so many treats for you, bubby."

I can't take my eyes off her smile, wide and bright. An energy exudes from her that I haven't seen before. If the sun cracked open for a second and landed on her face, this is how it would look. She's beaming.

I can't move. I don't even breathe. I stare, like a goddamn idiot, because of that smile. Fuck, I would do a lot of reckless shit to see her light up more often.

Back inside, I force myself into motion. I want her to be mine, but it's clear that she only needs Kong. I don't linger; I don't hover. I move around the apartment with mechanical focus, setting up the crate in a corner that feels calm. I place his blanket inside, showing her the food portioned out in the containers I brought.

I see she has gotten him a huge dog bed that's sitting right next to her bed. I turn to look for her, and I see her and Kong already snuggled up on the couch. He has his face nuzzled into her lap, and she is stroking his back and butt, giving him scratches on his cheek. I hear her talking to him, but I can't make out what she is saying.

I still can't understand how they bonded so fast. I don't even think he's sat with me on the couch. He usually lies on his bed. My heart warms, realizing he's going to finally have his person, someone who loves him exactly the way he is. No neglect or being left on a chain. No more pain. He deserves it. He's a sweet dog. Now, he has a gigantic bed, so many toys I can't even begin to count them, and he's already so loved.

Fuck, I'm jealous of a dog again. How it must feel to be loved by Olive.

"Food twice a day," I say, voice clipped. "He's picky, so wet it a little if he turns his nose up. It's normal for dogs to sometimes not eat when they are in a new environment for a day or two. I'm also giving you a can of wet food if you need to entice him a little. I know it's tempting, but watch the amount of treats you give him. You don't want them making him sick or fat."

She nods, watching me. I avoid her gaze.

I point to the leash and harness by the door. "He already knows this is his. I'll leave it here. Put it on before opening the door every time. And if you need me—"

"Loch."

I stop mid-sentence.

She's standing in the middle of the room now, arms crossed, not defensive, but holding herself together.

"Will you stay for a bit?" she asks. Her voice is gentle and unsure. "While he settles. And we can talk... about the other day?"

The words hit me square in the chest. Despite wanting this more than anything, I'm unprepared. I was ready to walk away and give Olive the space she asked for.

I blink. Almost apprehensive, because I'm not sure I'm ready for another letdown. I have tried to accept that she needs time and space, and that I need to give it to her. Accept that she doesn't need me. Nonetheless, I can't resist her.

"Sure. Yeah, of course."

She sits back down on the couch. I try not to be too eager, but my heartbeat picks up, and I'm jittery with anticipation. It's stupid to get excited about something so small. But she's asking me to stay. Whatever it is she's after, I'm here.

I take off my jacket and hang it on the chair on the island, and sit down next to her on the couch, but not too close. I give her and Kong their space. For a second, the silence feels heavy.

We sit in the quiet, watching Kong breathe, slow and even, on her lap. His chest rises and falls like he's always belonged here. Like she's home for him.

She glances over at me, then back at him.

"He's so sweet," she says softly. "I didn't think he'd be this gentle and affectionate."

I nod. "He's a good boy. Once he trusts you, he is a total lover. That's what's so special about the difficult dogs. They only show that side to a few people, and if you're lucky enough to be one of them, they reward you big time. They just need someone to give a shit. And it's clear to me that you're his person. He's taken to you in a way that, honestly, I've never seen. Circumstances compelled him to trust me; he chose to trust you."

She smiles again, smaller this time, thoughtful. "I've known a lot of pitties. Most of them smile, you know? That big dopey grin. But he doesn't. I remember from the picture in his bio that he looked sad."

I follow her gaze. Kong is still relaxed; his face is calm, neutral. But she's right, no grin.

"Maybe he just needs a reason to," I say. "Maybe you will give that to him."

Her eyes flick to mine. And for a moment, she gazes deep into my eyes, as if she's trying to tell me something with the way she looks at me. I don't know what it is, though.

Then she shifts, curling one leg up under her, sitting forward a little like she's trying to center herself.

"I have to say something," she says. "And I need you to let me get it out."

My pulse jumps. I nod.

She exhales. "I like you, and I enjoy spending time with you." The words are quiet, but they land like thunder in my chest. "When I'm with you, I feel... calmer, secure. Like—" her voice wavers, "like maybe I'm not so broken." Her eyes are glassy, suppressing tears, but steady and brave.

"I want to give you a chance," she says. "I do. But every touch takes me back to that night. It all comes back, his smell, his weight on me, my hands and mouth. All of it takes over."

My fists clench, and I grind my teeth to keep from saying anything.

She keeps going. "When I held your hand, it was nice. I was ok, but it took everything in me to get there, and I'm scared that one day you'll get bored waiting for me to be ok with the next step."

"I won't," I start, my voice rough. I feel her words in my chest, but also lower. Deeper. She lifts her hand to stop me.

"I'm not finished," she says, eyes soft. "I want to try to climb the mountain. I want you to help me. I want you to touch me. But I don't know when I'll be ready. I want you to help me push past this."

My throat is dry. My heart is pounding. And yeah, my dick's definitely responding to all this talk of her needing my touch. Wanting me to help her, like she doesn't know that's exactly what I would want, anyway. Jesus, get it together. This isn't about that.

I shift forward, leaning in, and place my hand on top of hers. She doesn't flinch. Doesn't pull away.

Her skin is warm, and my thumb brushes her knuckles. Nothing more, but enough to say, *I hear you. I see you. I'm here.* "I'll do whatever you need. However long it takes. However slow. I'm not going anywhere, Olive. You make me feel different, too. Like you won't judge me, you make me feel joy when I'm around you."

Her lashes lower, her breath catches, but she doesn't let go of my hand. And in the silence that follows, Kong lets out the softest snore.

The corner of her mouth lifts. And just like that... I'm back in. She hasn't let go of my hand yet, and I don't want her to. The quiet between us isn't awkward. It's full. Heavy in a way that anchors us.

"I don't know what it is about you," I say, thumb still brushing over her skin. "But you're different. I've been interested in you since the moment we met."

Her cheeks flush the prettiest shade of pink, and it's so fucking adorable I want to touch her and more. Her brows lift, a slight furrow between them. "Different how?"

"You understand what pain is. And what it can do to someone. I feel safe with you, too, like you won't judge me. Whatever it is, I think it's the same thing Kong sees."

She tilts her head, confused. "What would I judge you for?"

My jaw tightens. I can't tell her about the bad things I do. I need to change the subject to distract myself from the rising weight in my chest. But she's looking at me like I'm safe, and for a second, I believe I am. I want to be. For her. Olive is safe with me because I'm protecting her from the truth.

So, I let the words come out slowly. I want to lie, but I settle on a half-truth. "There's a side of me I don't show many people," I say. "A part that holds onto my past. A side that struggles to forgive and forget."

She doesn't speak. Doesn't fill the space with questions or sympathy.

She waits and listens with a curious expression, and fuck, that does something to me.

Then—

Buzz. Buzz.

I grab my phone out of my pocket and read the screen. Unknown name? But I know the number. And the second I read the message, the blood drains from my face and begins to boil.

Unknown: He's free, at his sister's home. 2841 N Middlefield Rd.

I clench my jaw and shove the phone back into my pocket. My whole body goes tense in a single moment.

"Loch?" Olive's voice is cautious. "Everything ok?"

I force a breath out through my nose. This couldn't be worse timing. My hand's already pulling away from hers, even though it kills me to do it.

"I'm sorry," I say, standing too fast, causing her to flinch. "I need to go. I'm sorry." Watching her reaction breaks me for a second. I hate that it has to be this way.

Her eyes widen. "Is everything–"

"I'll call you soon," I cut in. "I promise. I... something important came up."

She's nodding, her walls creeping back up like I slapped her. After she's finally agreed to let me in. "I'll come back," I add, softer this time. "Later. Tonight, if I can, otherwise, tomorrow, I'll bring you breakfast. I promise I'll be back."

She doesn't ask questions. Doesn't beg, or press, or accuse.

With a voice so quiet I almost miss it, she says, "Ok." I hate walking away. My chest aches and my fists tighten, knowing I have to leave and seeing the pain in her eyes.

My stomach twists in knots, not because of what I'm walking into, but because of what I am leaving behind, and what I have to do.

Chapter 21

Olive

A Tail of Injustice

I sit for a bit with Kong after Loch leaves. I feel like I've stepped off a roller coaster, nauseous and trying to recover from the adrenaline rush. It went so well, talking to him. I felt good about, you know, trying this thing with him. And then it took such a sudden turn. He just left.

But the quiet is louder now. I'm so thankful to have Kong here. I don't feel so alone. I can focus on his snoring and petting his soft fur. Kong still snuggles into me. Loch's scent lingers. It's clean and masculine, with hints of amber.

Something about the way he left, the way his face changed after reading that message... it scratched at something inside me. Was it someone from the rescue? Did something happen? I want to text him, ask if he's ok, but I stop myself. He said he'd call. I'll give him that space.

I glance at the TV, which has been murmuring in the background for the last hour. A picture of a pitbull on the screen draws my attention. I pick up the remote and turn up the volume. A news anchor is speaking in that clipped, rehearsed way they do when they're trying not to sound too emotional.

"...charged with multiple counts of animal cruelty and dog-fighting, Mike Thomson has been released from prison due to overcrowding after serving only ninety-five days of his six-month sentence."

I freeze, dread creeping in. A photograph flashes across the screen—a grainy, cold image of a backyard full of mud, chain-link cages, chains, and bones. Literal bones.

"Officials report removing over fifty dogs from the property. The majority of the dogs were emaciated, flea-infested, and scarred. Some were believed to be used as bait dogs. At least a dozen that they found were deceased; others were in such poor condition that they had to be humanely euthanized. Some animal activist groups have been upset over the lack of punishment for animal abusers. The groups have been showing up at the courthouse to protest his release."

I switch off the TV; my stomach twists in knots, and my hands tremble in a mix of anger and fear.

I fumble for my phone and start searching for more information on the case. Scrolling through articles, one after another—gruesome pictures, statements, and graphic descriptions and details.

Fifty-three dogs, dozens of remains from dogs that came before. Fighting and bait dogs. Neglected, starved, and tortured for years. Forced to fight to the death for hours and hours while sustaining brutal injuries.

My eyes well up. I blink, and the tears fall down my cheeks. I look down at Kong, curled up next to me. He looks so peaceful. His eyes are closed. He lies on his side with his head in my lap, curled into a ball. Seeing his relaxed body warms my heart, especially when I think of the day we met and how much he's learned to trust me. What did he go through before Loch saved him? I can't imagine Kong having to go through the trauma of fighting, his gentle soul beaten down into broken, discarded pieces. What if that had been him?

How many dogs like him don't get this happy of an ending? How many dogs are thrown away like garbage, unloved?

My hand clenches around my phone. I can't stop shaking, and then the thought hits me like a knife to the chest, sending shooting, hot pain throughout my body.

Six months. That's what that man got. Six months, fuck, and not even serving the time he was sentenced to. For breaking the bodies and spirits of animals who did nothing but exist.

And what about my abuser? My rapist? What will he get? What will his punishment be for hurting me, taking from me? Ruining my life? The one who shattered all of me, and I'm still trying to put myself back together.

What if he gets six months? What if he walks away with a slap on the wrist and a simple, don't do it again? The sob rips out of me before I can stop it. I press the heels of my palms to my eyes, trying to stop the tears. I'm so tired of crying over this fucking monster. But my chest tightens, my throat closes, and I can't swallow the scream building in the back of my throat.

It's not the dogs or even me. Not the system. It's unbearable knowing that people get away with this. That some things and some people are expendable. Some rules only apply to some people.

Walking off into the sunset, they leave behind a trail of hurt, used, and broken beings.

And those of us lucky enough to survive, we're the ones that carry the weight of it. We carry the pain, bruises, and fear every single day for the rest of our lives.

I curl into myself on the couch, hunching over in panic, tears soaking into my pants. Kong lifts his head, sensing the shift in me. He looks at me, and I look at him.

"I promise to always protect you." As if he understands me, he stretches his paws over my legs and pushes his head into my chest. Kong looks up at me with literal puppy-dog eyes, as if to tell me it's ok.

I reach for him with trembling fingers, and when I touch his fur, the sobs come harder. Not because it hurts more, but because in that one gesture, I remember. There is still good left in the world.

Rescued

He experienced trauma and survived. He was rescued, shown love, and taught to trust. Even if we are both a little broken by society's standards, he's mine, and I'm his. It's enough; it has to be.

Chapter 22
Loch

BREAKING BRAD

The house is silent when I walk in. The kind of quiet that seeps into your skin, stiff and thick. The familiar scents of dust and rot settle into my lungs and throat.

I've stripped the house of furniture over the years. The only thing I left behind is a single wooden chair and an old, splintered, and leaning table in the front room. A place that used to be someone's home, now left to decay. My boots echo against the worn floorboards as I cross the room.

When I open the basement door, the air is heavy with mildew, sweat, metal, and human waste. The odors invade my senses; my nose burns, and my eyes water.

The stairs creak under my weight, only stopping once I reach the concrete floor below.

I pull the small chain and turn on the light. The bulb hums above me, flickering in and out like it's trying to die.

Three pairs of eyes look up. Brad is stuffed into a dog kennel only big enough to sit, his knees pulled to his chest. His skin is smeared with years of old grime; feces dried against the bars. His hair is long, and he's completely given up. When I first brought him here, he would scream and holler at me all day long. Now, he watches–silent, hollow, and twitchy.

Roy is chained to a bolt on the floor. A thick metal collar is locked tightly around his neck, rust blooming at the seams, a padlock hanging from it, just like his dogs were. The collar cuts into his neck and leaves sores on his body. His movements are animalistic, full of rage, pacing tight circles in the three-foot range he's allowed. His fingernails are broken, and most of his body is torn up and bruised from fighting the chain. His mouth is always running, spitting nonsense and slurs that mean nothing down here, nothing to me. He's violent and angry, and full of spite.

And pathetic Greta, curled up in a five-by-five kennel, the only one with a blanket and a dented metal bucket. She doesn't speak much. Weighs maybe eighty pounds now. Her eyes used to be sharp and mean. Now they're dull and distant. She deserves worse, but I can't stomach looking at her for too long. I'm hoping she starves to death soon.

The room itself is no better. Mold creeps along the bottom edges of the wall. A drain runs down the center of the concrete floor–stained dark with things I stopped trying to clean. The only light comes from the single flickering bulb overhead.

I walk past them without a word. The only sounds are of rattling chains and a soft whimper from Brad. I hate coming here. I hate taking over this role. But someone had to deliver justice to those the law didn't think deserving. I'll bear that weight if I have to.

I grab a heavy chain–thick, welded, and rusted–off the wall. I go to open another large kennel like Greta's, unlocking it and preparing it. It won't be empty for long.

I slam the basement door behind me and leave the house. An hour later, I come back and pull into the garage.

The car door shuts, and all I hear is the quiet thud of my boots on concrete and then the scuff of something heavy, as I drag the body from the trunk behind me.

Mike doesn't fight. I sedated him enough to get him in my car. He moaned a little during the drive, but I don't think he realizes what's happening to him yet. I notice the cloth bag over his head is soaked with sweat as I haul him down into the basement. He's making sounds and twitching his hands; the drugs are beginning to wear off. I only have a little more time until he comes to.

The moment I flick the light on again, the others stir. Roy snarls, baring his teeth like a rabid animal. Brad lets out a low cry and curls in tighter. Greta doesn't even move.

I drag Mike forward and throw him inside the kennel. He falls hard, grunting through the gag, and I yank the sweaty bag from his head. He blinks, disoriented and barely awake.

Perfect.

I lock the kennel, twisting the metal tight and sliding the bolt in place. I crouch so I'm eye level with him. "Welcome, Mike," I hiss. "That's Brad, Roy, and Greta." I pause, letting the names settle in the air.

"They've been here a while. But you'll get to know them, and they can catch you up. Have fun." He tries to say something, but the gag muffles it. It doesn't matter.

I stand slowly, the weight of what I've done again, settling in. I want to be anywhere else. I'm so tired of looking at them and doing this; I don't even want to think about them anymore. Rage and a need for vengeance are the only things that keep me coming back.

I want to be there, on Olive's couch, with her hand in mine, talking about Kong and trying to get her to smile again. I want to hear how her voice gets soft when she says my name.

I exhale, hands on my hips, staring at the ground. I've never had a dog-fighter down here before. I'm not sure what to do with him. But I know he deserves worse than anything I can do.

Still, my mind drifts back to her. To the way she looked up at me before I left. The way she made me feel like someone worthy of knowing her.

I turn the light off and look at my phone to see it's after midnight. I'll just text her; it's too late to go see her.

Loch: Hey, Olive, sorry it's late, and I'm sorry about earlier. Just wanted to let you know I'd be stopping by tomorrow with breakfast. Have a good night. I want to continue our conversation.

And the basement goes dark again. The way it's supposed to be.

Chapter 23
Olive

Meat Cute

The knock at the door comes as I finish brushing my teeth, having just crawled out of bed.

Kong beats me to it—barking like someone is breaking in, his whole body launching from the rug like a missile. I gasp and jump to my feet, heart pounding as I move to calm him.

"Kong, it's ok," I coo, opening his kennel door and coaxing him in with a treat. He goes, reluctantly, still growling under his breath as I lock the kennel and turn toward the front door.

I look through the peephole to see Loch standing at the door, looking hot. He has on a fitted T-shirt and jeans, but his hair is a little wilder. And damn, I look haggard in a crop top, no bra, and sweats. My hair is probably crazy. Thank God I brushed my teeth. I take a deep breath. Kong is still barking his head off, and I want him to stop. I need to open the door and not worry about what I look like.

"Hey," I say, my breath catching the second I see him smiling at me. He's holding a paper bag out to me, the early light making his eyes look even more golden than usual.

"Brought breakfast," he says, offering an apologetic smirk. And I catch him looking me up and down. His eyes become dark and focused when they finally make their way back to mine. Given my appearance, I'm not sure how he could like what he sees. But my stomach warms, and I blush anyway.

Kong falls quiet as soon as he hears Loch's voice and settles. It's as if some invisible switch flips. I feel it, too. That calm I only seem to find when he's nearby.

"I wasn't sure if you liked bacon or sausage, so I got two of each."

I blinked at him for a second, then grinned, "I'm actually a vegetarian."

Loch goes pale. The silence stretches a second too long, his lips parting with his apology.

"I can go back and get you a potato burrito; I'm so sorry, Ol." I hold back a laugh, biting my lip.

"I'm kidding, I loooove meat," I say, with far more enthusiasm than I mean. His eyes snap to mine. Oh. Oh, no. Did I just say that out loud?! Now, heat flares in my cheeks.

My weirdness hangs in the air between us, thick and wildly inappropriate at nine in the morning.

I clamp a hand over my mouth, eyes wide, then snort. "God. That sounded–"

Loch shakes his head, smiling now. "I wasn't gonna say it." He sits down at the tiny island that serves as my kitchen table.

"Can I get you some coffee?"

"Please, black."

"Of course," I say. "I remember."

I pour two mugs and join him at the bar, pulling my legs up under me on the stool.

"So..." I start, wrapping my fingers around the warm ceramic mug. "Last night, you kind of disappeared."

Loch's expression tightens. He's not defensive but guarded.

"Something came up, something personal," he says. "It wasn't a big deal. I'm sorry for leaving in a hurry." His tone makes it clear that's all he plans to say.

I nod, letting it go, but keeping it stored for later. I don't want to push.

I open my mouth to say something else, then gasp and clutch my chest. "Kong!"

I jump up, setting my mug down and rushing to the kennel. "Sorry, buddy." I open the door, and he comes bounding out. He trots straight to Loch, tail wagging, and leans all eighty pounds of his body into him, desperate for the pets he'd been waiting for all night.

"He missed you," I murmur.

Loch looks down at him with a fondness that's so natural it aches to watch. "How'd he do overnight?"

"Perfect," I say. "I thought he might be anxious. But he ate all his food, passed out on his bed, and snored like a grown man."

Loch laughs, an actual, warm, heavy laugh. "Yeah, I noticed you bought him a bed. It's massive. I'm sure he loves it."

"He hasn't stopped rolling on it, like he's trying to rub all his smells on it. He thinks he's royalty now. Oh my God, it was so cute. I gave him that little stuffed duck, and he slept with it curled under his head like a little baby. I think I have 800 pictures of him sleeping. I sent 700 of them to Sophia."

I lean against the counter, watching Loch and Kong interact. "Can I ask you something?" He eyes me with curiosity, wrinkling his brow. "I want to know more about you," I continue.

Loch's mouth curves up at one side. "What do you want to know?"

"Where are you from?"

"Here. Always been here. Never left."

"College?"

He shakes his head. "No. Got my real estate license a few years after high school. And now, I manage a few dozen properties. That's what pays the bills while I focus most of my time on the rescue."

I nod, thinking of what else I want to know. "Family?"

"My mom's still around. I see her as often as I can. Dad passed from lung cancer about ten years ago. I've got a sister; she's fourteen years older. We were never close because of our age difference."

He looks down at Kong, smoothing his hand along his back. "I visit my sister once a year in Denver. Mostly for my nephew; he's seven, and he loves to fish, so I take him fishing every year."

I smile, watching him talk about his family. I can tell how much he loves them.

"I'm from Southern California, a small town called Carlsbad. I came here for college. Nursing school, originally. But I dropped out after a year. It didn't feel right. I loved the medical aspect, but it didn't appeal to me like I had hoped."

He nods, as if he understands the feeling.

"I've been bartending for a while now, maybe too long, but I haven't gone back to work since... you know. My parents have been helping me get by. They own this building, as well as many others. My dad is also in real estate. Now, I'm trying to figure it all out, I guess."

"What about your parents? Where are they now?" he asks.

"Still together in Cali. My mom's a nurse, still working. My dad retired last year from the brokerage company he ran. They're kind of invasive. I'm an only kid, so it's like they transferred all their hopes and fears to me. They can be a little overprotective and overbearing, but I guess I kind of appreciate that, too."

He chuckles under his breath. And it surprises me how easy this conversation is. How natural it feels.

"Hey, did you see the news last night? I saw there was a man released from prison after only serving ninety-five days. He ran a dog-fighting ring. It broke my heart to think about all those defenseless animals. Did you help with any of the dogs?"

He stills and looks at me with a questioning expression. Then, he scowls and pinches his brows.

His response to my question confuses me. "What? Did I say something?"

"No, you didn't. I just, yeah... I can't stand our system. There's no punishment for these people. I met a lot of the dogs on site; it was hard to see. We have two of them still in foster care, and one was adopted. They're looking good now, healthy and happy. But they have issues, which is why we took the more severe cases."

I need to change the subject; I can feel the tension radiating off him, as well as the pain and anger he holds.

I glance out the back window and smile. "Want to walk Kong with me?"

Loch lights up, like a kid in a candy store, and it makes my stomach flutter.

"Of course."

We leash Kong and head out back into the little clearing behind the building, where there are very few people around. Kong sniffs and wanders, eventually plopping onto his side and rolling in the dried brown grass. When he's done, he lies there with both his feet sticking out behind him, reminding me of a frog soaking up the sun in the cooler weather.

I giggle at his silly antics, and I feel Loch's hand tighten around mine. He pulls me closer, turning to face me. He kisses me.

His mouth is warm and familiar and still new, and I lean in without thinking. When he softly licks my bottom lip, I let his tongue in. Let him taste me, and taste him in return. His breath tastes like rich, nutty coffee. And when his arm pulls me a little closer, I let myself go completely, my body warms, and my core tenses, making me clench my thighs. A feeling I am still trying not to panic about.

His hand is large and presses into my palm, and his other hand reaches up to cup my jaw as his mouth envelopes mine. He pulls me even closer, holding me like I'm his salvation. I let him kiss me, and the grip on my jaw gets a little tighter.

I press my palm to his chest. Fear and panic set in, but instead of letting them take over, we pause. Every kiss allows me to lean in more and more.

But this is all I need—a pause, a breath. My hand on his chest is a silent voice telling him I'm trying.

He steps back, allowing for space between us, giving me a warm look. I can see the lust in his eyes.

We walk home. Side by side. His hand wrapped around mine, unaware he's shaken my world with that kiss. And Kong, blissfully trotting ahead.

We don't say much on the walk back to my apartment; my thoughts are spinning too fast to speak. You could cut the sexual tension with a knife.

As soon as I close the front door behind us, I feel it. Him. Loch steps into my space. Not touching me, but surrounding me. Forcing me back against the door. His eyes are dark, heavy, devouring. I stop breathing for a second. My gut tightens, heat rushes up my spine. It's overwhelming how much I want him, how much I fear myself for wanting him.

My breathing picks up, and my chest heaves in and out; I hear the blood rushing through my ears.

"I will not hurt you," Loch says, voice low and firm. "Do you trust me?" He puts one hand on the wall, blocking me in even more.

I nod before I can think. It's not fear of him—not really—it's the fear of what happened before. That my body doesn't always know the difference, and when I close my eyes, I can fall back into that night. The smell of him, the pain of his blows to my body, the restraints around my wrists. I need Loch to keep me here with him, where I'm not afraid, not of him.

"Say it, Olive."

"Yes," I whisper, my voice shaking. "I trust you."

He doesn't look away from me. "Give me a safe word. Say it, and I stop. If you can't speak, you can do what you did earlier. Put your hand on my chest and tap two times. That's the signal, ok? I will not push beyond your boundaries, but I need to know when you are at your limit. I want you desperately, but you have to tell me when it's too much."

He takes my hand gently and lays it flat against his chest. It's solid and strong. His shoulders are broad, muscular. His cotton shirt hugs his body. He's in shape, but he doesn't come off like a gym guy. Just strong and husky.

"Tell me a word, Olive."

I blink. My brain scrambles. "Peanut butter."

Loch chuckles and grins at me in surprise. "Good enough for me."

Then, he stops moving. His body presses up against mine, not rough, only applying pressure. His stare is unyielding, steady, and sharp enough to make my knees weak with lust and anticipation. His warmth seeps into me like sunlight.

"Olive," he says again, lips nearly brushing mine. "I want you. Do you trust me?"

I can't speak, only nod. My whole body is tight with nerves, electricity runs through my veins, and my clit pulses with need.

He kisses me. God, it's slow and tender. He tastes sweet, his lips soft and smooth. After several kisses, I can let my mind embrace the moment, to take notice of him. His hands find mine and hold them like they are something delicate, and then he squeezes my palms tight to remind me of his presence. His fingers move up my arms, feather-light, coaxing goosebumps to the surface. He's touching me like I'm something precious. As if it would hurt him to see me break.

His chest presses into me, making me feel grounded and alive. My breasts ache where they push against him. My nipples peak through my shirt at the sensations, the pressure, and movement causing friction.

Still, he doesn't rush. He doesn't grab, even though I can feel the tension in his shoulders and arms. I can tell how hard he is holding himself back.

His fingers travel along my arms again. Up. Down. Up. One hooks my chin, tilting my head to give him more of my mouth. I moan into him before I can stop myself.

His mouth moves lower, pressing to my neck, and I melt with need. It gives me space to breathe, but I don't want to breathe; I only want to feel.

Something dark takes over me. The pressure is suddenly too heavy, and I can't get air inside my lungs. I'm caught between two walls that will smash me to death. Hands are on my face, taking me back to that night when I was gagged, and my head was pushed into the table. Unable to make any sound.

The memory takes over. Not from Loch, but from him. Something has twisted itself around this moment, dark and cold and full of panic. I'm suffocating, unable to breathe or think.

I gasp and shove him back in a rush of anxiety. My chest heaves, trying to regain an air supply.

Loch doesn't back away, but gives us enough space to tilt his head back to look at me. He reaches out and holds my hands, squeezing them to remind me that I'm here with him.

"It's ok," he says, voice like stone, but still gentle, needing me to hear it. "It's just me. Look at me, Olive. It's me."

I hear him, I feel him, and I'm able to refocus on him now. Wide-eyed, breathing like I've just run a marathon, I look back into his eyes. And I see him. Really, see him. He's staring at me with pain in his eyes at seeing me so scared. He can look at me and see what I was thinking and feeling. His eyes remind me it's Loch, not the man from before.

My lungs calm, catching up with the air supply. The heat still burns between my legs, but there's a mixture of pain from the memory and need for the man standing in front of me. I hate how easily I fall apart, how hard it is to hold myself together. I want this, I want him. But every time I get close, the past pulls me under.

"You're stunning," he says, without question or thought.

He smirks, voice lower, playful. "Why do you tease me like that, wearing that sexy top? I can't stop watching your heavy breaths. It's torture. Are you trying to torture me?"

My laugh is jagged. "Shut up," I mutter, and shove him playfully. My cheeks warm at his tone. "I'm a mess."

I don't know what cracks inside me then. Maybe it's a shift. But the desire and compassion he shows in my most vulnerable moments make me reach for him. I grab the front of his shirt and pull him back to me, his face close to mine again.

"Can we try again?" Because it's him. Because I know it's him now, and I trust him. I may not always be in control of my physical reactions, but emotionally, I want him, and I trust him.

His hands land on my sides. I flinch again, but it isn't fear, not exactly. Just my body remembering, I steady myself again.

He touches my chin, lifting my face to meet his eyes. "It's me," he whispers. "Watch me, so you don't forget." He places the softest kiss on my lips and stares at me. He watches me watch him.

I nod, breathless. Nodding because I don't know words anymore. Stunned by the intimacy of having him look at me so intensely.

His hands slide around my sides to my back. I shiver when one large hand moves under my shirt, gliding across my spine. He stops between my shoulder blades and stares at me, seeing every thought I can't speak. His eyes narrow with lust, and they are doing all the speaking for us. Staring at each other, as he touches me, is the most erotic moment of my life. And the best part, it's working. I keep my eyes glued to him, and I'm staying right here with him.

Then one hand slips to the front, brushing my stomach and the hem of my shirt up. My breath stops in anticipation of where his hands will move next. His fingers brush up a little further, his fingertips touching under the swell of my breast, and I suck in a breath. His callused hands are so tender, I want him to keep moving higher.

He groans, like this is killing him, and he's desperate for more. Like he needs me, and is using every ounce of self-control he has. My pussy is throbbing watching him, seeing how turned on he is. I'm not sure I'm breathing.

He kisses me again, deep and full of need. He wants more, and so do I. He continues to watch me and hold my stare.

I am shaking all over; I can't control my own body anymore. But I don't want to stop. I don't want to be careful. I want to feel without it hurting. Without it echoing the past.

His hands are fire and comfort, worship and control. They are moving all over me with reverence now. My body pulses, deep in my core, for more of him.

Suddenly, one hand moves to my back and slides lower. He grabs my ass. Hard. Each finger cupping and pulling at my skin, and I moan from surprise, and from how good it feels to be wanted this much.

He's still watching me, eyes wild now, and presses me harder into the wall, enveloping my mouth again. He's losing control; his need is trying to take over. His thigh presses between my legs, his groin into my stomach. The pressure hits me all at once.

Closing my eyes. The memory comes back sharp. Too sharp, and I flinch.

"I can't, peanut butter," I say, pushing at his chest, shaking again.

He backs off immediately. And murmurs, "I'm sorry. Are you ok?"

His voice is steady but labored.

He helps me sit down, one hand on my back, afraid I'll collapse. "Eyes on me," he says. He's still here, and his intense stare brings me back to the present. He lets me calm down. I look up at him. "It's me." He never lets go of my hand. "You're perfect. Can I give you one more kiss?" I'm not sure if he meant to say that because he blushes, like it slipped out.

"Yes," I answer, and he leans down to kiss me one more time. He doesn't linger; it's to remind me that it's him.

After I calm down and have Kong by my side, Loch says, "I need to go check on the other dogs at home." He crouches in front of me. "I can come back in a couple of hours. Give you a break. Time to relax... maybe take a shower, since I woke you up this morning and ruined your routine? Would that be ok?"

I nod because that's exactly what I need—time to chill and reset my brain, attempt to unscramble it, and process what's happened. But fuck, that was amazing. I feel like I've climbed a mountain and ridden a roller coaster at the same time. I could use some time to sort myself out, alone.

He stands, watching me like he is trying to read my mind. And at this point, I'm convinced he can.

Chapter 24
Loch

Explosive Release

I slam the door to the old house hard enough to make the walls shake. The second I walk in, my nose burns from the sour smell of the captives in the basement. My boots echo down the stairs, every step vibrating through my bones like a drumbeat summoning violence.

The adrenaline is back, caused by the ache that consumed me when Olive used our safe word. Need courses through me, and I have to figure out how to suppress it, the white-hot surge that blurs the line between passion and frustration. I know what she needs from me, and I'm willing to be patient and give her that, but it doesn't mean it's going to be easy. My blood was already boiling before I even reached the basement, knowing what I needed to deal with. Fuck, even Olive saw what a piece of shit he was on TV. Of course, she didn't know the truth, and that he had it coming.

Mike's awake now, sitting against the back of the cage. I open the gate to his cage. He jerks when he hears me coming. Let him be afraid.

I stare down at him and take the gag out of his mouth. His face is puffy and sweaty. He blinks at the light, then looks up at me like a weak little man.

"What the hell, man, let me the fuck out of here."

He doesn't know who I am or where he is. He'll figure it out soon. He continues to shout and scream at me until I finally lose my mind.

"You're an actual piece of shit; you know that?"

He doesn't move. He finally shuts the hell up. That's smart, but it won't last. The rage bubbles up inside me, anger at what this man did to helpless animals for years. Anger at the man who attacked and hurt Olive. I could kill him for it. Anger at the fact that I lost my control with Olive and pushed her too far. I can feel my blood coursing through my veins, the adrenaline rushing through my body, making me see red.

I step into the cage, ducking under the low metal bar, and shut the gate behind me. He still has zip ties around his hands and feet. I hadn't formulated my plans for him, so I left them until I decided how to serve him justice.

"You like fighting cages, right? You like keeping dogs in fucking misery?" I'm pacing slowly in the small space. "There were scratch marks all over your fucking fight pit, Mike. Dogs trying to claw their way out of that hellhole. You remember that?"

He stays quiet. What a fucking coward. I kick him hard in the thigh. He lets out a small cough.

"There were dozens of chains pulled off your property. Each one was sunk into the ground like a goddamn headstone. Rusted. Short. Designed to keep them stuck there with no escape. And the puppies..."

I stop walking as the rage consumes me. My hands shake with anger. My pulse skyrockets, and my fists clench. My body is trying to break out of itself with adrenaline.

"There was a kiddie pool in the back of the lot. Six drowned puppies. Couldn't have been more than a few weeks old. Floating. Like trash. Who does that?! And let me guess, you made their mother watch so she would fight better? You sick fuck. I wish I could have your mom here to watch you die."

Mike starts panicking, yelling, and screaming. His pupils dilate into large black saucers. He's apologizing, already begging for me to let him go, promising he won't do it again.

Coward. My vision blurs, and something in me snaps.

I launch at him with all my fury. Sending all my anger and rage at him. My fists hit his face again and again and again. Cartilage breaks under my knuckles as his head bangs into the wall over and over. I hear teeth crack like glass. Blood gushes from his nose, into his mouth. His head bounces back and forth with each hit. I don't stop. My pulse thunders in my ears, my vision blurring. I want him to suffer. To feel something, anything, resembling the pain he'd handed out so carelessly.

"DEFENSELESS!"

Crack.

"HELPLESS!"

Crunch.

"FUCKING VOICELESS ANIMALS!"

I grab him by the shirt and slam his head back against the wall of the cage. His body goes limp, sliding down the wall, a smear of blood trailing behind.

"Do you feel like a tough guy now? Picking on poor animals?"

I freeze for a moment, trying to recover. My knuckles are torn; my skin is split open. Warm blood drips down my fingers–mine, his, I don't even know. My chest heaves. He isn't dead. But he will wish he were when I'm done with him.

I back out of the cage, knuckles throbbing, shaking the blood from my hands like water. I lock his cage and don't look back. The three other people glare at me. I've been cruel, but I've never lost control like that before. I need to release the tension that's been building up over the time I've spent in this disgusting house and the anger for what Olive has endured. Everything is coming to the surface. Forcing me to look in the mirror. I finish doing what I actually came here for; I don't care if they suffer, only that they survive. Food and water are dropped.

By the time I pull into my garage, my heartbeat has returned to normal. The storm has passed, and now the memory of touching Olive replays in my mind. The mask of calm is settling back over me like a well-worn coat. I have to check on the dogs and get cleaned up.

The moment I step into my house, I head for the bathroom. I strip off my clothes one piece at a time; my shirt sticks to me, half-dried blood and sweat pulling at my skin. My knuckles are swelling, crusted with split scabs and raw skin. My arms and shoulders ache from tension. The pain will be worse tomorrow.

The shower turns on with a hiss, and I don't wait for it to heat. I step under the icy spray and press my palms flat to the wall, letting the water slap against my face and trickle down my spine. It runs red, filling the room with the faint smell of iron.

The water stings my hands. My head drops forward, but I don't regret what I did. I never regret giving them what they deserve. I hate feeling like I'm a monster, like I'm actually one of them. But I don't regret it. As the water begins to warm, I surrender and let it wash away the bitterness I've been holding onto.

I can't take this spiteful energy back to her. Not to Olive. She deserves the part of me that's soft for her. She needs someone who's gentle and can protect her. Olive deserves the person I strive to be.

I close my eyes and see her face. The way her mouth curves when she smiles at me, her tongue when it peeks out to wet her lips. Ah, fuck her lips. She has perfect lips, large, plump, and beautifully shaped. That little laugh she tried to cover when I caught her staring at me this morning was adorable. Her scent is seared into my memory—citrus and sweet, and yet fresh and earthy.

And fuck, those tits, I couldn't help but stare at her large chest rising with each breath, and her nipples skimming my chest. The way they felt against me, soft and full. I would have done almost anything to touch those nipples, hard and peaking through her top.

I've barely touched her and I can't stop thinking about what she'd feel like pressed up against me—writhing, clinging, whispering my name in that breathy voice. Her eyes boring into mine with need. Lust replacing her sad eyes as I run my hands over her soft stomach and smooth skin.

My dick twitches and hardens, imagining her body in my head. I grit my teeth, wanting to resist thinking of her like this, but I can't stop. She's consuming.

My hand wraps around my dick, slow and tight, starting at the base. The water burns now that the heat has kicked in. I turn and let it hit my back. My strokes start deliberately. I have to remind myself that I have self-control. How she needs me. She wants me to take control.

Her voice is in my ear. Olive's moans seep into my brain from when I grazed the underside of her breast. Her skin flushed and trembling, her eyes wide and wanting. Watching me. I imagined everything I wanted to do next. Undressing her, my fingers sliding into her soaking pussy. Pulling her up and her legs wrapping around my waist, back arching as I filled her. Her nails clawing down my back as she begs for more.

"Fuck, Olive..." I hiss through clenched teeth, jerking harder now, needing it.

Stroking myself with one hand as I brace against the tile with the other, I'm working myself over, thumb dragging across the head, catching on slickness. My hips roll into it, fucking my fist. Sharp, rapid breaths echo off the walls.

I'm close. In my head, she's panting my name, looking up at me with that mix of trust and desire. Telling me she wants me. I see her straddling me, tits bouncing with each thrust, fingers clutching my shoulders as she whispers, "Don't stop."

My stomach clenches, release tearing through me in a long grunt that comes out like a confession. The high hits like a drug, pure, pulsing heat fading into calm. I slouch against the tile and let the water wash it all away.

When I step out, completely refreshed, I'm clean, clear-headed, and steady.

I dry off and pull on a fresh shirt.

I do a few things around the house, let all the dogs out, and play with them for a couple of minutes, to continue clearing my head. I need to get it back on straight before I go back to Olive. I want to go back, able to focus on her and her needs completely.

Chapter 25
Olive

Pizza and a Good Night's Sleep

I open the door, and Loch stands there, hands in his pockets. His eyes find mine, and I swear I see them soften. He gives me a gentle hug as he enters the apartment, and when he releases me, I see his injured hand.

"Jesus, Loch," I gasp, instinct pulling me closer before he can hide it. But he tries anyway, shoving it back into his pocket. "What happened?"

"It's nothing," he says, low and too quick. "Had an issue with one of the kennels. Scraped me up a bit."

I stare at him, my fingers already curling around his wrist before he can stop me. I drag his hand toward me and inspect his angry, red knuckles. They aren't surface scratches; they look as if they came from hitting something, not a dog run.

I say nothing at first, looking up at him, waiting for more of an explanation. He won't meet my eyes. What the hell is going on? Why is he hiding?

Something about this makes my stomach twist into a tight coil of unease. Why won't he tell me the truth? I see a flicker of something dark in him. It should scare me, but it makes me sad that after all this, he can't let me in.

"These don't look like—"

Before I can get the question out, his voice breaks the silence. "How's Kong doing?"

On cue, Kong trots up behind me, tail already wagging at the sound of Loch's voice. He pushes his head into Loch's thigh, and Loch crouches down, ruffling his ears with his uninjured hand. I watch them quietly for a second. The way Kong leans into him, he trusts him. I guess I should, too.

"I took a shower earlier," I said, breaking the tension by changing the subject. "Kong stared at me through the curtain the whole time like I had abandoned him. I thought he was going to jump in with me." I laugh again, remembering his sweet face checking in on me.

He laughs, standing up. "He gets attached fast."

I shrug, a little shy again under his gaze. Loch's so handsome and thoughtful; it's intimidating to look at him. "He's not the only one," I say, looking at Kong with utter adoration.

His eyes flick to mine again, and then down, taking me in. I'd thrown on leggings and a loose, low-cut blue tank that exposed more cleavage than I normally did, and tossed a black zip-up hoodie over it. Hair not quite dry from the shower, but I'd brushed it out and left it down for once. I even swiped on a little mascara. Not that I'd ever admit it out loud. It was stupid. We're just hanging out. But I still wanted to feel a little more confident.

"You always wear your hair up," he says, stepping in a little closer. "I didn't know it was this long." My breath hitches as his fingers brush a piece of hair behind my ear. His touch is barely there, but also everywhere. And I mean everywhere. How do guys do that? Putting a piece of hair behind my ear shouldn't send a shockwave between my legs.

"It's easier to manage up," my voice is quiet.

He doesn't say anything as he looks at me, deep in thought. We don't talk much after that.

We curl up on the couch again, shoulder to shoulder, and pick a random movie. At some point, I ask him, "Do you want to share some pizza?"

He says, "Sure, let me guess; you love meat?"

A beat passes, and I howl, laughing. "Yes, I do."

"Your laugh is adorable; I love how you snort when you're trying to hold back."

I smile at the compliment and blush. "Thanks, so glad you noticed I snort." I roll my eyes.

Loch orders the pizza, and while we wait for it to arrive, he advises, "You should put Kong in his kennel now, so that when the food gets here, he doesn't get so amped up." I do, and when the pizza guy drops off the pizza, Kong barks in the background, but is already contained and calms quickly. I make a mental note of that for the future. Putting the food in the kitchen, I turn around and see it. Kong is sitting in his kennel with a huge, full-faced smile stretching from ear to ear. That big grin that I've been dying to see.

I start crying, like fucking sobbing. Loch looks at me, alarmed, and I point at Kong's kennel. "He's smiling! Does he like pizza?"

"Loch chuckles, "Of course he likes pizza. He's a dog. But I think he's also just happy."

I barrel over to Kong, handing him a piece of pepperoni from one of the slices and letting him out. Kong watches me eat with intensity, the smile never leaving his face, but he doesn't beg. He waits patiently to see if I share any more. Loch watches us this whole time, pride filling his eyes at how perfect this moment has become.

After we finish eating, I move closer to Loch on the couch. His arm goes around me, like it belongs there. And when my head rests against his chest, his heartbeat is steady. His chest is soft enough to get comfortable, not all hard and stiff.

I don't even realize I've fallen asleep until the sun comes through the window on us the next morning. I wake up wrapped in his arms, feeling the weight of him around me.

It's the first time I've slept that hard in months. I'm used to the kind of sleep where I wake up with clenched fists and my body raging like a live wire. Or, I lie in bed with my mind racing and listening to every sound, unable to calm my thoughts.

But last night, I got real sleep. Deep sleep. Because he was here, and I'm not sure what to do with that. It was the first time in a long time that I hadn't been afraid to close my eyes.

I lean up, trying not to wake Loch, but as soon as I'm half sitting, his arm wraps around me, pulling me back down. I panic for a second, but hold his hand and take a deep breath, relaxing back into him.

CHAPTER 26

LOCH

TABLE FOR TWO, VIEW FOR FREE

It had only been a few days. Three, to be exact. Three long-ass days since I'd last seen her, and my body was going through withdrawals. My mind kept flashing back to the way she looked curled up against me on the couch, the smell of her hair, the way her breath evened out when she was in my arms. I watched her sleep for a while, so peacefully, and hoped I had something to do with that. It haunts and captivates me.

I needed to see her again, so I texted her.

Loch: Can I take you out? On a proper date?

Her response was instantaneous.

Olive: Yes. I'd love to.

So, now I'm standing outside her door, my heart skipping beats, then doubling up to make up for it. I exhale and close my eyes for a beat and look down to check my clothes before I knock on the door.

I chose navy pants and a white button-up shirt, leaving the top two buttons undone. The sleeves are rolled to my forearms, casual but clean. I took time to shave and style my hair. My hair is short on the sides, longer and messy on top, so it's pretty easy to get that messy-on-purpose look.

I don't care to look good for anyone but Olive. I want to impress her, to make her mine. The door opens, and everything in me stops. I can't breathe.

"Holy fuck," I mutter to myself, "Olive."

She's in this black one-piece pantsuit, tight in all the right places, hugging her hips and chest. The neckline plunges, showing off enough skin to short-circuit my brain. A few delicate gold chains sit at her collarbone, catching the light when she moves. Her hair is down in loose curls, soft, perfectly framing her face. She's wearing makeup, too. Not much, but enough to make my stomach twist. Her eyes are smoky and intense, but her look is still natural.

I forget how to breathe and speak.

"Wow," I finally manage to say, stepping closer. "You're stunning... Jesus, Olive."

She blushes hard, eyes dipping down, acting bashful, as if she doesn't know how hot she looks. I lean in to kiss her cheek, barely grazing her skin. "You look incredible."

"Thank you," she murmurs, her voice shy. "So do you."

I smile, staring down at her plump pink lips. They consume my dirty thoughts, and I cough under my breath. "You ready?"

She nods, then glances over her shoulder. "I need to say bye to Kong real quick."

I watch her kneel beside his kennel, giving him a treat like it's a ritual. She talks to him in that soft, baby voice she reserves for him, cooing sweet nothings I can't quite hear. Her hand strokes his head gently and closes the kennel door. He melts under her touch, his eyes glaze over like he's fallen in love. And I melt with the scene in front of me.

She doesn't know it, but at that moment, she's the most beautiful thing I've ever seen. Not because of the way she looks. But because of the way she loves. She's all heart, and she doesn't even realize it.

We head out the door; I rest my hand on her lower back. I open her door like a gentleman, and I can't stop glancing at her. Her outfit is revealing her tits more than I'm used to.

I'm trying my best to keep my eyes on the road. I picked a place I thought she'd like. It's a small family-owned place, tucked away, with warm lighting and a mostly local, seasonal menu. Nothing flashy or busy. Good food and atmosphere. We sit at a table facing a window with a beautiful view of the park across the street.

The way she lights up at the menu of handmade pasta and the fresh bread makes every choice worthwhile.

"I haven't been out of the house, like in public, for a while. This feels like my first time on a date. Sorry, I got so excited about the food and stuff. I just... thank you. I'm already having an amazing time."

Before I can say anything to reassure her, the server approaches to take our drink orders.

She orders wine; I stick with iced tea. We eat, we laugh. We share a dessert, even though she says she's full, and she steals the last bite of the cherry cheesecake while grinning at me, knowing she's a menace.

I can't stop smiling. I've never met someone like her. She's thoughtful, open, and easygoing. She doesn't seem impressed with superficial things.

Her laughter is easy tonight. Her eyes sparkle as we talk. She leans in when I speak, rests her chin on her hand like she's interested in what I have to say. Her hand brushes mine on the table, and she doesn't pull away.

By the time we finish, it's getting late, but I'm not ready to take her home. I want to stretch tonight as long as I can. I take her somewhere I haven't taken anyone else, nor been to myself in years. Not since I was a kid.

We take a twenty-minute drive out of the city, and we're pulling onto a gravel path that leads into a nature preserve. There's a narrow trail that cuts through the trees, and I grab the flashlight from the glove box before helping her out of the car. Then I grab a small bag that I packed.

"Where are we?" She's looking around, curious.

"You'll see."

She holds onto my arm as we walk along the path. Her heels are a bit wobbly on the path, but she's trusting me even in the dark. The trail opens up after a bit, leading to a quiet clearing with a wooded overlook that juts out over a slow, winding river. The moon is high, full, and silver, and the stars are everywhere. I couldn't have picked a better night if I tried.

"Loch..." she breathes, walking ahead to the edge of the platform. "It's beautiful."

"I used to come here when I needed to breathe," I say, stepping beside her. "I haven't been back in a long time."

Her hand slips into mine, and I hold it tight. She shivers, and I grab a blanket out of my bag to wrap around her, along with a thermos of hot chocolate. She accepts it with a sweet smile.

"You planned all this." Not a question, a statement.

We stand there for a long time, not talking, watching the water, listening to the breeze, the trees rustling around us. I turn to her, and her face is silver-lit, eyes wide. I can't help myself and pull her in for a kiss.

She tastes like chocolate and warmth. And when her fingers dig into the front of my jacket, drawing me closer, I swear I could live in that moment forever. She wants me too. She's letting me in.

"I didn't know a date could feel like this, even before everything..." she whispers against my lips.

I press my forehead to hers. "Me neither."

"Can you take me home?"

I jerk my head back, a little struck by her change in pace. "Is everything ok?"

"Yes," she gives me the sweetest look and bites her lip. Making me look at her mouth. "I mean, can we go back to my house?"

After holding my breath, I finally exhale. "Oh, uh, yeah. I would love that. I umm, well I hope this is ok, but I asked a neighbor to check on the dogs tonight," I take a breath. "So if you wanted, I could stay the night? There is no pressure. I just wanted to stay with you again?"

"Yes, I would like that."

CHAPTER 27

OLIVE

KERNEL DESIRES

The front door clicks shut behind us, and I lock it. Kong is waiting for us, tail wagging like he missed us even though we were only gone a few hours. His whole body wiggles when he sees Loch, like they have this secret bond I'll never understand. Loch lets Kong out, and he trots to me, still wiggling, and gives me that big goofy smile again.. It makes my heart tighten every time I see his grin. Loch chuckles and crouches down, scratching behind his ears, giving him a moment of attention before standing back up.

"I'll take him out real quick," he says, grabbing the leash from the hook by the door.

"Thanks," I smile, already walking backwards toward the hallway. "I'll change and get comfy if that's ok?"

He nods, smiles, and disappears out the front door with Kong, leaving me alone with my thoughts, which are suddenly very loud and scrambled. I press my back against the closed door to my room and let out a huge breath.

Ok, Olive. It's Loch. You trust him. You like him. You want this. You can handle this.

My heart's beating fast, my body is trembling with nerves and anticipation. My body is already alive from the way he kissed me at the overlook and how he's looked at me all night on our amazing date. How he touched me the other day flashes through my head, remembering his hands, wanting to feel him again. I want to be normal again. For him to be mine and me his. I want him. God, I want him.

I change out of the jumpsuit and heels, stepping into soft cotton shorts and a loose tank top. No bra, smiling to myself with devious thoughts about how much Loch will like the lack of a bra. My hoodie stays on the back of a chair; this isn't about hiding anymore. Not tonight. Not if I can help it.

In the kitchen, I make some popcorn and put it into a bowl. I settle on the couch, tucking my legs up underneath me, trying to act casual. Like my stomach isn't doing backflips, and my palms aren't sweaty, waiting for him to walk back through that door. I scroll through the channels on TV, looking for something for us to watch.

The latch clicks and the door opens. He's back. Loch steps inside, his eyes immediately landing on me. His lips twitch in a half-smile, but it's the heat in his eyes that I can't look away from—a deep, lust-filled gaze. There's something warm and familiar in his eyes. Like he belongs here, like this is ours. Even after such a short amount of time, we have our routine, our space, here on the couch together. Our night.

But there's also want. It rolls off him in slow waves, settling over my skin like steam.

He hangs the leash on the hook, takes off his shoes, removes his jacket, and walks toward me. Kong trots over to his fluffy bed and plops down like he knows it's time for us to be alone.

When Loch sits beside me on the couch, close enough that our thighs touch, and his hand reaches around my shoulders, electricity shoots up my spine. The sexual tension shows all over us. He says nothing, looking at me with dark, wanting eyes.

Chapter 28
Loch

I'M GOING TO WATCH

She's warm next to me, curled up with her legs tucked under that cute little body of hers, skin glowing from the inside out. The scent of her, grapefruit? It's clean but sweet, wrapping around me, and I can't stop myself from leaning closer.

The TV hums in the background, but I can't tell you what we're watching. I'm not paying attention. Not really. Not when she's sitting beside me like this. Bare legs, tank top, no bra, not that I'm trying to be obvious, but come on. I'm a man. I fucking notice when her nipples are peeking through her thin shirt. I can't stop watching her from the corner of my eye.

She reaches for the popcorn on her lap, grabs a little too much, and a few pieces tumble, bouncing off her fingers and scattering. Some land in her lap. One piece lands on her chest, between her tits.

Before she realizes what's happening, my hand moves. My fingers brush over the curve of her breast as I pick the stray kernel off her chest and toss it into my mouth.

Olive blinks. Her cheeks bloom with color, the flush spreading from her neck to her ears and down to her chest. She looks down at her chest, realizing what I had done.

She laughs nervously, brushing her hand over the spot even though it's already gone. "That was smooth," she says, her breath catching, not quite meeting my eyes.

She's flustered. She liked it, I can tell by the smirk in her smile. She just doesn't want to admit it.

I grin, leaning back into the cushions, letting my knuckles graze her shoulder. "Hey," I tell her, relaxing my voice, "Can't let popcorn go to waste."

She rolls her eyes, biting her lip to hide the smile. And that little move, God, that does something to me. She pretends she's annoyed, that she doesn't love how close I am.

I move a little closer until our legs are pressed together. I move my hand, innocent enough, tucking a strand of hair behind her ear, fingers grazing her cheek on the way back.

She turns to look at me, all soft and unsure. And I'm gone. Completely, hopelessly gone for her.

I adjust myself so that I'm leaning on the arm of the couch. I'm facing her, with my leg extended across the couch, trying to get my leg behind her, and I tell Olive, "Lean on me."

She lays her back to my chest, and I cross my arms over her, locking her in. Her heart is beating fast, but I can't tell who's is racing more. We lay there together, enjoying the moment. It feels so good, so comfortable to have her body on mine.

I envelope her in my arms, brushing my thumb softly over her smooth skin. I let my hands roam, slowly. Over her arms, hips, collarbone. So slowly, dragging out the tension and the desire, while also giving her plenty of time to stop me if needed.

I graze the underside of her breast like I did before, over her tank top. Her breath catches, the tiniest moan slipping out, like she didn't mean to let it go. But I heard it. Felt it. My pulse kicks up, wanting her to enjoy this, enjoy me touching her.

My other hand wraps around her waist and side, feeling her soft stomach. Her breath is now frantic. I press a kiss to her head, slow and reverent, barely holding myself together. My hands roam again, tracing the shape of her, learning every inch with aching restraint and enjoying every second. She arches back into me, offering herself up. Like she wants this, wants me to touch her.

"You're doing so well," I hum, my voice strained, rumbling my words against her neck.

I reach my hand inside the top of her shirt, fully cupping her breast; it's full, soft, bigger than my hand, nipple hard. Fucking perfect. I squeeze harder, pinching her nipple between my fingers.

I moan into her hair, barely able to contain my desire. My dick is getting hard; I can't think straight. Her hand grabs my thigh and squeezes like it's all she can do to control herself. I whisper in her ear, "Tell me this is ok, that this feels good."

She nods once and purrs, "Mmhmm," like a word is too difficult for her.

I lower my head, leaving a soft kiss on her cheek. "You remember your safe word?"

"Mmhmm."

In a low growl, I tell her, "Say the word so I know you know how to say it."

"Peanut butter." Her voice sounds strained, but it's there. I reach both hands around her tits, needing to squeeze them, touch her. I whisper in a groan, "You are doing so good for me."

I slide one of my hands down her body, my other still cupping her breast, teasing her. My fingers touch delicately along the band of her shorts. I want to see her reaction. See if she flinches. Her breath gets a little shakier, but she doesn't say anything, so I reach down on top of her shorts, moving slowly. I want her to have time to stop me.

I reach my hand between her thighs, widening them, cupping her between her thighs. She lets out a breathy moan and writhes under me, still holding my leg.

"Fuck, Olive, you are so fucking sexy. I can't keep my hands off you." I apply a bit more pressure with two fingers right on her clit. She moans out my name, "Loch." And I lose it; my dick is aching for her, I want to see how wet she is. I reach into her shorts, still giving her a moment to stop me, and run my fingers down her mound, through her slit and feel her fucking dripping for me. I let out a deep groan, loving that she's so wet for me.

I reach to touch her clit, and she freezes, her whole body going stiff. "Peanut butter," she mumbles. I pull my hand away.

"I, I need a minute." She turns to look at me, but her eyes are down, like she's ashamed. "Just a minute," she says again.

I reach for her chin and force her to look at me. "It's ok. You have as much time as you need." The need in me is overwhelming; I'm dying to touch her, to feel every inch of her. But I have to let her figure this out with me. A long moment passes, and she looks up at me again. Her eyes plead with me to keep pushing her. I give her a dark stare, waiting for her to change her mind.

"When you're ready, lie back on the other side, facing me." I insist so she knows what I want when she's ready. She knows that I'm on her time. But I'm also not exactly giving her any other option. I need to push her; she asked me to, and I want to.

After she takes a few deep breaths, she lies back against the side, our legs crossing over one another. She's staring at me like I'm going to eat her alive... and I want to. Although I can't tell if her eyes are full of lust or fear. Her breath is heavy, and her chest is heaving again.

I let her breath settle a little more, her body relaxes into the cushion, and in a low demanding voice, I tell her, "Touch yourself, I'm going to watch."

"What?" she replies. "I can't." Panic laces her voice.

"Yes, Olive, you can. I won't touch you, but I want to watch you touch yourself. You can leave your shorts on, and I'll use my imagination, or you can take them off. It's up to you. But I'm going to watch you cum tonight."

She pales, and I can see the wheels turning, deciding if she's going to say it again or if she's going to do what I tell her. She stalls and watches me. But she slides her shorts down; my breath catches watching her undress. I am panting like a fucking dog watching her. It's so fucking hot when she listens to everything I say. When she submits to me willingly.

"Good."

She opens her legs for me; her panties are still on, soft grey thong panties with a fucking wet spot that I can see from here. I'm hot and getting sweaty watching her take control, and it's making my dick throb painfully. I want to grab my dick, but this is about her, and I'm not going to do anything to ruin this moment.

She reaches down, her hands trembling, putting them inside her panties. She's fucking touching herself. I can tell she's making small circles, even though I can't see exactly what she's doing. She is rubbing that little nub that I know is soaking wet. She closes her eyes and tilts her head back in pleasure.

"Keep your eyes on me, Olive," I demand. She returns her eyes to mine, but I want more of her. Fuck, I can barely think with the lack of blood flow to my brain.

"You're doing so good, you're so fucking sexy."

She looks at me, biting her lower lip and arching her body seductively. I'm mesmerized by this beautiful woman in front of me.

"I want to take your panties off. Will you let me?"

She nods, lust blowing through her eyes. I lean towards her, turning onto my knees, and my hands dig into her thick hips because I can't fucking control myself. I pull her panties down, trying to touch her hips and legs as much as possible while I do, because I'm a fucking animal and I can't resist touching her again.

She has two fingers buried inside her fucking bare pussy, pushing in and out. I'm drooling at the sight of her.

"Fuck, you have such a pretty cunt. I'm dying to taste you."

She moans, breathy, but louder than before. I can see her body tensing, her legs starting to shake. I'm watching her fingers go from her clit, sliding inside her for a few pumps, back to her clit. It's the hottest thing I have ever watched. I palm my aching cock through my pants. I watch Olive's eyes follow my hand.

"You are so hot, Olive. I want to see you cum all over your hand."

She stops, pulling her hand away from her wet pussy. Fuck, have I lost her again? My mind races, wondering what the fuck happened to make her stop. I didn't touch her.

"Loch?" she whispers.

"Yeah?"

She holds out her fingers to me with lust in her eyes. I suck her fingers into my mouth, lapping at her arousal.

"I want you to touch me again."

Oh, fuck! Thank God.

"With your mouth," she breathes.

I close my eyes for a second to catch my breath, and stay calm and thank whatever god there is for the words that just came out of her mouth.

I don't even give her a chance to think about it or change her mind. I descend on her like a wild animal released from its cage. I lower my head to her, licking from her dripping cunt all the way up to her clit. It's not the best angle because she is sitting against the edge facing me. So I wrap my hands around her ass and pull her toward me, lifting her pussy to my face.

"Oh, God, Loch! Fuck. Oh!" she moans, a deep, throaty sound.

God, she tastes sweet; I want to fucking drown in her pussy. I hold her hips in place, licking and sucking her clit, driving her wild. Her hand comes to my head and starts caressing and pulling my hair, making me more feral, and my dick twitches with pleasure, knowing she likes this. I can't keep my eyes off her while I eat her like I've never eaten a meal in my life. Her eyes never leave mine.

Her body is squirming, back arching. Her hands are giving me more pressure, telling me all I need to know about where she likes it. She wants more, and I want to taste her more. I lick and suck her feverishly. Her body is tense, bucking into my mouth. Her moans are so fucking loud. Her eyes shut, mouth parted.

"I'm... Ahhh, I'm, I'm cumming..."

I fucking groan into her, wanting to watch her fall apart on my face, and lick up every single drop of the cum gushing out of her.

I want to taste her, all of her; I want her cum all over my mouth. I force my tongue into her cunt, as deep as I can get. She jolts into my face, more sensitive than before. Her cum on my tongue is making me ravenous. I lick her clean. Until her eyes open and her breathing returns to normal.

"Fuck," she stares at me. "Loch, I... fuck, that was so good."

I chuckle to myself, the feeling of making her cum, making her feel good... It's got to be one of the best feelings I've had. I'm overwhelmed with joy at seeing her flushed cheeks, her taste still lingering in my mouth.

I kneel again and wipe the back of my hand across my face, watching her every move. There is a devilish gleam in her eye. I believe I've awakened a beast.

"I forgot how good this can feel. I mean, I'm not sure much can compare to that. But you've given me back a piece of myself."

I see her eyes drift down to my crotch. I follow her gaze, then look back at her. Nervous energy and apprehension mask her face.

"It's ok, we don't have to do anything else tonight. That was all I fucking needed. Your hot cunt on my tongue. You're so fucking beautiful."

Her mouth parts like she wants to say something. "I want to..."

Fuck, my dick is so fucking hard, but I don't want to ruin this. Fucking hell, I wish I could think clearly.

"Want to, what exactly?"

With a sheepish grin, she says, "Fuck you."

My eyes bore into hers, trying to read her face, read her eyes. For a sign of hesitation, or fear, or anything else. But I don't see any.

I pause for a moment, thinking. My dick throbs, and my brain is barely functioning. And then her hand is there, feeling my dick through my pants, and my head falls back in surrender. Whatever this girl wants from me is fucking hers.

Chapter 29

Olive

HE LAID BACK, SHE SHOWED UP

I cup him through his pants. He's fucking huge. Dear God, what did I sign up for?! But it makes my core tighten more. I'm so turned on, so fucking hot from him watching me, and then eating me like a fucking feast. It's the hottest thing I've ever experienced.

There is an energy between us, like lightning flashing back and forth with every touch, every breath. My pussy is throbbing at the thought of his cock, and what it might feel like to have him inside of me. I crawl on my knees to face him as he leans back on the couch where we started. I unbutton and unzip his pants. My hands tremble with nerves. I reach in and pull him out. Holy fuck. His dick is huge and fucking thick. My mouth waters at the sight of his veiny, swollen dick. I look at his face, and he's wearing a cocky grin. He knows exactly what I'm thinking.

I smile, reassuring him and say, "You like this, don't you, watching me look at your dick."

"Yeah, I fucking do," with a shoulder shrug, like it's the most natural thing for him.

"Do you have a condom?"

His eyes widen. "No."

"Really?" I ask in an irritated tone.

"I didn't plan on fucking you tonight. I haven't been with anyone in..." He clears his throat like he's embarrassed. I look into his eyes and give him a gentle smile, letting him know it's ok, he can tell me. "Years," as he looks away for a moment. "I'm clean."

"Me too. I was tested after... well, you know. And I'm on birth control."

His eyes tighten and darken. He turns his body, so he is sitting on the couch like normal now, facing the TV again. He removes his shirt, unfastening each button slowly, teasing me as I watch him. His chest is wide, muscular, but not ripped like a bodybuilder. He's solid, and it's fucking sexy as hell. As I sit next to him, I take in every moment, savoring it. I see a tattoo peeking from around his side. There's far too much happening for me to get a good look, but it looks like it spreads onto his back. I focus on his eyes and breathing, trying to calm my racing heart.

He pulls his pants and boxers down more and pulls me onto his lap with ease. I can feel his hard dick pressing into my backside. It makes me shudder a bit, a feeling reminding me of the monster pressing into me, but I keep looking at Loch, reminding myself it's him. He kisses me hard, holding my jaw and neck, pushing his tongue into my mouth, making me taste myself on his lips. His kiss brings me back to him, back to the present. He pulls my shirt above my head, exposing my breasts, and I suck in a breath.

"You're going to look at me. The entire time your eyes stay on me. I won't touch you. I'm going to put my hands behind my head. This is for you. Take what you want from me."

"Loch, I want you to touch me," I stammer. I don't want him to feel like he can't touch me. I'm ok, at least I think I am. "I want this." His cock twitches under me.

"No, for tonight, this is you." He says it so calmly, knowing this is what I need more than I do. He's taking control by telling me to take control. It's so fucking sexy. After a long breath, I reach down, grab his dick in my hand. It's so hard, but smooth, and the veins pulse in my hand. I lift so I can notch him at my entrance.

"Eyes on me," he groans in a pained voice.

I'm still so fucking wet that I glide down his length. He stretches me, and he's so thick it burns for a second. His deep brown eyes are haunting and full of desire. We can't take our eyes off each other as I sink down further to the base of his cock.

The feeling of him inside me is so new, and... full. I grab onto his shoulders, his hands behind his head like you see underwear models doing in pictures. Looking all sexy and come-hither and shit. His mouth is tight. Like he's trying to hold himself together.

"Fuck, Olive, you're so fucking hot. I have been dreaming about filling your hot fucking cunt for so long. Ride me hard," his voice strains. "Now," he growls. I can see the need in his eyes. I can hear it in his voice. And it's making me even wetter, hearing him say such dirty things to me.

With my hands holding onto his shoulders, I move my hips and ride him. I can't help but let out a moan. I'm grinding my clit on his pelvis while I bottom out on his cock. Even though I'm putting on the show, I'm watching him. Watching to see his reactions, to see the pleasure in his eyes. I kiss him again, pressing my breasts against him, feeling my hard nipples rub his chest, creating a little bit of friction. I'm moving at a steady pace. I want to push him, make him beg for more. I don't know why, but I want him to lose his control.

He groans, "Fucking good girl, Olive. Does my dick feel good inside you?" His hips jerk up, forcing his cock deeper inside me.

"God, yes," I moan. I'm using his shoulders and neck a bit more to get more leverage and move harder up and down his length.

"Yes, fuck me harder. Take my cock."

His words are sending me into a spiral. I want to close my eyes and go wild, but he's keeping me present. It's erotic as fuck to have this much eye contact. My breath is heaving, pulse pounding. My pussy is clenching and throbbing around him. It feels too good.

"Oh, God, Loch."

"Yes, say my name. Fuck me, Olive. Your pussy is so fucking good. So fucking wet. I want to feel you cum on my dick. You're too fucking good, and I can't last like this. Cum for me, Olive!"

I could cum just from his dirty talk. It's so hot. I groan in pleasure, feeling that warm sensation down my spine, deep in my core. My body tightens, my hands dig into his shoulders. His hips thrust up, giving me more pressure on my clit, and I'm done. I shake, squeezing him and cumming hard. My eyes pinch shut, and my whole body thrums with pleasure.

"Oh, fuck," he moans. "I'm going to fill you with my cum." I'm still riding him, wanting to watch him lose his control. His body tenses; his thrusting becomes erratic. His hands come down on my hips and pin me into him while he thrusts hard into me, jacking his body into mine. It's fucking euphoric watching him come apart with me.

His body stills, his head collapsing into my chest. What we just shared was so different... so intimate and raw.

His breathing has calmed; mine has too. He leans his head up to meet my eyes, and I lean my forehead into his.

"Thank you." I've never understood the urge some people get to cry after sex. But I do tonight. So many emotions, so much healing. As tears fall from my face, I whimper.

"Why are you crying? I'm sorry I tried to resist touching you. I—"

"No, it's not that. It's a little overwhelming, in a good way. The emotions of it all are intense. I'm sorry, it's stupid."

"Stop, you have absolutely nothing to be sorry for. That was some of the best sex I have ever had. It was mind-blowing. And on top of that, I'm sure you're feeling so much more than I am. It's completely ok." And with that, his arms wrap around me, embracing me. Letting me feel it all, letting me cry it out. All the emotions, all the pain and suffering, that's slowly fading into the background. His dick is still inside me and I'm fucking sobbing. He holds me, letting me get it out. He speaks kind words and tells me how amazing he thinks I am.

I can't even put into words how perfect this man is. How can I be so lucky?

Still inside me, he holds onto my hips and stands. Holding onto me like I weigh nothing, which is definitely not the case. He walks us into the bathroom, setting me down. I feel the loss as he slides out of me and turns on the shower. "Get in," he demands.

There's not a lot of room for more than one person in my bathtub-shower combo, but I step in as he says. The hot water makes my body tingle and burn for a second until I adjust, but it's perfect. I let the water flood over my face, washing the emotions and dried tears off me. And then Loch presses his body into my back. His hands brush down my arms, causing a rush of goosebumps and a thrill to shoot through my body. I turn around. He reaches over and grabs my grapefruit body wash and looks at it.

"I swear I thought it would be your shampoo that smelled like grapefruit."

I smile and reach behind me to grab my shampoo and hold it up.

"Grapefruit and almonds." His smile grows wide. And he grabs my waist, pulls me in tight, and kisses me.

"Let me clean you," he says as his eyes darken.

"Mmhmm," I mumble, unable to use actual words.

He lathers my body wash between his hands and starts rubbing them all over me–my neck, shoulders, arms, chest, exploring and caressing. He reaches behind me and rubs the soap all over my back, pressing my soapy front to his mostly dry chest. His hands wander down to my ass; his finger slides between my cheeks. I freeze, my fists tighten, and I lurch back, my breathing shallow.

"Look at me," he whispers.

I do, and his eyes bring me back to this moment. He gets on one knee. He looks so uncomfortable; he barely fits in here. But his hands rub gently up and down my legs, lingering on my thighs and hips. He stands again, holding his hand between my legs, cupping me, and stroking my lips, washing all his cum off my body.

He helps me rinse off and wets my hair completely. He puts the shampoo in his hand and smells it, giving me another quirky smile before he turns me around and washes my hair. Massaging my scalp and gently pulling my hair as he gets the shampoo lathered. I turn back around and rinse my hair. His eyes wander up and down like he's taking me in all over again, and I decide to do the same, letting my eyes roam over his body.

The side of his torso has a snake tattoo coiling around him. "Can I see your tattoo?" I expect him to make a half turn. Instead, he turns to expose his entire back, covered in tattoos. Snakes wrap around several swords, with skeleton hands wrapped around the handles. It's intricate, detailed. And beautiful.

"What's it for?" I ask as my eyes continue to rove over his back and down to his round ass.

"Snakes are everywhere, and I believe in justice being served; nothing special really. It's just ink," he says, a little clipped.

"Well, it's beautiful," I tell him.

I condition my hair, and I let him watch me before he grabs my hips with his rough hands and changes places with me under the water. I keep watching him as the water runs down his body. There's something about him I want to run from, but he's so magnetic I can't deny the way I feel in his presence. I'm elevated, like I'm running on adrenaline, being in the same room as him.

Chapter 30
Loch

Snuggle and Spill

She's standing at the dresser, a towel wrapped around her body, her back to me as she rifles through a drawer. Steam still clings to her skin from the shower, and her wet hair drips at the ends. The soft light from the bedside lamp kisses every inch of her—the delicate slope of her shoulder, the curve of her spine, like the goddess she is.

I sit on the edge of the bed, towel around my waist, heart beating so hard it's damn near bruising my ribs. And for the first time, I'm scared of how much she means to me. Of how easily she could destroy me.

There have been times in my life where I've stared down the barrel of a gun, fist and face bloodied, skin split open, and I didn't feel a damn thing. Nothing as consuming as this. I watch her slide on a pair of soft sleep shorts and a tank top. She brushes her fingers through her wet hair, not knowing she's already carved her name into every hollow part of me.

I'm in her bed, and it's so simple and normal. But it feels like everything I've ever wanted, and the thought of losing it, losing her, terrifies me. I don't know how to be this new version of myself. The one that's soft, and the one that starts to wonder what it would feel like to keep her. To stop living like I have to make the world right and simply be.

I'm falling for her, and if I'm not careful, the weight of everything I've buried will crush us both.

She turns, catching me staring, and smiles–soft and sleepy. She doesn't say anything, flicking off the lamp and climbing into bed like this is second nature. Like this is our bed. She tucks herself against me, her cheek resting on my chest, one leg hooking over mine. I slide my arm around her, drawing her in tighter, instinctively possessive.

My hand rests on her bare hip, my thumb moving in slow, lazy circles. She feels like home. And all I can think is, if I lose her, if I fuck this up somehow... it'll destroy both of us. I bury my face in her hair, breathing her in, and hold her like I may never get to again. Maybe that's what love really is–terror and tenderness, wrapped so tightly together you can't pull them apart.

I didn't know it could feel like this, so intense, so quick. Deep down, the raw emotions for this girl are unreal. Not only the sex, although, Jesus Christ, that alone was enough to undo me for a lifetime. But the intimate time after, the stillness, quiet looks, and touches. Watching her tears fall from the release of it all, it fucking gutted me, the way she finally let me in. She let go of her past, at least a little, and let me touch her. She let me have her.

The weight of her body curled into mine right now is everything. The way my heart won't stop pounding is more than I expected. More than I was ready for. And now, all I can focus on is how I'm starving for more.

I press my lips to the top of her head. She shifts, curling tighter into my side, one of her thighs moving higher over mine. I pull the covers around us and let my hand rest on her lower back. But I have to ask, I need to know.

I clear my throat softly. "Olive?"

"Mmm?" she murmurs, almost asleep.

I wait a beat. Not wanting to push her too far, but needing to know. "Earlier, when we were together, when you asked for a minute..."

She tenses next to me. I soften my voice, thumb still moving over her skin. "You don't have to tell me anything you don't want to. But, if you can, I want to understand what happened that night. What you felt. What you went through. What I need to watch for. So I don't... hurt you."

Silence. Only the sounds of her breath and mine. I want to hear her tell me what hurt her. I know what the police report said, but I want to hear it from her.

Then, a small inhale. "You want to know?"

I nod, "Yeah. I do. I can't protect you from something I don't understand."

She's been quiet for a long time. And I let her. I don't fill the silence or rush it. I'm not sure if I expect her to say anything, but I hope she does. Her words, whenever she finds them, are going to matter more than anything else in the world because she chose to share them with me.

It comes out in pieces, fragments. Her voice trembles through every word, like the memories live in her bones, and she's pulling them out one splinter at a time. The gag in her mouth kept her from screaming for help. The knife he threatened her with. I'm so thankful she doesn't actually bear any visible scars from him. The emotion behind her words is enough to make my chest burn, enough to make me feel like I'm going to crawl out of my own skin from the rage building in my blood.

She continues to tell me how he restrained her and what he forced her to do. I can picture it without her having to say the worst parts. I can feel her fear and the loss of control in her voice. The helplessness. It makes me want to destroy something and take away all her pain.

But I don't speak; I don't let my fury out. I keep it locked away and solely focus on her—on the fact that she is here, breathing, opening up to me even though it's killing her to do it.

Her voice breaks as she talks about everything that happened before she blacked out. How it changed her, how the memories still live in the quiet. How traumatic it was to be left to die if no one had found her. She tells me about how Sophia found her and about the questions and the physical exam she had to go through. Her tears soak my chest, and I hold her tighter, brushing her hair back, pressing my lips to her temple. My heart is fucking wrecked. Her hands might as well be inside my chest, squeezing my heart like a stress ball.

I want to give her a world where none of that has ever touched her. I want to take every second of the pain she's ever felt and carry it in my own body instead. But I can't. All I can do is stay right here and not let go.

"Thank you," I whisper when she stops.

She tilts her head to look at me, eyes glassy.

"For trusting me," I say. "You're the strongest person I've ever met. And what you just did for me... that was brave as hell."

She doesn't respond with words, but presses in closer to me, and I wrap myself around her like a shield. I don't want her to carry that night alone anymore. Not if I can help it.

Eventually, her breathing evens out. She drifts off, still tucked in the curve of my body like she belongs there. I lie awake for a while, holding her, promising myself that no one will ever hurt her again, not while I'm breathing. If her attacker doesn't go to prison, I will end him.

CHAPTER 31
OLIVE

ME, HIM, AND THE DOG

I wake up tangled in Loch's arms. His arm is heavy over my waist, his chest presses against my back. For a moment, I don't move. I let myself exist in his warmth and safety, enjoying the strange feeling of another good night's sleep, something I haven't known lately.

His hands twitch in his sleep and pull me closer. My eyes flutter closed again, and I smile into the quiet peace.

When we finally stir and get out of bed, everything is slow and soft. We move around each other as if we've been doing this for years—brushing arms in the kitchen, passing coffee mugs between our hands, sharing looks that say more than words ever could.

Loch kisses my temple when he passes behind me, his hand ghosting along my waist, needing to feel me. And every time he touches me, something inside my chest heals, and my stomach tightens.

We spend the morning with Kong, letting him crawl up into Loch's lap while we sit on the floor, eating breakfast on the rug like kids. Kong's tail wags so hard it thumps against the couch. He is so happy, rolling onto his back for belly rubs with this goofy grin that melts me every single time. We play a game with him where I throw a ball down the hallway, and he fetches it. But he gets the zoomies and runs around every corner of the apartment before finally returning to me. We lie in bed for a lazy afternoon nap. Kong is the baby spoon, his head nuzzled into my shoulder with an adorable closed-mouth smile on his face. It's the most adorable thing I have ever seen. I'm the middle spoon squished between two warm bodies. Loch has his arm wrapped over me, resting his hand on Kong's side. It's so perfect it hurts.

Later, we take him out on a walk; all three of us bundled up in jackets. Even though the sun is shining, it's the middle of winter. Kong trots between us, leash held loosely in my hand. His tail is still wagging, and he hasn't stopped smiling since we woke up.

"He's a different dog," I say, watching him bounce ahead of us a few steps. He turns periodically to make sure we're still there. "He seems... happy."

"He is," Loch says. "You make him happy."

I glance at him, and he's looking at me.

"He liked me well enough when I had him," Loch continues, a small smile playing on his lips. "He was calm, felt safe. But he didn't act like this. This," he gestures toward Kong, who's stopped to sniff a patch of grass before trotting back toward me with a single little bark, "this is different. He's giddy with you. He lights up when you walk in the room."

My heart squeezes in my chest because I feel it too, that feeling of joy that has returned because of Kong.

"He needs you," Loch adds. "He was waiting for you. And," he reaches over and laces his fingers through mine, our arms swinging between us, "I think that's the most beautiful thing I've ever seen."

I swallow the lump in my throat, blinking up at him through the sunlight. "We all need someone to love us," I whisper. "And something to fight for."

His hand tightens around mine. "I love that we share this," he breathes. "That we have him. That he's not just a dog," he pauses, glancing at me again, and his voice lowers. "He's ours. You and I share a bond with him that no one else could ever understand or share."

I don't say anything. I don't have to. My heart pounds in my chest, and I nod, leaning into his side a little more as we walk.

It hits me then–somewhere between the crisp breeze and the soft sounds of Kong's paws on the pavement beside us–this is the beginning of something. It's not just healing or surviving; it's stronger.

This is the start of my happy ending.

Later that night, Loch sits at the island, a glass of water in hand, watching me make dinner like I'm the only thing worth seeing.

His gaze is searing into me, burning down my spine along the bare skin exposed from where my sweater has slipped off my shoulder. I try to focus on layering the pasta sheets and the ricotta, but every time I glance up and catch his eyes on me, I flush. He makes it difficult to concentrate on cooking.

"What?" I ask, grinning as I sprinkle shredded mozzarella on top.

"Nothing," he says, his voice low and warm. "Enjoying watching my girl be all domestic and adorable."

'His girl.' I like that he called me that. I bite my bottom lip, hoping he doesn't notice the blush coloring my face.

"You wanna help?" I ask, already knowing the answer.

A lazy smile tugs at the corners of his mouth as he shakes his head. "Nope. You said you wanted to make me dinner. I'm not messing with that. I'm here to enjoy the view, and I am fully enjoying it."

I roll my eyes, turning back to the oven and bending over to slide the lasagna in. "Well, the view is gonna burn dinner if you keep distracting her."

"The view can burn whatever the hell she wants if she stays right there, so I can look at her ass."

God, he is too much, but I also kind of like him looking at my ass, so I shake it a little for him.

He chuckles behind me, the sound is deep and full, and fills the entire space. I love the way his voice, rich and dark, curls around my spine, leaving me aching for more of him. He's an enigma, dark and broody but also kind and sweet, and so dirty.

While our dinner bakes, I sit down to talk, curious to know more about him. "Tell me something weird about yourself."

"Something weird. Hmm," as he ponders it for a minute. "I love pickle and peanut butter sandwiches."

I bust out laughing and make a fake gagging sound. "Gross! How did you ever find that combo?"

"During my early bachelor days. It was all I had, and then I loved it. You probably like some weird combo, too."

I laugh again, "Not anything nasty like pickles and peanut butter. But umm, I guess I have one weird thing—I like to eat my ice cream eighty to ninety percent melted. I know. I know. I like it all soupy."

Loch glares at me. "You're a psychopath, aren't you?"

We both laugh. He looks at me with lust-filled eyes, and I feel his hand on my leg, rubbing higher and higher. "I'm starving."

I stutter, "Dinner is almost ready; I can go che—"

"Not for lasagna, but I can wait until after dinner since you made such a nice meal for me."

I'm blushing again. We keep talking for a while longer about frivolous things—movies we love, and more odd facts. We share random memories that pop into our heads. He tells me about when his dad taught him how to drive. He tried to dodge a squirrel, because of course he did, and ran through a family's lawn and crashed into a fence. Our stories make me laugh so hard I have to clutch the counter for support. He watches me, soaking in every second, totally engaged and present.

Dinner is perfect. We sit at the island eating slowly from cheap, mismatched plates, savoring everything–the food, the company, the warmth. His hand finds mine halfway through the meal, his thumb brushing gently across my knuckles, and continuing to my wrist, giving it extra attention, and time slows for us.

There's something about Loch when he's soft, his armor slips; I see the man underneath, and the shadow he tries to keep around him as a wall. He makes me want to break it down. My chest aches in the best, most dangerous way. He makes me feel chosen and wanted.

I watch as Loch cleans the kitchen, putting the leftovers away and doing the dishes. He even feeds Kong for me. Now, I'm the one ogling him, being all domestic and adorable.

"I have an idea, Olive. But I need you to trust me and know that I would never hurt you."

I look at him warily. "What's your idea?"

"Tell me you trust me."

I look at his face for something, for a sign of anything. "Ok," I say, with nervous curiosity.

Loch grabs my hand and pulls me. I don't know what his plan is, but I think I have an idea of what it is once we go into the bedroom. He shuts the door behind us and turns to look at me with dark, smoldering eyes.

"Clothes off." He tells me in a serious tone.

I glare at him, questioning. For a long moment, he doesn't budge.

"Now, Olive. Don't make me ask again."

My clit pulses, hearing his dirty talk starting again. It's so fucking hot how he tells me what he wants and what he wants me to do.

I strip down, pulling my shirt over my head, and drop it to the floor; I slip my sweats down and step out of them. My fingers slide under the waistline of my underwear, and they come off, too. Feeling exposed and a little cold, I look at him. Waiting to see what he's planned.

Before everything happened, Loch would have totally been my type, domineering and powerful. It seems easy to slip back into something familiar, even though this is so much more intense than anything else I have ever experienced. I stand waiting. I've never been very shy, always comfortable in my skin, especially since I don't fit the stereotypical supermodel mold. My body has curves, rolls, and dimples, but I've always felt beautiful and sensual with men. Loch's gaze makes me feel more confident and more nervous than I have ever felt. My legs are shaky, my breaths come short, and he's making me wait.

"What now?" I ask.

"Patience, I'm admiring my view," he growls.

My body shakes with excitement. I'm fidgeting, unsure of what to do with my arms and trying to hide my vulnerability.

"Get on the bed, face up, arms above your head."

I do as he says, and my skin crawls with anticipation.

I watch him undress, removing his pants and his shirt, revealing his own bare body to me. "Fuck." He's so confident naked. Tan, built like a man who chops wood for a living–not chiseled, but thick and solid, with broad shoulders, soft stomach, and a strong chest. He strolls over to the edge of the bed, and I'm dying for his touch, for his mouth on mine, his hands on me, anything.

He wraps his huge hands around my knees and spreads my legs for him. He stands there and looks at me, at my bare pussy. The way he stares makes me shake, and my breathing becomes uneven. The slowness, the stillness, there's so much time to take it all in that I'm craving everything. I don't have any questions about wanting him anymore; I know I do.

His hand moves from my knee up my inner thigh, and his knuckle skims over my pussy. I'm already wet, dripping with need for him. His thumb moves down to collect my arousal, and he brings it between my lips and rubs my clit.

"Keep your hands above your head, and I'll give you what you want. Eyes on me, Olive."

He's gentle and slow at first, making me ache with need and anticipation. My core is tightening, watching him admire me. His pressure is steadily increasing, causing my hips to jerk, trying to get more from him. Without warning, his other hand leaves my leg, and he shoves two fingers into me. I gasp at the pressure, arching my back at the relief my body needs. He works me harder. I moan, panting and writhing. His fingers move at a faster and faster pace. He curls his fingers upward, rubbing my inner walls. He hits my G-spot, and he keeps rubbing, then thrusting, then rubbing, then thrusting, alternating over and over.

"You are so beautiful, panting like this. I love watching your body ache for me. It's so fucking hot seeing your dripping pussy waiting for me. Do you want more, Olive?"

"Yes!" I groan. Pleasure searing me, my body beginning to tingle in my core. I can feel an orgasm coming. My breathing gets heavy, and my body is shaking. And Loch pulls his hands off me completely. My body stills in shock at the loss. The feeling is gone. I was so fucking close.

"What? What's wrong?"

"Absolutely nothing."

"I was so close to cumming."

"I know, it was so fucking sexy."

"You know? Well then, why did you stop?"

"Your hands. Do you trust me?"

A little frustrated, I say, "I do trust you," and lay my head back down.

"Then you need to listen to me, leave your hands up. Do not lower them." He crawls up my body, first kissing my bare pubic mound, then licking up my stomach. I suck in with the feel of his mouth and his hot breath. He licks my peaked nipple with just the tip of his tongue. I ache for more, I need more.

"Your tits are fucking perfect." He pushes them together so he can lick them both, pinching intermittently and sucking hard.

"Fuck, Loch, yes." I moan.

His dick is hard. He rubs the head on my clit. I can't steady my breath with how turned on I am.

I let out a breathy cry, wanting more of him. My head is swirling with lust and the need to cum. I want to touch him back.

He crawls up to my neck, and then his mouth is on me. He's not gentle with his kiss. His lips are hard against mine; his tongue is thrusting into my mouth with force. I can't breathe, and he doesn't stop. His hands are still cupping my breasts, squeezing them hard. His dick is still teasing me. My body is so wild with want for this man.

"Please, Loch," I manage to get out, moaning into his mouth. His hips are moving, torturing me with sensations, but not entering me, and it's not enough. Between his mouth, his hands, and his dick, he is making me absolutely feral. I gasp and clutch my arms around him. I'm close. I just need a little more friction, and I can have the release I so desperately need. Then his whole body lifts off of me.

"I told you to keep your hands up. Since you don't listen to directions, get on your knees and suck my dick."

My eyes go wide, and I'm gawking at him in disbelief. He leaves me hanging again, and *now*, now, he wants me to suck him off. Which I am totally fine with, but after I cum, for fuck's sake.

"Olive, what did I say about making me repeat myself?"

"I, I don't understand why you keep stopping."

He growls like an animal, "Knees. Now."

Hot and frustrated, I crawl off the bed and onto my knees. Even though I'm frustrated, I'm also insanely turned on and want to taste him. He's standing in front of the bed, gripping his dick like he's irritated that he had to wait for me. But my mouth is watering now. I enjoy sucking dick, I always have. I love making a man putty in my hands and mouth. It makes me feel powerful, deciding how I want to give him pleasure. But as I stare for a moment at his cock, I gulp because his dick is so wide. I look up at him and see his eyes are full of desire, and it sends a pang of need to my clit. He wants this, and I want to be the one to give it to him.

I grasp the base of his cock and wrap my lips around its head, licking the tip. I suck and push myself further onto his cock, sliding my saliva down his length. Popping off, I run my tongue up and down, feeling his thick veins and smooth skin against my tongue. I open wide and take him back as far as I can. Bobbing back and forth, sucking hard.

"Fuck, your mouth is so good at this." His hand grabs the back of my head and pushes deeper into me until his dick is in my throat. I gag and tear up. His cock is so big I can barely fit him so far back. But he doesn't stop. His hips thrust harder into my mouth.

"You take my cock so fucking good. Oh, God, Olive," he moans with pleasure.

He's watching me; my chin is dripping with saliva, and he's so close.

"Suck, Olive, don't fucking stop."

He's going wild, dominating my mouth, and I love it. I moan on his dick.

He groans, "Oh, God," as his hand pushes my head down hard, forcing his dick deep into my throat. I take a deep breath through my nose to control my gagging and make a swallowing motion with the hollow at the base of my throat while he's deep.

"Oh, fucking hell. Your throat is squeezing my dick. Do it again."

I do, still breathing through my nose as he thrusts a few more times, cumming down my throat. "Swallow it," he gasps. His hands grip tighter and his body stills. I taste his cum and swallow as fast as I can, not wanting to waste a drop. I release him and lick my lips, tasting his sweet and salty release. Fuck, that was so hot.

I love that he was so raw, so carnal. That I could make him react like that.

"Get on your back," he breathes. He's still catching his breath, but his intent is clear.

Desire surges through my body. The second my back is on the bed, his head ducks between my legs. There is no slowness now, there is no patience or teasing. He devours my pussy, like it's air to breathe. His tongue is on me, thrusting into my center, flicking my clit. My legs quake, I'm writhing and moaning uncontrollably. He sucks my clit into his mouth, grazing my clit with his teeth, and I shoot off the fucking bed, moaning his name. I'm so sensitive after all the teasing from before.

He thrusts his fingers into me, looking at me with fiery desire in his eyes. "Hands above your head. If you drop them, I stop. Understand?"

"Mmhmm," I hum, the only sound I can make when we're naked.

He curls his fingers inside me again, touching that spot that I need. His tongue presses hard and flat against my clit, giving me the right amount of pressure. Finally, that feeling is back. My orgasm builds, and pleasure courses through my body.

The feeling crests, and I moan with pleasure. "Loch, oh, God," and he stops. My hands move down to push his head. Shit! I did not mean to do that.

"Oh, I see. You want me to restrain you the right way?" he asks before hopping off the bed and leaving the room.

"Where are you going?" I say in utter frustration. I drop my head, trying to reset my brain and figure out what the hell is going on. I've never been more frustrated in bed. He returns and stands at the end of the bed. He has something in his hand. As soon as I realize what it is, I'm frozen in sheer panic. Duct tape.

"What, what's that for?"

"Your hands, Olive."

"No, no, you can't."

"Trust me, please. I'm not going to hurt you." He pauses for a beat. "But the next time you see duct tape, you are going to think of nothing else besides the strongest, most intense orgasm you have ever had in your life. And nothing else, ever again. Can you trust me?"

I can't move. I can't speak. I'm frozen in fear, but I don't say no.

He walks to the side of the bed and takes my wrists, gently rubbing them like he did at dinner. This. This is what he had planned from the beginning.

"Breathe, Olive. You have to breathe."

He pulls my hands above my head and wraps them against the bar of my headboard. Not tight, and only once around. It won't be hard to rip my hands free if it becomes too much.

"What's your safe word, Olive?"

"Peanut butter," I breathe in a whisper.

"Good girl."

He looks me dead in the eyes, like he's looking into my soul. "I am not going to hurt you, but if you want this to stop, you say it, and I will stop and remove the tape as fast as I can. Ok?"

I nod.

I'm lying here like a lamb, waiting for him to take me to slaughter. My pulse pounds in my brain, my neck, and my throbbing clit.

His mouth is on me again, devouring and demanding. He sucks on my clit, licking exactly where I need it. Before I can even take a full breath, his fingers thrust back inside me. My brain is battling between pleasure and fear. I watch him between my legs. He's sending me right back to the edge. I have been waiting for what feels like an hour to cum, and that's all I can focus on. My hips grind into his face. He hasn't shaved since our date, and his stubble creates more friction. It's the perfect sensation. I am right there. And he stops, AGAIN.

"Fucking hell, Loch. I'm taped up—" He cuts me off without a word and moves on top of me. He thrusts his dick inside me, bottoming out with no warning. He's so big, but I can't get enough of the full feeling. It only takes a minute of him pumping his cock into me and I cum, hard. My vision goes black and spotty; I moan some sort of gibberish. My body is on fire, tingling from head to toe, a tidal wave of sensation that consumes me.

Loch doesn't let up, thrusting harder and deeper. As the tension leaves my body, he continues to thrust. My eyes fall back and I see my hands bound. The same thing I focused on once before, but now, all I feel is ecstasy. His body presses into mine, and I don't want it to end.

"Again," he grits out.

And just like that, my body is on edge again. His words twist my insides.

"Cum again, Olive. I want to feel more of you on my cock, feel you squeeze me like a good girl. And then, I'm going to fill you with my cum again."

That's it. Those dirty words send me right over the edge.

I moan, "Loch, oh God. Loch, yes."

"Yes, I am your fucking god. Cum on my dick."

His body tenses with mine. We both jerk erratically, cumming together, sweaty and panting. His body goes limp, falling next to me. I try to unscramble my brain and catch my breath for what feels like the tenth time tonight. His hands reach to remove the tape immediately. He holds my wrists, stroking them, kissing them.

"Are you ok, Olive?"

I fucking laugh, like shake with laughter. "Fuck yes, I'm ok, that was the best orgasm of my life. I mean, I had two of them, for fuck's sake. By the time you restrained me, I needed it so bad that I didn't even care. How did you know to do this?"

"I didn't know. I hoped. I enjoy using restraints, and thought if I could show you a good side of them, it would replace the pain with pleasure. I also like edging you," he says sheepishly. "I guess it's my thing."

"Well, fuck, yes, please. Sign me up for more of that."

Loch leaves the room again, but this time he returns with a wet towel. He's come to clean me up, and thank God, because I don't think my body could stand in a shower right now.

Chapter 32
Olive

Cuddle Between Choices

It's been a week of something that feels almost like magic.

Loch, Kong, and I have slipped into this strange, beautiful rhythm—mornings with sleepy smiles and tangled sheets, afternoons filled with lazy kisses, shared meals, and walks with Kong, where Loch sneaks glances at me and holds my hand. Loch only leaves when he has work he has to do. Otherwise, he's with me. We share nights where his body speaks every word and his mouth doesn't have to. I'm comfortable with him. His hands on me, his dirty mouth, it's... us.

Now, Loch's at work, and I sit on the floor of the living room, Kong sprawled out beside me with his gigantic head resting in my lap while I rub behind his ears. My phone rings, but I don't recognize the number. I answer, and something in my chest pulls tight; then I hear her voice.

"Hello, is this Olive Smythe?"

"Uh, yes, it's Olive. "

"Hello, this is Melissa from the District Attorney's office. I'm afraid I have some news." I hear the shift in her tone.

I sit up a little straighter, sweat breaking out on the back of my neck, despite the cool air in the room. "Ok."

"Yesterday, Mr. Wright's attorney submitted his case dismissal," she says, every word hitting like a brick to the sternum. "We–We did what we could, but unless you're willing to testify at trial, the case won't move forward. If you agree to testify, we can try to push for a trial. We've got three business days to file a notice of intent to testify and any additional evidence, and hopefully keep the case from being dismissed. I'm sorry I don't have better news. Would you be willing to testify in court, Olive?" I'm left speechless and in a fog. "Hello? Olive? Are you still there?"

"Yeah, I, uh, I hadn't really..."

"Think about it, and please call me when you decide what you want to do."

Three days to decide if I am strong enough to stand in front of him, as well as a room full of strangers, to tell my story. To have to look at the man who tore me apart and speak it out loud. If I don't do it, he'll walk free. He knows where I live; he could hurt others, not just me.

I don't say goodbye. I hang up and stare at the phone in my hand like it's betrayed me.

My breaths come quick and shallow. A buzzing starts in my ears, and my limbs are too heavy, like they aren't mine. I shrink back into the girl I used to be in real time. The girl who couldn't sleep, who triple-checked the locks, and who lived in constant fear and silence for months.

Kong's head lifts. He's awake now and watching me.

I don't speak, but something in my face must shift because he moves without hesitation.

He leans in, nudging his big snout under my arm and pushing until he forces his head into my chest. The sheer weight of him hits me like a wave; his body curls into mine with slow, deliberate care.

One of his front paws rests heavy on my chest, like he's pinning me down, not to trap me, but to hold me. That's all it takes.

I let go, burying my face into the side of his thick neck, sobbing quiet, shaky cries. I try to hold it back, hold it in, try to stay in control. I don't have to say a word. He knows that I've changed. His breathing stays slow and even, his heartbeat strong beneath my hand. He stays still and lets me cry into him.

At one point, he shifts enough to lick a tear from my jaw. One soft kiss before pressing his face to mine.

"I'm ok," I whisper, my voice cracking on the lie I tell myself as much as him.

His tail thumps once against the couch—light, like he's saying, 'I know. But I'm not leaving you.'

Eventually, I climb back into the cushions, and he climbs up beside me. The couch is large, but he tucks his massive body against mine so tightly, it feels like I'm wrapped in armor.

We stay like this for hours. I don't turn on the TV. I don't play music. I don't move; I shut down. I don't want to exist outside of this moment without him.

I think about calling Loch, about hearing the calm strength in his voice, but I can't. He's supposed to come by later, and I'll tell him then. Once I figure out how to tell him.

For now, I let Kong hold me the only way he can, in a fortress of muscle, loyalty, and love. I let myself fall apart quietly, in the safety of his chest and neck, utterly thankful for his presence.

The knock on the door startles me, and I scramble to my feet, hope rising in my chest. A sob builds in my throat, and the need to fall into his arms, to let him gather me up and piece me back together once again, swallows me. I need him so much that I can hardly breathe.

I open the door and see Loch. A subtle smirk curves at the corner of his mouth, but his eyes, those stormy eyes, are gentle as they drop to meet mine.

"Hey," he murmurs.

I step into him without thinking, arms winding around his torso, face pressed against his chest. His arms fold around me, and he rests his chin on my head. I let out a sob in his embrace.

"Loch," I whimper.

"I'm here," he replies, his voice low and warm.

"What's wrong, Olive? Don't get me wrong, I'm loving this welcome, but you're upset? Why?"

I stay like that for a beat longer than necessary, hoping the silence might hold me together and make it all go away. I pull back enough to look up at him. "I have to tell you something."

Loch's jaw flexes and his posture stiffens, bracing for impact. He nods once, "Ok."

I step back and cross the small space to the kitchen island. He follows, sitting beside me, his leg brushing against mine. His eyes don't leave me as I take a deep breath. I'm not sure why I'm nervous about telling him, but I can't keep my hands from fidgeting while I try to come up with the words.

"The D.A. called today. About... the guy. My case." My voice hitches. "He's going to walk. Unless I testify, they'll drop the case."

Loch doesn't speak. I watch as his fingers curl into fists and his jaw clenches so hard it ticks. His eyes flash with dark anger. Rage rolls off him in waves, testing his restraint. I've never seen that look on him, and it's terrifying.

He jumps to his feet and paces around the small room like a lion in a cage. My nerves peak, not sure how he's going to react or what's about to happen.

"He attacked you," Loch growls. "He should rot in prison."

"I know," I choke out. "But–"

"No." His voice is sharp. He turns to face me. "You shouldn't have to sit in a courtroom and relive it for others to believe you. This system is bullshit. The privileged people in this world never serve their time. The rules don't apply to them. You shouldn't–" His chest heaves with labored breaths as his hands shake. He's unraveling at the edges.

I stand, reaching for him; somehow now I'm comforting *him.*

He turns, yanking the chair away from the counter to reach me. His eyes are full of darkness. He grabs my waist and spins me around, pressing his chest tight against my back. The counter pinches my hips from his pressure. I try to find space, but he gives me none. His hands come around me on each side, trapping me in, pressing further into me with his body. He breathes on the back of my neck and drops his face to the side of my ear.

"Loch—" I plead, scared for the first time of his reaction.

"I want to hurt him," he snaps, his voice raw. "I want to end him for what he did to you," he says in a low, ominous growl, full of quiet rage. Only for me to hear. "I need to keep you safe." His voice is soft, but I hear a steel thread of warning.

I turn my face to look into his wild eyes, but there's pain in them, too. I arch my head into his neck, attempting to ground him.

"I trust you to protect me. I know I'm safe with you," I say. "You're already everything I need. I don't need anything else."

His breath shudders out. My words cut through the tension like light through fog. For a moment, he doesn't move. He looks at me like I'm the only thing holding him together. Then his hands are on me, desperate, strong, and demanding, needing me to stop the storm inside him. The air between us tightens. It's electric and jolting.

He's still pushing me into the counter, his chest to my back, and his hand lifts to cup my breast. His thumb brushes my nipple over my shirt, and it pebbles at his touch. I lean into it, and for a moment, neither of us speaks. We breathe and feel the tension and all the things we can't say out loud.

"You make it hard to stay good," he murmurs.

"Then don't be good," I say, pushing my ass into his groin as much as I can. "Be here with me," I moan. Feeling pressure between my legs. His arms consume me, pushing himself into me, all heat and desperation. He's not soft; he's hungry and out of control.

His hands are on my hips, my back, my sides, everywhere, like he's mapping me. He needs this from me, to lose his control, and I will give it to him.

He stills for a breath, causing me to hold mine, "I'd burn the world for you, and I will fucking kill him before I let him get away with what he's done."

"I know," I whisper back. "But right now... I want you to fuck me."

Without an ounce of hesitation, he moves on me like a rabid animal. He pushes down on my back, my chest falling into the cold countertop, bending me over. His fingers grab onto my hips and grab my pants and underwear, and he pulls them down to my ankles. I kick them away so I can give him better access. Before I can think or rationalize, his cock is at my entrance. I'm so turned on, but also a little afraid. He's different right now. He's dark and full of rage, but I'm trusting him not to hurt me. My blood is pumping, my clit throbbing. I look back at him over my shoulder. He's gone feral, his eyes blown, jaw tight, and his hands are back on my hips.

With one quick motion, he shoves his cock into me. There is no easing today. He fucks me with fervor, claiming me. His body is smashing me into the edge of the counter. I'll probably bruise, but this is a bruise I want. He has one hand on my back, pressing me down, and the other on my hip.

He snarls, "Fuck, nothing compares to fucking your tight cunt. I need to fill you."

He pounds into me at a relentless pace. I moan in short, jagged gasps because of the way he slams into me. His balls slap against me, sending sensations of pleasure to my clit.

"You're mine, Olive. Mine to protect; mine to fuck."

His words send me crashing into pleasure, heat bursting through me, sending a scream out of my chest. "Loch...I'm cumming. Fuuuck!"

My pussy clenches around him. He never stops fucking me through my orgasm, making sure every wave of pleasure courses through me. His hands move to grip my hair, needing more from me. Pulling me harder into him, rubbing my walls with his thick cock.

As his thrusts become erratic, his hands grip me even tighter, squeezing my shoulders and holding my body as he cums. The pain of his hands on me and the blinding pressure from his dick–both sensations mixing–send my brain into an enraptured daze. His dick twitches, and his body leans over mine. He kisses the back of my neck and releases me. He pulls out, and his cum drips out of me. It's almost to the crease of my leg when his hand comes down, his fingers sliding along my leg, scooping up all his cum, and then shoving his fingers into my cunt.

"Mine," he growls.

This is a new side of him, and my pussy clenches at his possessiveness and dirty words.

Chapter 33
Olive

Making Love and Decisions

As we lay in bed hours later, my breathing was still erratic from earlier. Loch had kissed me like he was trying to drag me into his darkness, as opposed to me pulling him out of it. But I let him, because it's what I wanted—his hands on my skin, his breath on my neck, the desperation of it all. It ignited a fire in me that I didn't know would ever burn again.

He took me like I was his, and I was. It felt good to be able to give him something, to put him back together for once.

There was something dark in him tonight, angry and vengeful because of me. His deep voice when he talked about my attacker, the wildness in his eyes, scared me because I could tell it pained him. It scared me because I liked it; I like the dark parts of him. It made the dark parts of me feel more normal.

The rage and possessiveness he keeps just beneath the surface threatened to break loose. He usually holds it back and hides it from me. But I want it, all the parts of him, broken and not.

Now, I lie in the dark, still trying to calm the hum under my skin. My body is sore in the best way; his touch still ghosting over me like a brand. I turn my head to look at him, the curve of his jaw sharp in the moonlight; his eyes are shadowed but open.

He shifts beside me and props himself up on an elbow, like he hasn't even tried to sleep.

"I can't stop thinking about it," he breathes.

My chest tightens. "Loch?" I ask in hesitation.

His face remains stoic, jaw locked, and body tense. He's holding back his rage, and it's a minute-by-minute task, costing him every ounce of control.

"I... I need you to know I'll back whatever choice you make." He continues, "If you don't want to testify, I'll support that. If you do, I'll be there for every second. But I hate that it's on you. That they put this burden on you. I'll make sure you are safe from him no matter what you decide, I promise."

I reach out, lacing my fingers with his. "I hate it, too." He waits, but he's restless like he's waiting for me to continue. "I'm terrified to testify," I admit. "The idea of walking into a courtroom and having to say those things out loud, to other people, and with him there, looking at me..." I swallow hard. "It makes me sick." Loch's grip on my hand tightens.

"But him walking free?" I whisper. "That's worse. Knowing he's still out there, living like nothing ever happened. Knowing I could see him walking down the street. He still knows where I live. It's like... he's still tormenting me every day. He still has power over me, even though I want to let it go. I want to let it go with every fiber of my body. To break his control over me."

Loch looks at me like he wants to tear the world apart and lay the pieces at my feet. "He doesn't have any control over you. He won't get away with it; I won't let him."

I nod. "I know. Not when you're here, not when I have Kong," my voice cracks.

His hand cups my cheek, his thumb stroking my skin. There's fire in his eyes again, but softer now.

"I'll never let anything happen to you," he says.

I reach for him, wrapping my arms around his waist, and he pulls me in tight. I believe him, even with that barely leashed darkness I'd seen earlier. Because deep down, it didn't scare me. It thrilled me. It turned me on that I was his. His girl. His weakness and his obsession. Maybe that makes me a little twisted, too, but I don't care. I want to be his, no matter how messy or broken. I belong to him.

I reach my hand down, turning more to my side. I push my hand under his boxer briefs and grab his thick cock. It's already half-hard. He groans like I hurt him, but he thrusts into my hand.

In a second, he's on me, hovering over me, his thigh nudging my legs apart and pushing in to apply pressure to my core. My body is bursting at the seams, so sensitive, still thrumming from earlier. I groan into his mouth as it crashes into mine. His lips press softer than before, his tongue more curious, like he's savoring my mouth. His lips move down to my neck, sucking and licking me, his breathing heavy already. My heart pounds, and my back arches into him. He touches his way down my body, taking my breasts in his hands, pulling them into his mouth, and he sucks hard on my nipples.

My hands can't help but do the same, wandering and exploring him. His back is broad, smooth, and defined; his arms and shoulders feel powerful and corded with muscle. His dark honey-brown eyes devour me. He slides his body down mine until he's on his knees.

"I want to show you what you do to me. Eyes on me."

I sit up on my elbows and watch him. My eyes drift over his chest, the way his muscles shift beneath his skin. His stomach isn't shredded, but it's firm, with enough softness to make him real. God, he is beautiful–raw, powerful, and mine.

Heat curls low in my belly as I drink him in. The dark ink of his tattoos, the faint sheen of sweat on his skin, and the steady rise and fall of his chest, all of it makes me ache with want.

He smiles, slow and wicked, and starts pulling off his briefs. He slowly fists himself, his predatory gaze watching me, full of lust.

My mouth goes dry. I watch his large, slightly callused hands move from the base of his cock in short pumps, and then long pumps going over his head and spreading pre-cum down his length. Fuck, it's so hot watching him, so hard and ready, all because of me.

"Pinch your nipples," he demands.

I begin playing with my peaked nipples, pushing my tits together for him. Biting my lower lip because he's making me feel like the most amazing thing he's ever seen. I can't think of a time I felt more confident and wanted.

"Touch your clit," he strokes harder.

As soon as I make contact with my sensitive clit, I moan in pleasure.

"Quiet, Olive. I don't want to hear a sound coming out of your mouth until I say so."

I nod once, understanding what he wants. Feeling so turned on, I'll do whatever he wants me to do. I need him.

His grip tightens around his cock, and his pace picks up. His smile fades, but the heat in his eyes doesn't. It only deepens until I can feel it pressing into my soul like a touch to my skin. Loch looks at me like he is unraveling me with his gaze alone.

He strokes himself, hard and deliberate, the air around us thick with something that might shatter me from the inside out. I can see the shift in him—his control is slipping, and I know mine is too, my fingers rubbing my clit faster and faster.

His eyes don't leave mine; I'm exposed in every way. It should make me nervous, but it reminds me of our first night. Looking into his eyes has become so natural and erotic.

"I can't fucking take it anymore," he hisses, his voice rough with restraint. "The way you look at me like that... like you want to be ruined."

"I do."

I reach for him, and he's there, hands cupping my face, mouth crashing into mine like he needs my mouth to breathe. This isn't frantic like before. It's deep and consuming. Loch kisses me like he wants to memorize me from the inside out, his tongue tangling with mine.

"You see what you do to me? I can't even resist you for a minute. I need you," he says against my throat, kissing down my neck. "Need to feel more of you. Need to be inside you."

"Please," I say in a breathy moan. I don't care how desperate I sound. I am desperate for him, for this.

When he finally presses his cock into me, it isn't fast. It is slow and achingly perfect. My fingers dig into his back as I pull him closer, needing more, wanting his cock deeper.

He moves like he's worshipping me, his forehead presses to mine, and our eyes lock. Pounding thrusts send waves of pleasure through me that are deeper than just physical. It's more than lust or want.

It's love, even if neither of us is saying it out loud.

My body wraps around his, our breaths tangle, hearts race in sync, and I close my eyes and let go completely.

He groans my name, and my pussy pulses and clenches around him. My orgasm hits me hard, like a wave I can't outrun. My body seizes around him, pleasure tearing through me so sharp it almost hurts. I cry out, his fingers digging into my ass. My hips lift to take him deeper as I shatter beneath him. I can't think, can't breathe; I only feel–us, the ache between my legs, the way he stays with me through every pulsing second.

My body is still trembling when I feel the shift in him, his grip tightening on my hips even more, his breath going ragged against my neck. He curses under his breath, low and gruff, and then he's moving harder and deeper.

"Fuck, Olive," he groans, his voice wrecked.

He buries himself deep with one final thrust. His whole body goes still, as he cums with a sound that makes my stomach twist and my heart stutter, raw and guttural.

He collapses onto me a second later, pressing his forehead to my shoulder, his body still shaking as he catches his breath. We hold each other for a long time because in this moment, we're connected; we're one. Breathing and panting, coming down from our high.

The next morning we wake up to our usual routine. Coffee, a walk with Kong, and shower time together. It's become so normal in a short amount of time. Today, there is a change, though; the air feels like it's charged with the power of the sun.

After last night's conversation about whether I'm going to testify or not, and the lovemaking without actually admitting it. It's a beautiful tension of unspoken emotion. Every ordinary thing feels brighter, colors sharper, and sounds crisper. Sweet moments of eye contact feel dizzying, like I'm actually soaring somewhere above.

I'm lost in a daze when Loch speaks up. "Olive, would you like to do some training with Kong today? Since he can't do a lot of outside activities, it's important to work his mind. He could use some mental stimulation."

"What kind of training?" I ask. "He's so well-behaved, I can't imagine him needing much."

"It's not about behavioral training; it's about keeping him engaged and his mind active. Not to mention the more he's trained to listen to you, the better you can control him if you ever need to."

"Sure, tell me what to do."

Loch lifts one eyebrow suggestively and gives me a sexy smirk. "You know I will always do that, but for Kong, how about I teach you?"

He goes to the kitchen and grabs a big handful of treats and gives some to me, and puts the rest in his pocket. We start simple with things he already knows. He sits and lies down. He even does a pretty good wait until you pass the thirty-second mark, and he gets distracted. We try giving the shake command, but he keeps jumping up on his hind legs and giving us both paws, making me giggle.

"Try asking him to shake with your hand at his eye level so he doesn't feel the need to jump up to your hand. Right when you say it, grab his paw so he understands what you want from him." He coaches me and never gets frustrated with me or Kong. It's making those tingly feelings even stronger.

"Ok," I say. I reach down lower for Kong's paw and say, "Shake." He does it, but not willingly.

Loch comes over to repeat the command and reaches for his paw. Kong complies. "Do it once more like before, and then after that, ask for his paw and wait for him to give it to you."

I have a huge grin because this whole thing makes me so happy I could burst into bubbles and glitter. But I refocus and repeat the command while I grab his paw. Then I stand and hold out my hand near his face and say, "Shake." With a flashback of that very first time I asked him to sit, he holds out his paw and shakes flawlessly, and my heart expands tenfold. I give him a treat and scratch his head. "Good boy, Kong! You did so good."

Loch comes over to repeat the command for him, and he does it again. We smile at each other, and he says, "If you can do this with him for five to ten minutes every day, learning new tricks and mastering others, he will be much easier to correct and control when you are outside and in public."

"But he listens to you so much better; I guess I'll have to keep you around too," I tease.

"He only listens to me better because he knows I protect him, like I will protect you. But I'm more than happy to hang around."

CHAPTER 34
LOCH

SLIP 'N SLIDE, BACKDOOR EDITION

We barely make it out of bed over the next couple of days. We only leave it when our stomachs demand something more than each other for nourishment, or the times I have to go to work. We get dressed out of necessity; when Kong gives us big, judging eyes that say, 'Take me out or I'll chew your shoes.' Otherwise, we're a blur of hands and mouths, gasps and laughter.

There's something different in the way she allows touch now. There's almost no hesitation; her aversion peeks its ugly head on a rare occasion. She isn't riding the edge of fear, and the best part is her trust. We have come so far in such a short amount of time. It's fucking with me in the best way possible.

Later in the afternoon, she lies on her back, her hair messy and cheeks flushed from whatever number orgasm I've just given her. She looks so goddamn beautiful it hurts. And that look in her eyes is so open and unguarded. But I haven't finished with her, and it isn't likely I ever will.

I need to claim the part of her that still flinches once in a while when a memory creeps in. The part that still sees ghosts when her mind goes quiet. I need to take that fear and erase it. I know I've taken a lot of the pain and changed it into pleasure, but the rest is deeper. I need to take all her pain and carry it for her.

I tie her wrists above her head again, not because I want to control her, but because she lets me. I love seeing her restrained, willing to do whatever I ask. Her skin is still faintly marked by the memory of my hands on her hips. I like the control and the trust she has in me. She is the sexiest fucking thing I've ever seen. She's bare, fully exposed, with her arms tied to the bed frame, her legs spread for me, because now, she watches me do it with calm desire in her eyes. The fact that it's not fear anymore is everything.

"You trust me?" I ask, voice gravelly.

She nods without missing a beat. "With everything."

"Fuck. You're such a good girl, and good girls get rewarded. Do you want that?"

"Yes. I want it all."

I brush my fingers down her arms, her ribs, her thighs–slow, reverent. She doesn't flinch. She opens herself to me even more.

"I'm going to give you the version of this you deserve," I croon, kissing against her stomach. "No fear, or monsters. Just me and you."

She whimpers, "Loch," lifting her hips, begging without words.

She's beautifully wrecked. Her hair is a tangled halo around her flushed face, chest rising and falling in uneven breaths, her nipples peaked, needing to be touched. She blinks up at me, dazed, lips parted like she isn't sure what I have in store.

I could sit and watch her writhe in front of me all fucking day. I take in every trembling breath, every shift of her hips, every shiver when my hands move lower again. Her body is exhausted, but it's perfect because she's too tired to overthink.

"Safe word?"

"Peanut butter."

"Good girl, tell me you'll use it if you need it."

Her eyes widen, and her throat bobs. "I will, I promise."

I whisper, leaning over her, my mouth brushing her ear. "Then let go for me, Olive."

She whimpers, already on the edge. She's soaking wet from her other orgasms and still has my cum in her from earlier. She is more than ready for everything I want to do to her.

My hands dip lower, brushing her little bundle of nerves. Pushing my fingers through her lips, slick with arousal, into her, feeling her walls clamp down on them. I bend my fingers, looking for her G-spot, and I don't stop until I find it. I want to make her squirt and need to find the spongy patch inside her. The sharp jolt of her hips, her back arching off the bed, the soft, broken cry that makes my heart flutter, and my dick throbbing painfully, tell me I'm in the right place. I watch her, reading her body's reactions as my fingers move faster over her cushiony insides.

Her body trembles, her skin is flushed and dewy with sweat, her breath comes in shallow bursts. She unravels right in front of me, and still–still–she's holding on, fighting the inevitable fall.

My fingers move with practiced pressure, fast and relentless. I know her body now–know how she builds toward release and how she tries to hold it in. I won't let her do that now.

"Let go," I demand, my voice rough with need. "Don't hold back. I've got you, Olive."

She whimpers, arching under my hand, her thighs trembling with tensed muscles. I move harder and faster now. Her eyes flutter shut, her mouth falling open, raw and beautiful.

Her orgasm covers my hands, and she screams in sync with each squirt, splashing me as her hips buck in the air.

Her whole body convulses, back bowing off the mattress as she shatters in front of me. She gasps my name like it's the only word she remembers; her release rushes out of her and she couldn't stop it if she tried. All the liquid runs down her pussy onto her ass and the bed.

I freeze in awe for half a second, watching this wild woman fall apart for me.

By the time her body stills, she's boneless, flushed from her face to her chest. Her lips are parted, her breath shaky, her eyes unfocused on me. Completely undone.

"You ok?" My voice is softer and more teasing than I mean it to be.

She smiles with a slow blink. "I've never done that before, squirt, I mean. It was amazing, but I'm sorry I made such a mess." As her cheeks flush.

"Never apologize for that; I wanted you to do exactly what you did. It was fucking hot to watch you squirt on my fingers. I love your mess. Now bend over, show me that beautiful fucking ass of yours, and let me fuck you."

While watching her adjust herself with her hands tied to the frame, I help her into a kneeling, bent-over position. I love how she does as she's told. I slap her ass cheek, hard, then the other cheek. She gasps. I wait a moment to see if she'll tell me to stop or use her safe word.

She's slick with arousal, her ass glossy with cum. I put two fingers back in her pussy, soaking my hand again. I run my fingers up to Olive's ass. This is mine, too. She just doesn't know it yet.

She jumps in surprise. "Loch," she stammers.

"What, Olive? You know what your safe word is if you want me to stop, right? Would you like to say it?"

I wait for a long, tense pause, moving my hands over her ass cheeks, feeling her skin. Her round ass sticking up in the air makes my dick unbearably hard. Nothing comes out of her mouth. She's not going to stop me.

With a slick finger, I press inside her tight hole, just a knuckle. Letting her adjust to the feeling. Olive is quiet and tense. "Relax, Olive, you trust me not to hurt you, right?"

"Mmhmm," she mumbles.

I use my thumb to press on her clit as I push my finger in fully. She gasps, tensing, and then, after a moment, she relaxes around me.

"That's my girl. My cock is aching to fuck your gorgeous ass."

After pushing in and out a couple of times, I slide in another slick finger, coated in more wetness from her pussy.

She whimpers, "Oh, Loch."

"Do you like this, Olive? You take whatever I give you so fucking well. I can't wait to fuck your ass."

She moans again, pressing back into me slightly, "Loch."

I slide in and out harder, stretching her, getting her ready for me. Fuck, she is so hot, and to my surprise, she hasn't stopped me. She's begging for more.

I wasn't sure if she would let me get this far. My gut sinks for a moment. She completely trusts me, and I haven't been completely honest with her. But now is not the time. I'll figure that out later. Her body starts pulsing with pleasure, pushing into my fingers for more. Thank fuck, I need to be inside her.

I leave my fingers in her ass and I sink my dick into her pussy, my other hand on her hip.

"Oh, fuck, Olive. You're so tight like this," I moan out. Her pussy is tight and wet. Reaching around her body to rub her clit, I lean over her, fucking her hard and changing the angle. Her moans are getting louder and more sporadic.

She squirts more on me, soaking my hand again, and covering my dick in her hot cum. She's panting and moaning. I love how loud and vocal she is. Her body is still shaking, like she's having a small seizure. It's so fucking hot to see her squirt over and over. I pull my dick and fingers out of her; her body slacks, and I notch my cock at the tight ring, now soaking wet with her own fluid.

"Loch, I can't," she stills.

"Then, say it," I demand.

She turns her head to look back at me. My eyes tell her to trust me, yet dare her to say it.

I pause for a long minute, waiting for her to decide. She nods, but continues to watch me. I can feel her stare lingering on me. Boring into me, to see that it's still me, that I'm giving her pleasure and not pain.

I push the head of my dick in, feeling her tight ring suck me in. "Oh fuck, Olive, you're so tight. Fuck, you feel so good. I'll go slow. Tell me when you are ready for more of me." I look back at her eyes, and moments pass, and she nods. I push inside another inch. Stretching her more. I see her hands clasp and tighten above her.

"Breathe, try to relax." Her eyes close, and I see her exhale, her body relaxing into me a little more. I push deeper.

She gasps, "Fuck."

I go still, giving her more time to adjust. I reach around to rub her clit again. Within seconds, her body moves, arching into me. Pushing back for more. Her clit is dripping wet. My fingers glide in small circles until she is breathing heavily. Her eyes finally open again, full of desire, and she gives me a nod.

"Oh fuck, my girl knows what to do," I tell her, letting her know how fucking hot it is to see her wanting me to fuck her like this. I push in to the hilt, and she cries out in pleasure. The need, want, and a bit of fear looking back at me send a pulse to my cock. I thrust into her, pulling almost all the way out and slamming back into her, watching her ass shake with every thrust of my hips.

"Fuck, your ass feels so fucking tight."

I watch my thick cock disappear inside of her. Making me jerk into her harder. Fuck, she is so beautiful like this.

She is everything—laid out beneath me, eyes locked on mine, lips parted in that breathless little way that drives me insane. Her moans are getting louder, her words becoming incoherent.

I move inside her, deep and steady, savoring every second. I can't believe I get to touch and fuck something this perfect.

God, she is so beautiful, so fucking sexy and pliable. Every sound she makes, every tremble in her body, every whisper of my name lights me up from the inside.

She spreads her legs further, allowing me to drive deeper into her, and I groan. God, she knows exactly how to drive me to the edge.

I pick up the pace, my hips grinding into hers, fast, hard, and deliberate. She moans beneath me, her hands gripping the headboard, turning her head back into the sheets.

"Look at me," I growl, my voice wrecked.

Her head turns back again, her eyes flutter open, glassy with pleasure, and when they meet mine, it nearly undoes me.

"You feel that?" I whisper, sinking deeper, watching her fall apart with every thrust. "No one gets this but me. No one else ever will."

She whimpers, her body clenching, legs tensing tighter, and I lose what little control I have left. I'm going to ruin her for anyone else. Over and over again, I move in and out until she tightens even more.

"Cum with me, Olive. I want to feel you as I cum inside your beautiful ass."

I keep rubbing her clit until she squirts on my fingers again. She screams, loud. I pump harder and faster. Shooting my cum into her ass, filling her up again. Some dribbles out down her leg. She is so full of cum that she can't contain it. It is my biggest fantasy and unbelievably hot.

Her thighs tremble, and I hold her through it. Her head lolls to the side, eyes heavy, close to delirium.

I kneel beside her, untying her wrists, bringing them gently to my lips before tucking her into me.

She shakes, small and quiet, like she has nothing left. Her energy is completely depleted, and we lie close, adjusting to what we did together. Once again, her emotions overwhelm her, but I hold her through it.

Chapter 35
Olive

Snouts, Doubts, and Winning Them Over

A knock rattles my apartment door. Loch and I both freeze, tangled in the blankets, naked and flushed from the last few minutes. Kong gives a low grumble from his spot on the floor, and I jerk upright, heart racing.

"Did you order food?" Loch asks, grabbing his shirt.

"No," I whisper, already on my feet, tiptoeing to the front door with Loch on my heels. I look through the peephole, and my soul leaves my body.

"Oh, my God!"

"What?"

"It's my parents."

Loch stands up straighter. "Are you serious?"

I spin back, panic setting in. "They're right there—my mom and my dad. I don't... Fuck! Why would they show up like this?"

"Why are they here?" Loch asks.

"I have no clue. Just hurry up and get dressed."

Kong is barking now, trotting toward the door like he knows exactly what chaos looms on the other side.

"Ok," Loch says, standing and looking around frantically.

"Get Kong in the kennel," I hiss, grabbing a sweatshirt and shorts, and tossing Loch his hoodie. "He's gonna scare the shit out of my mom." She doesn't even like dogs.

"I'm going, I'm going," Loch mutters, guiding Kong with calm, practiced words. "Come on, big guy. Let's go chill for a bit."

Kong is reluctant, but follows, his body tense and hackles up. I kneel by the kennel and give him a quick kiss on the nose. "Be good, ok? Please."

I take a deep breath, give myself one second to regret everything, and open the door.

"Hi!" I force a smile that, I'm sure, looks like I'm in physical pain. "Wow, this is–uh–what a surprise! What are you doing here, so, uh, unexpectedly?"

My mom wears a pastel sweater and pearls like she's headed to brunch at a country club. My dad stands next to her with a forced dad smile and a bouquet of grocery store flowers. He hands them to me, and I accept.

"Thanks, Dad," I say, a little too high-pitched, trying to be nicer than I want to be.

"You weren't answering your phone," Mom says, giving me a once-over and a frown. I'm sure I look like I just got fucked in the ass. Oh, wait, I did. Hopefully, I don't have cum running down my leg. "So, we figured we'd stop by. It's been two weeks since we've heard from you, Olive. With everything that happened, we were worried."

"I've been busy," I say, stepping aside and inviting them in.

Loch appears behind me then, cool and calm, hair still a little mussed. "This is Loch," I introduce him, "my, uh, well, my boyfriend."

Loch smiles at me; he wasn't expecting that. I shrug at him with an annoyed glare, trying to convey that we can talk about our status later and to roll with it.

My parents blink at him. My dad recovers first and steps forward to shake his hand. "I'm Jack. This is my wife, Barbara. Loch, is it?"

"Yes, sir."

Mom says in a judgmental tone, "That's... unique," and I fight the urge to cringe. Mom's eyebrows go up. "You didn't tell us about a boyfriend?"

Wanting to change the subject, I say, "And that," while pointing toward the kennel, "is Kong. My dog. My guard dog." My mom's eyes practically bug out of her head. Now I'm sweating bullets, and my throat feels like it's closing up on me with nerves. "I've been busy with him, getting him settled. He's got some stranger danger. It takes time for him to warm up to new people, and since you guys don't live here, it would be very hard to introduce you. So, sorry, but you won't be able to meet him."

The teeth-baring growl coming from the kennel punctuates my sentiment.

"Oh, Olive," Mom says, her lips pulling into a scowl as she clutches her fucking pearls. "What's wrong with him? He looks aggressive."

I narrow my eyes. "Nothing is wrong with him, Mom. He's just afraid of new people. Someone abused him, and he's a guard dog. I picked him because of that."

She looks at Kong like he threatened to eat her purse. "Pitbulls are not known for their good manners, and they are unsafe."

"He's not dangerous," I snap before I can stop myself. "He's protective. Which is kind of the point of a guard dog, Mom."

Loch takes a step closer to me, voice steady but firm. "Kong's one of the most loyal, intelligent dogs I've ever known. And I run a rescue. That's how we met. I work with dozens of animals every day."

My dad raises his brows. "Rescue?"

Loch nods. "Only Dogs. It's about forty minutes outside the city. We focus on high-risk, more unadoptable cases. Dogs like Kong, who need the right environment for them to thrive, but usually can't live in an average home."

Mom seems unconvinced, but then she glances at Dad, who nods.

Loch turns to me, then back to them. "If you've got time tomorrow, I'd love to give you both a tour to get to know you better. If you see what I've been building, it might change your mind."

There's a beat of silence, and my dad smiles. "I'd like that."

Mom hesitates and still wears a scowl, but gives a tight little nod. "All right. I suppose it would be nice to get to know you, since you're dating our daughter."

I let out a breath I hadn't realized I was holding.

Then she gasps. "Oh my, Olive!"

I turn so fast I almost give myself whiplash. "What?"

Mom points.

There, on the kitchen island, is my red-lace thong and duct tape, painting a very inappropriate picture. All of it lying there like it's part of a crime scene.

I make a strangled noise in my throat. Loch stares at the evidence of our afternoon activities in disbelief.

"Oh," he says. "Wow. That's definitely not mine."

"Jesus Christ," I mutter, diving to snatch the underwear up and stuff it into my sweatshirt. My face is on fire, humiliation runs through me, and I try to avoid eye contact with either of my parents. Dad coughs and looks at the ceiling, and Mom purses her lips. "We can come back another time, Olive."

"No, it's fine," I squeak. "I, um, it's laundry day."

Loch turns around, hiding his laughter behind his hand. "A very intense laundry day." He mumbles, only loud enough for me to hear.

"Shut up," I whisper under my breath, elbowing him hard.

He leans closer, his voice low in my ear. "I picked up a pair in the living room, too."

"I hate you."

He smiles at me, unfazed by any embarrassment.

I groan, turning back to my very confused and mildly scandalized parents.

"Coffee?" I ask, desperation in my voice. "Anyone want some coffee?"

"Olive, it's 5:30 p.m. It's too late for coffee," Mom says. "We didn't mean to intrude."

"We would love to meet you both for breakfast and then do the tour afterward. Is that ok?" Dad asks.

I look at Loch, and he nods, "Yeah, that's fine. We can meet you at the breakfast place around the corner at 9:00 a.m., and then all drive to the rescue together."

Loch squeezes my hand once and reaches to shake Dad's hand again. "It was really nice to meet you. We'll have a good time tomorrow."

The next day at breakfast was pleasant. Being fully showered and dressed seemed to help a lot. After breakfast, we all walked into Only Dogs together–Loch and I, and my parents trailing a few uncertain steps behind. It was early enough on a Sunday that the place was eerily quiet, a stillness that made you whisper with no need to. A couple of staff members moved through the space, nodding hellos in our direction as we passed.

Loch flicks on a few more lights, warm overheads that bring the main room to life. The front of the rescue is cozy, bright, and welcoming. Soft green and yellow paint covers the walls, and sunlight filters through tall windows with sheer curtains. Polaroids are pinned to a bulletin board showing dogs with wide smiles and goofy tongues. Each of them has a little handwritten name beneath it. A few 'Adopted!' signs hang in bright colors. The air smells of clean wood, detergent, and dogs.

I've only ever seen this waiting area, and I was in such a paralyzed state of mind that I really didn't even look around or take it all in. But today, I get the full tour like my parents do.

"Why is it called Only Dogs?" Mom asks as Loch steps forward, already leading us toward a hallway behind the front desk.

He glances back with that low, calm voice. "Because most of the dogs we take in need to be just that–the only dogs in their household. They come from rough starts, and they don't always play well with others. It's a passion of mine, helping the ones that get passed over because of quirks or special needs."

I stare at him, that little curl of pride in my chest tightening. I'd heard pieces of that before, but watching him explain it so simply, without apology, hits me like a jolt to the heart. Was I someone with quirks or special needs? Ugh, I'll stuff that down for another time.

Loch shows us through the door, "This is where our dogs stay; some are long-term residents waiting for a home, some are new arrivals and will find a foster."

The hallway opens into a long corridor of small rooms–at least thirty. Some on each side, leaving an exposed walkway. The top half is glass, so we can look inside. Each one is clean and spacious–five-by-five or bigger for some–with a split design that gives each dog access to both indoor comfort and a small private outdoor space. Some are lounging on elevated beds, others perk up at the sound of footsteps. A few bark, and everyone besides Loch jumps. They calm after a couple of minutes, and he tells us they're excited to see us.

"You take care of all these dogs?" Dad asks, eyes wide as he takes it all in. All the kennels are full; none of them are empty.

"My team and I," Loch says. "A couple of full-time staff, a few rotating volunteers. Jan, my dubbed manager who works for free, handles most of the admin stuff."

That's another thing I didn't know about Jan. I didn't realize she was so engaged with the rescue on top of owning the bar. I know she has a dog, and her picture is on the website, but based on what Loch said, she must do a lot around here.

He guides us halfway down the hall, then turns left into another door, into a bigger open space. There's a kitchen-style setup tucked into one corner, complete with a deep sink, a row of cabinets, two giant chest freezers, and two refrigerators.

Opposite that is a large open area, partially gated as a designated indoor play zone. Dogs must love that space. There's a huge garage door that rolls up, leading to a fenced-in outdoor area with agility ramps and grass. I can see a brindle mutt chasing a ball across the yard with what I assume is a volunteer or staff member, joyful and wild.

A massive pallet of bagged dog food sits stacked in another corner, and I catch sight of several storage bins labeled with names and feeding notes. It's impressive. Organized chaos, but in a way that's clearly working.

Loch motions to the far side of the space, where more rooms line the back wall. "That's where we quarantine new intakes. Give them time to decompress, make sure they're not bringing in anything contagious. We also use those rooms for puppies or smaller dogs, though we don't get many of those. They're not our usual demographic."

"And all this?" Mom asks, looking around. "You built this yourself?"

"From the ground up, it started with just a few dogs in my home. Then a couple of other guys joined early on, and it's been our 'pet' project ever since," Loch says with a grin and a wink, looking at me to see if I caught his joke. He shrugs, but there is weight behind it, and I know he's proud of what he's accomplished.

We step into a tiny office with two desks pushed into an L-shape, both buried under piles of paperwork, folders, and what looks like half a chewed rope toy. The walls are tacked with flyers and photos. There are drawings, clearly from kids, of dogs with wonky legs and hearts over their heads.

"This is where the magic happens," he jokes.

Dad chuckles. Mom looks overwhelmed, but in a different way now. Seeing him in his element and being his funny, thoughtful self makes my heart skip a beat.

We circle back into the kennel hall, and that's when Loch pauses beside a particular run. Inside is a tiny tan pitbull, her ears cropped, her body compact and wiggly as she stands up to greet him with a happy little bounce.

"This is Bellamy," he says, opening the kennel. "She's a favorite." We all light up.

He smiles, scooping her up. "We call her tiny but mighty."

Bellamy's tail wags nonstop, as we all follow him back toward the front of the rescue, into a cozy meet-and-greet area with chairs, a rug, and more windows. We all sit, and he sets Bellamy down, letting her wriggle free. She gives hugs and kisses, and hops directly into Dad's lap like she's known him forever.

"Oh," he says with surprise, laughing as she starts licking his cheek.

Mom's arms stay crossed, but her expression softens as Bellamy circles once more in his lap and then presses into my dad's chest. With a sigh, she rests her head on him. Dad holds her and pets her. It might be the sweetest thing ever.

"She's very sweet," Mom admits.

"She's one of the gentlest dogs we've had," Loch says, kneeling beside them. "She doesn't care for other animals, but she loves people. Loves kids, loves when the staff dresses her up for pictures and holidays; she's very tolerant. She's a Velcro dog."

"Velcro dog?" my dad asks, grinning, while Bellamy is literally pressing her body into his chest.

"It means she sticks to you like Velcro," Loch gestures at the dog.

My mom cracks a little smile. "She looks like she'd be happy to follow someone right out the door."

"Funny you mention it," Loch says, glancing at me. This is why I do what I do. A lot of people would give up on a dog like Bellamy because she needs to be an only dog. She's been in our care for over three years. Homes that will open their hearts to one of our dogs are rare. They're hard to find. This is more of a long-term care facility."

I feel it then, this warm, slow bloom in my chest. Watching my dad pet Bellamy like she belongs in his lap, and watching my mom finally let herself see a bigger picture.

This place is more than a rescue. It's his, built from nothing, with callused hands, a soft heart, and a passion for helping the voiceless.

And I'm falling harder than ever.

Chapter 36
Loch

ORAL AND OATHS

I barely open my eyes, a sliver of morning light cutting across the room, when I feel it.

I startle awake, feeling my dick warm and wet. I look down and there she is between the sheets. Olive's mouth is on me, sucking and taking me deep, acting like waking me up this way is the most normal thing.

"Jesus, fuck."

I run my hand between the sheets, threading my fingers through the soft strands of her hair as I watch her. She looks up at me with a devilish gleam, like she's proud of herself, and it undoes me. There is no hesitation in her, only pure lust.

How the hell did I get this lucky? This girl, this woman, she survived something that would've broken most people. She's clawing her way out of the dark, and somehow, she's here with me. She's soft and fierce all at once. And the way she touches me, like I'm not also damaged, not dangerous, makes me want to be better. I need to be better for her.

"Olive," I grunt, my voice coming out low and rough first thing in the morning, trying to focus on what's happening. She smiles around me, knowing exactly what she's doing to me. And in that moment, watching her, feeling her, I know something for sure. I'm hers.

I thrust my hips up, wanting to fuck her mouth. She feels so fucking good, her beautiful lips wrapped around my dick. She moans on my dick and takes me deep, swallowing her throat around my dick like she did before. She knows exactly what to do to finish me. I'm not awake enough to focus on anything but my own pleasure and ropes of cum going down her throat. Her mouth on me in the morning is hands down the sexiest thing I have ever experienced.

My heart pounds against my ribs as she curls up beside me and presses a kiss to my chest. She doesn't say anything, and she doesn't need to.

My head is a wild storm of emotion, not just lust. I know, in this moment, I love her. This kind of realization doesn't come easy. I love her. This funny, beautiful, selfless woman who somehow looks at me like I'm more than the weight I carry around, touches me like I'm not dangerous and smiles at me as if I deserve her.

But she doesn't know everything. Not the worst of it. And when she finds out... fuck, I'll lose her. I know I will. She couldn't love a monster like me. A painful pit forms in my stomach at the thought, and anxiety courses through my veins.

I lie here, staring at the ceiling, begging it for answers. I've done terrible things, and I'd do them again. Olive is full of light, survival, and hope. She shouldn't be with someone like me, but I'm going to figure it out. I have to because letting her go is no longer an option.

She stands up, stretching as she walks toward the bathroom, bare and unbothered like she owns the room, and damn, if she doesn't. She reaches for the towel on the rack and glances over her shoulder at me, her hair messy and her lips still swollen.

"I'm going to testify," she breathes.

I sit up. "What?"

She doesn't look back at me right away. She grabs a hair tie, pulling her hair up. "Yesterday, with my parents, I... I don't even have words. You impressed them, and I was beyond blown away. It's like I can't imagine my life without you anymore. And the other night, with all the orgasms, and well, you know." She blushes and looks embarrassed. "I overcame so much, and I'm healing, as much as I can anyway. I own my body again; you made me feel capable and assured. When you said you support me in my decision, it made me realize that I can actually do it; I'm not alone in it anymore."

My chest aches with a mix of pride, pain, and guilt. She shouldn't have to be strong. She shouldn't have to testify against that piece of shit to be believed. But she's doing it anyway. And I'll be here for her for every step. No matter what.

"You're incredible, and I can't imagine my life without you either," I say, my voice rough, the truth heavy on my tongue. She glares at me, her eyes soft and vulnerable. I stand and cross the room in three strides. My hand comes down in a quick, playful slap on her bare ass, and she yelps, laughing over her shoulder.

"Loch!"

"I'm not letting you shower without me," I say, stripping off my boxers. "Not after that kind of wake-up call." She is still laughing as I step in behind her, steam curling around us, and water cascading down my back.

I drop to my knees and lift her leg over my shoulder, and her laughter turns into lust. I hover my face in front of her wet pussy and inhale. Her addictive musk sends me into a frenzy. I devour her with my mouth, unrelenting and hungry for every drop. My tongue moves with purpose, delving into her heat over and over to drive her on, licking and sucking on her clit.

Her fingers thread through my hair. Her breath hitches. "Oh, yes."

Her thighs tremble around my head, hips jerking, fingers twisting in my hair, not knowing if she wants to pull me closer or push me away.

Her hips lift, pushing her cunt into my mouth, begging me not to stop; her breaths become ragged. I can't stop; I keep my rhythm steady, dragging my tongue through her slit, sucking her clit at a relentless pace. I slide my forearms up to her lower stomach, applying pressure, anchoring her to the tile when she starts thrashing.

"Loch! Fuck, Loch!"

A sharp cry tears from her throat as her whole body seizes, thighs clamping tight around my head. Her back arches off the tile, and I watch her come apart for me. She is completely raw, perfect, and all mine. Her walls pulse around my tongue, and I nearly lose it from the sound of her saying my name like that, shattered and breathless.

I continue licking up every single drop of her cum until the spasms slow and she squirms with too much sensitivity, laughing and gasping all at once. I kiss the inside of her thigh, letting her legs fall to either side of me as I look up at her. She's flushed, glowing, and wild-eyed, and I know without a doubt there is no going back. I'll never stop needing to be the reason she falls apart like that.

If this is all I get—these lazy days off, these soft touches, her trust—I'll give her every goddamn piece of me in return, even the parts she hasn't seen yet. But I need to figure out how.

I wipe my mouth with the back of my hand, still tasting her. I'm drunk on her sounds, her scent, the way she looks at me like I am the only man in the whole damn universe. I climb up her body, taking her in, watching her chest rise and fall as if she's trying to catch her breath but can't.

"You think I'm done with you?" I growl, brushing my lips against her jaw, her cheek, her mouth. Forcing her to taste herself on me. "I'm not even close."

She shivers beneath me, still trembling from her orgasm. "I'm going to make you come all goddamn day long, Olive. You will beg me to stop, but I won't." My voice is rough, dark, but reverent. "I can't take my hands off you. I don't even want to try."

The truth is there's something in me, feral and obsessive. I want to live in her skin, her breath, her wet cunt.

"Oh, yeah? You say that like a threat." She smiles up at me, all flushed cheeks and wrecked lips, not the least bit scared of what I said. I kiss her, slow and deep, and feel her melt into me again.

"All. fucking. day. You'll be desperate for me to stop by the end."

"Challenge accepted." She lets out a ridiculously loud snort, trying to stifle a laugh, and I pull back enough to look down at her.

God, she's adorable. "Was that a snort?" I ask, grinning despite myself.

Her hand comes up to cover her mouth, but it's too late; she's giggling, her shoulders shaking beneath me.

"Definitely not," she says between laughs. And I can't help it. I drop my head, laughing into her shoulder. Both of us erupt with laughter, giving way to joy you can get lost in, where everything else disappears except this one person and this one stupid, perfect moment.

I slide my hand over her soft stomach, slow and possessive, until my fingers find it. The spot on her side where it dips, between her ribs and hips, is the sexiest part of her. I'm not attracted to tiny girls with no curves. I want my hands to get lost, touching the different parts of her—her stomach rolls, her round, dimpled thighs, her bouncy tits—she is perfection. Her body fits so damn well against me. She is meant for me.

And just like that, our laughter melts into something heavier, warmer. Her fingers trace the back of my neck, and mine follow the curve of her hip, memorizing her all over again.

This is the part I never expected, never knew I wanted—the joy. She brings me pure, unfiltered delight.

Chapter 37
Olive

STRENGTH WRAPPED IN FUR AND FLANNEL

"I'll text you when I'm done," he whispers against my lips as he kisses me softly early the next morning to go to work. He kisses me like it pains him to go. Like, he hates leaving me in that bed alone. And then he's gone, and the room feels a little colder without him.

It's early afternoon before I rise from the dead, and the sun has painted the bedroom in soft gold tones. The last couple of days with Loch and my parents have been exhausting, but this morning, my body aches in the best way—sore and satisfied. My skin tingles where Loch's hands were hours earlier.

Kong trots in a minute later, hops onto the bed like he owns it, and curls up beside me with a big sigh. I scratch behind his ears and smile. "Guess it's just you and me today, buddy."

We lounge in bed for another hour. Then, I take a long shower and eat the first lunch I've made in weeks. Kong and I go for an extended walk while I attempt to process everything that's happened in the last week. Now that the sun is setting, I flick the lights on and curl up on the couch with a flannel blanket, Kong snoring beside me, and dial Sophia.

She answers on the second ring. "Ok, I've been dying. Tell me everything, girl! I have not heard from you in days. DAYS! "

I laugh, cheeks already hot. So, I tell her, not all the details, of course, but enough–how Loch touches me, how he looks at me like I'm his whole world, how it's not just sex, but something more. Something healing and visceral. I tell her about how he impressed my parents and me with the tour of Only Dogs.

"He's... God, Sophia. He's everything. He's rough and tender, and intense, and it feels like I can breathe again."

There's a pause on the other end, and then her voice comes back, softer. "You're so in love with him."

I say nothing. Because yeah, I am, but I'm not sure if I'm ready to say it out loud.

"And he's good to you?" she asks.

"Yeah, completely. Too good."

"Then, I love him, too," she says without hesitation, and I laugh through the lump in my throat.

We talk for a while longer about Loch and Kong. And about how my house looked like a tornado of thrown-off clothes and half-eaten takeout boxes when my parents showed up.

Then I take a breath and tell her about my decision. "I'm going to call the D.A. after we hang up," I say, fingers curling tight in Kong's fur. "To tell them I'm ready to testify. If I don't, they'll drop the case."

Sophia pauses. "Are you sure?"

"No," I whisper and take another breath. "But I can't let him walk away like nothing happened. I can't keep waking up wondering where he is or if he'll come back."

"You're doing the right thing. He doesn't get a free pass because he has money or a rich daddy. Testifying might not erase what he did, but it sure as hell might stop him from doing it to someone else."

"Yeah." I nod, even though she can't see it. "I need to do this. For me too."

"I'm proud of you. You're not alone in this, you know? And hey, if I'm not enough, at least you've got hot dog man over there acting like your personal emotional support man."

I giggle at her nicknames for him. We hang up a few minutes later, and I sit for a moment, letting the weight of it settle over me. I dial the D.A.'s office, and someone answers on the third ring.

"Hi," I say, my voice a little shaky but steadying with each word. "This is Olive Smythe. I'm calling to let you know I'm willing to testify." I'm on hold for a few minutes; they thank me, say that the court date will likely be in the next few weeks, and that they'll call to prepare me for the stand.

When I hang up, I stare out the window and watch Kong toss a new toy that my parents bought for him in the air just to catch it and chew it to death. Even though my hands are shaking, I pull my shoulders back, feeling more secure and braver than I have in a while. I've always had Sophia, but now I have Kong and Loch, too. And that changes everything. It's wild to think about how much has changed in only a few weeks.

I look down at Kong, now curled up beside me after killing his toy, his massive head resting on my thigh. His ears twitch at the sound of birds and people outside, but he doesn't move. There's not even a hint of the fear that I once saw.

A couple of weeks ago, when I met him, I flinched every time I got too close and he snapped. When I moved too fast, his lip curled, teeth flashing, and he came after me. I'm so thankful he realized he doesn't need to defend himself from me. I'd terrified him, just by existing, by reaching out with a love he didn't know how to receive.

And now, he follows me from room to room like a shadow. He sleeps beside me on guard duty, and nuzzles into my chest when the nightmares or fear come, grounding me with his weight and warmth.

Rescued

Different monsters wounded us both in different ways, and somehow, we found each other. We're two souls who didn't know how to trust again, but we chose to try.

He's not only my protector, but he continues to save me every day. In the soft snuggles and steady breathing. In the way his gigantic eyes find mine when I slip into the darkness. He sees me and all the cracked, frightened parts I try to hide, and he stays and helps me thrive.

My throat tightens, and I reach down, running my fingers through the fur behind his ears. "Thank you," I whisper, struggling to get the words out.

Kong doesn't lift his head, but he lets out a deep, audible sigh and nestles in closer to me, and I swear, in that moment, he knows. We rescued each other, and to top it off, he brought me Loch.

Chapter 38
Loch

TWO PEAS AND NO SLEEP

The past three weeks have blended in the most seamless way possible. My house has become little more than a pit stop—taking enough time to swap out clothes and check on the dogs before I find myself at Olive's door again. Every night, without fail, gravity drags me back to her.

I'm more than grateful to my neighbor, who is so helpful with my other foster dogs. He is an old retired man who comes over all the time anyway to spend time with the dogs. He can't have any pets because his wife is allergic, and he takes full advantage of doggy playtime at my house.

I grip the steering wheel while music plays in the background, in a daze of my own thoughts about how I got here.

Olive and I have become so normal and routine. I come to her apartment after work or checking on the dogs and find her and Kong snuggling together, waiting for me. She gave me a key, and now I walk in, and Kong doesn't even come to greet me. He pops his head up off her lap to bark once, a friendly hello, and to make sure it's me.

Then, he plops his big head back down while I come over to greet them, making both of us exchange smirks at his antics.

And the sex, I mean, it's so much more, but the exploration of each other's bodies and learning every inch of what makes her moan has been pure heaven. My mind flashes to a few nights ago when I torturously edged her for so long that she came from me sucking and biting on her hard nipples and grinding her clit on my leg. She's addictive. Every part of my body craves her; it's unrelenting. Even when I try to focus on something else, I fall back in, caught in her orbit–the way her eyes glimmer right before she kisses me, or her voice cracks a little when she says my name out loud.

But what kept getting me, what kept pulling me back every damn night, was the way she let me in outside the bedroom, too. We'd been living slow, nights in for the most part, where she's most comfortable. We cooked dinner together most nights, half-dressed and stealing touches every time we got a chance. Or ordering takeout and fighting over the last bite. We laughed at terrible shows, though most ended up abandoned ten minutes in, replaced with the heat of her mouth on mine. Kong would sigh loudly, roll to his side like we were the ones disturbing him, and Olive would bury her face against my shoulder, muffling her laugh.

The past few weeks have shown me more of her daily struggles. Coffee with Sophia a few times a week was always a big hurdle. One of those days, Sophia texted me because Olive had a breakdown at the coffee shop; a man bumped into her arm when reaching for sugar. The loud noises, grinding machines, milk frothers hissing, shouted orders, kids crying, and the personal contact sent her into a spiral. She shook so badly that she spilled her coffee while trying to make it back to the table with Sophia. Her hands trembled so much she couldn't even clean it up, and suddenly, she was sobbing because she felt exposed, trapped, and furious at herself for 'failing' in public. It was a rough day, and she skipped coffee for a full week.

I watched her try every day to overcome her fears; she never made a big deal of it, but I know how hard it was for her. When she did finally return to the coffee shop a week later, she came back to the apartment glowing because she didn't break down. Sophia and I were always there to pick her up, help her keep moving forward, and not let the small failures weigh her down. Even though I hadn't met Sophia yet, I admired their friendship.

And then there was the hard part—the thing that sat like a weight between us. The trial. The testimony. It was just a week away now.

We've been working through it together, every single day. Last night we sat on the couch, her voice shaky as she practiced saying what happened out loud. Her eyes flicked toward me to make sure I didn't look at her any differently. She still felt shame when telling her story, but all I saw was strength.

I hated it. Listening to her every single day felt like torture. Every word. Every detail. I hated knowing the things that bastard had done to her. Hated hearing her pain spill into the room like smoke, clinging to everything over and over. But if she had to carry it, then so would I.

She met with the D.A. to go over the trial. They had her practice hard questions the defense would ask. It made me sick, knowing they would try to say she asked for it, that it was consensual, or that her being a friendly bartender gave him some sort of impression that he could have her.

I sat with her, coached her, and helped her find the words that made her feel like she had the power again. We went over and over it until she didn't cry through it. Until she could hold her own voice steady and strong. Every time she looked like she was breaking—when the tears became overwhelming and the memories invaded her thoughts—I caught her, held her, and watched as she found her way through it.

Because that's what you do for someone you love. I haven't told her that, even though I think about it constantly. I want to tell her I love her, and how much she means to me, and I want to hear her say she loves me too. But I don't want to complicate things before the trial. I'll tell her after, in hopes she will be ready to say it back.

Now, driving back through the city streets after work, all I can think about is getting to her once more. I picked up our food tonight. I'm surprising her with her favorite meatball sub from the place across town that she usually says is too far. And now, I am only about ten minutes away.

Kong will greet me like always, tail wagging, eyes squinting with that lazy trust he gives us both. And Olive... she'll probably be napping under a blanket on the couch, waiting for me. My girl. My home. I don't know how the hell I'm going to keep them once she finds out everything about me. But I know one thing for sure—I need to be honest with her, somehow. I'll tell her the truth after the trial, all of it. She doesn't need any more shit on her plate before then.

CHAPTER 39
OLIVE

HE'S BACK FOR MORE

The sound of a knock at the door startles me. My head lifts from the pillow on the couch, groggy and disoriented from my nap. I blink my eyes open to fading daylight and the shape of Kong beside me. My body aches from the way I curled into him, but the knock comes again, firmer this time, and my heart jumps in anticipation.

Loch. Why isn't he using his key?

Kong is already on his feet, prancing beside me like he always does when Loch comes over. His tail gives a lazy wag, his tongue lolling out in a yawn as he reaches the door with me. But when I open the door, it's not Loch.

It's him. It's Jacob Wright. The world stops moving. Everything inside me seizes. I'm too paralyzed to even scream.

He stands in my doorway, holding a gun steady in his hand, the barrel pointed straight at my chest. He doesn't bother with a mask this time; he smiles with a twisted smirk, proud of himself, enjoying being back in my home.

"Miss me?" he sneers, stepping forward like he belongs here, like he's welcome. "You should've kept your fucking mouth shut, you stupid bitch. No slut is gonna send me to prison. You wanted it, and you know it. I guess I should have killed you the first time. You were such a slut at the bar that night, trying to act innocent. And then Father finally gets the charges dropped, and you agree to fucking testify. You should have kept your fucking mouth shut, you goddamn whore!"

My knees almost buckle. He pushes inside, closing the door, ready to take me out for good.

A horror I've never felt before crawls up my spine, clamping around my throat until I can't move or speak. My hands shake and my breath heaves, but I'm frozen in place as fear and shock consume my body. I can't think.

But Kong does. Before I can register what is happening, Kong lunges in a blur of fur and muscle and teeth. A vicious growl rips through the air as Kong tears into his side, jaws clamping down with savage precision on his ribcage. The monster's screams are loud and primal. He stumbles back, swinging the gun wildly, as Kong latches onto him like a machine made of pure protection and rage. The man kicks him off, sending Kong to the floor with a whimper, but Kong returns to his feet, lunging at him again. This time, he latches onto his forearm. I jump backward, gasping, my heart in my throat, as chaos erupts in front of me.

Fight or flight finally kicks in, and without thinking, I reach for the knife block in the kitchen to help Kong fight this man off. As soon as my hand wraps around the handle, I spin around, hearing a thud.

I see Kong on the floor again. He's hit him in the head with the gun; Kong lies there, hardly moving, his head bleeding.

Jacob strides over to me. I hold the knife in my hand, half-stunned and half-ready to fight for my life. He stands a few feet in front of me as I wave the knife around in a panic, trying to keep him away from me. He fucking laughs. He aims the gun straight at me.

"All you had to do was stay quiet. You made me do this by agreeing to testify and identifying me in the first place. Why couldn't you be a good girl and keep that pretty little mouth shut? Maybe before I kill you, I should at least get another taste of that sweet cunt of yours. Would you like that?"

"Fuck you, you piece of shit!" I scream.

He lowers the gun to his side and closes the distance between us. "Drop the knife, whore, and you and I can play a little before you die."

I'm crying and shaking my head as I attempt to back away. Praying that this will end. He cannot touch me again. And then there's another blur of blue fur in the corner of my vision. Kong attacks and bites down on Jacob's thigh, tearing his flesh.

BANG! BANG!

Two shots crack through the air, my ears ringing, and Kong falls to the floor.

"No!" I screech, the sound shattering the paralyzing fear holding me. I stumble forward, knife in hand, but Kong is already back up, staggering, blood pooling beneath him. Despite that, he charges the man again.

When he hits Jacob a third time, latching onto his hand, the gun skitters across the floor, stopping at my feet. He's kicking and punching Kong. When he kicks him close to a bullet wound, Kong cries out in pain, releases his hand, and falls to the floor like a rag doll. This time, he doesn't get up.

"No–no, no, no," I move without thinking, dropping the knife and reaching for the gun.

My hands grip the butt of the gun, shaking but pointing it at Jacob. He stumbles to his feet, eyes wide, when he sees me holding his gun. My finger trembles on the trigger, but I'm unable to pull it.

He pauses, bleeding and breathing hard. Then, he opens the door and runs away.

He didn't finish the job he came here to do, but I couldn't pull the trigger either. I drop the gun on the counter, like it's burned me. I slam the door shut, engaging all the locks.

I run, falling to my knees at Kong's side.

Blood soaks into the beige rug. He lies on his side. His breaths are faint and shallow, his eyes barely open, but he's alive for now. He saved me; he's always saved me.

My sobs come out broken and raw as I wrap my arms around him, pressing my face into his fur. "You're ok. You're ok. Please, please stay with me, buddy."

I wrap myself around his warm, bloody body. I rock gently, whispering to him through my tears, petting his head, and telling him how good he is, how much I love him. How proud I am of him. Comforting him just like he has me.

I don't know how much time passes, but it seems like forever before I hear the locks in my door jiggling. My heartbeat spikes into a sudden rush of panic at who might be coming through the door.

I see Loch walk through the door. "Loch!" I sob. He freezes mid-step, as his gaze locks on the carnage in front of him. Once his brain catches up, he lunges in my direction.

"Olive, are you ok?"

"He was here. He had a gun. He-he shot, he shot Kong."

He reaches for Kong, assessing the damage. "Fuck, Olive. What the hell happened? Who? Who shot him?"

I can't speak. "He had a gun, the man, the door, I, I, Kong, I couldn't." The words come out in broken pieces, sobs stealing my voice.

"Olive, I need you to focus; I'm here. What happened? Where is he? Was it Jacob?"

I nod, "Yeah, I-I got the gun and he left. But he shot Kong after Kong attacked him and protected me."

Loch's eyes are scanning, already calculating what to do next. He takes one look at me, wild-eyed, tear-streaked, covered in Kong's blood, and moves toward Kong. On his knees, he scoops my massive protector into his arms as if he weighs nothing.

"Get your shoes," he says, urgent and commanding.

"He's gone—" I choke. "He's not breathing, I—"

"No, Olive." Loch's voice cuts through my panic in a way only he can. Firm and fierce. "He's not dead. Look at me. We will not let him die. We have to try."

I look up at him, barely able to see through my tears.

"He needs you to be strong right now. Do you hear me? Put your shoes on. We're going to the hospital."

"I—" My knees and voice shake.

"Do it, Olive. Now."

And somehow, I do, because I have to, because Kong deserves it; he needs me, despite the trauma I experienced tonight.

Chapter 40
Loch

Vet and Run

She hasn't stopped crying since I picked Kong up off the floor.

Her eyes are vacant but streaming with tears, hands shaking in her lap as we speed down the road, Kong's blood staining her hoodie. Her breathing is ragged and shallow, as if she's drowning in her own emotions. And I'm gripping the wheel so hard I'm afraid it'll snap clean in half.

"Olive," I say in a soft tone. "Talk to me. Please. I'm sorry I wasn't there to protect you."

Her lip trembles, but she doesn't answer. She pulls her knees tighter to her chest like she's trying to make herself smaller; she's withdrawing. My jaw clenches. I want to give her space, but I need to know what's happening inside that head of hers. I need to understand what the hell happened before I lose my mind.

"Olive. Baby. What happened?"

Her breath hitches, and she finally opens her mouth. Slowly, the words come out, painful and choppy. She shakes her head, like she's trying to wake up from a nightmare.

"He was there with a gun. He said he wanted to kill me. That I was the only thing stopping him from walking free. He didn't want me to testify."

My whole body goes cold. I know I should have taken care of him before now, but I wanted to let the justice system run its course like I always do. And I failed her, and she is suffering again.

My vision tunnels, and my pulse is pounding so loud it drowns out the rest of what she's saying. If Kong hadn't been there... Fuck, I can't even let my mind go there. Thank God he was there, and he protected her when I didn't. A pain in my chest seizes thinking about how well he did his job. I'm so thankful for that sweet dog and all that he has done for Olive and me.

We pull into the emergency vet parking lot a little too fast, the tires squealing. I throw the car in park, jump out, and scoop Kong into my arms. He's heavy, his body limp. I don't think he's breathing, but I'm not about to say that out loud. I don't want to think about it.

Olive follows, unsteady, stumbling behind me, still covered in blood.

The doors fly open, and the techs rush toward us, a perk of knowing most of the vets in town. They see the blood and the stillness of Kong's body. I tell them he was shot, and they whisk him away. Thankfully, they don't ask me more questions right now because I haven't figured out the answers to give.

"We'll take him back." The red-headed tech says. "Please wait in the lobby. We'll update you as soon as we can."

I nod once, and they disappear through the swinging doors.

Olive sinks into a chair in the waiting room as her legs finally give out. I sit beside her, pulling her close to comfort her, but she flinches. She avoids looking at me, wrapping her arms around her stomach, trying to hold herself together. Her body quakes as a result of the serious emotional overload she's experiencing. She's retreating, sinking back into the darkness. I pull back, wanting to give her space.

I slide my hand onto her knee, and she flinches again. "He's going to be ok," I say, as steady as I can. "Kong's strong. Tougher than most people I know. And you did so good, you stayed with him, and I am going to take care of it. All of it."

She doesn't respond. Her face is still wet with tears. Her body trembles uncontrollably–shoulders shaking, hands spasming open and shut–as though fear itself is pulling all her strings. Her mouth opens, then closes again.

"I shouldn't have–" she starts, but I cut her off.

"No. Don't do that." I pull her against me, letting her lean on my chest. She still resists me, but I force her in. "You did nothing wrong. He did. And he's going to fucking pay. I will make sure of that."

She nods once, but her hands stay clenched, her nails digging into her palms. I wrap my arm around her, shielding her, trying to calm the tremors rolling through her body. We sit there like that for almost an hour. Her breath eventually slows. The sobs taper down to small, aching gasps, but she hasn't said anything else.

I can't sit still any longer; I need to clean up this mess. I know who did this, and he could have taken Olive from me tonight; he might have taken Kong from us. I have business to take care of. I stand slowly. Her head lifts, her body snapping alert.

"Where are you going?"

"I need to step out," I say.

Her eyes narrow. "What do you mean? You're not leaving me here. What about Kong? I don't even have a car."

I crouch in front of her, my hands on her knees. "I promise I wouldn't leave if I didn't absolutely have to. I need to go take care of this so I can keep you safe. I failed you tonight, and I need to fix it. It can't wait."

"But you don't have to." Her voice cracks, but there's steel under it. And then she sees it. I know she sees it. That flicker of something I've tried so hard to bury when I'm around her. The thing I keep behind locked doors, outside of my own house.

Her brows draw together in a scowl, and she suddenly realizes there are parts of me she hasn't seen yet. There are parts I've been hiding.

"Loch... what are you going to do?"

I don't answer because if I speak, I'll confirm everything she's afraid to ask. Everything I don't know how to say.

I press a kiss to her forehead and whisper, "Stay here. Take care of him. I'll be back to get you soon. I promise. I promise I will be back." And then I walk out, the door closing behind me. Only then do I let the anger rise through me. I let it take over, seeing red.

Chapter 41
Olive

RED FLAGS, THE ULTIMATE DEAL BREAKER

About an hour later, I receive a call from Sergeant Persimmons while I wait at the vet's office. Some of my neighbors heard gunshots, and when the officers arrived to check it out, I didn't answer the door.

"Olive, can you tell me about what happened tonight?"

"Sure," I say in a fog. "I heard knocking on the door, and when I opened it, it was Jacob. He had a gun." I told her everything that happened, except I left Loch out of the story because I didn't know what he was doing. Even though I was angry with him, I wouldn't get him into trouble.

"Thank you, Olive. Whenever you're free tomorrow, please come down to the station to give an official statement. Officers have already done a sweep of your apartment and collected evidence."

It's late when the vet tells me I can wait at home, that Kong is holding on for now. He is going in and out of consciousness. They can't make any guarantees, but promise me they'll do their best. They say if he makes it through the night, it's a good sign.

I don't even know how I stand and walk away from Kong, but I text Sophia and ask her to pick me up. She's the only person I can contact. I won't wait for Loch to come back. I'm so angry and upset with him for leaving me, but also too tired and traumatized to care.

Sophia lets herself in with my spare key. She helps me out of my shoes and my bloody clothes, and into the shower. The number of times she's helped me into the shower in such a short amount of time is more than any friend should have to do. I owe her so much.

After my shower, I walk out to find her cleaning up the mess in my apartment. She's thrown the rug away and is cleaning everything else she can. I fall apart again. How do I have such a good friend?

We sit on the couch, and I stare at Kong's kennel, his bed, his toys, and the hallway he runs down. She wraps a blanket around my shoulders. I must look as hollow as I feel because she doesn't say very much at first. She sits next to me on the couch while I stare into space, fingers clenched into the throw pillow like it's the only thing tethering me to this earth. We're back in a familiar silence, so much the same. Me, shut down. Her, a silent supporter.

Eventually, I tell her everything. The attack. Kong. Loch. The way he held me like he could keep the dark out if he stayed close enough. And then, I tell her about the way he left me stranded at the fucking vet to deal with Kong alone.

Her brows rise higher and higher until she finally leans back and crosses her arms. "Ok... wow. First, give me a hug, lady; I'm so glad you are ok. I hope Kong is ok, but more than that, I'm thankful that you are, and that he was here. Second, Loch left you alone after all of that? What an asshole."

I shake my head. "He said he had to go... and then just left. He wouldn't even tell me why, but I have a hunch."

"Red flag," she coughs theatrically. Her opinion is clear.

I sigh, curling into the blanket a little tighter. "He looked different when he left, Soph. Cold. Like something flipped in him. I've seen flashes of it before, but this time it consumed him. And I don't know... it scared me."

"Where do you think he went? After the guy? What do you think he's going to do?"

"I don't know what to think." I rub my palms over my thighs, trying to stop them from shaking and sweating. "But I keep playing it over in my head, how he looked, what he didn't say. And the way he walked away, like he had something to do and didn't care how I felt about it."

Sophia is quiet for a second, then she says in a gentle voice, "I know you like him a lot. But Olive... if he can't be honest with you, that's not love. You've already been through the flames of hell. You can't walk into a different fire just because he's holding your hand while you do it."

I nod, even though the lump in my throat won't let me answer. I know she's right.

"I think you need to ask him directly," she continues. "Whatever he's doing, he should have the balls to own it, and you can decide what to do with his truth. And if he doesn't open up? Then let him go and move on. It's his loss."

I want to say she's right, that I'd confront him and walk away if I had to. My stomach drops at the memory of his injured hands a few weeks ago. What if he's not who I think he is? What could he be hiding? Am I in danger? Again?

I'm drowning in the thought of losing him on top of everything else that has happened today. I don't know if I can survive it. If I lose Kong and Loch, and my attacker is on the loose, all in a single day, I will seriously lose my shit.

"Soph, will you take me to the police station in the morning? I have to go give a statement."

"Of course. Just let me know when you're ready."

After we return later that evening, Soph stays the night, but neither of us sleeps much. We stay curled on the couch, like before, Sophia's hand over mine.

A few minutes after 6:00 a.m., we turn on the TV. Sophia is pouring coffee for us as I scroll through my messages, hoping to hear from Loch or the vet. My heart is heavy and numb.

The news anchor's voice cut through the silence. "Breaking: Just in, this morning: Jacob Wright, the son of Senator Harold Wright, has been reported missing. He was last seen late last night, exiting a downtown parking garage alone. His father reported him missing when he failed to return home last night, and he is unresponsive to attempts to contact him. This comes on the heels of his recent release from jail on bail; he faces a court date next week, accused of breaking and entering and brutally raping a young woman. Police are investigating all leads to his whereabouts as well as the possibility that he's jumped bail, after his alleged involvement in another attack and a shooting last night."

I drop my phone.

Sophia turns, wide-eyed, and looks at me. "Wait, what?"

We stare at each other. The breath leaves my lungs in a single exhale. My heart drops and sinks into my stomach. "Oh, my God."

"Olive..." Sophia looks like she is trying not to freak out. Her back stiffens, and her voice trembles. "You don't know if Loch had anything to do with that. You still need to talk to him. But, fuck, what if he does have something to do with it?"

"I know," I whisper. Almost in disbelief that she thought I should still talk to him. "He was angry and didn't say where he was going. He looked like he wanted to kill someone. Him. My gut is telling me he did this. I don't know what he's done, but he's involved in Wright going missing."

We sit in stunned silence for a minute before I stand, grab my keys, and slip on my shoes.

"Where are you going?" Sophia asks.

"To see Loch," I say, my voice shaking. "I need to know. I have to know." And I walk out the door without another thought.

Chapter 42
Loch

DID YOU DO IT?

"Boise Emergency Veterinary Hospital, this is Becky. How can I help you?"

"Hi, Becky, it's Loch, I'm calling to check in on Kong and to see if his owner, Olive, is still in the waiting room."

"Oh, hi, Loch, I'm glad you called. I spoke with the doctor a bit ago, and Kong is still going in and out of consciousness, but he's holding strong. The doctor will call you both later this morning."

"Yeah, that's fine. I'm just glad to hear he's alive. As long as he talks to Olive, that's fine. Do you know if she's still there?"

"No, we sent her home a few hours ago. Someone picked her up."

"Ok, thank you."

An hour later, I pull into my garage and shut off the engine. The silence settles over me like wet cement, heavy and inescapable.

My hands are still tight around the steering wheel, knuckles white, jaw clenched. If I let go, if I so much as breathe, I'm afraid I'll completely unravel with rage and regret. Not from what I did, but from what I'll have to tell her.

What will she see when she looks at me? A monster? A killer? She could never love me now, a person like me. Fuck, she may even go to the police. But I had to do it. I couldn't let him hurt her again.

I climb out, close the garage door, and step into the house. The floorboards creak under my boots, but everything else is calm. It's deceptively quiet.

The dogs aren't even barking, as if they know what I've done. I go to check on them and let them all out. I strip off the clothes reeking of adrenaline, sweat, and blood, to shower, scrubbing until my skin turns red, sure there's nothing left of him on me.

Wright will never hurt her again. That's what matters; that's all that matters.

I lean my forehead against the cool tile as the water beats down on my back, trying to steady my breathing and calm the anxiety pulsing through my veins. I search for words that sound like the truth without being dangerous.

How do I explain that he deserved it, that justice was served? Because I need to tell her. God, I want to tell her. I just don't know how she will ever understand.

I want to look her in the eye and let her see it all, the fire, the wrath, the justice I serve when no one else will, but I need her to understand. The world is full of people like him, and I made sure one of them won't ever walk free again.

But, Olive won't see it that way; she'll see a predator. In my case, the monster only comes out for the other monsters, but it doesn't make it right.

This all started because the justice system failed me once, and I swore I'd never let it happen again. Rufus was my first real friend, my only real family back then. Someone poisoned him—they murdered him for no reason. And the man who did it walked free. "No evidence," they said. "Just a misunderstanding," they said. The city ignored every complaint, dozens of them, years and years of complaints. He was finally caught, and he got one year of probation. One. Year. Of. Probation. That was his punishment.

That was the day I gave myself permission to become what I am, a weapon, a ghost of vengeance for the voiceless and defenseless. They wouldn't hurt animals and get away with it, not in my city, not under my watch, but none of that matters if Olive walks away from me.

I did what I've always done. I protected someone who deserves to be safe. Like I protected Kong and Rufus and all the others. But for the first time... I want to stop. I want to be someone better for Olive. I know deep down what I do is wrong, and it's a never-ending cycle of anger and hate, fueling and isolating me.

I would stop if it meant keeping her. If it meant waking up next to her and Kong every morning, building something real, something lasting, with the only person who I've ever wanted to deserve.

How do you tell someone that you've locked people away? Giving them exactly what they have coming, and no one coming to save them? How do you explain holding them prisoner in a remote house with no daylight, no hope, no freedom, giving them an eye for an eye?

Maybe I should make up a lie that sounds better. A half-truth. And I can pray she doesn't look at me the way I looked at myself the first time I crossed that line. I hated myself for it, but I hated the idea of not doing it even more. This is the first time I've ever been afraid of the truth of who I am, the first time I've felt regret.

I dry off, pull on a clean black shirt, and sit on the edge of the bed. I haven't slept in over thirty-six hours. I'm exhausted, but I'm sitting on the edge of the bed. The same dead-end thoughts run through my mind as I try to stitch together a version of the truth I hope she can live with when she hears it.

A knock at my front door. I freeze. There's another knock, quicker and louder. Fuck.

Every nerve in my body goes still as I make my way to the door. I already know it's her. I feel her energy before I even look through the peephole.

She came here. "Shit."

When I open the door, my chest caves in at the sight of her. My body is tense, jaw tight. I'm trying to stay calm, but there is zero calm going on inside. Her eyes are red, her face puffy, lips trembling like she's trying to keep it together but losing the fight.

"Hey, what's going on? Is Kong ok?" I ask, stepping forward instinctively. "Are you ok–?"

She cuts me off. "Did you do it?"

I freeze. "What?" I say, as if I stall long enough, I can spin this into something else. But I see the fire in her. The accusation, the fear, and rage behind her eyes.

"Did you do it, Loch?" she asks again, her voice rising. "Did you do something to him?"

I don't answer. I open the door wider. "Come inside."

She doesn't move.

"Please, just... come in."

She crosses the threshold and folds her arms, telling me she isn't leaving without answers. I try to meet her eyes, but she won't give me that. She darts her eyes around the room to avoid me.

"Olive, I need you to listen to me."

"No," she snaps. "You need to tell me the truth."

I take a step toward her. She steps back.

I hate this. I have taken a hundred steps backward, and I don't know if I can make it right, or make her understand. "I never meant for you to get dragged into this. I only ever wanted to protect you."

"Then say it," she demands. "Tell me the truth if you care about me. You want me to trust you, and you have lied to me this whole time? Tell me why I should believe and trust you now. I saw him on the news. He's missing. What the fuck, Loch?"

I look at her, everything in me twisting in knots. "You won't understand."

"I might. But not if you keep lying to me. I can't trust you if you can't even tell me the truth." She turns to leave, her hand already on the doorknob.

"Ok!" I shout. My voice cracks, loud and desperate. "Ok."

She turns. Eyes searching mine, finally making contact, but wounded and wary.

"I'll tell you," I breathe. "Everything."

There's a long silence between us, thick with everything we're not saying. She doesn't speak; she waits.

"Come with me," I say. "Please. Let me show you."

Fear causes her to hesitate, and she withdraws. She slumps her shoulders, her face twisting in doubt. I see the war in her, but after a long pause, she nods once.

"Fine," she says. "But this better not be a fucking game. I want the truth. I don't need you wasting my time."

"It's not a game."

We get in my car. The drive is almost an hour, the silence louder than anything I could say. She doesn't ask where we're going or why I'm taking her. I see her stealing glances at me, with equal parts curiosity and dread.

When we finally pull up to the house, hidden deep in the trees, she shifts in her seat.

"Where are we?"

I kill the engine and turn to face her. "Come inside. There's something I need to show you, and I'll explain everything."

She doesn't move. I know this doesn't look good from her perspective. A man she thinks is a monster brings her out into the middle of nowhere to a creepy old house. Fuck, I'm really winning with this plan.

I reach for her hand, brushing my fingers over hers. She flinches and pulls away.

"Olive, listen to me. Please. I'm going to tell you the truth. All of it. But I need you to listen. No interruptions. No jumping to conclusions. Let me explain it all before you decide what you think of me."

Her jaw tightens. "You're scaring me, Loch."

"I know," I say, almost whispering. "But I swear on my life, I would never hurt you."

A beat passes, and she finally opens the door. We walk toward the house, her steps are slow and cautious. But she's here, and that has to count for something.

I unlock the door and step inside, holding it open for her to follow. Taking a deep breath before crossing the threshold with her. Now, she'll know everything, and I pray she doesn't walk away from me.

Chapter 43
Olive

WELCOME TO THE HOUSE OF HORRORS

The second I step inside, something shifts. The air is heavy, thicker, like it carries weight I can't see. The place is old and neglected. The sun has chipped and faded the white siding, and the inside is in even worse shape. Floorboards creak underfoot, and floral wallpaper peels from its long-forgotten walls. The only furniture is a wooden table standing alone in the center of the room, no chairs to keep it company. It's the shell of what it once was, once a home, and it gives me the creeps.

Loch says nothing as he walks toward the kitchen. My eyes follow his every move, so I'm not left alone here. He stops at a door off the kitchen. The basement.

As I move closer, I smell it. Something foul and rotting.

It isn't overpowering, but it's wrong. Like rot and sickness, like death, clinging to the walls in silence.

I cover my nose with my sleeve. "What is that smell?"

Loch pauses, his hand on the door handle. "I'm sorry," he mumbles. "It's going to get worse."

I take a step back. "Worse?"

He turns to me, something sharp and broken swimming in his eyes. "You're safe. I promise. But there are people down there."

I freeze. "People?" My voice cracks.

"Not dead," he blurts. "Not yet."

My stomach twists. "Loch–"

"I have nothing to lose but you, Olive. If you walk away after this, I won't stop you. But if you're going to hate me, I'd rather you hate me knowing why."

He holds out his hand. I stare at it, unsure if it's a lifeline or a cliff's edge, but I take it, too afraid to move without it.

Every step down the creaking staircase seems to take hours. The smell only thickens, sharp and sour. It settles in my throat, making my eyes sting and water. Halfway down, Loch pulls a chain, and a light flickers on, dim and yellow, casting long shadows against the stone basement walls.

Then, the shouting starts. Voices, all at once. Angry. Panicked. Animalistic. Screaming for help. I jump in surprise and panic.

"QUIET!" Loch's voice booms like a thunderclap, and the noise silences instantly, like dogs trained to heel.

That's when I see them. Cages. People in cages.

I stumble back, my stomach in my throat, panic crawling up my spine. I turn to run, to get out of there as fast as I can, but I slam right into Loch's chest. He doesn't let me go.

"You wanted to know," he says, looking down at me with tired brown eyes that aren't proud or smug, but resigned. "This is who I am. Now, I need you to listen to why."

He points to the first cage, and my eyes follow. A man sits curled in it, unable to stretch out. It's small, the same size as Kong's crate.

"Remember when I told you about the man who killed Rufus?" Loch said, his voice low and gravelly. "That's him, Brad."

I look again, and bile rises in my throat. He's in a cage for killing his dog? This can't be happening.

"Twenty years after Rufus, this man was found with dozens of cages in his basement, full of sick, abused, and emaciated dogs. Bloody collars, muzzles with teeth marks, and several dog carcasses were also found on the property. Some of the dogs were left in kennels to die a slow, painful death. There were dogs with broken bones, wounds, and burns. A stack of complaints had been made, and the system ignored them. Hundreds of dogs he had been breeding, beating, torturing, stealing, hoarding, and selling to dog fighters. He didn't fight the dogs himself, but he allowed the animals in his care to become emaciated, neglected, and sick.

"The police finally caught and charged him. He got probation. A fucking year of probation for over twenty years of animal abuse. That was the day I stopped believing in mercy. I was an adult by then, and it made me sick to think about all he'd gotten away with, and he got away with killing Rufus. It was personal."

I look at Loch again, my heart breaking at his story of all the helpless animals, and panic consuming me at the scene in front of us. He takes a breath, his jaw tight. "He's been in that cage for almost six years now. He was the first. He's never leaving that cage, and I can't bring myself to let him die."

My knees are weak. I don't know what to say, or if I can say anything.

Loch points to the next cage.

"That's Greta. She ran a supposed Rottweiler rescue out of her house. But all she did was hoard them. She took dogs from shelters, from homes, and starved them. Kept them locked in cages, with little to no time out of the kennels. She fed them a cup of food a week at the most.

"Many of the dogs they pulled from her property were already dead or dying. And for a long time, she swore she loved them. She never faced any charges."

Loch looks at her like she's already a ghost.

"I don't feed her. I'm waiting for her time to come."

I cover my mouth, bile pushing higher.

"And him." Loch points again to a man with a huge chain around his neck, attached to the floor. Although he has no more space than the others, the chain restrains him instead of a cage.

"That's Roy. I drove past his house every day for years, watching. At least five dogs at a time, chained outside for their entire lives; a few passed, but new ones came. Not pets, not working, not loved. I never saw them walk more than the five feet their chains allowed. All the dogs I saw were malnourished and abused. Dogs would be injured; they would starve to death, outside in all temperatures. I saw all five dogs freeze to death during one snowstorm. Complaints were ignored. But finally, after years of neglect, they removed the dogs from his property. He's been here for over two years. He was Kong's owner."

I gasp in shock and press my hand against my heart.

"I removed Kong from his property after he came here."

Everything in me twists into knots, my brain scrambling with all the information. I try to process the horrors I see with the horrors these people have unleashed.

The last cage held something different. The cage isn't as filthy as the others. This man is barely recognizable. His face is swollen and blackened; half-healed bruises cover his body. Dried blood covers most of his face and chest. He can't even lift his head. His arms and legs are zip-tied.

Loch's voice is ice. "He ran a dog-fighting ring, a big one. The biggest in the state. Police caught him, but thanks to overcrowding, he only served a few months of his six-month sentence, which was a bullshit sentence to begin with. He got off easy."

I remembered the story. I'd seen the grainy news photo on TV a few weeks ago. My stomach drops. This is where Loch had been that night, why his hands were so beat up.

"I saw that. I told you about it," I whisper.

"I know. I panicked, worried you would already know the truth because of my hands."

Lost in thought, I mutter, "I remember thinking... It wasn't enough. That he got off too easily."

Loch nods, stepping beside me. "That's what I thought, too."

I am shaking, my breathing ragged. My heart, my lungs, every piece of me aches with confusion, horror, and grief. All my emotions crash into each other, creating a storm inside my brain. I back away from the cages, but I can't get far. Not from them. Not from him.

"I don't know what to say," I'm still whispering, although I don't know why.

"You don't have to say anything."

"I'm trying to understand, Loch. I am. But this–" I gesture around me. "This is something else, unfathomable."

"The animals deserve justice. And these pieces of shit got what the system wouldn't give, and nothing more."

I look at him, really look at him. The man I've fallen for, who helped me heal. This gentle, thoughtful man, I trust. The one who makes me feel safe. And here he is–judge, jury... executioner.

I don't know if I'm afraid of *him*, or the fact that I'm not. Part of me still wants him. I understand him to some extent. His intentions are good, but his actions are dark and brutal.

I think back to when he told me about Rufus that day in his kitchen–his eyes were full of pain and hurt as he talked about his childhood friend. And I can't deny that these people deserve his vigilante justice.

Chapter 44
Olive

The Ultimate Decision

"I have one more thing," Loch says.

I tense immediately, not ready for more turmoil. I'm ready to leave this house of horrors.

I'm wound too tight and on the verge of collapse, but I let him guide me back upstairs. My legs move on autopilot as my heart tries to figure out what the hell it's supposed to do next.

He turns into a hallway near the front door. It's narrow, dusty, and dark. The light flickers above us, not doing much to light up the small space. He stops at a door, resting his hand on the knob for a second, as if giving me a chance to turn around.

I don't.

He opens it, inviting me to peer inside, and I stop breathing.

It's him. He's sitting in the middle of the empty room, taped to a chair, hands, feet, and waist. He's gagged and badly bruised.

His eyes meet mine and go wide with recognition. Panic sets in as he realizes why Loch brought him here.

My blood turns to ice, and my legs go weak. Every memory surges back in an instant. His hands, his body thrusting into mine, his words, the vile smell of him, the knife, and the gun. Kong, bleeding all over my rug and me. All of it rushes through me. My body quakes under the weight of my own terror. A tremble works its way through my limbs, my body trying to flee, even if my feet won't move.

He looks weak and pathetic. He's crying, fucking sobbing, and it makes me smile for a second.

Loch's voice is calm. This is normal for him. "What do you want to do with him?"

I can't speak. I can't think. Me? He's asking me?

"I..." Loch says in a low tone and swallows hard. "I can take care of him... for you. Or, you can take care of him yourself."

The words surprise me. My body is still motionless.

I look at Loch, my chest aching and seizing. He says in an even lower voice, like he's forcing it out, "But if you asked me right now to let him go, I would do that too. This is all for you, Olive. I'll let him go if you want me to."

A sob comes out, cracked, and I hate it. I hate that I don't feel stronger. That I don't feel like I can finish this. I stare at the man in front of me, the one who broke me. This man who I hate with every fiber of my being, but something else breaks open, something deep inside my chest.

He looks pathetic now. Begging for his life behind the gag, crying like the coward he is. The fear I've carried since that night is gone, nowhere to be found, and something worse has taken its place—white-hot anger and violent rage. I can feel my blood thrumming through my body and my temperature rising.

He ruined everything. He didn't just attack me; he stole from me. He stole my independence, my safety, my passion for life, and now my relationship with Loch. And he shot Kong. My sweet innocent boy, who had done nothing but protect me. Kong could die because this piece of shit believes he is above the law.

And yet... I can't move because I'm scared of what I'm feeling now. I see the huge blistering bite mark on his arm and hand, skin torn from the bone. It only makes me feel more enraged.

I look at Loch, my voice hollow. "I hate him."

Loch doesn't answer. He didn't have to. I turn back to the man, my hands curling into fists.

"Give me a knife."

Loch flashes me a pointed look. "Olive..."

"Knife." As I hold out my hand, waiting.

He hesitates, searching my face for something–doubt or fear, maybe a sign he should step in and stop me. But I don't flinch.

He reaches into his pocket, pulls out a pocket knife, flips it open, and hands it to me. It's cold and heavy in my hand, brown wood with black scrolls along the handle.

I walk to the man, my hand trembling, shaking with rage and anger, every breath shallow. My pulse roars in my ears. I stand inches from him, the tip of the blade hovering below his throat, at his clavicle.

He makes a sound. A whimper. I want him to feel what I felt. The fear and the helplessness. The knife's sharp edge looms, a promise of imminent pain and suffering.

He starts pleading behind the gag, his words muffled, begging, tears streaking down his cheeks. Pathetic. He's a small, pathetic man. I press the blade into his skin enough to make him stop talking. His body stiffens, like mine did when he had the knife to my neck.

I stare into his eyes for what feels like hours, deciding. But as I'm about to do it, Loch's hands wrap around mine, taking the knife from me. I release it, letting go of a deep breath, knowing I can't do it, that it will change me forever. Loch knows, in the way that he always knows what I need.

My body crumbles as soon as I let go of the knife. Sobs tear from my throat, violent and uncontrollable; the weight of everything is finally too much to carry.

No matter how much I hate him. No matter how much he deserves to suffer, I'm not this. I don't want to be like this.

He whispers in my ear, "It's ok, Olive, I've got you." I struggle to stay on my feet with the emotions overwhelming me and the adrenaline coursing through my body.

Loch wraps his arms around me, holding me like I'm the most fragile thing in the world. He whispers into my hair, again and again, "It's ok. It's ok. I didn't bring you here to take part. I brought you here to tell you the truth. The truth of who I am."

He's not the Loch I knew, the man I thought I knew deep down, but I understand and empathize with his pain and his reasons.

I barely register getting into the car. My eyes are still wet, and my heart has shattered into too many pieces to count. I can't even look at him; I'm too confused.

I don't know if it's because I feel betrayed by the person I thought he was, or if I'm angry at the real man sitting next to me. I hate what he's done, but I also understand exactly how he felt and why he did it. I was seconds away from killing a man myself, and I'm ashamed I couldn't do it, and somehow still glad I didn't. The more I think about what Loch has done for me, the less I actually care about what I've seen.

When we get back to his house, I don't say a word. I open the car door and step out, walking toward my car, my body stiff, my mind numb.

"Olive—" Loch starts.

But I can't speak. I need to go.

To breathe.

To be alone.

To think.

I shut the door behind me and leave him standing there, my silence louder than anything I could ever say.

Chapter 45
Olive

Secrets Blacker Than My Coffee

I walk into my apartment, and the first thing I see is Sophia pacing.

"Fuck," I mutter under my breath.

She turns fast, her eyes wide, like she's been waiting all day. "Jesus, Olive! Where the hell have you been? You left your phone, and the vet called—"

My stomach drops. "Shit! Did you talk to them? What did they say? Is he—"

Sophia's expression softens. "Yeah. Yeah, I talked to them. He's doing ok."

My knees go weak as the air whooshes from my lungs in gratitude.

"They said it's going to be a long recovery. He'll need to stay there for a while. Maybe a couple of weeks."

"As long as he's going to be ok," I whisper. "I'll wait. I'll wait as long as it takes." He saved my life. That beautiful, broken boy saved me in more ways than I can count.

I turn toward the hallway, needing only one thing. "I have to go to bed. I'm ok, but I need to sleep."

Sophia steps forward. "Wait, what happened? Did you find Loch? What–"

"I just need sleep, Soph," I say gently. "Please, I promise to tell you everything later."

Her face crumples with worry, but she nods. "I love you, Liv. " She hugs me tight and I let her.

"Thank you for talking with the vet. I promise I'll talk to you about it tomorrow."

"I can't leave you here alone; I'll stay on the couch. You get some sleep."

I collapse into my bed, fully dressed, shoes and all, letting the weight of the last twenty-four hours bury me. The attack, Kong getting shot, the vet, Loch abandoning me at the hospital, then... What do I even call the nightmare Loch showed me? The room spins, my mind spins faster, but mercifully, sleep comes at last.

I wake almost ten hours later with a dry throat and an aching body. I get up just to pee, see Sophia sleeping on the couch, and I crawl straight back under the covers. I don't want to think. Don't want to move. Don't want to feel.

When I wake again, it's to a knock on my bedroom door. My pulse quickens as I jolt up; I'm getting sick of people knocking on my doors. Sophia peeks her head in. "Hey girl, how are you feeling? Did you get some sleep? I bought donuts," she says, stepping in like she owns the place, waving the box of treats in the air.

"I haven't... woken up yet," I mutter.

She arches her brow. "You're talking and upright. That counts."

We walk to the kitchen, and I start the coffee.

The silence between us is heavier than usual, but I know she won't let me off this time. I don't want her to; I need someone to unload my life on, and I need advice. I'm completely overwhelmed with the decisions I need to make.

I pour the coffee into mugs and sit down across from her. She sees right through me. "You ready to tell me what happened?"

I stare at the steam curling above my mug, trying to find the words. I want to tell Sophia the whole truth, but I can't find the words to explain what I found at Loch's. The right lie or the least-broken truth may help me talk it out, without incriminating him.

"Loch's not who I think he is," I tell her.

Sophia doesn't move; she listens.

"He's... he's done bad things."

She leans in. "Bad things like what? Did he do something to Jacob?"

"I can't get into details, but yes," I deflect. "He has reasons for what he's done. Good ones. And that doesn't make it right, but... I don't know. If the reasons are good, but still technically illegal, what does that mean?"

Her eyes are skeptical. "Do you believe they're good reasons and good intentions?"

I swallow. "I think... I think I understand the pain and anger that make a person feel justified. Sophia, I know they were good reasons. I just don't know if it's something I can live with. Knowing he's doing dangerous things and could end up in jail at any time. I mean, I care about what he's done, but I'm not sure if it's enough to make me walk away or not. I—God, I think I love him, and his bad parts somehow make me feel more in love with him and more afraid of him simultaneously. I don't know what the fuck to do with that.

I don't want to lose him because of his past, his own trauma. I have no room to judge him for what he's been through. Our pains might be different in who hurt us and how, but he's suffered pain and loss, just like me. The Loch I know also helped to heal so much of my trauma; he encouraged me to live again, to try and grow. And all the dogs he has saved, he's the best and worst person I know."

She leans back, arms crossed. "Can you live with what he's done? And watch him continue to do it?"

I don't answer. I can't. I want to believe love could eclipse this, the way sunlight can trick you into thinking your world isn't burning by giving you stunning sunsets. But now I know what he does in the darkness.

He kidnaps people and throws away the key; he kills them. Monsters, sure. What they did to all those animals, Kong, and me... And maybe they deserve it; maybe the world is better without them, but who gets to decide that? I know his heart. I've felt it beat against mine in the time we've spent together. He's not evil. He's not. But loving someone who drags bodies into the shadows, even for the right reasons, is like planting flowers in a graveyard and calling it a garden. It's beautiful, but it's built on death. And I can't build a life with him like that, no matter how much I want to.

Sophia lets out a breath. "Look... I don't get it, I haven't met him. But I get you, and I know you're a good person. Be careful, Olive. Please. Love can make us see things in people that aren't really there. Or worse, make us ignore the red flags that are."

She's right, but it's more than a red flag. It's *the* red flag waving in the air as a bull runs full speed toward me, and if I stay, that bull is bound to take me out.

She looks at her phone. "I have to get to work; it's almost three. Call me later tonight, ok? I'm serious."

"I will," I say.

She kisses the top of my head like a mom would and leaves. The apartment falls silent again. I sit at the table alone as it all continues to flash through my mind.

How many more people will end up in that basement? How many will deserve it? Can I live with this? Can I love him, all of him?

He didn't show me the worst parts of himself; he handed them to me like a gift, like a test. He's been so gentle and tender with me, seeing what my soul needs. Maybe he needs the same in return—patience and understanding—but I don't know what his soul needs. If I can still love him after seeing his truth, maybe we have a chance.

CHAPTER 46
LOCH

SPRING CLEANING

A week later...

When I pull into the parking lot of the veterinary hospital, something cracks open in my chest. I'm here to visit Kong, the sweet dog who saved my girl. He's always had a special place in my heart. But now, there is no end to the love I have for this dog. I ask to see him, and because the doctors know me, they allow it. I don't know if Olive will ever let me see him again, but I had to see him at least once more to thank him for everything.

As soon as I step inside, memories flood me. The waiting room hasn't changed in twenty years—same cheap chairs, same stale air, the chemical bite of disinfectant clashing with the stench of urine and blood. The same flickering fluorescent light overhead hums like a heartbeat. I've been here many times over the years, but not to see a dog that I loved, and it's bringing back so many emotions now that I am.

The vet tech comes to get me and takes me back to the room. I can see him. I sit down in the corner, the same goddamn corner I curled into as a boy, ten years old and heartbroken. My hands clench in anguish. A lot has changed since then, but the ache in my chest is the same as it was the day Rufus died.

I didn't cry when it happened, not in front of my father, I didn't want him to know how much it hurt me, nor in front of the vet who showed me kindness.

But, later, at home, when the door shut, and the silence swallowed me, I sobbed so hard my voice cracked for days. Rufus had been mine, my only real friend. And that man, our neighbor, our fucking neighbor, poisoned him and left him to die in our yard like trash. And the world did nothing.

But sitting here now, older, blood on my hands that will never wash off, I don't feel powerful. I'm the same boy I used to be, trembling and helpless. I bury my face in my palms. My shoulders shake with the memory of losing Rufus and the thought of almost losing Kong. He protected my girl when I couldn't. Fuck, my gut turns at the thought of losing either of them.

I don't hear the door open, only realizing it has when the vet says my name.

"Loch?"

I look up. My face is wet with tears and red.

Then, I see him, Kong. A white, transparent cone hangs around his head, a muzzle covers his snout, and blue bandages are wrapped tight across his torso and chest. His tail doesn't wag, but his eyes—God, his eyes—find mine and my heart shatters.

He's alive, and I am so thankful he didn't lose his life at the hands of that fucking asshole; thankful that he saved Olive and was such a fierce protector.

"He woke up a little aggressive," the vet says with a tired smile. "Growled at everyone. We had to sedate him again to change the dressings. Hence the muzzle this round. He's protective, that one, but he seems to be warming up to a few of us. He's undergone three surgeries and will remain here for another week or two to make sure he doesn't get an infection. Kong is one tough dog. He had two bullet wounds and a major laceration to his head."

My vision blurs again, but this time it isn't from grief. It's from relief. I exhale, as if I've held my breath for years. My legs are unsteady as I stand and take a step toward him. His body is trembling slightly, and yet he stands tall. It's clear he's still doped up and on painkillers. He looks so strong and proud, as he should. He saved her. He took two bullets for my girl, and I can never repay him enough.

I drop to my knees beside him and give him a good scratch on his chin, making sure not to hurt him. "Hey, boy," I whisper.

He leans into me the best he can, despite his big cone getting in the way. My throat burns with bile and the thought of what I would've done if he hadn't made it. My hands tremble, I bury my face in his side, and let myself break open.

This isn't Rufus; this isn't the past. This is new.

And the realization hits me like a jolt of lightning. All the years I spent trying to settle the score, making the world pay for what it did to that little boy and his dog, were years lived in the shadows of my grief.

Kong is the first light that ever made it through that darkness. I don't think Rufus needs my vengeance anymore. Maybe I don't either. I've been carrying a broken boy's rage for twenty-six years, wearing it like armor. But armor rusts. It gets heavy, and it sinks you.

And now, if I can have Olive. If I can still have Kong in my life, I'll have something to fight for instead of against.

I can almost hear Rufus in the back of my mind, the way he used to bark when I came home from school, full of life. Rufus was the friend who taught me trust and love, and I am so thankful I had him for the couple of years I did. I feel like he is telling me to live, to live for him, instead of killing for him.

This is my second chance, my chance to leave the bad behind and focus on the good things in my life. I hold Kong and close my eyes. I let the warmth of him in this moment ground me. He's alive.

She's alive. And I still have time to make it right as long as they haven't given up on me.

I don't have to be that boy anymore, and I don't have to be the man he became. The burden of a life lived solely for revenge lifts from my shoulders. I can be better, be the man she deserves, the one she knew before. But I need to clean up the mess I've made and start fresh.

I enter the old house I've come to hate. The dark, damp scent in the air, the echo of broken, hopeless lives I've kept here. I can feel them all, those who deserve to die.

I've always lived by the rule of justice. When the system failed, I stepped in. They never knew what hit them. They thought they had gotten away with it. It was about them knowing what they'd done to helpless creatures, giving them a taste of their own medicine.

Until now, I never understood that vengeance, in its purest form, is a poison. A poison that will eat me alive if I don't stop drinking it. I will never be able to stop them all. It's held me back from living a real life and helping those who have suffered.

I make my way down into the basement. The prisoners, the ones who never saw the light of day after coming here, know I'm here, but they have no idea what's coming. The sound of their breaths, their eyes wide with terror, makes my skin crawl now.

They're still breathing, each one of them, trapped and suffering. Whimpering in the dark like the cowards they are. Like the animals they treated like trash. Should I end it now? The rage in my body threatens to keep them here like always, but this isn't about them anymore. It's about me; I want it to end.

What do I do with them?

Let them go? No. I can't. I won't. They'd find more helpless animals, more strays, more people like Olive walking home alone. They'd learn nothing, and it would accomplish nothing, and I would be at risk of getting caught. Letting them go is not an option.

But if I kill them, if I outright cross that line, I know what that makes me.

There's the rescue I need to consider, too. The life I built with long days, good people, and ones who I now consider friends. The animals we've saved, their soft noses and wagging tails. They are why I need to end this. The way Kong curls around Olive, like he was made to protect her, is why I need to change and do better. That's where I have the power and knowledge to make a difference.

Not here. Not with blood pooling on concrete floors.

Saving them, that's how I win. That's how I change things. Not by adding more bodies to the pile, but by giving myself a chance to thrive. That's how I honor Rufus. That's how I keep Kong's and Olive's eyes from seeing the worst in me.

But I still need to figure out what to do with the monsters in front of me. I stand in the ripe basement, looking at my mess, trying to figure out how to clean it up, how to take care of this as humanely as possible. For me, to live with myself, I have to be merciful. I cannot be cruel to them any longer.

Once I make the decision, I waste no time. I hurry to each prisoner. I have to move forward before I can think better of it. The best thing I can do now is make it quick and as painless as I can.

I pull out my pocket knife, the same one I took from Olive's hand.

Greta first. I open her cage and reach for her. She barely moves, only offering a glance up at me. I think she's days away from dying on her own. But I cut her throat and watch her body go limp.

Then, Mike, I don't want to waste a second on this piece of utter shit. He's screaming. I assume he now knows what's coming, given what he's seen, but I move quickly. His screams and thrashing tell me what an absolute coward he is. I slice his throat. Blood rushes down his body; his hands and feet are still bound.

Next is Roy. I walk up to him and his chain. This one would take a bit more effort because I don't have time to subdue him, and he can fight back. I'm not very concerned because of the amount of adrenaline rushing through my body, but I still need to be smart. He's already yelling and reaching for me like a feral animal. I rush him, tackling him to the ground like a linebacker. Fists fly in a tangled mess, both of us fighting for control. I take a knee to the gut, and when he stretches out his leg, I grab him, pinning him to the ground face down. I manage to get him in a chokehold with my knee to his back long enough to slide the blade across his neck, and his blood spills out.

I heave with my hands on my knees, trying to catch my breath. Half-ready to vomit, I look at what I've done.

I turn my head to face Brad. Fucking Brad. He hasn't left the small dog kennel in six years. He's disgusting, and I don't even want to touch him.

"Ok, Brad." I open his cage, and he falls out of the kennel, attempting to lie down, but his body struggles to move into that position after being cramped for so long. He offers his neck, stretching his gaze up to the ceiling. I take the hint and make it quick.

His body goes completely limp. It's almost anticlimactic after letting this man consume my life and my motivations for as long as I can remember.

By the time I finish, the room is silent. No more gasps, no more tears, all four of them dead within minutes. The blood pours, like it has for years, over this same concrete floor where I've spent too many nights convincing myself that it was justice well served. The stillness of death shares the same silence that echoes through the years of my life wasted by holding onto retribution.

I walk back upstairs to deal with the last man, Olive's attacker. I enter the room he is in; the monster in front of me is still taped to the chair, and his mouth is still gagged. I stand there, the pressure of all the deaths weighing on me. I never wanted to be a killer. I only wanted to serve justice, but I wasn't an outright murderer–until now. I hold the knife to his neck, close my eyes, and slice. One motion, no words, and I walk out.

And now that this is over, I have a chance to be better, to have a real life. I still have a chance to love Olive the way she deserves, and with any luck, she'll love me back.

I turn on the gas stove, letting a flame come to life. I grab an old cloth that I found in the basement and light the house on fire, throwing the flame into the basement to ensure it all disappears. I want to burn this house to the ground along with all of its horrors and nightmares.

It's almost too easy. I watch as the flames lick at the old wallpaper and rotting wood walls, consuming every bit of it; all my sins, burning to ash.

The fire rises, crackling in its fury. It roars, consuming everything I've done, everything I've justified in my own mind. The very fire I created to destroy my mess, now cleansing me of something deeper, of all the wrongs I've committed, of the man I never want to be again. The fire was forgiving me. I was forgiving myself.

The heat hits me hard in the chest, and for a moment, I almost let myself suffocate in the smoke right along with all my sins, but I have a reason to live. I walk outside, and as the flames dance higher, reaching into the night sky, the shackles that have held me for years finally loosen. The world will never make sense or be fair, but I can live with that now.

All I want is to protect Olive, Kong, and any other animals that I can. I want to be with her, to spend my life with her, loving her, making love to her, kissing her, and giving her a life worth living with me, for both of us.

We deserve a life that isn't defined by the ghosts of our past. I can't ask her to forgive me for all the things I've done. But I can ask her to let me show her who I will be after today. I can show her who I am now.

As long as I can keep her and Kong safe, as long as no one ever hurts her again, I'll be ok.

It has been nine days since I last saw Olive. And yeah, I've been counting every one.

I've called her so many times, texted, and left voicemails. I knew I shouldn't have, but on the first day, I couldn't stop myself. By the third, I told myself once every few hours was enough. Somehow, I thought that was more controlled. Now, I was down to one text and one call a day. One text message she leaves on read. One voicemail, a shot in the dark, hoping she'd hear my voice and finally decide to call.

But all I get is silence.

Kong is alive, but I haven't seen him since that day in the hospital. I miss him. I miss Olive, too, the simple routine we had, her scent. I miss lying in the sheets that smell like her. I'm miserable, depressed, and losing hope that I'll ever get another chance to tell her I fucked up, but that I've changed my ways. I know that I was wrong, but I don't know if I've lost her for good, and living in limbo might be worse than knowing she's done with me.

The thought that I won't get to make it up to her or tell her what I did hollows me out. It leaves me pacing the walls of my mind, trying to figure out what the hell to do next. How do I fix this? How do I show her I'm still the man who would burn down the world to protect her?

I keep replaying the last time I saw her, the way she wouldn't meet my eyes. The hurt in her voice and the tremble in her hands when she turned away from me. God, she looked like she was shattering into pieces, and I let her walk away. I didn't know how to fix what I did; I couldn't do anything to make it better. I told myself she needed space. That I needed to give her room to process it all.

But the truth? My fear is that when the fog lifts and her heartache subsides, she'll see only the monster I am. She won't see the man who held her through the nightmares, the man who showed her how to feel again, or the man who would carry her pain like it's his own. She'll only see the weight of my past, the shadow of every dark thing I've ever done cast over us.

I can't lose her like this. She is everything, and I won't give up on us. I'm not done fighting for her.

I have to find the right way to reach her, the right words. The right moment.

An idea pops into my head. If I get another chance, I know exactly what I'll do.

Chapter 47
Olive

Kong's Home... Now, Let's Address the Other Beast

Kong's nails click against the hardwood as he walks around the apartment, sniffing every corner like it's all changed in the weeks he's been gone. He looks healthy—a little skinnier, a little slower, but alive and breathing. He's mine again.

I sit on the floor beside him, once he settles. My fingers smooth over his fur, his warm body presses against my side, and for the first time in weeks, my chest calms and I breathe easy. He's home. Even with that weight lifted, the ache still doesn't leave me, though.

The pain of not having Loch around crushes me every day. It's been almost three weeks since the attack, and it's been so lonely here. God, I miss him, his voice, his hands, the way he used to look at me like I was the only thing in the room that mattered.

I miss how well I slept beside him and showered with him. But mostly, I miss the way I felt when I was around him—stronger, safer, and more whole. When he was around, I could carry all the dark memories and still move forward.

Rescued

I haven't slept a full night since the shooting. And maybe that's why it feels so loud and quiet at the same time.

I thought Kong coming home would help. I'm so glad he's ok, and is back home, but it still feels empty here; even Kong seems to feel it.

Luckily, everything with Jacob seems to have blown over. I received a call a few days ago that they were closing the case until further notice. The police suspect that Jacob Wright skipped town thanks to his father's money and connections. They said he was likely on the run in another country. So, Loch is free of any investigation that might lead to him.

I grab my phone off the couch before I can talk myself out of it.

Olive: Kong's home. He's ok. Just thought you should know.

I stare at the screen, thumb hovering, stomach twisting. Maybe I shouldn't have. What if it opens doors I'm not ready to walk through?

But the reply comes fast. So fast, my breath catches in my throat.

Loch: Thank you for telling me. Can I see you both? Please. Just let me talk to you. Let me explain.

I hold the phone tighter. My heart wants to say yes. My pride and my brain want to throw the phone across the room and delete his number.

I don't know if I can forgive him. But I'm not ready to let him go and cut him out of my life either. I'll keep it about Kong. No commitments.

Olive: You can come to see Kong if you want.

A pause. Then, before I can blink, I get his reply.

Loch: I'll be there soon.

I press my forehead to Kong's shoulder and exhale. I don't know what is going to happen next. But the moment is coming, whether I'm ready or not.

Chapter 48
Loch

THE GRAND GESTURE

My hands tighten around my phone, nervous anticipation setting in with relief that I'm going to see her and Kong. Except this time, the relief hits harder than the adrenaline. She didn't have to text me. She didn't have to let me in, but she did.

I stare at the message for ten seconds too long before I'm already moving. I grab my keys and head to Olive's.

The drive feels longer than it is. Every red light taunts me. Every second I'm not near her is another reminder of how far I let her get away. I need to tell her about the changes I've made, and beg for her forgiveness. I need to tell her I stopped for her and Kong.

I stand at her door, staring, trying to breathe and remember everything I have to say. Then I knock. The door creaks open, and there she is. I let out the breath I didn't realize I was holding.

"Olive."

She has her hair pulled back into her usual messy bun. Her eyes seem almost colorless, only a few flecks of blue visible, as if holding secrets behind a veil of fog, calm and unreadable. Her sad eyes have returned. The look on her face says she's exhausted. She looks like she hasn't slept in weeks, but she's still the most beautiful thing I've ever seen.

Kong pushes past her legs and sniffs at my boots before nuzzling his head into my thigh. She opens the door, allowing me past her. I follow Kong into the apartment, careful not to let my eyes wander too much. I don't want to make her uncomfortable. I don't know where her mental state is after the last attack and everything I put her through. I don't want to push her. I'm letting her set the tone for how today is going to go.

Kong drops to the floor in the living room like nothing's changed. Like he didn't take a bullet for her and almost die. He acts as if I'm here to watch a movie and hang out like normal.

I sink to the floor beside him, fingers working through the fur around his neck. His eyes flutter shut, and I see his little closed-mouth smile. Something in my chest unclenches.

"You scared the hell out of me," I whisper to him as I hug him. "You little asshole." His tail thumps against the floor once. He doesn't move otherwise; he leans into the contact like it's all he's been waiting for.

I stay like that for a few minutes, grounded by the contact with him, by the sound of his breath, steady and warm. So thankful that he's ok, and that he protected her when it mattered. I'm very thankful that she let me see him again. I love seeing him smile now, and he even smiles at me, but I know it's only because of her.

Olive says nothing for a while. She allows me to love on him. And I don't look at her until I feel her eyes on me.

"Thanks for coming to see him," she mumbles.

"I would've come sooner," I tell her. "I wanted to, every day."

She stares, puzzled, eyes flicking from my face to the flower lei in my hand. "What is that for?" she asks quietly, forcing her words, like it's taking all her effort to speak to me. It makes me sad for a moment, knowing that I was the one who caused her pain.

I glance down at the garland. "Will you come sit with me? I'll tell you; I want you to be a part of it."

She hesitates, and I mentally brace for her to deny me. But without a word, she saunters across the room and sinks down beside me on the floor. She's close enough that I feel the warmth of her, and I get a whiff of her grapefruit scent.

Kong presses his giant head into her lap like he's been waiting for her to settle so he can, too.

I smile, brushing my fingers over the petals, ready to make my move and hoping for the best. "There's this tradition in Nepal. It's called Kukur Tihar. During the Festival of Lights, a whole day is dedicated just to dogs."

She glances at me, curiosity softening her jaw. "They thank them," I continue. "For their loyalty. Their friendship. For being protectors and companions. They make these garlands for the dogs to wear, called mala, to honor them. And they apply a red mark, a tika, to the dogs' foreheads as a sign of respect, blessing, and love."

Olive's now glassy eyes drop to the mala in my hand, then back to Kong. Her expression flickers–something between wonder and ache. Seeing her eyes water makes my own heart ache. We both have so much to thank Kong for.

I lean forward and drape the garland around Kong's thick neck as he looks up at us. The bright flowers settle clumsily into his fur, awkward and perfect all at once.

"King Kong," I whisper. "Protector of queens. Thank you for your loyalty and protection." He huffs, pleased, and settles between us with a contented groan. Then, I reach into my jacket pocket and pull out a small leather bag. I open it and reveal the crimson powder inside.

"I thought..." My voice tightens and cracks, but I push through. "I thought you might want to do the tika."

Olive blinks, surprised. "Me?"

"You're the reason he fought so hard," I say. "And the reason he's still here." I extend the bag toward her, the vermilion catching the light like a flame.

She takes it with both hands, holding it like it's fragile. She looks at it, admiring it, almost like she's praying over it or blessing it. I watch as she dips two fingers into the powder, then pauses, looking at Kong like she's trying not to cry. Then, with the utmost reverence, she presses a soft, red mark into the center of his forehead. Starting from between his eyes and moving up to the top of his head.

Kong closes his eyes. And for a moment, everything is still. Not silent, still. Like the world stopped spinning so we could witness this a little longer. And beside me, Olive exhales a trembling breath, telling me she feels it too. Tears tiptoe down her face.

"Thank you." Her throat moves, and her voice cracks like she's trying to swallow words she's struggling to get out.

I want to move closer, to comfort and kiss her. My whole body is aching with the need to soothe her, to get her back, but I stay where I am and I wait for her to tell me if I'm allowed.

Olive leans back and says, "Thank you, that was very thoughtful." She stands and paces. I catch her reflection on the TV screen, bare feet, arms crossed. She's fidgeting with the hem of her sleeve like she wants to crawl out of her own skin. She's trying to build the courage to speak, but the words are barbed.

I wait. Kong sighs and rolls onto his side, kicking his back leg when I scratch the right spot. It should make me smile, but there's a tension behind my ribs that won't let go, won't let me relax.

Then, finally, Olive breaks the silence. "I can tell he wanted to see you, too."

I lift my head and see she's not looking at me. Her eyes are on Kong.

"I replay it," she says, her voice tighter now. "Over and over. The sound of the shots. His yelp. The way he dropped. I don't want to imagine what could have happened to him." Her voice cracks, and she covers her mouth with her hand like she's ashamed of it.

I'm on my feet before I can think. "Olive."

She shakes her head once and puts her hand out in front of her. "Don't. Please don't."

I don't touch her or cross the room. I stand there, close enough that she knows I would if she allowed or wanted me to. "I know you don't want to hear this," I say quietly, "but if he hadn't been here, if something had happened to you."

"I know," she snaps, and then flinches, wrapping her arms around herself like she didn't mean for it to come out that way. She exhales, slower this time. "I know," she repeats. "I just... I can't stop thinking about if I had lost him, if that man took something else from me."

My fists curl at my sides. "You did nothing wrong," I say. "Not then. Not now. You did everything right. That's why Kong is here today." She looks up at me then, the first time our eyes lock since I've walked in. It hurts seeing her like this. All raw edges and sleepless nights, seeing her fall back into her shell. She was cocooned in that shell when I met her.

My jaw tightens; I can see that she needs me, but I don't know if I still have the right to touch her. I want to hold her and make all of this better, but I'm afraid it'll make things worse. I've spent every day since the shooting trying to figure out how to make myself into someone worthy of standing in front of her again. Trying to figure out how to get her back.

"I want to talk to you," I say. My voice sounds rougher than I mean for it to be. There's too much tension behind it, reaching for hope.

Olive's expression doesn't shift, but something behind her eyes hardens. She shakes her head. "I can't, Loch." My chest goes still.

"I'm not judging you," she adds. "I need you to know that." I stay quiet because I already feel the sting of the rejection coming.

"I won't say anything to anyone about what you've done. I get it, why you did it. I do." Her voice breaks again. "And maybe, in another life, if we were different people, or if we had met under different circumstances, or been through less..." She trails off, tears brimming. She blinks them back, desperate to hold herself together. "But I can't be with someone who lives that life. Someone who's willing to cross those lines. I can't carry that weight, Loch. Not after everything I've already been through. I can't worry about what you're out doing every single time you leave."

The worst part is she's not angry, not even close. She's kind and gentle, empathetic in the exact way that makes it hurt more.

"I want to be with you," she says, almost in a whisper. "So much. You have no idea how much. But that part of you, it's too much for me."

I step forward before I can think. "Olive, please—"

"No." She lifts her hand again, but it's softer than before. Her eyes are pleading. "Please don't. Let me finish." I stop and swallow hard.

"I believe you're good," she says. "I believe you've saved people and innocent animals who needed saving, but I need to feel safe too. I need to know that when you leave, you're not putting us in danger. I can't watch you run off every time someone goes free. I need peace, and I don't think you can give me that."

I'm hollowed out. Her soft words land like a knife straight to my heart. I've tried so fucking hard to be something close to good, and all I've done is remind her of everything she's trying to outrun.

There's a sharp little ache that lives in my throat when I'm near her. "I'm sorry," I whisper. "For everything."

I look at her, and I can see she's not saying it to hurt me. But I can't hold it in anymore. I have to lay it all on the table and try to change her mind. If I fail, then I will walk away knowing I tried. "Olive," I say, the sound splintering as I speak. "Please, let me talk to you before you decide."

She tilts her head in a slight nod, and I break my silence. It all comes out in a rush, raw and stripped down. "I ended it. All of it. Seeing Kong bloody on your floor and your face, I knew I couldn't keep living that life. The look on your face when I showed you who

I am, who I was. That part of me died when you left that night. It died when I knew Kong survived. I'm so sorry for hurting you. You deserve better. I couldn't risk losing either of you again." My throat is tight, and it's hard to breathe, but I push through because I need her to hear this.

"I don't want that darkness in my life anymore. I don't want justice or violence or... whatever the hell I thought I was doing. I want peace. I want you. And I know I can't protect you, or have a real life with you, while I'm still drowning in all of that." Her eyes glisten, chest heaving, but she doesn't look away.

"I made sure it's over," I say. "All of them, including him, they're gone. You never have to fear him again, ever. But I'm done. That life is behind me. I cleaned up my mess as my last act, and I am ready to move on. I would like to do that with you. We had something I've always wanted, and I'm begging you to give me another chance."

She's still silent, but something shifts in the air. I hope I'm getting through to her.

"I want a future, a life, for us both," I say. "I want us to let go of the past, not just mine, but yours, too. I want to give us a shot at something real. Something good." And then I say it. No hesitation. "I love you, Olive, so fucking much. I will do anything to keep you." Her lungs seize for a beat. "I love you, Olive. I want a chance to build a life with you. Whatever that looks like, I want it with you." I wait, my heart exposed.

She doesn't say anything right away. Her cheeks are tear-stained, lips parted like she wants to speak but can't find the words. Whatever she's feeling is too tangled to pull free. I can see it in her—the way she wants to come closer, but something inside keeps her still. Doubt has its fingers hooked beneath her ribs, holding her back.

My chest aches with the weight of it. So I reach for her, slow and steady, and slide my arms around her waist. "Please, Olive." She doesn't pull back, but she doesn't lean in either. She's trembling; her breathing is ragged.

"Do you still trust me?" I whisper.

She doesn't move, doesn't even blink. Her chin dips in the smallest nod, afraid to admit it, but that's all I need. Holding her still feels like home, and I hold her tighter than I should.

I lean in and kiss her, soft at first. I don't want to scare her away from me. Her lips are warm, unmoving, but they don't pull away. She lets me linger in the moment.

I pull back only enough to breathe against her. "Tell me what to do to get you back." She looks into my eyes. She doesn't stop me. Her eyes swallow me whole. I move closer, crowding her space, guiding her back into the wall behind her. My hands slide to her hips, holding her there, anchoring her in place.

"Please let me remind you that what we have is real." I wait as long as I can. "I hate that I let my actions twist what we have into something else. I never meant to hurt you."

She looks up at me, eyes wide, breathing shallow. Her body quakes, but her hands lift, slow, tentative, and curl into the fabric of my shirt, not saying a word. I kiss her again, deeper and rougher this time.

Her fingers clutch tighter. I feel the moment she stops fighting. Her body calms, and her mouth is on mine, returning the kiss with passion. My mouth and hands are calling her back to me.

Chapter 49
Olive

Where Love Stands or Breaks

His kiss reels me back in too fast. My brain screams at me to stop, to think, to take a breath, but my heart's already putty in his hands. I watched how gentle he was with Kong, that garland of bright, beautiful flowers. The way he spoke about honoring him like he was more than a dog, like he was family. It wasn't just a gesture; it was him. His soul was so bare and aching and sweet, in a way that hurt to look at, but I couldn't look away from.

God, he's trying; he's really trying. But is that enough?

He says he's changed. That he's done with the violence. The man who stole from me is dead, and he killed him. He says what's left behind is the kind, thoughtful man I've come to know.

My head is full of questions, but none of them matter when his lips press into mine. His mouth is warm and insistent, and I taste the underlying ache behind his kiss. He's starving for something only I can give, and I've been starving for him this whole time, too.

He draws me in closer, his hands sliding over my waist until my back hits the wall harder. I let out a gasp.

I want this; I want him, even if it breaks me again. I still love him, and I don't care what he did; he won't do it again, and I can live with that.

It would have been easier to walk away, but love can't be flipped off like a switch. Loch isn't his past; he's so much more. He's smart, patient, kind, and compassionate.

His vanilla and amber scent, wrapping around me like a warm blanket, takes me back to our nights together and falling asleep in his arms. His hands are greedy, splaying across my ribs and hips. His thumbs brush the skin beneath my shirt like he needs to touch every inch to prove I'm real. As his hands roam over my body, I arch and moan into him, my breathing becoming rapid and needy.

"Olive, God, I have missed you," he whispers between kisses, low and desperate.

My pulse is throbbing almost as much as my clit. Without thinking, I wrap my leg around his hip, encouraging him on. He groans into my mouth as his hand slides down and grabs my ass and thigh, anchoring me tighter against him.

I can feel every inch of him pressing into me, unrelenting and mine. And through it all, my thoughts race, tangle, and then scatter.

He loves me.

He loves me.

And the truth is, I love him, too.

His mouth trails down my neck, and I whimper as he presses a kiss beneath my ear.

"Olive, I'm begging you to tell me you're mine," he growls against my skin, rough and low. "Say you're mine."

I should push him away. I should take time to think about what he's told me, and what I want. I shouldn't be so quick to forgive him, but my hands are in his hair, and my body has betrayed me, knowing exactly what it wants.

"I'm yours," I breathe, and the thought of it nearly undoes me.

His hands are everywhere now, up my shirt, squeezing my breasts, pinching my nipples with his fingers. They move down the curve of my back, fingers sinking into my thighs as he lifts me and pins me harder against the wall.

"Tell me to stop," he murmurs. Not because he wants to hear it, he doesn't. He needs to know I still trust him, and I don't want him to stop.

I'm vibrating with need. My pussy is soaking and pulsing. His rock-hard length presses into my stomach. His skin is hot and sticky with sweat as I run my hands along his neck, shoulders, and back.

I lean in, my lips brushing his, and whisper through the heat between us, "I love you." He freezes.

In the space between heartbeats, I watch something in him morph. His whole body goes still, his eyes tighten like my words hit some tender, shattered part of him. His forehead presses to mine; his breath trembles against my lips.

"Fuck, Olive," his voice breaks. "You don't know what hearing you say that does to me. I didn't think I would ever hear you say it, or if I would ever get to have you again, to keep you."

He closes his eyes as if it hurts to feel this much raw emotion. "I don't deserve it, I don't deserve you. But Christ, I'll spend the rest of my life trying to. I fucking love you."

I cradle his face between my hands, pulling him close so he sees me, sees that I mean every word. "You deserve me, Loch," I whisper. "Because you want to be better, because you are here now. When we met, I was a mess. I could hardly function without Sophia. But you helped to change that. I lost the person I was before my attack, but I love the person I've become. The fact that you saw me, you saw through the sweatpants and sloppy exterior, and helped me through the hardest part of my life. You gave me Kong, who saved my life. You mean everything to me."

Loch's mouth finds mine again, slower this time, deeper, more ragged. His shirt is gone in seconds, thrown to the floor, and mine follows, tossed somewhere around us. His fingers trace every inch of my skin like he's learning me all over again. He removes my pants and panties, and his eyes eat me alive.

When his mouth moves down over my chest, I close my eyes and allow myself to feel him explore. He moves to my stomach and pulls my leg over his shoulder. I arch into him, every nerve alive and shooting off like fireworks.

"I need to taste you," he breathes hot air on my clit, and it's making me even wetter waiting in anticipation. "You taste like the best damn meal I've ever had, and I thought I'd never get to have you again."

He licks me from ass to clit, my whole body tenses and shakes with the contact.

"I could survive off your cunt. It's an addiction I never want to stop." He spears me with his tongue, my body contorting with pleasure. My breathing increases. His tongue feels so good.

He continues to lick me and suck my clit, sending a wave of need coursing through me. My orgasm is building, sensation surging through me like a storm gathering strength, impossible to contain. Impatient with his own need, he climbs up my body and says, "I'm sorry, I can't wait any longer to be inside you."

He pulls his throbbing cock out, fisting it once while his gaze rakes over me again. Loch grabs my legs, pulling them up and around his waist, holding me up and against the wall. Without waiting one more second, he slides deep inside me. In one powerful thrust, we're both panting.

I look into his eyes, feeling that familiar intimacy. His grip is brutal; we're both on the edge within minutes. With every thrust of his hips, I feel the grief, his want, and our love, finally releasing.

We move together. I roll my hips into him like we're relearning the shape of each other's bodies. His hand wraps around my wrists and holds them tight above my head, restraining me. His other hand grips my hip so I can't move. I'm completely pinned to the wall, like he's afraid I'll disappear.

"Fuck, you are so goddamn beautiful. Keep your hands up. Do not lower them until I say so. I want to watch your tits bounce as I fuck you."

I've missed his dirty words and demands. He thrusts into me harder; he can't hold back anymore. He needs to break loose and completely lose control. Each movement is deep, purposeful, and unfiltered, like he's trying to bury himself in me for good. Him claiming me again is the only way he knows how to say everything his mouth can't.

His breath is hot against my ear, voice ragged. "I need you. I am so lost without you. I love you, all of you, Olive," he groans my name like a vow.

This isn't just physical; it's coming home after a long, painful trip. It's surrender and salvation, all wrapped up in skin and sweat and gasped declarations. And when we finally fall apart together, breathless and clinging and undone, I know one thing for certain—I don't want to let him go again.

Ever.

Chapter 50
Olive

PUPPY BREATH AND ASHES

I haven't stopped smiling in weeks. I'm talking about the stupid, giddy, cheeks-hurt kind of smiling that feels like sunlight coming out of your bones. That dangerous joy you get when you realize you've fallen hard, and you're not even trying to catch yourself anymore.

I told Sophia everything. Every beautiful, messy, impossible detail, and true to who she is, she didn't judge me or Loch. She hugged me, squealed, and called Loch a "smoke show with a tragic anti-hero complex." She might've also threatened to kill him if he ever broke my heart, and I believe her.

Even now, even happy, I still don't go out much. I wish I could say it was all behind me, but fear doesn't work like that. It lingers, especially after the second attack. The fear builds tiny nests in your ribs and waits for something random to show its face. But it's quieter now, less prominent.

Kong, sweet brave Kong, makes it better, too. He's healing, slow but steady. His fur is patchy where they had to shave him, and the small, angry pink scars curl over his shoulder and chest, but he's alive, he's mine—ours.

Somehow, almost a month later, he still has a little bit of red dust from the tika on his head, clinging to his fur. He wears it like a badge of honor and knows what it's for.

This morning, Loch texted and asked me to come down to Only Dogs with him. I'm looking forward to seeing some of his coworkers and Bellamy again. I can send my dad a picture of her.

The last time I was at the rescue with my parents, everything felt so far away from the world I once knew—bartending, partying, drifting. Galavanting was my constant, but now it feels... small. Not bad, but not enough for me anymore. I have zero desire to go back to work at the bar, and I can't live off my parents forever. I'm finally ready to figure out what's next and consider my future.

The rescue is busier than I remember. It's warmer somehow, more comfortable because Loch and I are in such a different place in our relationship. We greet everyone as we walk into the building. Jan is there, and I give her an enormous hug.

"Hey, Jan! How are you?"

"Olive! What a surprise! What are you two doing here?" She glances between Loch and me. I assume she doesn't know what all we've been through, but it's pretty obvious what we are now.

Loch chimes in, "I have some things to show Olive. I told you Kong is back from the hospital, right? He's doing great."

Jan replies, "Oh, that's wonderful, so glad he's on the mend. Olive, what's going on with you? Do you think you'll be coming back to the bar anytime soon?"

Well, there's no time like the present, right? "Um, well, no. I don't think I'll be coming back. I planned to tell you soon, but I kind of just figured it out."

"Oh, honey, no problem at all. Besides, it looks like I'll see you around here more often," she says as she winks at Loch.

I'm grateful for her understanding. "Thanks, Jan, I really appreciate everything you've done for me. I wouldn't have Kong... or Loch if it weren't for you."

"Yes, things sure worked out well with that. Now that my divorce is final, I need to find a good man of my own." She jokes and laughs.

Loch smiles at our girl talk and says, "Thanks again, Jan, I'll chat with you later, ok?" She waves us off and goes back to whatever she's working on.

We wander around. Loch introduces me to a couple of newer dogs that they've taken in. One sweet boy named Gary, who is a tiny version of Kong, with adorable floppy ears. I wish Kong had his ears; it breaks my heart to think someone butchered them for looks. Finally, Loch leads me to one of the private rooms behind the kennel room, and when I look inside, I nearly melt.

A mama German Shepherd lies in a kiddie pool covered in blankets; she's curled around five tiny, squirming puppies.

Loch opens the door and lets us inside the room. My chest clenches tight, and I drop to my knees beside them, their mama trusting us instantly. Five little squirming, barking–well, if you can call it barking–bundles of fluff. Their cries are pitiful. Two of them jump on my lap, and I snuggle them in, holding them to my chest.

There are two tan and black pups who look like mom, and three almost all black pups. They're playing, jumping on each other, and they have the cutest growls. I hold each one. Loch tells me they're all named after a vegetable–Carrot, Asparagus, Tomato, Zucchini, and Potato. Each one has its own little personality already. Some want to wrestle and bite like little sharks, and some want to snuggle and breathe their yummy puppy breath in my face. I decided one little girl, Zucchini, is my favorite. She's a snuggler and puts her little paw on my nose when I hold her to my face, like she's booping me. She does it every single time I put her to my face. Loch and I laugh at her antics and how adorable she is. So sweet and full of puppy breath. She's almost all black with two little tan socks and a white diamond on her chest. Watching her walk around on wobbly legs is the most adorable thing I've ever seen. I can't help but continue to cuddle her.

"I'm so in love with her."

Loch sits beside me as I cradle her, her head on my shoulder, fast asleep, her tiny heart fluttering fast against my palm.

"Where did they come from?" I ask, not looking up.

He says quietly, "Someone dumped them. Left on the side of a freeway. The puppies were in a bag tied up. Luckily, a good Samaritan pulled over, seeing mom, and checked the bag. There were six pups. One was already gone by the time she found them all."

I stop breathing, eyes filling with tears. I can feel the heat rising in my chest; my stomach flips with rage. How could someone do that? How could anyone look at this sweet mama and these fragile babies and decide they were trash?

I meet Loch's eyes, and I see the same fire there. It's a cruel reminder to us both of why Loch had done what he did. The same quiet, deadly kind of anger fills us both. We don't need to say a word. We both know exactly what kind of person does that, and exactly what they deserve.

Loch softens, breaking the tension with his voice. "We found a foster. She's incredible with moms and pups. And since we don't take puppies often, we've already got a waitlist of approved adopters. They'll get great homes."

I look down at the little black pup. She yawns, showing me her little mouth with the tiniest pink tongue, and my heart completely unravels.

Loch leans in, almost teasing. "You know... Kong might accept a little sister," he pauses, "if you want to try."

I stare at him, blinking fast. "Are you serious?"

He nods. "She'll need to go out, meet people, and socialize. You'd have to take her places—coffee shops, parks, for walks and hikes. Shepherds can't sit at home all day. They have more energy and need a job and training. Stuff Kong can't do." He smiles, soft and knowing. "It might help you, too. If you're up to it, we could even train her to be an emotional support animal, so that if you ever get nervous in public, she can help. I know Kong does that for you now, but he can't go out with you."

Tears prick my eyes, stupid and sudden. How does he always know exactly how to push me, how much I can take, and what I need, even before I do?

"I'd like to try," I say, my voice small but sure.

"Then we will, when she's old enough, but don't get your hopes up in case it doesn't work out with Kong, ok?" he says, and leans down to kiss my temple.

I nod.

"But first, I've got one more thing to show you."

I struggle to set the sleeping puppy down, not wanting to disrupt her.

He leads me to the office, where he pulls out a massive rolled-up paper from the corner. He spreads it across the desk, anchoring the corners with office supplies and mugs.

"Blueprints?"

"Recognize it?" he asks.

I frown, studying the lines and the shape of the land.

"Should I?"

He takes a deep breath. "It's the old house... the one that I... I burned down. It's fifteen acres. A few others from the board and I are turning it into a sanctuary. It's time we expand."

I don't speak; I can't speak. I listen.

"This," he points, "will be the main building. Indoor kennels with large outdoor runs; each dog gets two hundred square feet outside. Comfortable beds inside, even comfy little couches for the ones that like to curl up like they're at home."

He slides his finger across the page to another section. "And here? Four tiny houses with room for more, for volunteers or visitors.

So dogs can spend the night with people who love them. We'll partner with local programs to help unhoused people in need, or women coming from domestic violence situations, too. It will be simple housing, but we are hoping we can reach people to help, and in return they can help care for the dogs. Kind of an animal therapy deal. We still have to work through that part."

My soul shatters into a million pieces. Loch has the biggest heart of anyone I've ever known. I press my hand to my mouth, trying to hold them back, but the tears come anyway. He watches me, eyes full of warmth and longing. I whisper, "It's beautiful."

He shrugs, like it's no big deal. "It's what the dogs deserve."

I look at him. This man, who holds so much pain and still gives back, is rebuilding what he broke with his entire heart and soul.

And with absolute certainty, I know I'm in love with him. The real him. The one who builds sanctuaries from ashes and protects me from the monsters.

CHAPTER 51

LOCH

INTRODUCING TROUBLE WITH A PINK BOW

I sit outside Olive's apartment with a damn pink bow, bigger than the dog's entire head and a stomach full of nerves. The nine-week-old little diamond-chested girl is curled up in a small kennel in the passenger seat. She's completely unbothered, while I'm sweating bullets.

I asked Sophia to take Olive out for coffee and a walk. She's giving me the window of time I need to try this, because if this goes badly, if Kong doesn't accept her... I'll have to be the asshole who breaks Olive's heart, and I can't bear that. We really haven't talked about the puppy since that day about five weeks ago. She brought it up once a few days after, and I told her I would let her know when they were old enough. I hope I can surprise her again.

I carry the kennel in and set it down in the middle of the living room. Kong is here, tail thumping in the kennel when he sees me. I kneel beside him, open the door, letting him out, and rub his big head.

"Hey, buddy. Missed you, too. I need you to meet someone, ok?" I glance toward the kennel. "She's your new sister. You gotta be nice and protect her."

Kong's back legs shift into a guarded position, ears perked. He sniffs the air and takes a cautious step toward the crate, his nose still working. The little puppy isn't making a sound. His hackles go up, and my breath hitches, but he's only posturing. No teeth or growling, just curiosity and a little tension.

"Good boy," I soothe. "You're doing so good."

I give it ten minutes and let him settle down a bit. When he drops into a sit beside the crate and tilts his head, I take a chance and open the door.

The pup perks up and stumbles out into my hands, legs too short to be taken seriously. She yawns, then looks up at Kong like he's the biggest mountain she's ever seen. He watches her, still and alert, but he hasn't lunged or reacted. I hold my breath. Kong looks at me, and then at the puppy, and then back at me. He's calm and curious, so I set her down.

I'm there, ready to pull her back if needed, but also trying to see what he does. Kong has been friendly with dogs that are smaller than he is, so I hope he'll understand she's a puppy. She immediately runs to Kong and tries to climb up on him.

Kong startles backward, gives a sharp bark, and snaps at the air, not close enough to touch or hurt her. She flinches, takes two steps back, and plops down into a sit. This sweet little thing raises one tiny paw, holding it up in the air like she's trying to boop his nose without getting in trouble. The same thing that she did when Olive met her. It's the cutest fucking thing I've ever seen—assuming Kong doesn't eat her.

But that's it; that's all it takes. He sniffs her little face. She stays where she is, and Kong looks up at me like, 'Seriously dude?' And just like that, the vibe shifts. Relief crashes into me like a freight train.

I sit back, hand running through my hair, laughing under my breath. Jesus Christ, I thought I was gonna have to tell Olive she couldn't have this damn puppy.

The puppy trots off to explore, her little tail wagging in a blur. Kong watches her like he's not sure if he wants to play or babysit. He settles for a spot in the middle of the room, in guardian mode.

I pull out the bag I brought: toys, a puppy bed, the tiniest little collar, and I tie that huge, obnoxious pink bow Jan insisted on around her neck. It looks ridiculous, but Jan is right; it's fucking adorable.

I text Sophia.

Loch: All clear. You can come back whenever.

About an hour later, the door clicks open. I don't even have time to stand before Kong and the puppy charge the entryway, tails wagging. Olive's laughter erupts into a scream as soon as she sees them barreling for her. She walks in, and her face–God, her face. I don't know if I've ever seen her light up like that.

"They're–oh my God–Loch, they're–Kong! Look at you!" Her words come out in excited, incomplete sentences. She drops to her knees, arms wrapping around Kong, smothering him in kisses and praise. "You're such a good boy, buddy. Such a sweet, brave boy. I love you so much."

Olive scoops up the puppy and squeezes tight, like she's hugging something she can't live without. The puppy wriggles under her arm, climbing up to lick her face.

I can't stop smiling; my cheeks hurt from it.

She turns to me, eyes shining. "So she's staying?"

"If you want her to," I say, nodding. "Kong passed the test. We'll still need to monitor them and watch for any behaviors that can arise as she gets more comfortable and bigger. But I think they'll do fine together."

Olive sets the puppy down on her lap, stroking that little white diamond patch. "What's her name again?"

"You get to decide. We only name the litters for marketing and adoptions. What would you like to name her?"

She's quiet, thoughtful. The way she always is when something is important.

"Nova," she says. "It means new. A star that burns bright again after going dark. A new beginning."

My chest tightens all over again. "Nova," I repeat. "Yeah. That's perfect."

"She's a light," she says again, her voice warm and sure. "Just like you've been for me."

I can't say anything. I kneel beside them, wrapping all of them up in my arms as Kong lays his head on Olive's knee and Nova climbs over my thigh like she's already a little queen.

I pull one last gift out for Olive, another keychain, like the one I gave her with Kong's face engraved. This one has Nova's face, but I left the name blank so I could add it later, once she had one. Her eyes well with tears, and she hugs me back even tighter. We have our own little family, a little piece of heaven here.

We're not just surviving anymore; we're starting to thrive.

Chapter 52
Loch

PAYBACK'S A PLEASURE

The apartment is quiet. We're snuggled in bed.

Kong is passed out, belly up and snoring softly in the corner of his oversized bed. Nova is curled into the crook of his leg, wanting to be close to him, not in the bed we bought for her. I've watched these two creatures bond, like she's always been his. It makes something hot and protective stir in my chest every time I look at them and think about how far Kong has come. A rough journey, but a beautiful one.

Olive is tucked beside me, skin warm against mine, her fingers tracing aimless patterns on my chest. Her heart beats in sync with mine, slow and steady in this rare peace that we've both fought so hard for.

She tilts her head back to look at me, eyes soft in the dim light. "You know I'm really lucky, right?" she utters softly.

I turn to face her, brushing a strand of hair from her cheek. "Yeah? Why's that?"

She smiles, but it doesn't reach her eyes, not until she speaks again. "Because you gave me so much. You gave me Kong, my freedom back, my life. You loved me when I wasn't sure I could love you back. And now, Nova... It's so much, I–"

She trails off like it overwhelms her to say it all out loud.

"I haven't given you enough," she finishes, eyes glossy.

I catch her hand and kiss her knuckles. "You give me everything I need by being here. Loving you is not something I have to do; it's something I get to do. You deserve all this and more. I'll spend the rest of my life making you as happy as possible."

She stares at me for a long moment, then her smile shifts and turns a little crooked, a little mischievous.

"Well," she said, pushing herself up, straddling me, and letting the blanket slip off us. "I've got something for you anyway."

My brow arches as I watch her crawl over me, my hands running along her soft thighs and hips. "What is it?" I ask, breath catching in my throat, and my dick getting hard with her on top of me and her huge tits right in front of my face.

She reaches into the nightstand beside the bed, pulling something out with a sly glint in her eye, and drops it onto my stomach. Handcuffs.

"They're for you," she says, her voice low and full of heat. "So you can restrain me without tape. Do whatever you want to me whenever you want."

My pulse thunders, and my dick twitches. My hands grip her thighs tighter, reaching around to cup her big ass. God, this woman. I tip my head back against the pillows, already imagining all the ways I was going to make her regret this in the best fucking way.

"After I'm done with you." She grins. "Do you trust me?"

I stare at her, breath shallow, muscles tight. "Yes."

She smiles, slow and sure, and guides my wrists above my head. I don't resist, not even a little. I want everything she wants to give me. There's something in the way she touches me, with confidence and in control. When the cool snap of the cuffs closes around one wrist, then the other, locking me to the bronze bar that I've attached her to several times now, a low breath hisses out of my lungs.

Olive sits back on my hips, eyes roaming over me, taking her time, taking in every inch.

"You always take care of me," she hums, trailing her fingers down my chest. "Always making sure I'm sated and safe."

I swallow hard. "That's never going to change."

Her smile turns coy. "Good. But tonight, I'm taking care of you."

Her fingers tease lower, skimming the edge of my stomach, her nails just barely grazing my skin, sending goosebumps down my chest. I flex my arms against the cuffs, not to fight them, but because not touching her is already driving me out of my goddamn mind.

She leans down, pressing her lips to my throat, then to my collarbone, then to the hollow of my chest. Her mouth is warm, soft, and a little maddening. Her pace is torturous.

"Olive..." I rasp.

She looks up at me from where she kisses below my ribs. "What?"

"You're going to kill me."

She laughs, quiet and breathy, her fingers tracing low enough to make me strain against the cuffs again. "Maybe," she says, as she bites me on my chest hard enough to leave a mark. The pain did nothing but make my dick harder.

Every kiss, every touch, every wicked look she gives me from under those lashes—she's in control, and she's stunning. The broken woman I'd once met is now powerful, playful, and so full of life. I watch her tease, worship, take her time because she knows she owns me.

Her hands go to my hips, but her tongue licks the head of my cock, making it jerk onto her lips. Her tongue runs up and down my shaft. She wraps her lips around the tip of my head and sucks hard.

"Fuck..." I grunt. I am so fucking hard, and I want to push her head down and fuck her mouth, but I can't. She pops off my cock and sits back up, climbing back up my body. That wasn't enough. I can feel the blood flowing through my body with anticipation. She kisses me, too quick, and moves higher, dropping her full tits in my face, her nipple falling into my mouth. She squeezes them together so I can suck on them both. My hips jerk, I'm so fucking turned on, but I need more. She pulls her tits away, climbing again.

"I'm going to sit on your face. Be a good boy and make me cum."

Her wet cunt lands on my mouth, and she grinds on my face unapologetically. She's so fucking sexy. I love seeing this side of her. She's dripping with arousal, and fuck, she tastes so good. I jerk my hands again, begging to touch her and pull her down harder, but the cuffs only jingle.

"Ride my face harder," I growl with lust and frustration.

She complies, even from on top, and she does what I tell her. Blood rushes through me, my pulse on fire with need and want. I lick and suck her clit; she grinds on me. Her body is tensing and jerking, getting louder and louder.

"I'm close, so close," she moans. "Make me cum, Loch."

The sound she makes, it's so hot–a raw, breathless cry caught between gasps and my name. Her back arches, thighs trembling and squeezing around my head, fingers digging into my skin like she's holding on for dear life. I know she is on the cusp, and I bite down on her clit. Just hard enough, sending a searing sensation to push her over the edge. I watch her come undone, every part of her unraveling, tasting and licking up every drop of her cum.

With shallow breath, she says, "Good boy, you use your mouth so well." The smile on her face is full of sass and dirty thoughts.

The restraints are fucking holding me back. I want to touch her; I need to fuck her. But before I know it, she's back on my dick.

"Oh fuck, thank God," I mumble, as my dick hits the back of her throat. My hips jerk up in pleasure. I'm so on the edge already, and her hot mouth on my dick is so wet. Her hand moves from my hip to cup and gently tug on my balls, her head bobbing up and down.

She licks my sack, her tongue running up and down and flicking the underside.

I grunt with pleasure.

"Fuck Olive, you're so fucking good at sucking my cock, please uncuff me so I can touch you, and fuck your mouth."

Her eyes flick up and gleam. She turns her head back and forth to say 'no' while her tongue is on my balls, running back and forth with the motion.

"Fuck," I groan.

Her hand grabs the base of my cock and she's stroking me hard. Her mouth is back on me. Her muffled moans cause her throat to vibrate around my dick. She lifts her other hand and spits on it. I look at her, watching her to see what she's doing. She keeps sucking, deep-throating me, gagging and tearing up.

I'm on the edge. Fuck, she feels so good and I can't hold back anymore. Then I feel it. She reaches around and is rubbing her wet fingers that she just spit on, on my ass. I flinch for a moment, but honestly, I don't even fucking care. I'm so fucking turned on and it feels good. Her finger presses in. I feel a slight sting, but mostly pleasure knowing she is taking what she wants. My cock is lodged in the back of her throat, and she does that thing where she swallows and her throat squeezes my head. I'm in such euphoria; I'm not sure what to feel or even what to focus on. Her finger presses in further and then hits my prostate.

I never imagined I'd let someone see me like this, touch me like this. But this is Olive, the woman who shattered all my walls without ever trying to. And then–fuck.

It's like she hit a switch inside me. My whole body tenses, a sharp gasp tearing out of me as pleasure surges through my spine like lightning. My hand clenches around the headboard bar, and I can't stop the sound that spills from my throat, deep, raw, and involuntary.

My orgasm slams into me like a wave prickling throughout every inch of me. Every nerve lights up, every muscle locks tight. I groan her name, desperate and hoarse, as I spill into her throat, completely wrecked. I cum so hard, my vision goes black. She licks her lips, swallowing every drop of my cum. I can see it in her eyes. She wants more.

She is watching me fall apart in her hands like I've never done for anyone else. This woman owns me in the most intoxicating way, and I'd let her do it a thousand times over.

"Such a good boy." She leans over and uncuffs me, wearing a devilish smile.

My hands slide to her waist, and she hums against my skin, nuzzling her face into my neck. "I love you," she says.

"I love you, too," I jingle the cuffs at her.

"You know what happens now, right?" I ask, my voice gravelly, low, still wrecked, but already hungry again. "You've woken the beast."

She bites her bottom lip, eyes gleaming with challenge, and leans in close like she's whispering a secret straight into my bloodstream. "Then, what are you waiting for?"

"Get on your knees, bend over. You have been a very bad girl tonight. I'm going to spank you and fuck you so goddamn hard." She flips on the bed, putting her ass in the air, and starts to pull her hands to the headboard. I reach for them instead, gripping her wrists and pulling them behind her back. She offers herself up without hesitation.

"Goddamn, Olive, I love this view."

I slide the cuffs into place with slow, deliberate clicks, watching her eyes flutter closed at the sound, trusting, wanting, and waiting. That's all I need; that's all I'll ever need.

"Fuck," I glide my hands over the globes of her ass. "Are you going to take me like a good girl? You wanted to tease me, Olive," I taunt as I slap her ass cheek hard. She gasps; I slap again, her gasps turn into moans. Slap, slap, slap. "Did you enjoy teasing me? Riding my face and cumming all over my tongue?"

"Yes," she breathes.

"Are you mine to use however I want?" My mouth brushes her ear; my hands glide down her sides, claiming every inch of her.

She breathes, "Always."

And I'm gone again, completely feral for her. Starving for her. I'm determined to leave her trembling and undone, and fully aware that giving herself to me like this is the most dangerous mistake she'll ever make. Now she's mine to devour.

She turns her face to the side, her ass high in the air, hands cuffed behind her back. I kneel there, on my knees, looking at her, watching her breasts hang in the air, her chest heaving. Her pussy glistens with arousal. I wait a moment. Letting this sit in the air, admiring how fucking gorgeous she is for me like this. Taking it in like it's the best thing I'll ever see. My dick is hard again. I palm it, relieving a little tension, stroking up and down my shaft, taking my time.

"Beg," I say with control in my voice.

"Wh–what?" she stammers.

"You want my cock? Beg for it." I run my thumb along her slit, just to see how sensitive she is. I can feel her patience unraveling, see it in the way she leans toward me, trying to get more friction from my touch.

"I want you," she croons, breathless.

I chuckle low in my throat, the sound dark and thick with control. "I know you do."

Her eyes lock with mine, wide and needy. "But wanting isn't enough."

Her breath hitches. "What... what do you want?"

I drop to a slow crouch in front of her, our faces so close we share the same breath, the tension coiling between us like a fuse. My voice is a growl when I say, "I want you to beg for me."

She freezes for half a heartbeat, like the command hits her straight in the chest, and then her lips part.

"Please, Loch," she whispers. "Please touch me." Her voice breaks, her eyes glassy. "I'm aching for your cock. I want your hands, your mouth, everything. Please."

I swear my blood heats like fire under my skin. Then I give her what she's begging for. I shove my cock in her. I'm not slow, nor easy. I fuck her hard and deep. I reach forward and pull her wrists and cuffs into my hand, arching her back and lifting her off the bed. Pulling her pussy even deeper into me. She screams out, "Oh fuck. God, Loch, yes!"

"Do you want it harder?"

Her breathing is rapid, her voice shaky. "Please, fuck me harder, Loch." My hips piston into her cunt. Her body is trembling and tense. Her orgasm is coming.

I stop. I'm going to make her beg for this orgasm. She startles, looking back at me with disbelief.

"Noooo," she cries.

I smile with a cheeky grin. I put a single finger into her wet cunt, slowly sliding in and out.

"You'll need to work for another orgasm, Olive. You wanted to tease me earlier, and now you're going to pay for that."

Her breath hitches the moment my fingers graze her puckered hole. I can feel the tension coiling under the surface, tight and trembling, like she's been holding herself back to unravel now. Every time I touch her, I am learning her all over again—how her body responds, how her hips tilt into me, how the smallest moan from her lips lights something primal in my chest.

Using her own arousal, I push that same single finger in hard. Her hands tighten into a ball, knuckles going white, and I swear I can feel her pulse under my fingertip.

With a single thrust, I shove my dick back inside her pussy. Oh, fuck, she is so tight. I fuck her hard. Her hips buck back into me for more. I push a second finger into her ass, gripping her wrists and cuffs again, filling her more, giving it to her harder.

She's clenching around me, trying to keep me there, like she doesn't want a single inch to get away. Every time I move, she gives this breathy little moan that wrecks me.

"Cum with me, Olive. I'm close." I'm losing control of myself; she feels so tight. Her moans and desperate pants pull me in closer. She arches into me as if she's been waiting for this, too. I pull her hair, arching her neck to find her lips pointing at the ceiling. She leans back into me. I lean over her, pulling her into me. Her lips brush mine as if we've never kissed before, as if this is the first time every single moment counts.

We finally cum together, and the world shifts. There's no past. Just the two of us, lost in something that's so damn real.

I release her hair, and she falls forward with a breathless sigh. We both collapse, letting the sensations course through us. Unable to move. Unable to breathe. I pull out of her, but don't release her hands yet. I turn her to the side and lie down facing her. My arm reaches around her, between her back and arms. She's still mine. Still in my control. And her forehead dips to rest under my chin. "You are stunningly beautiful, and I fucking love you."

Epilogue

Olive

Nine years later.

Our home sits on the far edge of the sanctuary, past the tree line, where the noise from the dogs quiets, and the air always smells like pine and earth. It's tucked back far enough to give us space and privacy. We enjoy our little piece of heaven back here. It's a world of our own that still beats in rhythm with the one we built to save others.

Our living room is warm, lived-in, full of love. Sunlight spills through tall windows, pooling across the wooden floors. A well-worn leather couch sits beneath shelves lined with old books, dog-eared novels, and framed photos of every animal that ever left a mark on us.

And here, near the sliding doors that overlook the pasture and tree line, is where his and Nova's beds have been for the last five years. His thick gray memory foam-padded bed, faded from years of use, is shaped to his body. His red collar rests on the edge of the bed, right where we left it, the metal tag catching the light and reflecting it into the house.

Loch and I are kneeling on the soft blankets laid out next to Kong's bed. Our little old man lies curled up, barely more than a shell of the giant protector he once was, his battle scars still hairless and visible. His breathing is shallow, his body trembling from the effort of staying awake. His head rests to the side, and his cloudy eyes track us with tired warmth. His cancer has spread; he's weak and tired.

He knows we know. He's a brave boy until the very end.

I reach out to brush the grizzled fur around his face, and I choke on the sob in my throat. "You saved my life," I whisper, my voice trembling. "You were the first one who made me feel safe again, and we had so many good years together."

My hand shakes as I run it down his side. His ribs press through his thinning coat, and yet I still see him as he once was—majestic, strong, and powerful—a beast with the biggest heart, the king of our little world.

"I didn't know I needed a friend like you. You changed it all." My heart cracks open with each word. "But you have been everything I needed. The best decision I ever made in my whole life was choosing you." Unstoppable tears stream down my face.

Loch doesn't speak. He can't; he's crying too, his firm hands wrap around mine, our fingers tangle together, knotted with grief, holding each other together on Kong's chest.

Kong's tail gives the faintest flick, like he's trying to comfort us even now.

"You rescued both of us," Loch says. "Without you, we wouldn't have had this. You brought her to me, you brought her back to life, and then you saved me, too. We could never repay that debt in full."

We fall silent, caught in the ache of the moment. He's almost fifteen years old, and he's lived a good life—close to ten years with us. Ten years of birthdays, walks, and car rides. I still remember his first birthday party. We went to a remote park with the few people in his circle. We made him wear this silly, gold, glittery birthday top hat.

He acted like we had condemned him to a life of eternal humiliation. He had a big red dog cake and got lots of new toys.

Then, there were the years of watching Nova curl around him every night like he was the only thing in the world that mattered. Kong and Nova became inseparable. Somehow, they have a bond almost as close as Kong and me. Nova sits next to us, calm and patient, watching us like she knows, too.

Ten years of watching him transform from a guarded, growling beast into a wise, gentle guardian. Kong is a teacher and a healer. Special doesn't even seem like a big enough word to describe who he is to us. There's something about him, a sense of joy that he spreads around, and everyone that he lets into his circle feels it. It could be because of the pain he suffered at the beginning of his life. Maybe he was grateful for his new chance at life, somehow knowing how lucky he was to be in a loving home and alive.

Loch reaches into his pocket and pulls out the small, foil-wrapped chocolate, a Hershey's Kiss. I am sobbing even harder now, unable to see through all the tears.

I unwrap it, the silver foil trembling in my fingers. "One kiss," I whisper to Kong, holding it near his muzzle. "Your last kiss, sweet boy." He doesn't move much, but his nose twitches, and I press it to his lips. "Goodbye, my love."

Loch presses his forehead to Kong's. "You did good, old man. You did so good. We'll see you again someday."

Kong's breathing slows even more, each exhale softer than the last. The syringe is already in my hand, my heart aching so violently I don't know how I'm still upright. But I owe it to him to make sure this is gentle. That it's peaceful and that he knows he's not alone. He lived a long, fulfilled, happy life. We spoiled him rotten every chance we had, but I knew I had to do the right thing. We couldn't keep him any longer. It would be selfish, and it was time to let him go.

I inject the medications with steady hands and a shattered soul. He drifts in seconds. His chest rises, and then it doesn't.

A hollow kind of silence fills every space in the room. Loch wraps his arms around me, and I fall into him, sobbing against his chest. “He was mine; I can’t believe he’s gone,” I say through my tears. “He was the beginning of everything.”

Because of Kong, I found safety and love. I found my purpose thanks to him. I became a vet to help more dogs like him, through a private practice, as well as providing free or cheap care to all the dogs that come through Only Dogs. I want to give back what he gave to me. We built a home, a sanctuary, and a life all because of one very special boy, Kong.

Because he loved us.

Because he rescued us.

And because we loved him back with everything we had.

THE REAL KONG

The Real Kong, who inspired this story, is pictured below. Details, like his age and certain behaviors, were changed to fit the fictional story you just read.

I met Kong when he was ten years old. He was emaciated, had a huge lump on his leg, and was chained to a truck. The top of his neck was wounded from the heavy chain that was embedded in his skin, from the amount of time he'd been left in that condition. Beauties and Beasts, Inc. was able to get the owner to surrender him, and he became a Beauty. My husband and I thought he was only weeks from passing and took him in as a hospice foster. He lived over a year with us, bringing so much joy and laughter into our lives. He not only learned to meet new people, but he also began thriving in our home. He loved his toys, his people, and nothing could stop him from trying to get more treats. Since he was a hospice dog, he got many, many treats.

The first picture you see is Kong's real first birthday party. The others are from the day he was rescued and show his terrible living conditions. The last picture is from the day we took him home to foster. He had the best last year with us, and we are so thankful to have been the ones who got to love him.

To learn more about his rescue group, check out their webpage, beautiesandbeasts.org. They rely on private donations for support, and if you're able, please consider donating. It would mean a lot.

All the dogs mentioned in this story, besides Kong and Nova, are up for adoption, waiting for their people.

How we found Kong the day he was rescued

Kong's last day on a chain

Kong's first birthday party

Kong's first day in a foster home